MW01148098

WEARING
THE LION

ALSO BY JOHN WISWELL

SOMEONE YOU CAN BUILD A NEST IN

WEARING THE LION

WEARING
THE LION

John Wiswell

DAW BOOKS
New York

Jacket design by Adam Auerbach
Interior design by Fine Design

DAW Book Collectors No. 1983

DAW Books
An imprint of Astra Publishing House
dawbooks.com
DAW Books and its logo are registered trademarks of Astra Publishing House.

Printed in the United States of America

Library of Congress Cataloging-in-Publication Data

Names: Wiswell, John, 1981- author.
Title: Wearing the lion / John Wiswell.
Description: First edition. | New York : DAW Books, 2025. |
Series: DAW Book collectors ; no. 1983
Identifiers: LCCN 2025004198 (print) | LCCN 2025004199 (ebook) |
ISBN 9780756419547 (hardcover) | ISBN 9780756419554 (ebook)
Subjects: LCGFT: Mythological fiction. | Fantasy fiction. | Novels.
Classification: LCC PS3623.I8486 W43 2025 (print) |
LCC PS3623.I8486 (ebook) | DDC 813/.6--dc23/eng/20250204
LC record available at https://lccn.loc.gov/2025004198
LC ebook record available at https://lccn.loc.gov/2025004199

First edition: June 2025
10 9 8 7 6 5 4 3 2 1

To all the gods I cannot please.

THE TWELVE LABORS OF HERACLES

1   Fetch the invincible skin of the Lion of Nemea.

2   Defeat the immortal Hydra of Lerna.

3   Catch the evanescent Hind of Ceryneia.

4   Defeat the man-eating Boar of Mount Erymanthos.

5   Clean the entire Augean Stables in one single day.

6   Defeat the man-eating giant Birds of Stymphalia.

7   Defeat the Bull of Crete, child of Poseidon.

8   Steal the man-eating Mares from the warlord Diomedes.

9   Steal the war belt of Hippolyta, Queen of the Amazons.

10   Steal the world-famous Red-Haired Cattle from the Three-Headed Giant Geryon.

11   Fetch the Golden Apples of the Hesperides from Hera's Garden at the Top of the World.

12   Defeat Cerberus, Three-Headed Guard Dog of the Underworld, Pet of Hades.

Part One
The Rise

Hera 1

"Good news, Heaven," announces my dipshit husband. "I've made a new king of the mortals."

It's that same boasting tone he used the morning he conceived Perseus, the slayer of monsters and first King of Mycenae. The same tone he used when he'd conceived giants, and heroes, men who wrote history with their footsteps. This tone beckons me to celebrate that he has sired his newest favorite child, since I am the Goddess of Pregnancy.

I have never celebrated these children for a simple reason: I am his wife, and we haven't fucked since the mortals discovered bronze.

"Bastard!" I reach for the ivory javelin that a priestess once carried across half the sea to lay at the foot of my temple in Delphi, ready to finally break it in. My aim will be true. I want to get him through both testicles and at least one eye.

Immediately my entourage betrays me and descends. Até is first, the quickest of foot, looping both of her slender arms around my right shoulder so I can't throw. She's stronger than her slight frame looks. Até has always been poison disguised as wine, her sunny complexion often leaving her mistaken for a nymph. Being the Goddess of Ruin, she's destroyed many people who thought she was less than she was.

Spittle flies from my teeth as I yell, "You should be on my side!"

Then Granny's leathery wings fill my vision, and she is on me too. It's been a long time since anyone called her a goddess; now they call her kind "furies." Granny is the oldest of her kind, predating the Erinyes triplets. Great bat wings extend from her shoulder blades, and brown vipers grow from her scalp instead of hair, although with age the vipers are more sloughed-off skins than venomous threats these days.

"Dear, please." Granny's face is as creased and leathery as her wings. It is less age and more the stress of her eras of work. She lives in my entourage as a sort of retirement from this kind of stress. I see her dull eyes begging me to look into them, to slow my violence. "Don't let anyone make you hurt yourself."

Até still wrestles my right arm. "And let go of the damned spear."

"It's a javelin!" I yell, stampeding forward, dragging them both with me across the halls of Olympos. They are immortal, but I am the Queen of the Olympians, tall and unbowed. The Amazons may kiss Artemis's ass, but when they want something done, they pray to me.

Até groans, trying to bend my arm downward. "Hera, honey, there's got to be a better way."

Granny pleads, "I want better for you."

"Heraaaaaaa!"

That's neither Até nor Granny. That's the tone again, demanding that I adulate him for his great gift to the world of fertility.

"Hera, come look! He's going to be my best work yet!"

There are not enough gods on Olympos to hold me back.

Olympos is an evanescent place, more an idea than a reality. Our great temple reshapes itself to our wills, providing any chambers, or towers, or dungeons as we need them. Architecture is to us what a syllable is to a poet. Every room that I run through hews itself out of living white marble, not painted as the Thebans treat their temples. Doorways open through solid rock, obeying my rage as I race closer, permitting me passage as I grow closer to my dipshit husband's voice.

There is only one permanent feature atop Mount Olympos: the rim. The great circle of unbroken marble was chiseled from the greatest slab of such rock anyone on the Aegean Sea could find, long before Perseus's time, and was offered to us to earn our favor. It is the very edge of our temple atop the unclimbable mountain. It is the boundary between our infinite possibility and the mortals' affairs.

There, at the rim of our temple, stands my dipshit husband. Immense in height, his white beard thicker than brambles. His robe made from the wool of golden lambs is cast away, dangling from one hip. His shoulders block out the sun.

He stands at the very spot on the rim where we used to sit and kiss and gamble on the futures of mortal lovers. A small notch rests in the marble there, the only scratch on the entire rim. It marks where my dip-shit husband dropped his thunderbolt in the midst of our . . . better times.

This is the spot where he first called me Queen.

This is the spot where he now calls, "Come look. This kid is going to be your favorite."

Most of the Olympian Twelve have come out to watch in their curiosity. Zeus's enormous brother and God of the Seas, Poseidon, stands closest to him, his thick brow dripping with brine. Hestia, Goddess of Homes, and my son Hephaistos, God of Craftsmen, skitter out of my way, opening a space at the rim for me beside another of my sons, Ares, God of War, who swallows hard and avoids meeting my eyes.

As I come close, I'm distracted enough that Até catches the back end of the javelin and tugs it from my grasp. All I manage is to shove my shoulder into Zeus's side. To my disappointment, he does not fall over the edge.

This close, I can't resist taking a look. The mortal world is right there. The reason to be angry. The thing my dipshit husband has done.

There, along the wine-dark sea, in the south, within the fruited land of Boeotia, within the walled town of Troezen, within a bedroom streaked with oil and bodily fluids, is the insult.

I am the Goddess of Mothers, and no conception is outside my perception. The bedchambers are wide, thin sashes of blue dangling from the ceiling. The wide-shouldered Queen of Troezen, Alcmene, brown skin aglow, is hurriedly explaining something to her husband, the lumpy King Amphitryon. By her gestures, already she knows she is with child, and she is way too happy about it. She should be apologizing.

At least her husband will be angry with her. I'm rooting for him. His wrath will be a good outlet. Maybe I'll pick up a few revenges from him to visit upon Zeus.

Except the next time I glance into their bedroom, they're not arguing. They're necking so intensely the rest of their bodies get in on it, and next they tip over the bed in their passion.

I hope they hear me say, "What the fuck?"

It's impossible. That they'd be happy about this, and that my dipshit husband was so bad in bed this human woman still had strength for more. He must have been off his game. Back in our day, we split mountains with our lovemaking.

"See?" says my dipshit husband. "Everyone is excited. This kid is going to change everything."

I throw my hand at the image of this blissful king and queen who defy the bounds of marriage, willing my javelin to split their roof. Giving them a good impaling will send the right message.

Then I remember my hand is empty. That damned Até stole my javelin.

My dipshit husband boasts, "He'll be more man than man. More god than gods. He'll hold the world on his shoulders and extend Greece's greatness for centuries."

Time is so much thinner on our side of the marble rim. I blink, and already Alcmene's belly bulges. She kisses her fingertips and then holds them over where her baby grows.

My dipshit husband mimics the gesture, kissing a hand and then placing it to my shoulder. He rubs my flesh and beams with pride down at the mortal world.

"You watch over this one. I'm making him king."

His touch dries up my interest in mortal-watching. I bat his hand away and jab a finger into his chest. He won't treat the world as his domain alone. It took us both to slay our father, and I can kill again.

I say, "You're done making kings. Your son won't rule a fruit stand."

"Come on," he says to every other god in attendance, like I'm being difficult. "Goddess of Pregnancy. Goddess of Mothers. Goddess of Family. You can't hate a kid."

"You're a fucking child and I hate you."

"Plus, this is two kids."

"Twins?" I ask. "You made two demigods for me to look after?"

I wonder if I can beat a god to death with his own dick.

"Only one is mine," he says, leaning an elbow on the marble rim. "The other is Amphitryon's. Balancing each other out."

I wrinkle my brow in the way a countryside wrinkles in an earthquake. I say, "That is not how pregnancy works."

"I'm having a new son! I'm being liberal with the miracles today. It's a celebration. Everybody's babies will be more handsome than average. You can do that for me, right, oh Goddess of Mothers?"

I'm reaching for his throat when another goddess proclaims, "That's brilliant!"

I want to kill her before I even recognize it's Até. My Até, my Goddess of Ruin, the person I soonest turn to to shit-talk this dipshit god. She pushes right up against my side, holding my ivory javelin, her face beatific and radiant up at the King of the Olympians.

She says, "Give your son a mortal twin who is himself better than all other mortals. Bless the shit out of the kid."

"Exactly!" Zeus says, gesturing to her like I should be taking notes. "See? She gets it. You should listen to her."

Até prattles on, "And you won't stop at his twin, right? Everyone born on the same day as your heir should be more beautiful than any mortals before them."

Zeus puffs out his chest. "Because they live in the era of my generosity. All these babies are going to make grown men blush. You'll see to it, yes, Hera?"

I don't know how Até is still talking. I should be strangling her, but I'm dumbstruck. What is she doing?

Até says, "I heard he's to become some kind of king, too?"

"The greatest of kings! He has my blood, and the blood of Perseus!"

"Do you have a date picked?"

"Oh, it'll be the solstice. Everyone loves a festival."

"So it's destiny, then? No waiting. The child born of yours and Perseus's line on the spring solstice shall be king?"

"He shall be king of all he surveys!" Zeus said, thunder resonating from the clap of his hands. "Yes. It shall be the law of Heaven and Earth."

Até looks me full in the face, with that same beatific expression, not dropping it at all. It's only then that I realize the Goddess of Ruin might be misleading someone.

I keep the disgust on my face as I ask, "Destiny? For the child of Zeus and Perseus's lineage born on the spring solstice?"

Até clutches at my elbows. "You've got to be happy for the King of the Olympians. This is going to be wonderful. For us."

That pause. That "For us" is what finally gets me on board. This is why I keep such a smart entourage. I'm lucky my dipshit husband doesn't figure it out himself, but his eyes are glued to Até's ass.

While Até starts spinning up possible names, I return my attention to the mortal world. They had only to speak this law, and now every oracle in the lands is spreading the same mythology. The one born of Zeus and Perseus's line on the solstice shall be king of all he surveys.

Great states are already sending tribute to Troezen, to fatten the wealth of King Amphitryon. Queen Alcmene reclines on a bed of feathers, with attendants rubbing her swollen feet. Those feet are going to be swollen longer than she expects.

I sort through souls like a librarian sorts through documents. Perseus was almost as horny as his father, and has left plenty of fools in his wake. For instance, King Sthenelus now rules both his father's Mycenae and Tiryns, really living up to daddy's rapacious desire for power. He's a bully; he exiled his nephew Amphitryon to Troezen in the first place. If his child is king, it might put some impudent whelps from Troezen in their place.

He is a weight upon his suffering wife, Nicippe, who would have done great things had so many power brokers not traded her around. There she is, pregnant with a boy she could shape into something worthwhile. She deserves the ear of the powerful.

And look at that? She just so happens to be due in the spring.

What a coincidence.

It's an invitation for him to catch me. To see what I'm doing. To struggle against my plot, and to scheme back. To fight with me like I deserve to be fought with. To be defeated, like he deserves to be defeated. Those are the only drives that keep our marriage going these days.

And my dipshit husband doesn't hear me.

He's boasting to all the other gods, jumping between them, his tone like his sentences want to fuck their ears.

"So then I said, 'You know, I can look like your husband tonight.' I mean, I could look like a swan if she wanted, but sometimes looking like the husband spices things up just right. And she turned this color, you know, like the dawning of a new day, but that dawn is somehow bashful?"

I rear back to slug him, and there is Até, capturing my hand one more time. She wraps her fingers around mine and squeezes. She still wears the beatific smile of false innocence.

She whispers, "Got the plot?"

I love this evil weirdo.

With the look we share, I find enough calm to wait.

"Look at that!" Até says, so loud that nobody could mistake her for actually surprised. "It's a miracle of the gods down in Greece."

My dipshit husband stops in the middle of miming something like eating a fig. With a grin as broad as any tyrant's ambitions, he leans over the marble rim and to the mortal world. The days have burned by, and the solstice is upon the Aegean Sea again.

"Now you all better bless his kingdom," he commands. "Especially you, Hera. No tricks."

I squeeze Até's hand. "I would never play a trick on the King of All He Surveys."

"That's why I married you. You know when to follow—wait."

The hairs of his white beard curl further, like they are winding up around a spindle. Static sparks pop around his eyebrows. He grips the marble rim of Mount Olympos, probably not noticing that his left hand rests over the old notch he once made. He leans so far over that he could spill down into Greece.

"Who is that in the palace?"

I pretend to look. "Why husband, that is the King of All He Surveys."

Not a single idea on our plane of existence dares move. Everything becomes taut, tensing with anticipation for Zeus's revelation.

"What the fuck?"

I brush Zeus's bare arm as I lean over the world again, to watch. There are so many processions of states and tribes pledging their allegiance to the new king of kings. The infant who carries with him the destiny of Zeus.

He is a skinny baby with little brawn in his frame, but he will grow strong enough to wear his crowns.

"King Eurystheus," I say with a cold laugh. "Strange. I don't see twins."

I watch until the procession from Troezen arrives. King Amphitryon has to swallow his bile and kneel before someone else's newborn. Behind him, his wife Alcmene struggles to hide her disappointment—or maybe that's her going into labor. I'm sure her children will be worth the wait.

Temptation overtakes me. I start to slip down into the palace, in the guise of a midwife who will really be able to rub this in. They thought they would control the world through the insult of a child my dipshit husband gave them. Nobody insults me.

I feel the chill of the stone floor under one foot and am about to put the other down when I hear the thunder cracking. The skies are shining and clear, and yet thunder fills the air and stings my nostrils.

In a tone I haven't heard since the last great war, I hear my dipshit husband ask, "Até, aren't you the Goddess of Misfortune?"

"Yes, my lord. Why do you ask?"

"Then you should've seen this coming."

I'm back on Olympos in time to see Zeus lifting Até in one hand. She is less than a feather in his grip, and he straightens her as stiff as a javelin. Her entire body crackles with lightning, her face a portrait of agony. Her cries are imprisoned in her throat. Nothing save sizzling sounds escape her lips.

With her captured in a thunderbolt, Zeus raises his arm. No Olympian dares catch his arm.

He hurls her downward, and she passes as a shooting star over the palace, and across the islands. She hits the sea so hard that Poseidon crosses his legs.

Zeus holds his bearded chin high. "Até is exiled from Mount Olympos. She will never set a misfortunate foot on this mountain again. That is part of the new era, too. Am I understood?"

He does not actually wait for the Olympians to agree. Perhaps he knows I'd shout him down. I'm already parting my lips to argue when he continues.

"And her domain is vacated, as well. Ruin. Misfortune. Whatever the fuck she thought she was peddling, any of you can have it. Who wants it? Hm?"

That piece of shit Apollo immediately raises a hand to claim it. He's been a thief of domains since the day he was born. I don't let him speak, elbowing him aside and shoving him into Ares. Ares will know enough to shut him up.

"You had no right!"

"I am the King of the Gods! Olympos is my war-won domain. No one but me has the right."

"You fucked around and you found out."

"Do you want to see more lightning?"

"Do you want to see a javelin pierce both your testicles and at least one of your eyes?"

"That's . . . imaginative, but no. No more disobedience."

I slap a hand down on the marble rim, and it cuts my hand. Shocked, I realize I hit the notch in the stone.

What pulls me out of the surprise isn't my husband's swearing and threats. It's the wailing of twin babies. Never have newborns begging for milk made me sick to my stomach before. I could vomit across the mortal plane.

Both Zeus and I look down, together, upon that household in Troezen. There is a crib of wood so freshly lathed it must have been built this very week. The parents must have built it on the journey back home.

There they are. The twins. The mortal, and the insult. His face is wrinkled, his arms flail erratically. There's nothing unusual about him. And yet I hate him from my depths.

Zeus is still looking at his newest favorite son when he says, "You are done, Hera."

"No," I said. "I haven't begun to get my justice."

From the crowd of Olympians comes Granny, who must feel out of place. She is the only non-Olympian left here, with Até being exiled. She knows she could be next, and still she comes to my side to rub my back and coax me away.

I will not be coaxed. I look upon the aging vipers of her hair and take inspiration.

"I will not suffer that insult to live. I'll put fucking snakes in his crib."

Zeus says, "Do not put snakes in his crib."

"Oh, like you'll even notice. You'll be too busy turning into a fence to have sex with a rake, or whatever you're into at that point."

"I'm the King of the Gods. I run the mortal world. Of course I'll notice."

Heracles 1

Dear Auntie Hera,
    Thank you for the snake friends. They are very wiggly. We played a lot. They are sleeping now.
    Please send more animal friends. Do you have cats?

Quit praying to me, you little shit!

Also, nobody prays like that. A prayer isn't an application to the academy.

Also, how the fuck is a toddler capable of talking like that? You're tiny. Your father is a fucking idiot. Where did you get that sort of wisdom?

Oh, I see her. I know where you're hearing those insipid words. Those false pleasantries meant to sway me. Your mother, Alcmene, with a darkness under her eyes that fades at no time of day. She looks behind her more than she used to. That's what has her bothering my temple every morning, and droning at me three times every day.

There she is on her knees before the bust of my visage she installed in her courtyard, as though her household had ever praised me before.

"Goddess Hera, you are the Goddess of Mothers, and so . . ."

I turn away from the marble rim of Olympos, already bored with your mother's latest prayer. She thinks I've never heard a suck-up before? She thinks words will earn forgiveness?

Granny is waiting there when I turn around. She takes my shoulders in her taloned hands and says, "Dear, this mother prays to you three times a day. There must be some conviction to her."

I turn up my nose. "It's not enough. She's lucky I don't send you down there to drive her mad and get rid of the child."

Granny releases me to grab at the desiccated snake skins of her hair, pupils dilating. "P-please, no."

"No, no," I say, softening my voice. Granny trembles at the idea of having to work again as a fury, and now I hold her. "Your time is done. And my fight is not really with her. It's with that insult."

My eyes betray me and return to your world, as Alcmene lifts you from your crib in the dead of early morning. It's the first of many times she carries you into the courtyard, to where my visage lies in the small shrine. My dipshit husband gave you strength, so you can stand at a very early age. You wobble over, peering oafishly at my stone eyes.

As your mother recites yet another prayer, you put one of your grimy palms over my mouth. You hug your teetering weight on it and call it "Auntie Hera."

Granny moans in pain. "Dear, you're holding me very tight."

I realize some of my fingers are digging into Granny's side. I release her and shake my head.

"Sorry, Granny."

"It's all right, dear. Please, take it easy. I know this is going to upset you."

"What is?"

"Well." Granny makes a show of clearing her throat. "Alcmene has named the child."

"Dipshit the Second? He already has a name. He's 'Alcides,' named after some other useless mortal in his family." Your mother named you after one of Amphitryon's ancestors, to try to appease him. "What do I care if she heaps extra names onto that living insult?"

Down in the courtyard, in front of my visage, Alcmene coaxes, "Go ahead and pray to her. Go ahead, Heracles."

Wait.

Heracles?

Heracles?!

If Granny weren't standing in the way, I would dive off Olympos and strike them down myself.

"Heracles?" I repeat. "She's calling that thing 'Hera's Glory'?"

"She's showing reverence to you."

"Because nothing makes me feel as revered as my husband cheating on me. I'd kick his balls up through his skull if he was around."

Like always, the King of the Olympians has managed to disappear right after his infidelity. I'll find where he's hiding, in time. I'll deal with him.

First I'll deal with you, Alcides. *Heracles.* Your name is an insult, and your existence is an insult. You will never be king. You'd grow up to be just as bad as your father. You look like him, and you smell like him. Like stale milk and staler leaves. You'll think like him, too. You'll have no fear because you are too godlike in strength, and you'll have no perspective because you are too mortal in wisdom.

I survived the horrors that came from the generation before mine. I toil against the horrors my generation creates. You will not get the opportunity to make the world worse. Your kind of story only ever ends one way.

Heracles 2

Auntie Hera,

How they sing our name. Can you hear them all the way up from atop Mount Olympos?

The crowd amassed around my stepfather's villa, hundreds of people in any direction, waiting for a glimpse of the two great brothers of Troezen. They did not chant my name. They sang it in a sweet repetition, like locusts droning together. The passion. The yearning to see us work.

How do so many people know our name? People were calling me by it before I knew what it meant. Isn't it funny, to have a name before you have a self?

I am Alcides, proud son of Alcmene.

But I am also Heracles, proud son of Zeus.

"Alcides" honors my forebears, ancestors of my mother and stepfather. But "Heracles" is a title that honors all your virtues, and all your lessons of how important family is to us. When a crowd sings for "Hera's Glory," they praise you as much as they praise me. It's the name that brings us together.

"Al, come on," calls Iphicles, my twin brother. He beckons me with both hands to step inside the arena we have built beside his father's stables.

Auntie Hera, have you met Iphicles? I was born wrestling him, as though we were racing to see who could enter the world first. He is a born athlete. Mama Alcmene says the night she conceived of me with Zeus, she also conceived of Iphicles with her husband. It boggles the mind such a thing could happen. I assume it was a miracle from you. You preside over all births, so you must have had a hand in this. Thank you for blessing me with this constant companion, who doubtless will be as legendary as myself when we are grown men.

"It's time, dumbass!"

Iphicles gets a little impatient with my constant prayers. Please forgive him. He's royalty, and royalty deranges people.

Iphicles stands naked before the throngs of admirers. Every muscle on his relaxed frame is more defined than when a grown man flexes. You could not build more muscle onto a body than he does. He approaches the stone he selected yesterday, the largest one yet. It's a great gray slab, taller than he is and carved with stars, so it can resemble the sky that Atlas keeps aloft. It took four of Iphicles's servants working together to drag it into the arena.

Iphicles stoops on the sanded-dirt arena floor, blowing kisses at the blushing virgins sitting on the benches in front. He collects a palmful of dust and beats his hands together so he'll have a drier grip.

The rock doesn't stand a chance. He clasps it from the base and hoists it to my father's sky. Up it goes, grit crumbling off where he holds and tumbling down onto his dark curls.

How the throngs cheer for him. I cheer, too, beating my hands together. This is his personal record.

Then it's my turn. Most of the crowd goes quiet as I stride out, staring at my chunky thighs and the paunch wine has given me. Someone murmurs, asking if I'm a servant boy. The one person who cheers is Themistocles, a boy a year older than me, who has the sweetest singing voice in the city. We've only flirted a couple times before. I wink to him, and his cheeks go afire.

I come right up behind my brother, into the shade that his slab gives us both, and stoop. I touch my fingertips to his heels. With knees trembling, he steps first his right foot onto my palm, and then his left. I feign agony at how heavy he is, letting the crowd worry this won't work.

As the first person snickers, I hoist Iphicles straight into the air, up into my father's sky. I hold my brother in one hand, directly over my head while he keeps the stone above his.

Surely you hear them chanting.

"Hera's glory! Hera's glory!"

Poor Themistocles falls onto his bench from the passion, and he isn't alone. Many need quenching for their hoarse throats after our display. Boys and girls our own age run up to give us baskets of nuts and dried fruits, and fans of the blue and brown feathers of cuckoos. Do you see them? I only accept cuckoo and peacock feathers, as they are your favorite birds.

While show-offs try and fail to lift Iphicles's slab, I collect half of the offerings of food, and all of the cuckoo fans. These I carry to the little shrine to you that is tucked behind the fruit vendors. It was disheveled when I first found it, but I make sure to clean it daily. You are as beautiful in a stone bust as you would be in person.

Locals wish to replace the bust, saying your image shows disdain in its gaze. But when I gaze upon your bust, Auntie Hera, I see your poise and determination. I will never let them take it down.

There's an older woman at your shrine today, already down on her knees, her face deeply creased from the intensity of prayer. Her red raiment has gone shoddy from years of use and lack of care.

"Please, Glory of Hera," the woman says to me. "Answer my prayer."

I put out a hand. "I am not god enough to be worth praying to. But if you are hungry, you can come have lunch with me."

Her voice croaks as though she's worried sick. "It is not food that I hunger for."

"Please, my lady. What is the matter?"

She remains on her knees as she turns to me. "The Lion of Cithaeron is so great that it can shatter a carriage with one swipe of its paw. It destroyed my sons' business, and still their caravans must travel through those mountains to bring our city's tribute to the Minyans. If the lion is not defeated, my sons will not come home next time they venture out."

"That is a terrible burden, my lady."

"No god has intervened against this horrible beast. Yet here you are, before Hera's visage. The Goddess of Mothers. As a mother, I beg you to be the miracle that spares my sons."

As she speaks, my brother Iphicles catches up with us. He looks tentatively upon her, as though to ask whether I want her sent away. I wave him to come closer.

"Iphicles," I say. "How would you feel about hunting a lion today? It would make a great prop for you to lift at our next public display."

Iphicles comes not one step closer to us. "I don't know, Al. I need to get ready for court with King Eurystheus. He will be in the region soon to deal with the Minyans, and Father wants me to strengthen our relationship. The fate of Troezen hangs on it."

Auntie Hera, do you know King Eurystheus? He was born shortly before myself and Iphicles, but was much less fortunate. You see, Papa Zeus proclaimed the first child of Perseus's lineage born that day would be King of All He Surveys. Eurystheus was so unlucky that he was born before dawn, and now he has grown into a life overburdened with responsibilities. I see my stepfather King Amphitryon trapped in court from dawn to dusk every day with complaints from the people in his little territory. Eurystheus must be miserable. Praise be to you, Auntie Hera, that I was born too late and am free from the weight of crowns.

And I didn't realize Iphicles was so busy. All he's talked about is lining up dalliances with his admirers. I feel guilty for even asking him. Poor royals, you know.

"Please," says the mother, bending her head to your shrine. "There is no counting how many children that lion has taken from mothers."

Iphicles says, "Al, the Lion of Cithaeron is supposed to be a nightmare. I know a poet that sang of it, and it tracked him down and ate him too."

I try to imagine that. "That's a lot of work for a lion."

"This thing is vicious on another level. They need Ares, not us."

"Ares is not answering their prayers. This mother needs a hero."

"Seriously, Al. Drop it. You know what happens to heroes?"

I look upon my brother, and then to this terrified mother. But it was the gaze of your bust that convinced me. What would the Goddess of Family want me to do?

I say, "Anything for Auntie Hera."

Hera 3

I lean back on the marble rim of Olympos and kick my feet up, resting them on a cloud. On the mortal plane below, everyone is doing exactly what I planned. I love being good at my job.

In a voice mimicking the follower I sent, I say, "Oh please, great Heracles, won't you solve all my problems by getting eaten by a lion?"

Only shitheels turn down a mother in need. I didn't even inspire her to get on her bare knees like that, though. That was great stuff. If that woman wants to get married again, I'll pick out a handsome prince for her myself.

The satisfaction is so sweet that I half-expect my dipshit husband will appear and spoil it. I haven't seen the bastard in what feels like years.

Yet it's not Zeus who ruins my beautiful solitude. I hear the talons scratching on the marble floor, and I know it's an owl before I smell it. I hate that she always shows up in the avatar of an owl. Like predator birds are special?

I ask, "What do you want, Athena?"

I wave on my blind side, hoping I'll smack her by accident and send her down to the mortal world. She doesn't belong up here, especially when I'm feeling this good. She erupted from my dipshit husband's head one afternoon long ago, and is quite likely the only child of his who isn't the product of infidelity. She's a literal headache who thinks she's the Goddess of Wisdom.

"Your Grace," Athena says in that neutral inflection she always uses, like she has no opinion on anything because she's above facts and opinions. "I am merely curious of one detail in your grand scheme."

"Whatever the question is, the answer is you should leave me alone."

Her white-speckled brown shape waddles into my peripheral vision.

Of course she won't leave me alone. There's something she doesn't know, and nothing bothers the Goddess of Wisdom more than that.

She asks, "Why the Lion of Cithaeron?"

That's what she doesn't understand? My head lolls back, the tips of my golden hair brushing the floor.

"Because if you go to its home region, and you examine the creature very closely, you will find it is a big fucking lion that kills everything."

"Yes, Your Grace," she says. "It's just that I recall Cithaeron is the mountain where you and Zeus used to go make love outside of the titans' purview. When you were youngest and most in love. I believe you called it your one private hiding spot."

"It's not very private if you know about it. You weren't even born back then."

Those talons claw closer, and I can feel her chill near me. Most gods and goddesses have very warm auras. This goddess, though, always leaches my heat.

She says, "The question compels me. You looked for a place to send Zeus's son, and your thoughts went to a place where you and Zeus were happy and carefree. Why?"

"Because a killer lion lives there. I thought you were the smart god."

"There is a much larger lion that lives in the west, which you could have—"

I wheel around to lash out at her, but at that exact heavenly moment, another god's voice rings out across Olympos. Every room and space in the temple shakes with the voice of Apollo. He jumps up on the marble rim of Olympos, both hands grabbing hanks of his golden hair. He's so transfixed by whatever is happening in the world below that he loses his luminescent crimson robes, and they fall away, fluttering to the mortal plane as though they're a present for whoever just entertained him.

I give him a withering look. I already have Athena here; I don't need a second headache.

I ask, "What happened now? Did one of your mortal suitors steal the moon for you?"

"The kid has already slain the lion."

"No. The fight can't be over."

"It wasn't much of a fight, unless you think a hand swatting a fly is a war."

It was a cosmic second ago. He can't have fought it. It's going to kill him, and I'm going to watch.

I peer over the edge of Mount Olympos, down at Mount Cithaeron, into the ravines where roads wind, those great clefts that Zeus and I once broke into the earth when we were a little too zealous in our lovemaking. We were foolish and I didn't know him better yet.

Nowhere on the mountain can I find the great lion. It has to be prowling somewhere.

Then it emerges from the shadow of the ravine, and its golden fur drinks in the light of the sun. It raises up toward the sky, toward Mount Olympos as though it is looking at me. As though it questions why this day has dawned.

But there is no actual life in its eyes. Its body rises and falls, rises and falls, as a single man parades it along the road toward Thebes. It's that damned bastard, his smile splitting open his beard.

He bellows, "Thank you, Auntie Hera, for giving me the strength to survive this ordeal!"

I have sparred with Artemis. I have been pummeled by hundred-handed titans. But his words feel like a slap across my entire cosmos.

I reel away, and find Athena isn't peering over the edge at the sight. She's watching me, casually, as though she already knew the outcome.

Oh, I could go for roast owl right now.

I say, "Apollo. Athena. Get me something deadlier. Let's drive some other heroes mad and slaughter the bastard that way. Is Oedipus still alive? He's easy enough to fuck with. Just tell him he's related to Heracles and that'll do it."

They're cowards. I can see it in them. Apollo shrinks up, finally realizing his nudity in his discomfort, and actually crosses his legs for modesty. That shrill, gray-eyed owl, Athena, shifts on the rim of Olympos.

I grip the marble rim and peer again upon the mortal plane. At that insipid half-god, bouncing along the path to a city, proclaiming he's slain a thing in my honor. Leaving the mountain that should have been his deathbed behind, leaving more tainted memories in a place that should be special.

I could send him to fight another lion. A bigger lion.

I could, if I was an idiot who was out of ideas.

A beast like the Lion of Cithaeron has broken a few dozen men.

But there are things that break far more than that. There is no beast greater than war.

I look along the shores of the Aegean Sea, for the unrest that terrifies wild animals into abandoning their homes. Throughout the entire region of Boeotia, no one is as feared as the Minyan Army. Their bronze blades hold an edge longer than any other, and each man in their ranks wears a breastplate that turns arrows. The Minyans take tribute from every other people who dare raise their heads. Even Thebes would not stand against them, angry as Thebes is becoming with their demands.

The Thebans will fight the Minyans eventually, no matter what we gods do. They are bullying each other back and forth. Humans always become petty with power.

But if they went to war soon, then Heracles would have to join his stepfather, King of Troezen, regent of Mycenae, in the call to defend Thebes.

Let's see how you like a war, dear boy.

Heracles 3

That was fun! The Theban elders say a war has never gone that well. Did you see the look on their king's face when I threw a boulder over his entire encampment? Iphicles swears he saw King Erginus soil himself. I think—

Oh, I'm sorry. I was too excited and lost my manners.

Auntie Hera, please hear my prayer.

I sacrifice this meal and this wine to you in gratitude.

Thank you for leading Thebes to overwhelming victory over the Minyans. I know it was you who kept my neck safe from their blades, and who diverted the arrows so that they landed in the dirt. Iphicles says I have the reflexes of a deer, but I know my fate is more than my own work. You smile upon me, and so I do this for your glory.

It would have been a slaughter if not for your beneficence. Thebes is a great city, but it had too few arms to mount an appropriate defense against the entire Minyan host. I heard Thebans crying in terror for want of blades as I was attending your temple. Had I not been in your temple at that very moment, I would not have known that keen spears and keener arrows decorated the walls.

You're a clever one, Auntie Hera. You inspired me to hand them all out so the Thebans could defend themselves, didn't you?

Of course, having a son of Papa Zeus on the battlefield helped a little, too. I do not like to brag in prayers, but I will never tire of lifting the ground out from beneath a hundred warriors and sending them spilling like droplets of water in a current. So many of the soldiers threw down their painted shields and abandoned the cause.

The great city of Thebes is safe tonight. Poets sing that no army west of Thrace is so formidable as the Minyans, and surely they do own more bronze armor and brush-headed helmets than any I have seen in one place before. Now the Thebans have collected the weapons those terrified extortionists dropped as they fled, and arm themselves with the shields of their oppressors, all painted with the three-headed dog Cerberus on them. I'd love to meet that puppy someday.

Soon it will be the Thebans who demand tribute from the Minyans.

But that way lies violence, and I know you abhor senseless killing. So when my business in Thebes ends, I shall travel the land and meet with any of their leaders. If we can have them discuss their grievances, then fewer mothers will mourn children fallen on battlefields. I know that must be your desire. And you know I will do anything for you.

As I returned within the gates of Thebes, I called for everyone to hear what you did.

"See what is the strength of Zeus? See what is the provenance of Hera?"

And I had a decent audience, as many had witnessed my feats upon the field of battle. Again, I do not wish to brag in prayers. But you saw that moment where I caught the spear out of the air and shattered it with my teeth, yes? That's everyone's favorite anecdote. Guaranteed to be in poems by next year.

A sharp-eyed poet whose hair and beard were the exact same texture, all long and curled, asked me, "What name should we celebrate?"

I gestured with both hands in the direction of your shrine on the hill. "Hera's Glory, my friend. The name of Heracles."

The poet scoffed. "You cannot be Heracles."

"Heracles?" balked a second Theban, who was still carrying the sword I'd handed him at your shrine. "We are all indebted to you, good foreigner. But you cannot be Heracles."

They led me to a marble statue of most impressive proportions. It is quite tall, in the shape of a man I recognize. He is enormous, muscles bulging from his shoulders and thighs, and his beard so thick it could house a family of birds. He also hadn't covered himself when someone had chiseled his likeness, and so I recognize other parts of him as well.

I stood beside this marble giant and struck the same pose, glowering downward with a fist on my hip. It looks much less assuming coming from me, as I'm shorter, and my arms are much thinner. It's hard to bulk up when divine strength lifts everything for you. Where his exposed belly is taut, mine protrudes.

"This is *a* son of Alcmene," I said, holding back laughter. "He was born moments after me. But you bought a likeness of Iphicles. Please tell me you haven't been worshipping it."

One woman cackled like a rooster at dawn. She was particularly dark of complexion, like King Creon of Thebes himself, with broad cheeks and broader hips. She carried with her several quivers of arrows, and it was clear she had ferried them to the front lines for the siege.

People tried to argue with me, and I wished I could just introduce them to Iphicles. He's somewhere in the city, although he always tends to disappear when there is battle. Despite his great size, he is a politician.

Left to defend my identity alone against all of Thebes, I decided to climb my brother's marble likeness. I proclaimed to them all, "I will prove that I am Hera's Glory. Any Theban who doubts me may arm-wrestle me to test the strength of Zeus. If I best a challenger, it will cost you one cup of wine. If you best me, then I will bring you wine whenever you please for the rest of your life."

Local sellers immediately began mixing wine with water for the festivities. I thought it would be a good way to get a couple drinks and start some conversations. A little revelry after our godsent victory.

But there is probably a shorter line leading to the underworld. My challengers queued up around the courtyard twice, and then their numbers stretched from there down the road. The one laughing woman from earlier checked and reported the line ended in a bathhouse, where the last of my challengers were washing up in excitement for the endless wine they would soon win.

They quieted down after the third man crumpled in defeat from a squeeze of my hand. I was trying to be gentle, but got too eager. Yet everyone got excited again by the fifth, and certainly by the tenth challenger. Their being incapable of winning became the joke. These Thebans were not flighty hedonists who drank every night away. They had survived an invasion, and I'd made myself an excuse for a party and a release that they needed. That's a part I was happy to play, with or without a fancy statue dedicated to me.

I pulled the Lion on Cithaeron's skin off of my shoulders and laid it across my seat, so that the head of the beast would gaze out across the courtyard and at the line of waiting arm-wrestlers. I usually wear the head as a cowl.

A lion makes an imposing thing to wear to new places. It starts conversations.

That laughing woman now loitered to my left, within the dead gaze of my lion. To the left were no challengers, so she was not threatening me. Not with physical violence, anyway.

She asked, "You killed that animal?"

I answered, "It was a monster."

"And you killed it?"

"That's how I remember it."

With surprising venom, she said, "You are just like Perseus."

I joked, "Did you know him?"

"I know enough about his type."

"Be kind to his name. He is my great-grandfather, father to the father of my mother Alcmene. He did great things in his time."

"Perseus was crueler than monsters. Unless you think how he treated Medusa was right."

I slammed down the next man's hand, a little too hard. I apologized to him, and gave him two cups of the wine I'd previously earned so far as compensation. I kept arm-wrestling and winning more cups as I chatted with this blasphemous lady.

I bested the next challenger and said, "Medusa was a monster. She turned people to stone with a suggestive look."

The woman gave me a suggestive look. I did not feel hard as stone right away.

She said, "Perseus did not even have grievance with Medusa. He boasted he could get any gift necessary to woo his lover, and the corrupt King of Seriphos held him to it and demanded Medusa's head."

"I believe it was a little more complicated than that."

"Perseus had grievances with the king, not her. If he was a hero, he should have beheaded him instead."

"You know, he did slay that king."

"He also slew an innocent woman. If my gaze turned people to stone, would my life be so worthless that you could behead me in pursuit of whoever you lusted after?"

Those words could haunt a man. As it was, I nearly lost focus and the next arm-wrestling match. The centaur, Nessus, strained all the way to his haunches trying to best me, his hooves clacking against the floor. I put his hand down to the table, but without the fervor for sport. My mind was elsewhere.

I turned to the woman. "My lady, what is your name?"

"Call me Megara."

"Megara, what god guides you to such wisdom and blasphemy?"

She blew a strand of hair from her face. "Why don't you guess?"

"Is it Hera?"

"She is the August Queen, but I do not pray to her."

Forgive Megara, Auntie Hera. She didn't know better.

"King Zeus? He who commands the sky?"

"I live on the ground."

"Athena? The Goddess of Wisdom? All the smart girls love Athena."

"You think I need a goddess to bring me wisdom?"

"Well, we can all use some assistance in wisdom. And she is the greatest of strategy. She has all but supplanted Ares as the Goddess of War because of her cunning nature. Yours is a city in need of defense."

"I do not need both wisdom and conflict," she said, signaling the server for a cup of wine. "I pray to my god to bring me the right conflicts. I handle them swiftly, for I have all the wisdom I need."

No. It wasn't possible.

"You can't worship Ares."

She said, "I believe I can."

Megara received her cup and set it on the table. The last of the challengers bold enough to wrestle me was thwarted, leaving the seat open. A groove is worn into the surface of the table from all the elbows of the people who challenged me and lost their wine.

She thunked her elbow into that groove and invited me with her palm. One more challenge.

Around us, a city of survivors danced and fell in love. We linked hands, and leaned in until I smelled the bitter air of her breath.

I lost.

My arm went straight down. I am the son of Zeus, and the beloved of Hera. But I fought a whole war, and arm-wrestled every bold man in Thebes. I'm weary, tired, and she had Ares on her side.

What a mighty woman. I tell everyone in court how strong she is. I beg the poets to sing of this great saga; it was my loud boasting that got the attention of her father.

You see, nobody in Thebes was more surprised than her father, Creon. As in *King* Creon, monarch of Thebes and all Boeotia. He descended upon us with all of his servants and retinue, saying he had searched everywhere for me. To show his gratitude for my defense of the city, he would grant me anything.

I looked into Megara's dark eyes and said, "Well, I owe her a lot of wine."

She's very strong, Auntie Hera. I think you would like her.

Hera 4

There is no door and I kick it open anyway.

I always know when Aphrodite is on Mount Olympos, because a vast territory of the marble restructures itself into the many private chambers she desires. Any unused area becomes part of the Goddess of Love's palace of fertility. She takes it up with her powders and oils, and mirrors and paints, and wigs and wardrobes—all worthless human artifice. Any goddess can change her avatar by sheer will. Divinity makes tools unnecessary. Yet the Goddess of Love is unhealthily attached to the mortal world and mastering its constantly shifting ideas of beauty.

And there are never doors into Aphrodite's private palace. She insists on vast space and vast privacy.

I find the specific room she's in by following the sounds. She is also the patron Goddess of Geese because of certain noises she makes when she's enjoying herself. I circle three outer walls until I hear her nasally honking away in bliss.

I put my foot through the marble, reducing it into a cloud of dust. Beyond is Aphrodite, reclining on a bed festooned with pearls, and myrrh bushes, and red anemones as bright as her lips. All she wears is that golden girdle, which must be uncomfortable, with her bare legs both hiked up high in the air like her toes are saluting me. Just looking at the position makes my lower back ache.

But I'm not here for her.

At the foot of the bed, down on his knees, is my son. Ares, the God of War, the scourge of battlefields, crouches between Aphrodite's thighs, face buried in there, giving peace a chance.

Aphrodite goes bolt upright, a flock of doves flying from the bed to take cover in her golden chariot. Then her gaze turns withering, and she drops her head and brilliant hair onto the bed.

"Really?" she says. "You picked right now? You couldn't have waited six months? I was close."

"Mom, seriously!" Ares says, like I'm cleaning food off his face. I am *not* going to clean what's streaked in his beard. "At least knock."

"Get up this instant." I point out through the hole I kicked and toward the marble rim of Olympos. "Give that foolish Megara girl some divine inspiration to dump Heracles. She worships you."

Ares asks, "Who's Megara?"

He starts to stand up, and Aphrodite grabs his beard to keep him in place. She says, "Some aging princess with no marital prospects and a lot of luck. And shouldn't you be asking me to break them up? The Goddess of *Love*?"

No, I'm not hearing that shit today. "I am the Goddess of Mothers, Family, and Childbirth. I'm more the Goddess of Love than you ever will be. That's why I'm ending this Heracles and Megara thing immediately."

Ares says, "I don't really meddle in love stories. My realm is more the wars that come from them going wrong."

Aphrodite rubs the heel of one foot on Ares's shoulder. "Yeah, and also that boy is, what, twenty years old now? He's strong as Zeus. He's never had a lover who survived ten minutes, and Megara's built like a donkey. Let them have fun."

That's what love sounds like? How does anyone worship her?

"Ares," I say, pulling my voice taut. "You know you are my son."

I can hear the concessions coming in his tone. "Yes."

"And you know I love you."

"I never doubt that out loud."

I tilt my brow forward, running my tongue along my upper teeth. "How do I feel about infidelity?"

Ares sits halfway up and shares a blank look with Aphrodite. I have seen dogs share more thoughtful expressions.

He says, "Is it really infidelity if I was going to marry her but Hephaistos got there first?"

"Yes!" I say. Maybe I'm a little too loud, as my voice sends all the rock dust swirling into whirlwinds and out into Aphrodite's other rooms. "Yes, it is! So go quash this Megara thing or I will tell Hephaistos what you are doing with his wife."

I despise that Ares's response is to look to Aphrodite.

Aphrodite rubs some of the juices off Ares's chin as she says, "Look, my relationship with Ares is a secret, but not that kind of secret."

And Ares adds, "Also, what is the God of Blacksmiths going to do to the God of War? Forge a bunch of invisible chains to catch us the next time we sneak in here?"

Aphrodite thinks for a moment. "Are you into chains?"

"Hm. I could be."

They are not changing the subject, and especially not to that. "Heracles won a war without your blessing. You will do as your queen says and end his engagement immediately."

"He actually did have my blessing."

"What!"

It is not a question. It is a curse word, and anybody who thinks it isn't hasn't been a disappointed mother.

Ares shrugs with his wrists. "He was defending Thebes, and I have a lot of followers there. I'm cultivating my lineage. I know everyone likes the Aegean people's sculptures right now, but trust me, war is what they'll be famous for."

I nearly charge into the chamber to dash his brains against his mistress's pelvis. "This is why people call you the worst God of War!"

Aphrodite rolls her eyes. "You're only saying that because Athena is standing behind you."

She is not. Nobody can surprise the Queen of Olympos.

Only, when I glance behind me, she is.

So that's how I soil a perfectly good dress. Do you know how hard it is to get stains out of stardust?

This time she's in her humanoid avatar. She is one of the tallest goddesses, with an olive complexion, the fine robes of a senator matched always with the plumed helm of a charioteer. It's as though she's ever ready for work.

"Your Grace," in that same neutral tone. Her tone makes me want to pour molten bronze down her throat. "I wanted to make sure you were all right."

I warn her, "Do not mock me."

"This age has put a great deal of stress on your shoulders. You deserve more compassion than you receive."

"Oh, fuck off," says Ares. I can feel the daggers he's glaring at Athena. She has been trying to steal his spot as God of War since the afternoon she was born. She thinks that he's a mere thug while she's all tactics. A lot of people think a lot of things.

"Oh, fuck off," I say. "Zeus sent you to spy on me. Do you want me to carve your eyes out with a spoon?"

Her eyes crease with the faintest concern—concern for me. That's what gets my stomach roiling.

Still placid of tone, she says, "I assume your outburst is because of the news?"

"Which news? You're supposed to be the smart goddess. You know everything."

"The news about Heracles."

I'm ready to grab her by the robes and drag her to the marble rim. Maybe this second-string Goddess of War can disavow Megara's affections for me. "Heracles is not getting married."

"Your Grace," Athena says, "he's been married for some time."

Damn. How long has it been while I've been arguing with Ares and Aphrodite?

"I'll have to do something . . ." I say, yet all that comes to mind is another lion. There has to be a better solution than lions.

"Their marriage is not the news I thought upset you, Your Grace."

Now I do grab the insipid goddess's robes, feeling my face heat up like a blade in the furnace. "Tell me one thing that would upset me more than that idiot getting married?"

Auntie Hera, hear my prayer,
You have blessed me throughout my life. From before I could stand, to the day I marched to war at Thebes, I have always known your grace. But never have I needed you more than I do now.

I'll never forget when Megara first told me. She followed me right into the bathhouse, sending naked elders scattering in all directions. She plunged right into the water and grabbed onto me, looking like she'd seen the shades of our ancestors. But no. She'd seen our future.

"We are having a child."

I celebrated until towers shook from my voice, and militias arrived thinking I was a beast that needed to be put down. I paced all around the wilderness of Thebes twice. The wild dogs have grown fat because I kept throwing them more food to celebrate this gift you gave to us. Our family was growing! Anybody who was building a house, I snapped the trees myself and split them into lumber with my bare hands.

Oh, Megara makes fun of my splinters. She mocked me to Ares.

But something is wrong.

Her father summoned the finest midwives from across Thebes, and further ones from Gia and Athens. They say Megara shows the signs of a troubled pregnancy, and hers will be a hard labor. They say she is old to bear children, and that bearing the greatness of a demigod's lineage would challenge anyone. History is littered with lost parents.

The pregnancy is Megara's choice. I have implored her to put herself first, but she is steadfast. She wishes to bring lives into this world.

There is no one who greater understands her passion than you, Hera, Goddess of Mothers, Goddess of Childbirth, Goddess of Family. No one has seen more lives come into the world, nor has anyone protected more vulnerable souls under Atlas's sky.

Her father went to the Oracle at Delphi, and learned that Megara will give birth in the next three weeks.

So I sacrifice this calf to you, the fattest from my herd.

So I sacrifice this goat to you, the hardiest in my herd.

So I sacrifice this wine to you, every cup that I might drink.

I shall fast until the morning after my child is born. Please help a mother, Auntie Hera.

I am the Goddess of Marriage and Family. Do you know who beckons me? Every ruling family, every family of politicians, every family with a soldier in it claps their hands before my shrines and begs me to resew the tapestry of fate for them. From goats not yielding milk to ships sprouting leaks out at sea, people always bend the story to ask for my intervention.

In other words: I am busy.

I do not just answer every petty prayer. I am a goddess, not a waitress.

An Achaean stable maid is dangerously underweight to be delivering her child, and I am there.

A groundskeeper who lives his truth as a man, but who in doing so has lost the support of his family, must give birth with no one to even wipe the sweat from his eyes as his contractions hasten, but he is not alone, for I am there.

A foolish woman with contractions growing closer together seeks to climb Mount Olympos so the gods will see her baby, in defiance of the divine order. Approaching divinity itself will kill any mortal. As she ascends, boils raise on her flesh, and her limbs weaken until she cannot stand, much less climb. She is about to slip and perish, but she is not alone, for I am there.

Cities around the Aegean Sea are teeming with new life. I can't be bothered to look in on everyone.

A shriek rings out from Thebes, and I stiffen my spine. It is too like a sound I once made. When I was alone.

I am so struck by the sound that I do not realize I have company. Standing to my left is that gray-eyed know-it-all.

"Will you help them?"

Athena's voice makes me jump, and I nearly expose myself to the mortals. I scowl at her and make a lewd gesture with one hand, while using the other hand to weave a blessing over the newborn.

I spit out, "Why do you all think I don't have other things to do?"

A foolish Lefkadan couple who are rowing out into the Ionian Sea for some late-term dalliance, to recite poetry at one another and contemplate the clouds. Her water breaks just as the island of Lefkada dwindles to a speck over their starboard side. They'll have to deliver with her feet up on his bench, surrounded by water, dreading that Poseidon will vengefully take their baby's spirit. But he won't touch this baby today.

Everything will go fine for everyone.

Everyone giving birth tonight will have the most painless experience in recorded history.

Athena questions, "Every person?"

"Silence. I'm working."

"She will not survive this birth. You could save her, and with ease."

"She's strong enough to do it on her own. If she can put up with that oaf of a husband, then she must be a—"

Another shriek rises up somewhere in Thebes, and then is cut off right in the middle, as though the mother's throat collapses from the power of the noise. My eyes water from the sense of how she must feel.

In the momentary silence when her voice is quieted, up comes another prayer.

"Auntie Hera, please . . ."

I am busy. I do not even look in their direction.

Maybe once. One peek with my all-seeing eyes. Just one peek won't ruin my schedule.

Heracles 5

Auntie Hera,

I have never seen the like of this child. King Creon's men meant to take him away and banish him, but I wouldn't let them. They'd have to kill me first.

I washed my son's brow, first with water from a nearby stream, and then with new wine. When I held this child to my chest, something pricked my flesh. The baby's hand dug deep at my skin.

That was when we discovered his hands and feet were not those of normal children. Not normal human children.

The flesh of his palms is rough and pink, like the pads of a lion's feet. His fingers are short, and the nail of each is surely a claw. They extend when he exhales his breath. He doesn't know it, but he gave me quite the scrape. I nearly lost a nipple. We wrestled a little, as I tried to swaddle him so he wouldn't injure himself with these miraculous gifts.

The rest of him is perfectly human, and he's eager for Megara's breast. Human eyes that have yet to truly start seeing. A human back and shoulders, upon which he would carry the weight of his life. He's no more a monster than I am. I wonder what he'll grow up to become.

This is your doing, isn't it?

Mama Alcmene reminded me that when I was very little, I used to pray to you to see cats. She says I asked you for them three times a day.

Is this your way of delivering cats to me? Is this your sense of humor?

Thank you for answering those prayers. I take my son's paws as a sign of your love on my household.

His name is Therimachus, son of Heracles and Megara. Therimachus the Lion will be as dedicated to you as I am.

Hera 6

So you spared Megara's life after all."

Can I have one fucking moment to myself? I was up all night answering prayers. I reek of mortals, and now I have to deal with this?

Athena is behind me, because that weirdo always appears behind me. She probably does it because she knows if I saw her coming, I'd avoid her.

"I did no such thing!" I say, turning away from the marble rim. It's time for Olympos to make me a private temple. I'll steal Aphrodite's idea and leave no doors. Maybe a single window, with a bird feeder full of poison. "I don't even know what you're talking about."

She's in her owlish avatar again, feathers speckled white. She perches nearby, twisting her head at me with those wide eyes. "I have not heard a single parent this morning who does not praise you for your intervention."

"What's that? Mortals making mistakes and thinking they're special? What a novelty. Thank you so much for bringing it to my attention."

"You didn't oversee every childbirth in Greece last night?"

"I didn't oversee all of them, you feckless twit." I gaze at myself in a mirror of polished bronze. I fix a few strands of my hair. "A goddess chooses."

Athena persists. "Did you look in upon anyone in Thebes last night?"

"I looked in on many people in many places. I thought you were the smart goddess."

"Queen Hera, did you look in on Heracles and Megara?"

"Shut the fuck up, Athena."

Slender hands take my shoulders, and I rise up ready to smite whoever made that mistake. But there are the happy snakes of Granny's hair, all flicking their tongues, their eyes as glassy and content as her own. The fury rubs my back with her taloned fingers, such a glow of pride in her typically sallow features.

"I knew you'd overcome your resentment, dear," Granny says. "You're not petty. You're not capricious. That's a shell that shallow people can't see through."

I scrunch up my nose like I'm balling up a fist. Of course Granny was behind Athena's interloping. Why else would the Goddess of Wisdom be pestering me so much? The old fury put her on my path to try to change my mind. Furies think they're good at that.

With an elbow, I push Granny away from me. I give both her and Athena the chilly stare they deserve.

I say, "I could still wipe out that entire family. I'm not out of serpents to put in cribs."

Granny reaches for me again. "Dear, you are magnificent."

"Maybe I'll skip straight to lions and put one in the baby's crib."

Athena says, "Why do you always pick lions?"

The javelin is in my hand before time itself knows it. I thrust it at that damned owl, and she flutters her pudgy wings to get some distance.

It's Granny who saves Athena from being perforated. She puts a slender hand on the haft of my spear, just south of the blade. Her hand trembles, and I know it's more from the toll of time than it is fear for me.

I could calm myself faster than I do.

"It doesn't have to be lions," I say, looking at Granny. "I could send you."

Her fingers retreat from the spear and hide themselves in the folds of her robe. Even the heads of her snakes hide against her scalp. "Please don't joke about that."

"It would be simple. Send you on a short trip down there, into Heracles's mind. Make him destroy himself with the very strength he says I gave him. That would show my dipshit husband."

"Please . . ."

What am I doing?

I assure her, "I wouldn't."

It comes out faster than the javelin. The pleading tone of someone so tired, despite so much rest. The need to assuage her fears is too great, like I went from a deep breath to suffocating. I will not treat Granny like my dipshit husband treats everyone else.

Yet Granny's face shuffles, clearly trying to muster the conviction to tell me that she knows I wouldn't. That she can't say it immediately makes me ache. This isn't right. This isn't what I want for her.

A safe distance away from us, from the marble rim of Olympos, comes Athena's voice. "What are you truly mad about?"

"I'm complex. I'm capable of being mad about more than one injustice at a time."

"That is true." Athena says it like she's the authority on truth.

Despite myself, some part of me is pleased that she agrees with me.

I say to Granny, "I knew you sent her after me."

Granny stares at me, while her snakes stare at the owl perched on the rim of Olympos. "But I didn't."

"Don't lie to me."

Granny touches her own chest, right over her heart. "I can't order the Olympians around. Even if I could, I would never manipulate things behind your back."

"She didn't summon me," says Athena. "I would tell you if she did."

The Goddess of War who stole her position through tactics and strategy says she wouldn't lie. I have some room to doubt her here.

"All right," I say in a clear tone that indicates that this isn't and will never be all right. "Tell me, Goddess of Wisdom, what has you riding my ass?"

"The King of the Gods sired a child he claimed chosen above all others. But he has scarcely been a part of his son's story."

I will ram my javelin right through that owl. "I am not Zeus's secretary. Go ask him why he sucks at parenting."

Athena shuffles on her bird feet so that she can gaze over the mortal world. "Don't you find it suspicious that Zeus would be so enthused over Heracles and then ignore him? Where is he?"

"I do not spend every waking moment thinking about my dipshit husband. I spent all of last night racing across the entire world, from birthing chamber to birthing chamber. Why would I know where he is?"

"This is why I approached you."

I'm halfway sure that Athena is playing me, and Zeus is watching this. This is a trick they're playing on me. "You're serving his ends again? You always suck up to your father."

"I am not in his service."

I sweep my vision around Olympos, and I don't sense his aura anywhere. If he's hiding, he's doing better than usual. "What do you mean? Where is he?"

"That is the puzzle, Your Grace."

The words come out a little faster than I intend. "You're the fucking Goddess of Wisdom. You know all kinds of shit. Where is Zeus?"

"I cannot find him in Crete, or Arcadia, or Thessaly. Not in the Aegean Sea, nor the Ionian Sea. He is not typically difficult to find."

"Oh, please," I say, glancing over the marble rim to the mortal world. "If you miss him, check under the nearest nubile virgin. He disappears to fuck around constantly."

"You think he's being unfaithful?"

Given that she's in the avatar of a bird, it wouldn't do anything if I shoved her off the mountain. But I still consider it.

"Yeah," I say. "I have some evidence he's unfaithful."

"Your Grace, your domain includes all families, and all parents, and all children."

"Are you trying to earn the domain of Goddess of Rote Facts now? What is this?"

Now she peers at me with those gray eyes, and I see an ancient shade of gray in them. A shade that hasn't appeared in storm clouds since the titans died.

Athena says, "It has been years. If Zeus is philandering, he would have gotten a woman with child by now."

I almost joke that I'll have Granny burn the woman's house down so that there are no annoying offspring this time.

Then I get it. I don't want to get it, and I turn from the goddess and the world.

Waiting there is Granny, arms already halfway raised to offer me the comfort of an embrace. She's put it together, too. I can hear how it troubles her to say it.

"If the King of the Gods was philandering and got someone with child, wouldn't you know it?"

It's a reflex. I can't help checking the mortal world, just a real quick peek at everyone and everything. Every person late on their period. Every growing womb. Every milk-hungry cry. Every toddler taking their first steps. I know it before they know it, and I know everything.

It has been so many years since that mistake Heracles was born. And not a single other mistake has been made on the entire Aegean Sea. I stare at the islands. I have to have missed someone. Zeus never stops fucking around. What made him go chaste?

Wait. There's a bigger question. Because I don't see my dipshit husband anywhere in our domain.

I ask Athena, "Where the fuck is he?"

The Goddess of Wisdom stares down at the mortal world with me and says, "I don't know."

Heracles 6

When I row a ship off to do battle in your name, it's not the threat of injury that bothers me. Iphicles's boy, Iolaus, often comes with me, and he sees how badly I want to return. It's the same when I drag a boulder to irrigate farmland, or drag carts of grain to towns hit with famine. In all of it, the heaviest burden on my shoulders is the time away from them.

Life feels eternal until I hold one of my sons in my lap. All three are healthy: Therimachus, Creontiades, and now Little Deicoon. Each of them deserves so much time. So why is it only then that time goes so much faster? We scarcely begin a footrace and then it is time for supper. No archery lesson is long enough. I feel the time with these boys falling between my fingers, days as grains of sand.

Auntie Hera, can't you slow the hours for fathers when they see their children?

As I enter the house this afternoon, none of the boys is present. I set down my club and cast off my robes, enjoying the coolness of my home for a moment, and expecting them to come running to me.

But I don't hear a peep.

I call up the stairs, "Boys?"

There is a strained silence. There is perhaps one titter, half a giggle, before a hand is clapped over a mouth.

They are testing me again. They want to ambush their papa. They will slay a hero tonight.

So I tread heavily up the stairs, putting all my weight loudly into every step. When the three of them pounce, I am aghast. I am dragged to the floor, and three boys promptly climb on top of my fallen body.

"Mercy!" I beg. "I have not been bested so horribly since I arm-wrestled your mother!"

Megara snorts from across the room. She is sprawled across the bed, clearly enjoying having all the space to herself. She is more asleep than awake, but her amused expression says she is still paying attention. That is good, because any time she closes her eyes, Little Deicoon demands she pick him up.

I am home tonight, and so I care for them and grant her some time to recuperate.

Creontiades holds my beard in one hand, while the other is aloft, hefting an imaginary sword. It is as though he is Perseus, about to behead a gorgon. I wonder if his mother will sass him.

The eight-year-old conquering hero demands, "We will only spare your life if you show us the lion!"

Little Deicoon says, "Give lion! Give lion!"

Against such a fearsome enemy host, how can I not surrender?

I bring out my old traveling cloak. The hide is a little smaller than I remember, but I put it at the east wall of the room, and unroll it, and unroll and unroll, until it nearly touches the west wall. The old lion's head still has all its teeth, and its eyelids are eternally open, gazing upon me with a wrath it will never make good on.

Therimachus is the only one who dares look the old lion in the face. His face goes slack with wonder, and then he examines the soles of his own hands and feet. He compares the thick pink flesh there, and his small claws against those of the mighty beast that preceded him. Besides his extremities, he has always looked human to me. Perhaps he has a feline cunning in his gaze, but that is more from his mother than anything.

He tugs at the pelt, just below the lion's head. "Will I grow this big?"

I laugh softly and kiss his hairline. "Perhaps you will. Your cousin Iolaus is getting quite tall, and his father is huge."

Creontiades asks, "Will I grow that tall?"

"Yeah," asks Deicoon, his voice so nasal. He always has to tip his chin upward when he wants to speak full sentences. "Will I be big as lions?"

Creontiades and Deicoon have never displayed any of the unusual traits that their older brother does. They are strapping boys, each sprouting up to broad shoulders and long legs far before they have any use for them. Creontiades, I notice, is nearly as sharp with a bow as I am, but only when nobody is watching. He has yet to master his abilities under stress. I wonder, and I worry, whether he will master such things, and someday become a legendary archer. Will the divine blood from his grandfather manifest in this boy's eagle-eyed archery?

What will come of Therimachus as he ages? Will he sprout a mane, and an appetite for flesh on battlefields?

Will Creontiades and Deicoon become more like unto lions as they age? Who is to say their eldest brother didn't merely have a head start, and their whole generation will grow into a voracious pride that will rule the entire Aegean Sea?

I catch myself hurrying in my thoughts, rushing past the moment tonight, on to their futures. On to the men they will become, instead of enjoying the time I have with them as boys.

You answer my prayers, Auntie Hera. I understand how to control time.

I do it by slowing myself down. I gather all three of the boys to my chest, and I lay them down on the pelt of the Lion of Cithaeron. Then I climb onto it with them, as though we all ride on the back of the great beast.

I ask the boys, "Who do we thank for time as a family?"

In unison, all three of them yell, "Thanks, Great-Auntie Hera!"

B eneath the tall columns of Zeus's temple in Olympia, a narrow-faced priest with overgrown fingernails speaks about how the King of Olympos witnesses all. In an extraordinary coincidence, a flock of flesh-eating cuckoos descends on the temple in the middle of his lecture. They peck only at Zeus's loyal priest and chase him off the platform.

Coincidences. Aren't they funny?

I linger outside the temple, squinting through the oncoming twilight for his outrage. Zeus will blight the land and salt the eyes of all who saw this. Poets will live happy lives just on retelling the tantrum he's about to throw.

There is no outraged eagle. No thunderbolt splits the oncoming night.

"Come on, you dipshit."

Does he think he can ignore the Queen of Olympos?

I clench my fists so hard that my human avatar bursts like a jug of wine on a hot day. Gore gets everywhere. It'll take the worshippers weeks to clean that up.

My next avatar is a cunning disguise. The robe falls a little too deeply over one creamy shoulder, every speck of my new flesh pale in the way mortals are now pretending is attractive. My hair is woven from Helios's own sunshine. I wear the voluptuous figure that my dipshit husband always goes chasing after. This avatar is a list of everything that makes him make mistakes.

With bare feet that never pick up a single scratch, I walk from Kalydon to Thermon, and from Thermon to Delphi, and from Delphi to the east. This beautiful avatar crosses all of northern Greece.

The wrong attention follows me a few times. Those men become goats, and those goats become stew meat at temples that pray to me. I drop off the donations on my way past them.

If any of them were Zeus, I couldn't overpower them so easily. As far as I know, he's never pretended to be stew to get laid, although I wouldn't put it past him.

Yet I find myself at the shores of the Aegean Sea and he still hasn't showed up. What's keeping him? He couldn't resist this. I've caught him far more easily before. I keep walking.

The first shrine is unintentional. It's barely a shrine, with one room and the road-facing wall left open so anyone can come within. Its foundations have washed out over centuries, and the decaying wood of its walls bow westward down the hill. Within is the only thing of value, the chiseled marble visage of the King of Olympos.

I exhale too hard, and the whirlwind sends the shrine to tatters. The bits go skittering down the hill, digging up clumps of weeds as they go.

The only thing that stands is the visage of Zeus.

Still in the avatar of a human woman, I step into the remains and put my hand over his stone mouth. With a simple shove, it goes backward. The crash reverberates through the soles of my feet. It's the best music I've heard in ages.

Then I am the wind, and I am foul ideas, flitting from mind to mind, and town to town. Along the roads the devout have left images of Zeus as protection and places where travelers can pray. The closer I get to Thebes, the more I knock them over. I leave my husband's image in the muck of the mortal world.

"Well?"

Another goes down.

"Where is the king?"

This one splashes into a puddle of horse piss. I linger over it, with my back to the sky, daring him to strike me. Let him show how ferocious he is.

The blow doesn't come, and so I keep going.

I strike, and I shove, and I hurl the likeness of the absent god to the earth. I dare him to show his face. To defend himself. To show that I'm worth fighting.

I get so riled up that I nearly smash the wrong statue.

Here, in the shadow of a high-walled city, in a stretch of land that reeks of ill-tended vineyards, is a statue with a proud chin and gentle eyes.

It takes me a moment to realize I'm looking at myself. Some artist with cheap stone and cheaper tools, and a misconception that I'm something soft.

Looking at her eyes makes me touch my own. My face feels clammy, despite my being in that gorgeous avatar. My face is painted with ambrosial oil, and now all it feels like is a cloying mask.

He wouldn't protect his shrine, nor the visages on the side of the road. He wouldn't lift a hand.

"Where the fuck are you?" I ask him as I raise my hand, ready to strike down my own visage. This is the vision of the goddess that he made queen. This is the image he's supposed to fucking cherish. The greatness that keeps the world running. If he wouldn't defend himself, will he defend what he's forced me to be?

I grab a loose rock off the ground, jagged edges of its underside digging into my palm. I squeeze and let myself bleed, and raise the stone to strike my visage down.

"Stop."

There he is. I know the power in that voice. The lightning that reverberates in it.

The first thing I see is that curled beard, thicker than deepest night. He's made it black, though, instead of the white it's been since we slew our father. Is he pretending to be young?

"Please put that down."

It's not his face. It's his beard, and his broad cheeks and thick brow. But this isn't Zeus.

He holds out one broad hand, thickly callused from a harder life than my husband ever had to live. His face isn't Zeus's, because Zeus never looks like he's understood anyone else. All this man is doing is imploring me, when he should just drive me into the ground. The way this shitty civilization treats women, one blaspheming could be killed in a heartbeat. I want him to fight me.

"That's my aunt there," he says, less lightning in his voice now. "Whatever your problem is with her, it's got to be a misunderstanding. She doesn't hurt people without reason. If we think about your problem together, I'm sure we'll find a better remedy than smashing statues."

I can't see his shoulders because he's carrying the biggest boar I've ever seen. One hand holds two of its hooves, keeping the dead beast in place. The other hand stretches out to me, like he's both offering it to shake and to take my weapon.

The rock is deep in my palm now. Blood trickles between my knuckles. I say, "I'm not trying to defy her."

"That's good, because you'd probably break your hand. I made that statue myself, and it's harder than you think."

It's easier to look the dead boar in the face than the live man. Its eyes are open, like death made it curious for the first time in its life. It's at least three times larger than the man holding it aloft.

I say, "What are you doing with that thing?"

"It's a long story," he says, shifting weight to his other foot, not like he's tired, but like he's fidgeting from social interaction. "It was plaguing the vineyards and the silver miners. The threat's over now. I'm taking it home, to my personal courtyard. I'm actually on my way to offer it to her."

He nods his head down at my crudely chiseled visage.

Then he asks me, "Are you headed into Thebes? You can come with me. Sometimes travelers get accosted on the roads around here if they're alone. We could even talk out your problem."

Weakness seeps out of his face, this facile openness, beckoning me to fill him up with my problems. Shoulders holding aloft a monster sag as though a demigod could be demure. His sun-cracked lips smile as though the women in his life misled him into thinking he's sweet. That smile sits in a familiar beard. I know him.

I jab a finger in his direction. "You do not understand me."

He'll back down and apologize now. He'll weasel out of his generosity. I know mistakes when they're made.

Except he stands his ground. His voice still gentle, he says, "That's why I asked what was wrong. Are you sick?"

"You stand there thinking you can comprehend what I go through? What a god has done to me? That you can judge me while a dead animal leaks shit on your shoulder?"

"I didn't mean to—"

I don't let him finish that. "Don't you dare pity me. Think you'll show me a little mercy, and then what? I'll fuck you behind your wife's back? That I'll help you fall into more glory?"

His eyes dart around, like he's wrestling with what to say. All my harsh words, and he's still trying to figure out a way to help. That pity makes me seethe until the flesh could melt off these bones.

Before he can give me some asinine advice, I leave. I drop the bloody rock at the foot of my own statue.

Heracles 7

Aunt Hera,

I'm covered in grime and fly bites. I've got the feces from three different animals in my mouth. I nearly lost an eye.

Never has a boar hunt gone so wild. This thing could burrow deep underground at will in a blink. Twice I had to plunge my hands into the earth to pull it out, and still it dug its way around them. They say it had gone from dragging the goats into its underground caves and was now attacking silver miners.

Tonight, the miners can rest easily, knowing the boar hunts no longer.

It would have made a fine trophy. And every butcher in Thebes would have paid me handsomely for it.

I lug it home over one shoulder, and lay it down to rest before the altar in my courtyard. Before your stone visage. May tonight's offering honor you.

I look upon the bulk of its back, and think, there is so much meat here. So much flesh.

I know Megara feels she has not appropriately honored your son, Ares, for some time. Will you begrudge me if I invite her to take a portion of the boar? To sacrifice for her god, and in doing so, honor a parent and a child?

I think of all the gods, you will understand doing something for your spouse, and doing something for your child.

The air in the house is still. I'm home so much earlier than I typically arrive. Megara isn't working in the craft room, but I hear a scuttling somewhere, like feet are hurrying.

"Megara? Are you home?"

It's not just still in the house. Within these walls of baked mud bricks, it's stifling. It's so much hotter in here than in the courtyard mere steps away.

Megara isn't home.

Except there's a wet sound, like breathing through an open mouth. It's coming from upstairs.

"Boys?"

When I start climbing the stairs, I hear a muffled giggle, like it's covered by hands. A little voice shushes someone.

I smile, realizing an ambush is waiting for me. I keep climbing the stairs to walk into the danger.

Hera 8

Petrichor and testicle sweat. I smell him before the static frizz builds in the air, and before the winds kneel and lower their currents. Before Aphrodite can complain about the clouds killing her lighting, and the rains fall at the feet of Mount Olympos. The clouds swell like ill thoughts, billowing across the horizon. Soon midday is smothered, and Helios flees, leaving our temple as dark as pitch.

Flickers rise from deep inside the clouds, flashing their contours with brilliance. Flashes that surpass white for brilliance. The thunderbolts the Cyclopes forged for him.

He's home.

Before I can reach the marble rim, Granny sprints into my path. Her leathery wings spread wide, as though she can shelter me from this weather.

"Please, dear. Don't do this to yourself."

My voice is steady as though some dimwit chiseled it out of granite. "I just want to see my husband."

"Think of all the children you've helped deliver this year. Why don't we go look in on them?"

"Perhaps. After I'm finished here."

She gets up on her tiptoes and still can't match my height. She tries to take my hand. "Let him wait. Let him dread facing you. There's no reason to rush this."

"Thank you for your counsel, Granny," I say, and keep walking toward where he'll have to enter.

They're all here, at a safe distance. Aphrodite and Hephaistos hold hands from beside an anvil, watching me. Ares isn't far away. Hestia and Dionysus have put down their jugs of booze to watch, and Hermes and Apollo crowd alongside them. Artemis stands in her doorway, a hand on her bow. Poseidon and Demeter go unseen, but I can feel their elements in the atmosphere. They are watching from safety. Eavesdroppers in Heaven.

I bang my lotus-headed scepter on the floor of Olympos, and all its walls obey me. Doors and windows snap shut, forming a perfect wall of white marble. There will be no other entrance along the marble rim, other than in front of me.

Any Olympian who wants to watch this will have to come out here and brave my company.

Who answers that challenge?

Perched at the top of the walls I've formed is a gray-eyed owl. The Goddess of Wisdom has her answer now. She knows where Zeus is.

I ask her, "What have you got to say for yourself?"

She's smart enough not to say anything.

It's Granny who says, "I want you to have fewer regrets than I do."

Thunder rolls from the south, and all the polished floors of Olympos light up as though his fingers grope every speck of the place. His light is everywhere. He's definitely here.

Except the marble rim I've left exposed in the south is vacant. No hand clasps the rim. He doesn't drop out of the sky on a thunderbolt, nor does he climb up. How dare he keep me waiting?

Overhead I notice Athena, still in the avatar of the owl. Her head twists northward. She's not watching where the thunder rumbles.

I look north, and there he is. He used the thunder as a distraction, to sneak into the palace.

How dare he look meek? That mountainous figure, with shoulders for days, but slumping, crouching along like he's pathetic. He pulls his waist-wrap up along his side, clutching the red fabric like he's suddenly cold. Like he is the one with something to fear. Like he's put upon in his own kingdom.

He won't even look at me. His eyes are on the solid walls I've erected, as though he's imploring all the other Olympians behind them to come out and defend him.

I say, "You."

He goes stiff like he's been struck by his own thunderbolt. His face turns only halfway to me, eyes threatening to dart away from me at a moment. He's about to turn into a bull and run for it. I know it.

"Hey, Hera," he says. "Love the crown. Is it new?"

"No," I say, despite the fact that yes, this polos was actually forged for me a year into his disappearance by Hephaistos, with a veil running down the back of the head. It looks great on me, but now I'd like to take it off and beat a man with it. "Who is your newest mistake?"

He dares to look perplexed. "The newest what?"

"You heard me. Who is she?"

He turns a little more toward me, an arm holding conspicuously to one side of his robe. He's hiding something in there.

He asks, "Who are you talking about?"

"I don't know what power you cooked up to hide yourself in Greece, but I know how you'd use it. You're spitting in my face. Tell me who you've been off fucking."

He glances over his shoulder to the marble rim. "I haven't even been gone that long."

"Where did you get the power to hide yourself from me?"

"You always get jealous when you miss me. That's one of my favorite things about you." His voice warms, too pleased. The dipshit thinks he sounds charming. "I guarantee you, I haven't been hiding."

I throw my scepter to one side, and Granny catches it. I didn't realize she was still there, and I'm so mad that I forget just as quickly.

I follow after him. "Then what were you doing?"

"It's not what you think."

"It is always what I think with you. You have never once been surprising."

Those shoulders tense and his robes fall away, and I think he's finally going to swing at me. I'm barehanded and I'm ready. I'll remind him that it took both of us to defeat the titans.

Then he falls against the marble wall, one brawny arm bracing his body. The robes spill further away from his side, and I grab onto them to see what he's been hiding. All the disgusting trophies he's smuggled here over the ages. I won't let another one of them into our bedchambers.

The fabric is wet to the touch. At first I think it's sweat, but it's too sticky. It spreads red across my fingers.

Then I see his flesh. On his side, just below his ribs, leaks a long gash.

It's so deep that I can see twitching organs inside him. I can't tell if this was a sword or a bull's horn. Immediately he cups the wound in a palm to slow the bleeding.

He's bleeding, on himself and onto me. I'm squatting with him despite myself, putting both hands over this impossible injury. We can't be harmed like this.

I ask, "What happened? What did this to you?"

"It's nothing. I'll tell you about it later."

"What the fuck, Zeus? Who wounded you such that you couldn't erase it immediately?"

He tries to stand up, and has to reshape the marble wall to give him a handrail to do so. He trembles like a baby cuckoo caught in a storm. He says, "I'll be fine."

"No, you talk to me," I say, grabbing his beard so he'll look me in the face. "What did this? What have you been doing?"

He yanks his head out of my grip, losing a clump of curly white hairs in the process. The hairs feel wrong in my hand. All the tips are singed, and I realize he smells more of burned hair than lightning.

The walls fold outward for him, and he slips through on unsure feet. Is he staggering down the hallway? I follow to check, and the marble closes up behind him, bricking me out. I am sealed outside, with my husband's blood on my hands.

"No."

No, I'm not sealed outside of anything today.

The wall crumbles like good intentions facing reality. I climb through before the rock dust has finished settling, and before the marble has any chance to brick itself back up and obey its king's wishes for privacy. Zeus's robes drag along the floor, and I snatch at them to stop him.

I demand, "Get back here and talk to me."

He winces to his right, an arm covering his bare side. That wound is still bleeding. What could even do that to an Olympian? Nothing has threatened us since we overthrew the titans.

"Hera, baby," he says in this forced casual tone that makes me want to slap him. "Don't be so rough on the architecture. Relax."

"Relax? You're bleeding to death on my floor."

"No, I'm not. I'm great."

"Look!" I point at his side, and of course that's when his wound vanishes. He's summoned enough focus that his avatar obeys his self-image. There isn't even a mark where once was the thing that scared the life out of me. But it's not damage to an avatar that kills a god.

He pretends it's fine, as though he doesn't wince when he tries to keep walking.

I keep hold of his robe. If he's going anywhere, he'll go naked, and he'll go pursued by me. I'll throw him through a wall next if I have to.

"What were you doing out there?" I ask, as though I know where he's been. "Who did you fight? What is happening?"

He shows too many teeth. "It's going to be great."

"What is?"

"You're going to love it. Just be patient."

The next time he tugs on the robe, I release just to see him stagger. He catches himself against the wall, and he definitely clutches his side. Whatever stabbed him, it's more than superficial. It's cut him deeper than his avatar.

"Let me help you," I say. I don't mean to say it that way. It just comes out, from the part of me he's hurt. "It took both of us to bring down the titans. We can get all the Olympians ready, if you'll tell me what it is. We can do this together. What are we going to war with?"

"This is better than a war."

The pride in his voice, like he's sure I'll be proud of whatever he's not telling me about. The tone that says whatever folly he's up to, the surprise and the hurt that follows will be my privilege.

I ask, "Then what is it?"

I mean to scream at him, but I realize something. I'm looking up at him.

We're supposed to be the same height. I never let my avatar falter and become shorter than him. And he hasn't grown in the last moment.

Am I making myself smaller? Am I losing my grip?

He's the one to speak first. Concern crosses his brows, like he's just now sensed something is wrong with me that only he can fix.

"Has my little queen missed me? I do love the look of that new crown on you . . ."

"Missed you?" Now I do come at him, reaching up to claw at his beard. "What are you fucking doing out there? What are you hiding?"

His look sours, like I spoiled the moment. "Haven't I earned a little damned patience?"

"What is it? What can't I be a part of?"

He pushes my hands away, daring to turn his back on me again. "I can't talk to you when you're like this."

"Is it the titans? Did you somehow let them free from the underworld?"

"You're not ready to know yet." His laugh is a keening, almost nervous laugh. "You're going to love this. I'm doing this for you."

My threats aren't off my tongue before the air splits open. All of Olympos is swallowed in violent brilliance, shaking the marble from floor to ceiling. The king's lightning has come for him.

I shout, "Don't you dare leave without m—"

The thunderclap deafens all sound. I can't argue with it, no matter how I scream. My whole body is singed by the lightning, and still I reach for him. No matter how far I reach, my grasp can't find him.

Zeus is gone.

There's nothing to hear in all of heaven, like thunder kidnapped all the world's other sounds with it. So many gods, hidden behind their marble walls, holding their breaths.

One thing stirs at the head of the hallway, where I kicked through the walls. The flutter of dusky wings, bolting from their perch. Athena has seen her fill.

I want to chase her down and make an example of her. I want any of Zeus's bastard god children to laugh at me right now. Let one god of any origin step out of line. Tell me I'm smaller. Tell me I can be left behind.

"Zeus! I know you can hear me!"

I don't know. But he has to be watching. The self-absorbed prick always wants to see what his mind games do to others. We're just effects to his whims.

Rubbing inexplicable tears from my face, I whirl right, and then left. Let me hear a god who thinks they know me. Who wants to trifle? Who wants to speak to me tonight?

"Auntie Hera, I'm covered in grime and fly bites . . ."

Who the fuck is praying to me?

No, I don't need to hear another word to recognize that voice. All the other prayers in Greece I ignore like individual droplets of sunshine on one's skin. His is the one voice that always irritates and demands hearing. That power that thinks it's humble.

Does Zeus hear his insult praying to me?

I call, "Granny!"

There is another god in the heavens tonight. When I call her name, I see a bat wing twitch, and I fly up the hallway toward it. Granny, that old fury, tries to escape my sight. I shut all the walls of Olympos in her path. No one else is allowed to hide from me.

I tower over her. Nothing will make me small now.

I command her, "Go down there and shut him up."

Granny's face wrenches up in a panic. Her snakes bite at each other, and she twists her hands like she wants them to come off. "I don't know if I can anymore. It's been so long since I've besieged someone's mind. I'm still so weak . . ."

I say, "Zeus needs to see this."

She dares beg like I'm being unreasonable. "Please."

"Do you disobey your queen?" My voice is so hard that cracks open in all the walls around us. Dust bleeds out from those irrational wounds. I choose not to heal them.

"N-never, dear."

"Then get down there," I say, pointing over the marble rim to the cesspool mortals have made of their domain, to that place where an insult like Heracles could be seen as a hero. "Show my dipshit husband what a monster he is. Take the power Zeus gave him and make him destroy himself."

"You don't mean this."

Immediately I am nose to nose with the old goddess. "If I ever hear that little shit praying again, I will have you back to work every night tormenting dreams."

Granny's lips quiver. Her wings clutch to her back. Her agony isn't my fault—this is Zeus's work. Another mistake he's sent out into the world, just like his favorite son. But the mortal world will be better without Heracles. Quieter. His wife deserves someone who knows the weight of life. His sons will grow into better men without his oafish example.

I am the Goddess of Families. I protect them. I'm going to protect this one from its father.

I point down at Thebes and command my fury, "Go!"

Heracles 8

Are those wings beating? They sound hurried, like an eagle is desperate to return to Papa Zeus's sky. I look up in time to glimpse something dark whirling upward, perhaps the wings of a creature, but as quickly as I see it, it's gone.

The vision makes no sense, but my eyes sting and my vision blurs. I rub knuckles into my eyes, and the blindness only worsens. The dust mixes with oil that coats my face and beard, the fumes threatening to suffocate me. Where did the oil come from? Did I spill it while burning the offering to Auntie Hera?

And what is that smell? A septic reek and roasting hair. Everything is so hot, and my nostrils fill with the heat and the reek, like the nauseating odor is trying to climb inside my skull.

That roasting meat and fur smell has to be the boar. Did I get drunk and forget the whole offering?

That's not possible. I won't drink until tomorrow. I'll fast until the offering to Auntie Hera is over.

"Therimachus? Creontiades?" I call out for my sons. "Deicoon? Did you spill Aunt Hera's oil?"

I remember them laughing from upstairs. They were going to ambush me. Did one of them strike me with an oil jar, and it broke? Creontiades needs to rein himself in or someone will get hurt.

The air rushes around me, and I gag on smoke. That's when I realize I'm not on the stairs anymore. I'm not indoors. I reach to the left and feel the heat grow. The fire pops and crackles nearby. This has to be our courtyard. Damn it, did I actually get drunk?

I call again, "Boys?"

I wouldn't sacrifice the boar without them. They need the blessings of the gods more than I do.

I fumble my way to the drinking trough. Water splashes thinly under my fingers. There's not enough. The boys should have refilled it this afternoon. I cup as much water as I can and dribble it into my face, to clear at least some of this mix.

The courtyard is covered in ash. It coats the oil jars, all tipped over. More ash coats the stone wall before the road, and the flowers. We burned up everything.

The bonfire got out of hand. Creontiades must have doused it in his zeal. He wants to impress his Great-Aunt Hera into talking to Athena, so he can become a great general.

Beside the wall of our courtyard is the great form of the boar. It's as huge as it was when I slew it. Nothing has been cut from its hide. All its bristly fur is coated in the same layer of ash as my skin, like we're two of a kind. The boar's snout lies across the ground, pointed at the bonfire.

This makes no sense. What's in the fire?

It blazes, flames reaching as high as the roof of our house. It could consume everything. We must have used too much oil. It spews ash up into the air, sending dots of it swirling like gray dandelions down on our courtyard.

Yet I make out shapes in the fire. There's ample wood there, that I cut down myself yesterday before the hunt.

At first I think it's just wood in there. But some of those long limbs aren't branches. They're skinny legs, the wrong shape to be a boar. And the boar hasn't been cut up. I wanted to offer it whole.

"Megara?"

I don't know why I call for her. I need her. I need her to make sense of this.

Something hard forms in my guts as I approach the fire. I wave my hand, as though to part the flames like they're drapes. There are shapes in the fire. Bodies, with limbs twisted as though writhing. They look like people. A blackened arm is extended, forever stilled in a desperate attempt to reach for me. Begging for help.

This can't be happening. This can't be real. I look at the oil and ash streaking my hands, and then back into the blaze.

At the end of that reaching arm isn't a hand. It's a lion's paw.

His kids . . . ?

I can't get them out. They're wilting down to nothing, just bones in what was supposed to be a glory to the gods. I keep reaching in, and the fires billow outward, scorching me and driving me back.

My hands. Look at my hands. These ashes. I'm covered in my boys.

I rub at myself, rake my fingernails at my elbows. The oil is mixed too deeply with them, and I can't get them off. They keep smearing across my chest, and they're all that I can smell now. I killed my children and now they're smothering me.

I grab handfuls of my skin and yank. If I can't rub it away, then I'll tear it free. This has to come off somehow. This has to be a mistake.

Please, Aunt Hera, take this back. Fix my mistakes. What did I do?

Behind the boar, and behind the wall, out in the road glint bronze-tipped spears. So many men ready to fight. There's a whole garrison out there, like they're assembling to defend against the boar if it wakes up from death and rampages again.

But the boar isn't the monster here. I am.

I reach over the wall, begging any of them for his spear. Let me peel away the flesh stained with my mistakes. Let any of them come at me.

And all those brave foot soldiers back away, smacking into each other in fear. How many of them saw what I did? What I can't even remember?

I got so drunk and so full of pride that I did this. Noises escape my mouth, no meaning in them, no prayers. It's just animal pain, because I'm no better than that boar. I'm worse. I've destroyed my family, and I've despoiled your glory, Auntie Hera.

"Auntie . . . Aunt . . ."

I can't even say your name. I don't deserve to.

This isn't a prayer. Can I ever pray to you again?

Can I ever do anything again?

There's only one thing I deserve.

To burn.

I grab a jug, and it's empty. All the jugs are kicked over by the bonfire, leaking onto the ground. Most are smashed, like I hurled them onto the bonfire with my boys. How did I . . . ?

Bile surges from my throat. My empty stomach heaves and I fall onto the boar, its bristles sticking into the burns on my arms. I clutch at its back, rocking the creature, feeling the ground shake under me. I can't stop wailing. I beg my boys to come back. For this to be a nightmare.

Instead what I get is one last ceramic jug. It's trapped between the wall and the boar, safe from whatever rampage I went on. Its contents slosh as I thrash with the boar, and immediately I drop the animal.

I heave the jug overhead, and the suffocating stench of oil douses me. It's too cool to the touch, like diving into a refreshing pond. But I'll burn soon enough. I'll be with my boys, even for a second.

Jug still in hand, I turn for the fire. My vision is blurrier than ever, and I close my eyes against the sting. The heat of the fire beckons me to turn to ash. It won't be long.

I'm sorry, Therimachus. Creontiades. Little Deicoon. Papa Zeus. Auntie Hera.

I'm so sorry.

"No."

A hand against my chest, pushing through the oil and the ash. It isn't nearly as strong as I am, and I could trample it. But I can't. Not tonight.

I shy backward at the touch of a woman I can't see.

She says, "Don't you dare."

Both hands force up against my chest, insistent, and I submit. I stumble backward, until the backs of my thighs hit the boar. There's no seeing who's attacking me.

I plead with them, "I don't deserve to live. I got drunk and killed my boys."

"I've known you drunk."

That voice. The hardness without an edge.

Megara. My poor wife. What have I done to her? How did I not think of her this entire time? She deserves to run me through with every spear in the city.

She says, "I've seen you at your worst. At war, and drunk out of your mind."

There's more than hardness to her voice. It's irate without anger, like it's constantly on the verge of screaming. How can she do anything but scream?

I say, "The oil is all over my hands. Our poor boys."

I feel her standing before me, like if I charge into the fire, then we're both going.

How I want to hold her, and I'm the last man who deserves to touch her.

Half a sob. That's all she lets out, before somehow she finds the strength not to cave in.

She says, "This wasn't you."

She's lost her mind. She doesn't want to believe I could be as cruel as I must have been.

She goes on, "I saw the winged nightmare fly out of our house. The creature sent from the skies. Something was inside you."

Despite the oil blinding me, I look up. All I see is burning.

I ask, "What do you mean?"

"Someone made you do this to us," she says. "Some god."

F uck.
      Fuck fuck fuck.
Fuck!

This can't be happening. Granny was supposed to make him destroy himself.

They were supposed to be protected. They were supposed to be looked after. They should have been spared. Zeus did this to them! Zeus did . . . he did . . .

He did nothing.

Three little boys, slain by the Goddess of Mothers. I keep summoning them out of the fire, to climb free, to shake off their wounds. But I can't. Their shades no longer walk that courtyard. They'll never lay their heads down in that home again. Never go foot racing their rivals. Thoughts of families are now bygone lies they told themselves.

Wake up, boys. Please, shake off the mistakes of your gods.

I would reach for them with my own hands, but my avatar has fallen apart. Long arms and strong fingers chip like aging clay. I am a sculpture of myself, dry and crumbling. My own dust becomes a mess on the floor of Olympos. I'm alone with regret.

Wait. Am I alone here?

I feel him behind me. The great chill, the massive body that overshadows me. Zeus rises behind me, doubtless staring at what his wife did in her rage. The mother of our children did this to those children.

As much as I can move, I hold my head up, stretching my neck long. Clumps of my hair snap off and drop to the ground like debris. I expose myself to him. Let him strike me down. There is nothing he can do that will match my shame.

I wait. It could be eons, except I know time isn't passing that long, because I can hear Heracles sobbing down in Thebes.

The blow doesn't come.

I have to see his face. I have to know the judgment, to know what's coming.

My neck splits as I turn. I have to hold my chin and crown to keep my head from falling off to the floor. To keep myself together for one more moment, to face him. I look up.

Zeus isn't behind me at all.

It's Athena, in her tall human avatar, built of supple flesh and a scholar's robes. Her gray eyes gaze upon me with a neutrality that hurts worse than hatred.

Of course he wouldn't come himself. He must be in worse state than I am.

"So you're summoning me for your father?" I ask. "What does he demand? To kill me? Banish me by thunderbolt?"

A moment passes.

Then Athena says, "No, Your Grace."

"Then what does he want?"

I swear her voice aches as she answers, "I do not know."

She doesn't know?

"Is he on his way? Is he going to do it himself?"

"No, my queen. I do not think so."

"What do you mean?"

"I cannot find King Zeus. He's gone again."

He's gone.

All my terror. All my preparation for him to fill the void of my worth with pain and retribution. And he didn't even see this tragedy. This whole maelstrom of regrets, and he wasn't looking.

He isn't going to fill the void.

He is a void.

That's when I drop my head. My polos crown hits the floor first, and breaks off and rolls over to the marble rim. The clattering of my skull on the floor covers my crying, at least for a moment.

I force my words out through disobedient teeth. "Athena."

She is quick to reply, "My queen?"

"Can you follow those boys into the underworld? Make sure their shades pass safely?"

It's too small a thing. It cloys to say it, because it's such a petty thing. I owe them so much more. But everything I have is out of reach.

Athena says, "I can do that, Your Grace. But . . ."

But? Anger punches through my entire avatar. I'm not ready to hear her judgment. To know what the Goddess of Wisdom sees in me right now.

I ask, too sharply, "What is it?"

"It's Heracles," she says. "He's waiting for you."

I whirl to the marble rim of Olympos so quickly that my body leaves my head behind. Every part of my crumbling self whirls down over the rim, to stare at that broken half a man. A half a man who stands in the Temple of Delphi, with the Oracle of Delphi, the Pythia herself who foresees all things. He's asking her something.

Alcides 10

I'm not myself.

I don't notice moving. I'm at the fire, and then I'm at the temple. I stand before the court of the King of Thebes, and then I'm on a dirt road dotted by a drizzling sky, and then I'm in Troezen for the first time in years. People with soft voices suggest something, and I guess I do it. Part of me is eager to do it, because doing anything kills thinking.

People call me "Heracles" and the name slides off me, like it belongs to someone else. When I sit still, I swirl down that drain of grief, where I want to tear my hands off so I won't have to think about what they did.

I'm in my Mama Alcmene's house, and she implores me to dispel the rumors. Her eyes threaten to fall from their tired sockets. I stand with her as she crumples to the floor, and weeps and tears at her hair. I barely know why she's so hurt, because I'm doing something.

As soon as I leave, as soon as we're finished talking, my first thought is whether the boys have eaten yet today. It's a moment before I catch myself.

I fall on my knees in the garden and want to douse myself with oil again.

This keeps happening. I forget and remember, and I forget, and I remember.

"It's a good idea," says my nephew Iolaus. I keep thinking he's Therimachus, except he's too tall, his beard coming in. "You've always had a special relationship. Go ask her."

When did I arrive in my brother Iphicles's court? And what did I propose that was a good idea? Or could I have said anything, and my nephew would have assured me it was the right thing, because his father wants me gone from his home?

I don't touch Iolaus on my way out of his court, just as I didn't hold Mama Alcmene. I can't do it. I can't risk it. No one should trust my hands.

"Do you want to sleep out here, Uncle Al?"

My nephew's voice again, and again I think he's Therimachus, but he's too tall and too alive and I'm wrong. We're not in his father's court. I try to rub ash grains from my eyes that aren't there, to clear senses that don't want clarity. Iolaus's breath hits my side, smelling of stale barley chewed and unswallowed. I step away from him, not wanting him to get too close. He can't touch me. He can't let me touch him.

Uncertain where we are, I tell him, "You belong home. Be with your mother and father. Keep growing your life."

"You're part of my family, so you're part of my life."

He even sounds like my boys. He has to get away from me.

"You deserve a bigger life than that."

"I had a teacher," he says, staying put. "He's the man who taught me the strength in being gentle. After his sons died in the Minyan war, he kept insisting on being alone. He needed to think. So I gave up my classes with him, and Father gave him leave." He swallows nothing. "I was the one who found him. We're not leaving you alone."

How I want to hold him, this youth with the likeness of my son. I want to kiss my nephew and thank him.

Instead, I try to walk away from him, to get him away from whatever curse hangs over me. I trip over fir logs, and sprawl before a woman. Megara. My wife, sitting on a log, wearing a dark veil over her face. Still, I look her in the eyes. She doesn't wipe away her tears. I can tell they spill because they leak down along the hollow of her throat.

Right, we're not in the court. We're out in the open, in a camp in the absence of a fire. Under the shining tapestry of stars, I make out the temple. Three times in my life I've visited the Temple of Apollo, to best other champions at sports. It is a regal building, and its columns will stand for all time, built into the side of Mount Parnassus, the peaks of which loom above as though to shelter it from the world.

Here lives the Pythia, the greatest oracle of our age. I think of the oracle, and I remember why I need to talk to her, and I have to muffle my mouth when I remember.

Megara and Iolaus let me weep, for a time.

"Alcides," Megara says, her voice a warning. "Listen. You need to actually hear us. Don't just walk through the world like you're a shade."

I turn from the Temple of Apollo, and to the young man who looks too much like a son. Iolaus has a softness to his expression, a barely disguised pity.

He says, "The Pythia gains her oracular insights from the gods themselves. That's why you need to be careful."

I repeat, "Careful?"

"I've consulted everyone my father can reach. There were other men in my garrison, who saw the same creature that Aunt Megara did."

Megara tilts her head upward, as though the winged creature will return. Like she's challenging it.

When nothing strikes her down, she says, "It was a divine fury. That's what came after our family."

Iolaus adds, "Furies are primordial gods, from before Gaia birthed the titans. No scholar knows how many of them there are. They respect few forces, and obey even fewer. If Eros or Nemesis were to command a fury to drive someone mad, the furies would mock them."

He looks to Megara, and Megara says, "The furies answer only to the twelve Olympians."

Now I look up, but not for a fury. I yearn to pray to you, Auntie Hera, to bring that fury down. If they have to obey you, can you kill them? Bring justice to our family?

No. I wish I could, but I can't pray, any more than a man with a broken back can stand. As badly as I want, I don't deserve you.

It's Megara who breaks my self-flagellation. "Did you hear me? An Olympian god commanded them to kill our boys. That means there are twelve suspects."

"No."

I can't hear this. I cover my ears. That's too far. Apollo's temple is right there, and he is a capricious god. We can't incur his wrath after all this. What will he make me do to the rest of my family?

"You owe this to us," Megara says. "Don't leave us again."

How is she keeping herself together like this? Where is she getting her strength?

I want to ask. I need that same strength. But I know better than to pull that stick from the bottom of the stack. The whole stack will tumble if the thing supporting it is disturbed. Her resolve has to go unquestioned, especially unquestioned by me.

Iolaus clears his throat. He's barely a man and doesn't know how to resolve things between Megara and me. If we don't, he can't be asked to.

So he tries to move us on. "I've marshalled emissaries to temples around the Aegean Sea, to find out what they can. We need to consider which Olympians did this before they make another move against us."

I say, "That's blasphemy."

And Megara's voice is sharper than any bronze blade. "The truth is never blasphemy. You want to talk blasphemy? Ares could despise me for marrying a man who worships other gods, and for having a shrine to only one goddess in my own courtyard."

"No, no," I say, without having an objection, beyond that she has to have done nothing wrong. It was me. "You had an altar to Ares in your private chambers. You had his figurines in all the parts of the house."

"How do I know that was enough? I lapsed in my worship more than I should have."

Her tone. She sounds like how I feel. Her head tilts down, and through the veil, I can tell she's staring at her hands. Maybe she wishes they could come off.

It takes everything I have not to cross the camp and hold her. "You can't blame yourself."

"So far, I've found I'm capable of blaming everyone." Her voice dries up. "I'm very good at it."

In an act of mercy, Iolaus interrupts us. "In fact, Ares, Artemis, and Athena are all gods of violent conflict. Any battle you have endured could have defied destinies they wrote for a war. They could have been supporting a champion whose path you curtailed. They have cursed many people before."

Ares? Artemis? Athena? All children of Papa Zeus. My half-siblings. Would they come for me, without Papa Zeus striking them down?

"Athena is Creontiades's favorite goddess. He prays to her daily. Why would she—"

Remembering that he doesn't pray to anyone, and never will again, hits me like a tidal wave and sends me to the ground.

Megara exhales slowly through her nose. "Just because you revere someone does not mean that feeling is returned."

Iolaus jumps in. "I passed no judgment. I'm sorry, Uncle Al. I'm trying to help. I'm trying to help you figure out how best to talk to the oracle about who this is."

Such softness in his voice, coating an emotion unrelenting. A strength I wish my sons would have grown up to have. I have to hold onto it. Hold onto what they should have been. That's how I'll find justice.

"For us. For you, Megara. For Papa Zeus, Mama Alcmene, Auntie Hera. We'll find a way."

The way Megara regards me through her veil, I assume I've sworn this oath a hundred times in my blackouts.

But that's not why she's regarding me that way.

"Any of the Olympians could have commanded this," she says. "Any of the *twelve*."

"That's not true," I tell her. "It isn't."

Megara says, "Listen."

I don't. I go off. "I was on my way home with meat and oil to sacrifice to Papa Zeus and Auntie Hera. Why would they interrupt an offering to themselves? Why would Zeus kill his own family line? Why would Hera burn children? Have some sense!"

Megara is so much quieter than me, and that makes me listen to her. "Sit down."

Anger beaten into a tiny sliver, condensed until it could pierce anything. I feel the hatred of a woman looking at her children's killer. I sink.

But I can't stop seething. Zeus and Hera would never. The heavens have to be weeping with this loss.

She says, "If the oracle does not know which Olympian did this, then have her tell us how to find it out ourselves. And do not let her look away from *any* of the twelve. No matter whom. You owe us that."

Us.

It pierces me, all right. That anger is on behalf of all of us. Mother, father, and children, divided by death, and still united by the harm done to us.

How badly I want to kiss her. To hold her. To not be a threat to the last survivor of our household.

I have work to do. I leave my wife and my nephew in each other's company, and ascend to the temple of a god. I don't let my mind fade as I walk, refusing the comforting numbness of motion.

I tell myself, "I owe us more than that."

The ceiling of the Temple of Apollo is lower than I remember, the confines feeling closer because of all the darkness. A mere three braziers burn deep within the temple, near a bowl several meters wide, filled with still water. The stone floor leading to the bowl is covered in woven rugs dyed brown and green to the likeness of serpent skin. It is the remembrance of the terrible Python, whom Apollo slew to free Delphi from tyranny. These serpentine rugs lie only on the floor, so visitors will tread upon Python's memory.

Feeling the stiff wool underfoot, I think only that it is regrettable a monster had to be slain. It's no better than a wasted boar. How distant I feel from ever celebrating the end of a life.

"Heracles!"

Such revelry in that voice. Nobody should utter my other name with such excitement. The voice is nasal and naïve, as though it's unaware I am no longer worthy to be called Hera's Glory.

Reclining against the great bowl is a woman with skin nearly as bronze as the braziers. She has a hook nose, and her left leg is shorter than the right, both sticking out from a feathered skirt. A red scarf collects her frizzy hair. She waves a green laurel for me to approach, then uses it to fan some of the white vapors from a crack in the floor toward herself. She inhales them like she's sipping water.

I come to within ten steps of her. Still on the serpentine rugs, I say, "I come to beg the assistance of the Oracle of Delphi, the Pythia."

"Uh, yeah," she says, smirking with the right side of her mouth. "I know."

So this is her. The Pythia is awake in the middle of the night. It must be destiny.

"You know who I am? Because of your connection to the gods?"

"Well, also I heard you screaming outside with a voice like thunder, so it wasn't hard to guess. Thanks for waking me up early. I had some laundry that needed getting to."

I almost step back, but retreating from truth won't help me.

"Then you know?" I ask. "You already know what I've done?"

She taps two fingers together like scissors snipping. "You're not the first person to have a fury take everything from you. I know everything I need to, except what you want me to tell you."

I grit my teeth and pull my lips down to hide it. This is the destruction of everything I am. How can an oracle be so flippant?

"How can I?" the Pythia asks like I've already voiced the thoughts. "When I was little, I asked why the gods were so cruel. They answered by giving me this job. It turns out everybody is heartbroken the first or second time everything awful falls on them. But, you know, betrayal after betrayal, war after war, storm after storm? It becomes business."

"I see," I say, even though I don't.

"You got used to doing impossible feats. So did I." She waggles those two fingers again, casting shadow puppets from the fire over her legs. The shadow looks like a bird. "So you're here to wriggle out from underneath all your guilt? Heroes always need purification."

Purification sounds relieving. How good it would be to get forgiveness, even from eleven innocent Olympians.

I kneel on the likeness of Python. "Oh wise Pythia, I beg you. It is clear that one of the Olympian gods sent the furies to unleash havoc upon my house. I ask you only this: who is responsible?"

"Oh, wow." She smiles with more teeth than most people have in their whole heads. "I love a surprise. Is this a path of revenge? Because remember those Minyans you beat up at Thebes were out for revenge, and that didn't work out great for them. Revenge against the gods is going to be even steeper."

"I seek justice."

She taps a fingernail against her crooked teeth. "Justice is a great virtue and I have never once actually seen it in person. It'll be good to see what it looks like."

"Can you divine which god did this to my family?"

"I'll look it up for you. Wait a breath."

The Pythia raises both palms to her temples, fingers peeling back as though they no longer belong on her hands. Her breath makes her entire body billow, and I swear there is some golden glow in her face that is not a blush. Is this divinity?

"Oh," she murmurs. "Oh, no. Oh!"

Then her eyes snap wide open, her lips puckering into a perfect circle. I lean forward, needing to hear the revelation she's just had.

The wisest oracle in the land says, "Fuck."

Hera 11

Fuck!"

I shoot over the marble rim and reach down into the mortal realm, seizing the Pythia by the throat to stop her from spilling another word. That ditzy seer is going to ruin everything. Fortunately, any god can influence an oracle; they draw their foresight from us and our relationship to time. Apollo probably wasn't even paying attention when I intervened with my own inspiration.

Except . . . what do I make her say now? What exactly do I want?

Down in the mortal world, Heracles watches on one knee, awaiting the identity of his family's executioner. He's expecting divine wisdom.

The moments pass as I wrestle for any possible thing. Do I point the finger at Zeus? He's never around and won't even notice if his son hates him. I need time. I need . . .

For the first time in the history of history, I'm glad Athena is looming over my shoulder. That gray-eyed know-it-all is behind me again, watching, like she wants to write my memoirs when this is over.

Still holding the oracle's tongue in Delphi, I ask my fellow goddess a question in Olympos. "What am I supposed to do here?"

Athena answers, "Win."

That's it? That's all she says? I bounce my head, willing her to elaborate. When she doesn't, I say, "Win? You don't win at grief."

"You got what you wanted, my queen," says the Goddess of Wisdom. "Tell him you did all this. Inform your most devoted supplicant that you have despised him from the moment he suckled milk, and you orchestrated the destruction of his life. That you, the source of his virtues, made only one mistake: not killing him, too. If you tell him that, he will be undone. Every age hereafter will hear of your victory over him."

She is right. It is that easy.

I will the words, and nothing leaves me. Not a drop of inspiration.

"You're supposed to be the smart god," I say, with less venom than I want. My heart's too torn up to be appropriately snide. I can't even get the satisfaction of talking down to her.

"What did you say, Pythia?" asks Heracles, who probably just heard gibberish escape the oracle. My head snaps down at him.

The mortal world is slipping through my fingers, and soon Helios will drag the sun up on his chariot and this whole plot will be even more obvious. I can't let him see through this. But I need time.

Stalling, I try to inspire the Pythia to dump some divine bullshit.

Her mouth moves and she says, "The wisdom of the gods is not easily attained. If you want to learn the answer to your question, you will have to labor across Greece. First bring a tribute to King Eurystheus. Bring to him something of unparalleled rarity. A bounty that no mortal has ever captured. A thing that . . . a thing that . . ."

Fuck! What is it supposed to be?

I hope the Pythia didn't just yell that.

But what is something a mortal can't easily do? What will stall him forever until he forgets what he's up to? What's a monster that no human can slay? I am renowned across the world for my cunning, and damn it, my mind locks on one fucking thing. I try like hell to imagine anything else. Some war he can wage. Some sea he can swim. I'm blank with panic.

I don't have time to come up with something better. If Athena laughs at me, I will stuff her back inside her father's head.

"Athena," I say, already regretting this. "What's the fiercest lion in the world?"

She hides her expression behind a hand.

Alcides 11

As I emerge, Helios is riding his chariot across the very lip of the sky, so that shadows wane. His chariot is drawn by those divine twins, Sleep and Death. Only with their might can great Helios return the sun to its proper place, and shatter night with day's radiance. Golden strands of sunshine wash my face, and for the first time in too long, I feel a little cleaner.

I make sure to stand still in the dawn. To be motionless for a moment, and make myself think. Still I feel their ashes in my eyelashes. No amount of wiping will clean them from me.

But justice is possible. Where I walk from here, I will bring their memories something better. The hands a god stole from me will wring justice out of the sky.

"What did she say?"

It's Iolaus, his voice tentative. With the sun dawning behind him, his shaggy hair looks so much like Therimachus's.

I can't bring myself to touch him. I tell myself it will come, in time.

Instead I say, "The Pythia struggled with her revelation. She says this will be the beginning of a long series of labors, unseen since the time of Theseus. But we can learn the name of the god if we do as she says."

And I believe the Pythia, not that I have the words to explain it to Megara and Iolaus yet. I felt the glow. The power of your presence.

"Alcides." It's Megara, standing at the bottom of the few steps into the temple. No sunshine dares land on her, not her bare shoulders, nor her dark veil. She remains a silhouette in the dawn, as though night won't let go of her. "If she didn't give you the name, then what did she ask from you? What offering does she want?"

"It's not her," I say, gesturing back inside the temple. "And the vision was overwhelming. She's out of sorts. We should bring her some water."

Iolaus says, "I can do that. But what exactly did she say?"

Using the sun to orient myself, I squint toward the south. "I am traveling to Peloponnese, to the place called Nemea. It is where my father's greatest temple resides."

Megara says, "What are you doing at this temple?"

"Defending it from a lion."

Megara balks. "Another lion?"

Iolaus isn't balking. He puts his hands to his hips, steadying himself from his thoughts. "The Lion of *Nemea*? The creature whose fur is mixed with gold, and whose hide has snapped a thousand spears? It's invulnerable. Literally no weapon has ever scratched the Nemean Lion."

Suddenly the Pythia's words make more sense. This is going to be harder than I thought.

I have to tell them. "I'm not to simply drive the lion off."

Megara sounds like she could spit. "You have to kill another monster lion?"

"More than that," I say. "I'm to bring its hide to King Eurystheus."

From the sound, Iolaus does spit up. "You can't skin the Lion of Nemea. The gods made its flesh unbreakable. I'm telling you, I've known great Thebans who have tried hunting it. None of them lived to return home."

This is why they demanded it. I'm asking for impossible knowledge, and so they require impossible labors.

Gazing upon the gold of that rising sun, I imagine the lion's mane. I've fought lions unarmed before. "I'll find a way."

Megara climbs the first step, so that we are closer together. She doesn't force me to touch her, but her hands make it obvious she longs to do something to me.

She says, "If we have to, then *we* will find a way."

I love her so much that I can't keep my eyes open. I close them, and imagine her face beneath her veil.

I imagine your face, too. I don't deserve to think of your visage, but please grant me this.

Aunt Hera?

Please hear my prayer.

Because I know it was you.

From the moment the Pythia struggled with the weight of the revelation, I knew you were inspiring her to put me on the right path. I know you want justice for my family, because it's your family, too. We'll make this happen. There's nothing you and I can't do together.

With me laboring on earth, and you laboring in heaven, we'll find who did this to us.

Part Two

The Family

Hera 12

On the outskirts of Nemea is a newborn who will not see dawn. Her parents are millers who pulverize so much barley that flour smelling of it has been under their fingernails for years, no matter how much they wash. They keep clay figurines of all twelve Olympians on their tiny shrine, although they work such hours that they have not cleaned them. The couple's brows are sodden with sweat as they try to bundle their daughter in more clothes, wrapping her in every robe and sheet they own, to save what little warmth she's born with.

They don't know that their daughter was born with half of a heart, and it fights harder than they have ever fought a thief just to beat. They have done nothing wrong. They think they have. Mortals can be wrong about the worst things.

I hold the unnamed newborn to my forehead, and I breathe in her fluid scent. I breathe for her. I exhale into her lips, so she takes in air that I have blessed. Until dawn is long gone, and Helios has dragged the sun halfway into the sky, I breathe for her again and again, blowing the billows of her lungs and heart.

By the time I release her, she has the heart of a lioness. It will never fail her. Her parents will never have to worry about it failing. They never see me, not even as I stoop and exit through a closed door.

Above me, on the roof of the home, is a gray-eyed owl. She doesn't have to say anything. I know what she's thinking.

"This wasn't enough," I yell up at her, annoyed that she's making me say it. "Don't tell me what I know. I know this undoes nothing."

I stop beside the shrine, looking down on the simple figurines of the gods. They have no facial features, and most of them lack arms. I pick up one figurine, rubbing my thumb over her until all the grime is dispelled. Now at least one Queen of Olympos will be clean.

I set the clay figurine down beside her king. His face is small, with a mighty brow, and an extra glob of clay for his beard. I'll leave the grime on him. He deserves it, I think. Or maybe I'm afraid to touch him.

"Athena."

"Yes, my queen?"

"The Lion of Nemea is the right choice."

"Yes, my queen."

"Its hide is impenetrable. Bronze bends on its fur."

"That is the legend."

"The whole point is that he can't do it. He'll never accomplish the task, and therefore he'll never end his journey. He won't have to learn the thing that will break him."

Her head twists, like she needs to see me at another angle. "You are making him fight a lion out of mercy?"

Inside, the baby squalls, as though my chatter has disturbed her. But none of the family hears us. Her heart has beaten enough that she's hungry. I almost smile. I would, if I weren't looking at that bearded figurine on the altar.

"Athena?"

She answers, "Yes, my queen?"

"Do you think I'm the same as he is?"

"That is a matter of opinion, not wisdom."

Despite myself, my voice heats up. "I asked your opinion. Do you think me vile?"

The gray-eyed owl regards me for another long moment. "What does our goodness matter to our victims?"

Alcides 12

She wakes before I do every morning. In fact, I can't remember the last time I saw her asleep. A cook at the Gulf of Corinth said she woke before anyone, to look at the sky. Every day I catch her looking up there.

Is she praying?

Or plotting?

Megara says Ares brings her conflicts and it is her task to handle them with reason. I don't see how reason gets someone through this. And I know she prays to your son, Ares.

But please.

Hera.

Goddess of Mothers.

I beg you to look after Megara. Give her the strength I lack.

She is the first to approach the Nemeans, to get us a lead. A rumor of a man who's fought the lion before sends her walking past dusk, even through the plains beyond the vineyards, where no guards dare patrol. It's like she's daring the lion to come out. It's like she's hunting before we have spears in hand.

A one-armed man is building a new house using pulleys to raise the stone slabs to the second floor. I take the rope from him, and send up every brick he wants to lay in moments. He stares at my paunch, and the flab of my arms that barely strains at the weight.

It's Megara who turns his wonder into something useful. She spins sentences like threads on a loom. I can't even follow the stream of their conversation, much less join it. My mind keeps drifting toward silence, toward the relief of not thinking. It's the only way to prevent fantasizing about how the boys would run races around this man's house, with Little Deicoon insisting they go again, over and over, until he won one.

The one-armed man says, "I know the look of you. Hunters?"

Megara says, "Something like it. You've encountered this lion?"

"Yes, I know that damned beast," he says, his voice so gruff that I surface from drowning in my thoughts, feeling like I'll have to defend Megara. I don't. It's another false instinct. The man nods to the wad of bandages below his right shoulder. "It got a taste of my arm. I'm the only one out of ten hunters in the party who got away."

Megara asks, "Does its skin truly turn away swords and spears?"

"That's the word. If you want a real fight, it's your game."

My nephew Iolaus asks, "How do you approach such a thing?"

"There's no point in chasing it. It knows if you're hunting it. It's nested in a cave under the hills, one that's old, that dragons bored out in the time of the titans. There are five holes leading into the cave system, so the lion can escape through any of them. You can't flush it out unless you've got an army to station at each one. Otherwise, it'll come out and get you from behind. That's what happened to us."

I open my mouth and start to turn, to warn my sons to stay behind. Then I remember. My head collapses into my hands. I'm an embarrassment. I have to pull it together, for her.

It's Megara who mercifully draws attention to herself, producing a parchment map. I don't remember when she got that. She unfurls it against the side of the man's unfinished house, and says, "Can you point out where the exits to the cave are?"

I lead the way to the caves, going first, so that if the lion springs, Megara and Iolaus will at least have time to react. We carry torches in broad daylight, a silly idea, like fire will protect us from a monster. Megara keeps at least five paces away from me the whole time, giving me the distance I need so I'll feel she's safe from me. I know what my hands did. I'm no better than the lion.

She asks, "You lost yourself again back there. Are you all right?"

I nod. "I let myself get distracted."

"All I am these days is distracted. It feels like my feet walk on their own."

"Where's your mind?"

Her breath hitches, and she reaches under her veil to fix something I can't see. Eventually she says, "You know where it is."

My throat tightens at the desire to tell her what a great influence she was, and how much the boys would love seeing how strong she is. I don't let myself weep. This isn't about me.

"When I don't think about them," she says, "I think about this lion. I wake up every morning thinking about it."

"I know you don't like the treatment of monsters, Megara. But the gods willed this. This isn't caprice. We aren't doing this to prove how great we are, or for glory. This is going to lead us to answers."

"That's not it."

"You're not upset that we're maiming the invincible lion, the way Perseus maimed Medusa?"

That hand disappears beneath her veil again. It's a while before she speaks again.

"I imagine it lunging on top of me. I imagine fighting it. Being torn apart. How quickly my shade would pass to the underworld. How it wouldn't be so long before I saw them again."

My feet would never move again from the shock, except I have to keep up with her.

"Megara. You don't deserve that."

"Our boys didn't deserve to burn."

"We need to do something for you. Do we have to stop this journey right now, and get you somewhere? Get you help?"

Megara's fingers coil, until they're not so different in shape from the paw of a lion, or the paw of our son. She mimes digging claws down her collarbone. She says, "The only help is getting through this."

"You're always so thoughtful. You wake up first. You kept me from burning myself." I gesture to the space between us. Then I drop a couple steps back, closer, a hand open. An offer to touch her, if she needs to be held. To feel something other than an imaginary lion's claw. "You always give me what I need. What do you need?"

She slows until the gap between us is wide again.

"I don't blame you, Alcides. But I can't have your hands near me."

I wait to hear more. I want her to rant about how dangerous I am. Blame her waking up early on feeling unsafe. There's a hideous connection between us now, knowing we both fear me in the same way.

I get further ahead of her. With Iolaus scouting for us, we find most of the cave openings soon enough. I dig my fingers into the earth and fill the holes with rockslides. I have always been good at ruining things.

Then we stand before the last remaining entrance to the lion's lair. It's narrow enough that I'll have to stoop to get inside. I make sure to stand in the way. I can hear Megara shuffling, struggling with how to get around me and inside when she doesn't want to come near me. She and her fantasies of being torn apart are stuck behind me.

Noises stir from down in the caves, like bones clattering, and a great body thrashing around. The lion is running to another of its exits, and it's in for a surprise. Soon it will find there is only one.

"Iolaus and I will watch the exit." Megara closes some of that gap to hand me a torch. "You better come back to me, Alcides."

It's a horrible thing, to want to be torn apart, and to need someone else to not be torn apart. That's why I don't kiss her goodbye before I climb down into the dark.

The torch grants little sight down here. I hold it far from my body, and the flames dwindle from the lack of air. I brush the ground with the soles of my bare feet, feeling discarded bones against my calluses.

My eyes water from the smell. Everything down here that isn't limestone and dirt is rotten. Bones strewn about, cracked from the teeth of a giant beast, marrow sucked out. Scraps of flesh dangle before my torch's light. What the lion hasn't eaten is rotting away, and that prickly, musty smell speaks to me. My stomach rolls, a hunger pang piercing the nausea.

I've spent day after day avoiding cooked meat, because I can't handle the smell.

Now I'm hungering for rot.

A paw swings in from beside the torchlight, coming straight at my head. I jerk an arm up, catching the lion's leg below its paws, and its limb hits mine like a great oak falling on me. In the fire's light, its fur is golden as the sun. I barely catch it in time, swatting it aside, and hear the entire beast fly across the cavern and thud into the wall. When I move my torch in that direction, it's already gone, off in its next hiding spot.

This is its home. It knows this place better than I do, and I'm unarmed.

My feet kick broken bows, their strings trying to tangle in my toes. So many snapped spears lie against the walls, from other heroes who came to kill it. I lower the torch and find a perfect bronze sword, thicker than any normal blade in Thebes, like it was designed to hew trees and monsters alike. There are no scratches or nicks on it. The owner died before they got to swing it a single time.

I could pick it up. Test the hardiest of Hephaistos's bronze against the monster's skin. Do what the gods demand.

Looking at the hide-bound handle, my palms sweat. No, I can't pick it up. The thought of it in my hands brings bile to my throat, worse than anything the rotting smell has done.

Then the cave is noise. The lion's roar fills every open cranny in the limestone walls, like we are trapped in a great throat. I know it's in front of me and still I hear from behind, and to my left. It's coming. I feel its heavy thudding footfalls before it's in the sight of my torch.

I drop the torch, the only light in this underworld, just in time to catch the beast by the jaws. Saliva trickles around my knuckles, and one of my thumbs wraps around a long fang. It tries to bite down, and I muscle its jaws open, forcing it backward, kicking that bronze sword behind us as we go. I force its back against the wall, and it swipes its paws against me. The blows sound like someone beating a hide drum over my heart, and I force myself in closer, so that its forelegs are pinned between its chest and my own, until I feel its heart hammering against mine.

It thrashes, and I won't let go of its jaws. Sharp teeth dig into my flesh and I hold it still. I could snap its neck like a fatted cow. I should. I know I'm supposed to.

One of its paws is trapped against my sternum. It can't even fidget, hard as it's wrestling to free itself. Its claws extend, pricking the bare skin there.

Pricking a place so similar to where a newborn child's paw once pierced me.

In the dark, does it matter that I close my eyes?

Do you hear me call it by another child's name? I won't repeat it. I can't.

Do you see as I pull the lion down into my arms, forcing its muzzle against my shoulder? I clutch it by the scruff of its neck, trapping its mouth shut without harming it further. My tears wet its mane, and it tries to bite at me. It can't get the angle. It's never wrestled someone who didn't want to kill it before.

I have to flay the skin off a thing that never asked to be invincible. That never asked to live alone in a cave, and I don't hear a lioness or cubs. Is this lion the only of its kind? Is it another wayward child of gods, lost and unsure of what to do? Something pursued by uncountable hunters, of whom I am just the latest one?

Between my chest pinning its forelimbs, and right arm trapping its head against the crook of my shoulder, it cannot escape. There's nothing wrong with using my free left hand. I rest it atop the lion's brows, and I stroke it from brow to mane. I hold it like I wish I could ever hold my son again.

Those things, I never meant to do and will never forgive myself for doing.

This thing, I choose to do.

The lion's head thrashes one more time, and I stroke it again, like it's a fitful child who can't sleep. If it can tear me apart, let it try.

We go on like that, until the torch burns out. I barely notice the light fading until it's gone. Then I startle, and my grip slips on the lion's scruff. It gets loose and immediately pushes its muzzle at my ear. I feel its teeth.

Then I feel its tongue.

Fetid breath washes my shoulder as the beast licks me from neck to hairline.

I stare at the monster than I can't see, and I stroke its head. Before I can finish the stroke, it licks me again. Its next growl is a demand, and continues until I scratch behind its flicking ears.

So many killers have come after this lion. Has nobody ever thought to pet it?

Hera 13

"Y ou are fucking kidding me?"

I reel back from the marble rim. Torch or no, I can see everything that is happening in that damned cave. His thick beard drips with the lion's saliva, and its tongue gets thick with his curly hairs. They rub at each other, and stagger around, the lion's paws coming to his shoulders like it's actually going to play with him.

Beside me, Athena says, "This hasn't happened before."

I shove her in the shoulder. "You told me that was the most dangerous lion in Greece!"

"It is," she says. Then her voice lowers. "Or it was."

"How the fuck did it get pacified that fast? It's a man-eater."

"There is no record of the origins of the Lion on Nemea," Athena says, as if this lack of knowledge offends her on a moral level. "No normal lion would dissolve into affection this quickly, especially not after so many humans have hunted it. There has to be something uncanny about it, like a god created it as a harbinger at some point."

The creation of a god? I squint down at that oversized cat.

"If that fucking lion is one of my dipshit husband's children . . ."

"It does live near the Temple of Zeus."

"You're not helping—wait, it bit him!"

I jump over the marble rim to see it maul Heracles. Except after one nip, it returns to shoving the crown of its head into his hands. He wasn't petting it the right way and had to be punished. He goes right back to rubbing its head, and it rumbles again.

I object to all of this. "Lions can't even make that noise! It sounds like a house cat."

"That is another feature that suggests it's an unusual creature."

"And what is that noise, anyway? Every house cat in Greece goes 'whurr.' I know cats. What is 'purr' about? Is it possible that beast is just trying to annoy me?"

Athena makes an appraising sound. I know the next thing out of her mouth is going to be annoying. "Did you want it to kill him?"

"I wanted it to stall him! Does he look stalled to you? I need time!"

That touch-starved man holds onto the lion's neck, swinging around with it. He's found perhaps the most durable playmate in the world. All his fears of destroying his wife or nephew melt away. He's not worried about breaking the lion.

"There's some upside here."

Athena nods. "It could provide some catharsis to him."

That sentiment is like cold water unexpectedly pouring down the crack of my ass. I shove Athena again.

"I thought you were the smart god," I say, not deigning to glare at her. "The one advantage is not only is the lion's skin impenetrable, but now it's his friend. Let's see him bring that thing's skin to King Eurystheus now."

Heracles 13

The citadel greets me with six hundred bronze-tipped spears. These walls were built by the Cyclopic Titans themselves, from stones so enormous that no mules could have dragged them to the top of the hill here. It took the work of giants. No mortal can see over the walls to the grounds inside. When mortals inherited the citadel, they found a Temple of Hera lay in the path of the wall, and they dared not demolish it. Instead it became another brick in that wall, and your presence became a blessing the soldiers still revel under. No army has ever breached the Citadel of Tiryns, home of the King of All He Surveys.

Yet the King of All He Surveys has these walls guarded by six hundred of Greece's finest soldiers, the sweat on their skin nearly as bold as the bronze of their breastplates. They clutch their spears as though they'll turn them on us at any moment. All their faces wish they were behind those walls, rather than guarding them.

I put up the palm of my free hand to calm them. "It's all right, boys. The King of All He Surveys is expecting Heracles."

From my left, Iolaus says, "Uncle Al, I respect you. But this isn't going to work."

"I am to bring the king the hide of his lion, and so I will. Come."

While the Lion of Nemea's weight is no trouble, his bulk engulfs me, paws dragging on the ground from either side of my shoulders. Even my brother Iphicles would disappear under such a beast. I return my right arm to the back of the lion's head, palm smoothing along his brow above his closed eyes. His head bobs limply with my steps, as though he's dead to the world. My right hand always stays on his body, supporting his haunches and holding onto its tail. I can't have it swaying happily right now.

This beast would chew a hundred swords and spit them out. But it melts into a puddle of laziness after an hour of petting.

His belly is full of game meat. I keep petting across his brow with my left hand, to keep him pacified. As far as the king's guards are to be concerned, this lion might as well be dead.

When the Pythia commanded me to bring the King of All He Surveys the skin of the Nemean Lion, she never said I couldn't bring the rest of it.

I stride forward, and the sea of shields and spears parts. Horrified feet shuffle away, losing their tight formations at the sight of the "slain" beast's visage.

"See? The King of All He Surveys is most hospitable."

It's untrue, but it needs to be said. My tone is jovial enough to float up to Papa Zeus's sky. Someone needs to set all these servants of the king at ease.

The gate of the citadel is more a long hallway running alongside the main buildings, with a dirt floor, and walls so tall and close together that it feels like the stones themselves are watching me. From over the sides, more soldiers watch, waiting for a mistake I won't make. It would be cramped even if I wasn't carrying the lion. Megara and Iolaus have to follow along behind me.

I speak in a low tone. "The Pythia sent me on this path. Her insight is from the gods themselves. So if things go wrong here, remember, keep alert. This isn't about being honored. It's about seeing what opportunities the gods open for us."

Megara eyes the soldiers watching above us. "Unless the god in question is the one we're after."

Iolaus says, "I hope it's only one."

As though you would allow several gods to attack me? No. Auntie Hera, I believe in you.

I carry the slackened lion all the way into the citadel's central court, a wide space of dirt that is packed with even more armed soldiers, their bronze shields set side to side like the scales of a dragon. They form three curved lines in front of the throne room of the King of All He Surveys.

The throne room is through a wide opening with no doors, Doric columns supporting either side of its roof. None are allowed inside, even when an army isn't protecting the entrance. Beyond all those shields, there flicker braziers, and the armored champions of the king. Atop a great throne of wrought gold is King Eurystheus himself.

Or, he should be there. When I squint through the poor lighting of the throne room, I only see his head and his frilly hair. He's hiding behind the back of the throne, using it to shield himself.

We're cousins. I was hoping this would be more fun. But I can't blame anyone for not wanting to be near me. Not after what the gods made me do.

In the central court stands a well, its rim made of stones hewn into rectangular bricks. Facing the throne room, I walk up to the well and plant one foot on it. After scratching the lion behind its ears, I lift it up, and it's as limp as overcooked lunch.

"Great King Eurystheus," I say. "I have traveled long under the commands of the gods. I bring to you the skin of the most feared monster in all of Nemea."

King Eurystheus covers his mouth, chattering with some of his champions.

Then he says, "You were only supposed to bring its skin."

"I kept all the skin intact, my king. You can examine it if you wish."

I stretch my arms forward, extending the drooping lion to them all. Its tail threatens to swish, and I hold onto it as hard as I can without pinching. Nobody needs an angry lion in the middle of a forest of shields and spears.

Several of the soldiers lose their intense gazes, trading them for awe. The man nearest to me gawks, not at the lion, but at the loose flab on my arms. Surely they've seen strongmen before, who are never shaped like my brother. Still, it must be unusual for someone of quite my shape to be lofting the largest lion in Greece.

King Eurystheus calls, "How do you lift that thing? Is it hollow?"

"The lion is quite full," I say, since I'm the one who stuffed his mouth with meat this morning. "You may have heard I'm a little strong. Papa Zeus had a plan for me, as he had for you, King of All He Surveys."

"So it seems."

I gesture to bring the lion a little closer, and immediately the king drops his head, diving fully behind his throne. All these men ready to fight me for him, and he couldn't look more spooked if he were hiding inside a bronze urn. The life of a king must stress you out.

I wonder how you two manage your stations, Papa Zeus and Auntie Hera. If his burdens have him falling apart, you two must have wills harder than bronze. Mortals could never do what you do.

From behind the throne, the king calls, "That's enough lions for today! And all days! Take it away. Gone from the citadel and don't bring it back."

This at least lets me pull the lion back to myself. He's starting to squirm when I hug him to my chest, so I cradle his head to the crook of my neck again. My fingers scritch through his mane, where nobody can see, and I keep his head squished down to my breast. The lion is so content there that I'm already thinking of names for him, should he decide to stick with me. He'll be another part of the family. He's such a brave lion that maybe I'll name him for my great-grandfather, Perseus.

Except with the happy noises he makes, he will be Purrseus.

I think that will make Megara smile, and I move to share the idea with her, but her mind is elsewhere. She asks, "Isn't he supposed to give us information?"

I nod to her, and call, "Thank you, Great King Eurystheus. I'll get rid of this lion for you. It won't trouble you again. But the oracle led me to expect you would tell me what I must do next in my path. You are of the lineage of Zeus and Perseus. What wisdom do you have to share? What is my next labor?"

The king stares at me like he's going to demand his guards drive me out of the citadel. My legs tense, and I double my grip on Purrseus. I can't have a massacre on my conscience.

Iolaus says, "Come on. He's got to know something."

Megara says, "Do the gods really care about us?"

Auntie Hera, I need to know. I didn't come this far for nothing. Did you really want me to slice this animal apart?

The throne room rumbles, as though an earthquake has hit just one room in all of the world. The ceiling clatters against its pillars, and all the champions fall away from the throne.

Behind the throne, King Eurystheus stands bolt upright. His robes shine as brightly as the gold of his throne, and he steps around it like fear has fallen apart from him as easily as the waters from a bath. He points to me with his golden scepter.

"Heracles," he says in a booming voice befitting my father. "You will travel to Lerna in Peloponnese, and there you will battle the many-headed hydra. It is a beast from before the dawn of Olympos, jaws greater than any lion, breath more poisonous than any dragon. If one of its heads is chopped away, two more shall grow in its place. Solve its living riddle."

I could run into the throne room right now and kiss that cousin of mine. I knew my faith would be rewarded.

I ask, "This is how I'll find the god responsible for my family?"

"I have spoken!"

He tosses his scepter away, and it clatters across the floor like a demented musical instrument. It resounds through the throne room, and the noise makes the king startle. Immediately he shrinks away again, clutching at one armrest of his throne. He's fixated on the lion in my arms.

"Aren't we done here?" he says. "No more lions ever. Are they banned from the citadel grounds yet? Ban them."

On our way out of the citadel, my head buzzes like a wasp's nest. Not merely an enemy I don't want to kill, but one who can't die. One who constantly grows. It feels like a metaphor for the unsolvable mystery we're chasing.

I wonder aloud, "What could a serpent have to do with the furies?"

"Something," Iolaus says. "It has to be something. I've never seen divine inspiration before, but that had to be it. We're onto something, Uncle Al."

Megara sucks in a slow, noisy breath. "Are we?"

I reel at her, nearly dropping Purrseus. "Didn't you hear him?"

"I heard. We're chasing another monster without any clear idea of what it means."

"This is the doing of the gods, though," I say. "They'll guide us, as sure as bronze will always be the strongest metal."

As she exits the gates, she mutters something that only I can hear. I know an argument is coming. We haven't had a fight since before the fire. Before I was stolen from myself.

What she says is just a tease for what we'll be arguing for days to come.

"Are the gods the only way to find the truth?"

Hera 14

One of the worst sounds is owl talons clacking against marble. At first, I refuse to look. I know she wants attention. She doesn't deserve it. This hydra business will stall Heracles and give me time to think what to actually do about him. I deserve a moment to drink and exhale.

"My queen?"

That know-it-all thinks every hour belongs to her. That must be why she inspired the mortals to discover recordkeeping.

"My queen?"

She sounds like a mortal now, having changed her avatar out, like she thinks that will earn my attention.

"My queen?"

Fine.

"Yeah?" I say. "What now?"

"Why did you select the Hydra of Lerna specifically?"

"Are there other hydras? I'd never even heard of this one before. But it's turned the Lake of Lerna into an uninhabitable marsh just by living there. It's got to be good."

I turn. To my surprise, she isn't facing me with gray eyes imploring details. Both her arms are folded against the marble rim, and she's watching something intently. It's not Eurystheus's palace, but another part of Greece entirely. She's watching something in Lerna, and chewing the inside of her cheek.

She says, "This hydra is quite formidable. Lesser gods have struggled against them."

"I bet it's tough. It's got, like, what, ten heads?"

"They currently have several heads, yes, each head the size of that of a large dog, each along a serpentine neck. If a head is cut off, two more will replace it in short order. They don't replicate sexually. They just grow more of themselves."

I wave off the idea with a hand. "So Heracles will never be able to kill it. Great. That buys me the time I want."

"The heads are . . . ornery. When wounded, they bleed a blood unlike any other living creature. It's a poison beyond anything humans have divined. Its effects on flesh make fire seem tame."

I hug my middle for a moment. I don't love the mental images that fire brings to mind right now.

Still. Heracles isn't going to be able to hug his way out of this one. This will stop him.

Things are going better. So what's this tension in my chest?

"My queen," Athena says. "You didn't answer. Why did you send him to fight this specific hydra?"

I gesture for her to make her damned point already. "What's your deal? Are you scared for the hydra here?"

"I have some concerns about where this is going."

Her tone is too measured. She needs to be goaded into spilling what she's thinking. She better not have thought of an angle I haven't.

I say, "If you think you'd do a better job as Queen of Olympos, go ahead and say it. You'll be banished by morning."

"It's not that. I have knowledge of this hydra."

"You're the Goddess of Wisdom. You've got a lot of knowledge."

"Specific knowledge."

"Specific? Specifically what? Out with it."

It is an unendurable moment, so long that civilizations rise and fall waiting for this goddess to get to the point. Mountains are worn into deserts by wind. Stars die.

Finally, Athena says, "We dated."

One of those stars must have taken my listening comprehension when it died. I didn't just hear that. That is not possible.

"What the hell, Athena? You fucked a snake?"

"They are not a snake."

I gesture to her pristine senatorial robes and that plumed charioteer's helm on her head. She couldn't be more of a virgin if she worshipped Artemis.

"You? You just do knowledge stuff. You're asexual."

"Sexuality and romanticism are not the same thing." She looks away, to the mortal world. "But I get mine. Discreetly."

"From a snake!"

"As I said, they are not a snake."

"You fucked a snake! No wonder you know the burning sensations its fluid emissions give. Athena, you, of everyone, dated, of everything, that thing?" I have to remove my polos in order to rub at my prickling scalp. The surprise almost takes my hair off. "How did your dating go so badly that you made King Eurystheus send Heracles to kill the thing?"

Athena's face goes abruptly pensive. "I didn't give Eurystheus the idea. You did."

"No, I didn't." I wag an index finger before her nose. I know I didn't, because I didn't have a good idea for what Heracles should do next. I was thinking of sending him after the mad king Diomedes and his man-eating horses or something. And I haven't set foot in Eurystheus's palace since the day he was born. This isn't my work. "Fess up. Why did you send Heracles to kill your ex-snakefriend?"

The tension in those gray eyes. Her lids flutter, like she's trying to think with every living mind in Greece.

Athena says, "Someone gave Eurystheus the idea. If it wasn't you, my queen, then there's another problem."

I lean on the marble rim, still rubbing at my scalp. Rather than down at the mortal realm, I squint into Olympos's marble halls.

"What other god would interfere with my plan?"

Heracles 14

The poets sing that Lerna was once a fishing village, with crystalline waters that trickled down to the farmers of Argos. People from the across the land came to anoint themselves in its waters, and to pray to Papa Zeus and Auntie Hera.

The poets haven't been here in a while.

A cloud of black flies swarms into my eyes as I near the marsh's shores. Swatting seems to make them swarm harder around me. The marsh reeks of sickness, and the waters have mostly dried up, reduced to brackish ponds around tiny outcroppings of land. We make camp under the thickest bunch of trees we can, although they're so limp we have to prop some of them up.

Iolaus says, "This is all the hydra's doing. The slime from its scales tainted this place down to its roots."

Purrseus pads along down to the edge of the water. He raises a paw with claws out, like he wants to slap this lake into behaving. I doubt he'll want to join me on this hunt. Cats and water.

"Are you sure you want to do this?" Megara asks.

I promise her, "I'll come back to you. I'll always come back to you."

She's going to reproach me, but Iolaus strikes the torches. We set them around the periphery of our camp, along with two quivers of hollow arrows. They're filled with oil. Iolaus tests the tip of one, and it ignites right away. He uses that to light the last torch, which he hands to me.

"If you call, we'll rain down fire on the monster. It might not be afraid of losing a head, but nothing likes burning."

I tell them, "I'll be counting on you both."

Megara has the bait in a sack; the inedible parts of our most recent meals attract more flies than anything. I reach for it, and she withholds it.

"You can stay. Wait until tomorrow."

Tomorrow wouldn't be enough for either of us.

I say, "I'd rather be back before tomorrow. This is going to get us what we need. I owe this to us."

I take the sack and trudge into the marsh. One step and my entire foot is submerged in slime and warm moss. I flex my toes in my sandals to get used to the feeling. Immerse myself in discomfort. There's no sinking into thoughtlessness today. I need my wits.

As I trudge further into the marshes, something splashes behind me. I turn to look, and am surprised to find Purrseus is following me. He won't let me go alone.

I guess I'm not alone out here after all.

Thank you for this, Auntie Hera.

Hera 15

Nothing is easier than hunting Apollo. He is the most try-hard of the Olympians. Look away from your domain for an instant, and he'll have a franchise in it. He's the God of Laws, despite most laws coming from Zeus and Athena. He's the God of Archery, despite Artemis basically inventing the bow. He's the God of Protection when literally every fucking god protects things.

If you want to catch Apollo? Show up at dawn.

There he is at the marble rim, wearing a slim red cape over his boyish physique with his ass hanging out, and a laurel on his brow that glows like it wants to shed light over the world. Apollo is always there at dawn, eye-banging Helios on his ride across the heavens to raise the sun. Apollo scribbles notes about how Helios performs, and how he could do it better. He's determined to steal that God of the Sun shtick.

I snatch the gilded laurel off his head, then shake it at him like a toy rattle. I'll turn him into a musical instrument if he says the wrong thing even once.

Apollo gasps. "Huh? Queen Hera?"

I'm not buying it. "Are you fucking with Heracles, you little shit?"

"Wait," he says, shrinking from his laurel like it's already a knife. "I thought you were fucking with Heracles."

"Don't use that kind of language with me."

"Didn't you murder his entire family or—"

"That's irrelevant! I know you trifle with human affairs constantly, with your inspirations and your oracles. You put that thought of the Hydra of Lerna into Eurystheus's court, didn't you?"

Something worse than confusion crosses Apollo's delicate features. There's an envy, like a snake that's spotted the first sunbeam to warm up in. He's not just afraid of my assault now.

"Whatever you're doing right now," he says, his tone speculative, "is someone the god of it yet?"

I reel back to smash his laurel across his face, and a dirt-streaked hand catches my arm. I've been too enraged with Apollo's possible interloping to notice my son Ares step from around me. His avatar is taller than us both, the bronze shoulder pads of his armor streaked with the blood of unknown soldiers who died praying for his help. He gets between us, like a personal eclipse.

"I've got this, Mom."

His voice is as cooling as a small wave lapping across my toes. I rise to demand he show proper outrage, but before I can, his voice turns into a storm surge.

"There's been a misunderstanding, Apollo. My mother thought you interfered in her affairs. Of course you would never."

I try to interject, "He would—"

Ares continues, "Because you know what we'd do to you if we caught you."

"I didn't tamper with anything," Apollo says, his face a forced mask of steadiness. He's trying too hard to look like he isn't shaken. "But you know, she fed arcane information to the Pythia. That's my big oracle. I'm in charge of who the Pythia talks to."

"You're done here, Apollo."

Ares stamps a sandaled heel on the floor of Olympos, and the marble walls slam with his gesture. Doors close between us and Apollo, boxing us away from the marble rim. Now I can't watch what's happening below or further interrogate that prick.

I ask, "What do you think you're doing?"

"Apollo knows who you truly suspect."

I get boxed into a private room in the middle of an interrogation, and somehow, someone let Athena in here? I turn a fuming gaze on both Gods of War. These are two more than I need right now.

Ares says, "Mom. It's not him."

It probably wasn't Apollo. He's too obvious in all his machinations; that's why oracles can read him so easily. He would've cracked and coughed up anything he knew.

Then my son says, "It's not Zeus."

Cracks spiderweb out along the marble below both of my feet. "Who said it was him?"

"You only get this angry over Dad. But I'm telling you, wherever he's gone, he's not the one messing with Heracles. I've got lesser gods watching out in the mortal world. I'd know."

This is the same man who I found vacationing between Aphrodite's thighs? What made him get his shit together so quickly? And now he's on the watch for my missing dipshit husband?

Athena gets the full wrath of my glare. "You told Ares about this behind my back?"

"No, my queen."

"No," Ares agrees. "I don't talk to her. I figured it out because this is all less secretive than either of you think."

"Less secretive, huh?" I ask. "Then which of the Olympians sent Heracles after the hydra? Was it Artemis? I never trust virgins."

"I'm only one God of War," Ares says with so much passive aggression that I'm briefly proud of him. "But I've been moving through the ranks of Olympos. I don't think your enemy is on this side of the marble rim."

He must have a point, because Athena looks pensive. Did the Goddess of Strategy get out-thought by the God of Brute Force?

I ask him, "What do you mean?"

"It's not only Olympian gods who meddle in mortal affairs. You need to look at what gods are roaming the earth."

Athena says, "There are thousands of lesser gods in Greece. Every stream. Every sport. Every significant house claims protection from some lesser being, and every significant road claims perils from another."

Ares puts one foot up on the marble rim, his calluses thicker than the stone. "We'd better get looking. Because whichever god is after Heracles, they're already down there. They could be closer than any of us know."

Heracles 15

"Ahhhhhh!"

At least it's not hard to find the hydra. In hunting Purrseus, I had to rummage around in caves until he attacked me in the quiet. He could have been anywhere in the dark. Whereas today, hunting this Hydra of Lerna?

"Ahhhhhhhhhhhhh!"

Theirs is a chorus of phlegmy voices, all marching toward me like a choir to the God of Pain. Is there a God of Pain, Auntie Hera? There must be. It's such a part of life.

The purpose of bait is to choose the arena. I toss the sack into the murk beside a wide shelf of stone—it would make a great roof for a temple if Lerna ever gets tidied up. The footing is firm, and with a thicket of cypresses sprouting behind it, I can trust the monster won't get my back.

Politely, they come at me from the front. Their heads tear through the waters, murk dripping down their opening jaws, revealing rows of fangs. Chewing anything with that many mouths much be exhausting. Their necks are longer than any snake, and many are thick as my calves. There are so many churning serpentine lengths that I can't see their central body. Most of the heads train on me, slime oozing over their eyes, and they shout in unison.

"Ahhhhhhh!"

I heft the great bronze cleaver in my right hand, a weapon taller than I am. The flat of its blade will make a good club. I'm not sure that crushing the heads isn't a better idea than decapitation—will one grow back if it's flattened and not removed?

In case any of those heads understand human gestures, I put aside the cleaver and hold up a hand for them all to slow down. "Feel free to eat this offering before we brawl. Or you could surrender in advance. We have options. Do you know anything about the furies?"

A few heads trample the bait sack and tear it open, promptly munching on the free meal. This doesn't slow down any of the other heads, which bite onto any nearby earth to drag the whole mass of them toward me. They haul themselves forward, and whenever a mouth releases its hold, it goes right back to screaming.

They sound like they're in such pain. I'd offer to help if they weren't about to devour me.

As I heft the bronze cleaver, Purrseus darts in. He roars into those serpentine faces, like Zeus's own thunder daring them to strike. The nearest head opens its mouth to strike at me, and Purrseus snaps his jaws down. He tears the entire skull off the hydra, and a forearm's length of neck to go with it. Immediately the lion whips his head back to swallow his prize.

"No!"

I try to get to him, to make him spit it out. Already Purrseus's body seizes up, forelegs going rigid against the stone. He gags hard, and liquid spills out of his maw. He vomits the head down, mixed with his own blood. He shrieks and scampers away from the hydra, pawing at his mouth, trying to attack the pain from the hydra's fluids burning his insides.

The hydra chases after him, one head rearing up to strike while Purrseus is still convulsing. Others tense, preparing to follow. I can see it: unable to pierce the lion's hide, the hydra will drag him under the waters to drown him.

It's a mistake and I can't stop myself. I swing the cleaver overhead, lopping off the first of the heads and letting the blade clang against the rocks below. I stare down the other heads, not letting them anywhere near my lion.

The two headless necks tremble, seams opening along their underbellies. Before I can move, they split, new mouths sprouting from their fronts. They swell up to the size of the other heads, and eagerly snap their new jaws at me. Where there were two heads, now there are four.

Damn it. The exact thing I'm not supposed to do to a hydra.

"Ahhhhhh!"

They don't sound happy about it either.

As the many necks wind around each other, slime oozing from their mouths, I have one brief opening. All the hydra's necks are bundled together for the moment, focused only on me. One giant swing with the cleaver could sever them all. Will that stop them? I have to try, if only to buy Purrseus enough time to run.

I raise the cleaver high overhead, like I am going to chop a forest down. I brace both my feet against the flat stone, letting all my weight rest behind me. All the hydra's heads stare at the blade as if fascinated. Almost as if they want to be beheaded and to spew their burning blood everywhere.

"Ahhhhh!"

My feet and calves are stinging, like dozens of tiny mouths are nibbling on me. That ankle-deep water froths, and for a moment I think the hydra has burrowed into the slate I stand on. But orange claws break the water, and rounded shells. They swarm up, little creatures climbing on each other to get at my knees. It's a swarm of . . . crabs?

Yes, those are crabs pouring out from under my flat clearing. Their legs click-click-click against the surface as they climb my legs to get at me, bigger ones emerging all the time, with claws the size of my fist, all snapping at me. They lap up like living waves, clamping onto my calves and knees, trying to climb and engulf me. They're everywhere, dwarfing the hydra, shoving their necks away like they're nothing. Mounds of them fall on us like rain, like they want to drag us under the waters to their home.

"Ahh!"

Hera 16

If you want to stop divine intervention, then what you need is more divine intervention.

You taught me that, Zeus. How many titans did we interrupt in the middle of their grand schemes? How many gods have you surprised by lying in wait for them to act?

You can hide yourself. You can convince Ares that you're entirely missing. No matter what our son says, you won't fool me. Perhaps you're being discreet because you know you have a hand in what happened to Heracles, too. Perhaps seeing him heartbroken is what got you to finally act.

You're why that lion licked him when it devoured everyone else.

You're who put the ideas in King Eurystheus's head. I made him king, and you made him into a puppet to mock me.

So I lie in wait, like an angler on a boat made of clouds. Heracles is my bait. You'll make another move around him, and when you do, I'll be here.

Athena says, "Are you actually watching over Heracles? The way he always thought you did?"

"Shut the fuck up, Athena."

I banish her from my clouds to go hunt the lesser gods she and Ares suspect. This is no time for nonsense about something as ludicrous as me having an attachment to Heracles. This is no time for sentimentality and nonsense. I need to concentrate.

Even when the skies are clear, I am above casting a shadow. I browse the arguments he's having with his wife—all natural, all two-sided ignorance, both of them too hurt to understand what they're doing. That's mortal stuff, not the work of a god.

That lion follows Heracles around everywhere. As he shoulders his quiver of arrows, it rubs against his thigh for more attention. More mortal business.

They descend into the marshes, and every one of them, even the demigod, gags at the air. It is fetid and poisoned by the hydra. There's nothing divine about it.

How do the other gods watch this all day? I can barely stand to stay above them a moment longer. Heracles encountering the hydra livens up nothing. I've seen men maul monsters before, and monsters make meals of men before. Their epic struggle is as tasteless as a bite of straw.

I start turning away to check if Athena has discovered anything when the waters move in a way they shouldn't. That's not wind over the surface, and nothing that lives down there could do this. A whirlpool opens in the lake, and orange crabs begin pouring out, snapping their pincers at Heracles's feet.

There are no crabs in Lerna. If there ever were, the hydra's poison would have killed them off centuries ago.

You're a heavy-handed fool, Zeus. I've got you now.

Fast as one of your thunderbolts, I shoot unseen into Lerna, dashing the avatar of crabs into smithereens. My impact spares just one of them, which I pluck up by the top of its shell, outside the range where its pincers can reach. It wiggles its feet in futile confusion. I refuse to let the god take its former shape. You're stuck in this avatar until I say otherwise.

The waters recede to their proper height, sending Heracles and hydra back up to the surface. The sudden reverse of a whirlpool might spit out Heracles at a safe distance from the monster, but I don't intend it. He gets lucky, that's all.

I rest my feet on solid marble caked in kelp and ichor. With the waters returning to their proper height, I realize this is a long-submerged building. A small temple from bygone eras. The receding waters haven't only revealed a god in the form of crabs; they've revealed the god's place of worship. There's a single statue inside, and I recognize its thick brows and dense beard.

With a fraction of my strength, I squeeze on that shell. How easy it would be to shatter my husband's tiny avatar.

"Zeus, you goat-licker. Where have you been?"

"Hera!" the crab squeaks in a feminine voice that's all too familiar.

That's not my dipshit husband. "Wait, wait, wait. Don't let Heracles get away. We've got him right where we want him."

I bring the crab up closer to my face, dumbstruck by a voice I haven't heard in so long.

"Is that you, Até?"

Heracles 16

I land with all my weight on a broad patch of moss, hitting hard enough that my heart rattles around inside my ribs. I skid along the earth until I hit a patch of reeds, and catch them to stop myself. As soon as I stop, I grope over my chest, then down my legs.

Not a single crab has a hold of me. In fact, not a single one is in sight. They've vanished as quickly as they came.

Thank you, Aunt Hera. There's no mistaking your touch. I knew you were looking over me.

I'll do the rest now. For all of us.

But where's my cleaver? Did it sink to the bottom of the lake?

"Ahhhhhh!"

The hydra screams on the next patch of land over from me, furious they were spit out of the whirlpool. Many of their mouths clutch at something that shines darker than gold in the muck.

I wipe my eyes and see the worst. They've got my bronze cleaver, coiling around it, like they're dragging it into their fold to become a new head.

Streaks of flame cut through the air, snagging in branches and catching anything dry ablaze. From far away, Iolaus and Megara are loosing arrows at us. A burning arrow zips in and plunges into one of the hydra's faces, straight into soft flesh under its tongue, which goes up in flames immediately. Every head shrieks together.

"Ahhhhhhhhhhh!"

It's my chance, given by gods and friends. I run to the edge of the water, then hurl myself across. Serpentine heads swing at me like fists, and I bat them aside, until I find the hide-wrapped handle. I grasp it with both hands and yank, and it doesn't budge, instead dragging the entire hydra closer to me.

Too many of its coils are wrapped around the cleaver. They pull the blade toward themselves insistently, as though to steal it from me. As though to sever their own heads with its edge.

So I give them what they want. As flaming arrows pelt its many necks, I plunge forward and swing. A horrid sweat pours off me, washing away the filth of the lake. My grip slips on the handle because my hands are shaking. I'm doing violence with these hands again. I'm no better than a monster.

I drop the cleaver and fall to the ground, clutching both my hands together so they don't do anything else. I fight to breathe and look away from the maimed hydra. I can't look. I can't see this. Megara was right.

"Ahhhhhhhhhh yeeeeeeeeees! Yeeees, more of that, please!"

I'm too baffled to control myself. Those words make no sense. The voice is ecstatic. The hydra still has a voice?

One head slithers out from the mass of its brethren, every bit as dripping and fanged as the others. The skin around its eyes narrows as though relaxing for the first time in its existence. I can't believe what I'm seeing. It has to be another trick. The crabs were easier to understand.

"Hey, kid," says that one surviving head. "You wanted to know about furies, right? I'll tell you everything I know. Just do me one favor."

The head isn't screaming. It's the same voice, with composure. With needs. It needs me.

"Anything," I say. "What do you want?"

Another flaming arrow flies down, digging into the earth and catching a bush ablaze. The surviving head points at the brush fire and says, "Get some of that and burn my other neck stumps. I can already feel them trying to grow back."

I look at the sheered sides of this head's neck. Flesh bubbles there, like they're brewing themselves into another batch of serpents. Their purple blood pours out of every wound, smoking in the air. It's a magic like nothing I've ever seen.

I say, "You don't want to save them . . . ?"

"Quickly! Quickly or some of me will eat all of you."

The panic in that voice. I can't question it. I can only help.

I uproot the burning bush and treat all of those bubbling wounds. The hydra shudders a few times at the first burns, then pulls their body around to offer more of those neck stumps. By the time they're all gone, and the hydra is reduced to a single serpent's neck, with a single tail and a single head, they make a sweet noise between hissing and humming.

"Love you humans," the hydra says, slithering down to rub their burns in cool mud. "I always knew you guys would amount to something. Terrible at regrowing body parts, but a beautiful species."

I crouch before the mighty hydra, offering palmfuls of water to soothe the burns. "You speak?"

"Observant species, too. Of course I can speak. Didn't you hear me screaming this whole time? That migraine was a beast."

Maybe this makes more sense if you think about it with multiple heads. I ask, "One of your heads had a headache?"

"A headache? Fa! At two heads, I got a buzzing through my skull. At three heads, I couldn't keep food down anymore. After a dozen, I barely knew where I was. The world was fire and agony. I thought you were an ocular and olfactory hallucination. There was a good century where I hallucinated the smell of roasting pork everywhere."

The hydra makes a gagging noise. I didn't know serpents could gag.

"Migraines," says the hydra. "They're real motherfuckers. I spent at least three hundred years hiding in dark crevices hoping for a little relief. Couldn't even concentrate enough to get out of that lake."

The head upnods at the nearby waters. It's such a human gesture that I struggle to believe this is the same creature that was rampaging before.

"And trust me. I wanted to leave."

"I'm glad I could help you."

"Help me? You saved my life. What's your name?"

"Alcides. Or Heracles. Whatever you prefer. What do I call you?"

"I'm not big on names. Mostly people just scream at me. But the smartest person I ever met called one of my heads Logy. So you can try that on and see if it fits."

This is going to take some getting used to. I start by saying, "Hello, Logy."

"Al, buddy, good to meet you. Carry me anywhere but here and I'll tell you anything you want to know. I'm going to lie in the sun somewhere, all by myself. No other heads stealing my idea and getting in the way. No more competition with myself for food."

I smell Purrseus's breath before he can strike. I reach out with my right arm, and he comes pushing in. I capture him in a headlock, stopping him in place so he won't maul the remains of Logy. He's sopping wet from our adventure, and wriggles with displeasure. He's earned a few ear-pettings.

As I try to subdue Purrseus with grooming, Logy says, "The Lion of Nemea's still around, huh? You can't kill a classic."

I study this hydra's sole remaining head, with its scales and perpetually squinted eyes. They certainly sound sincere.

I ask, "You know him?"

"I was around back when he was a cub. One of Zeus's spawn, when he was going through a feline phase. He sired this lion to scare some worshippers into line, but forgot his plan midway through when he noticed a shapely local maiden. I'd recognize this guy anywhere. Scary as death itself, but sweet if you don't treat him like shit."

I smooth a palm along the top of Purrseus's fuzzy scalp. "So we're brothers? Is that why you're gentle? You smelled Papa on me?"

Purrseus doesn't care about our fraternity. My newly discovered half-brother just wants head pats. And he gets them.

As I scritch behind Purrseus's ears, I ask Logy, "Do you know many creatures like Purrseus here?"

"Sure do. Back in the day, I was trying to catalog all of us. Until I got stuck in Lerna. It's a long story."

I have to ask, "What do you know about the furies?"

"Everything. I was around when the titans fired them," the hydra says, matter-of-factly. "But I think what you want to ask is: do I know how to hunt the furies?"

I lean in closer, until I'm nearly on top of Logy. "Do you know?"

I may be first mortal to hear a hydra's laugh. It sounds a lot like screaming.

I could get used to it.

Até throws herself at me, blond hair fanning behind her head in every shade of gold the sun neglects. Her hands clamp onto my shoulders and she crushes our chests together with abandon, her voice a honeyed hum. There's such warm glee in every iota of contact between our skin.

Nobody touches me like this. My husband couldn't feign it if he wanted to. This isn't Zeus in disguise.

It's really her. Her eyes are so keen they belong on a peacock's feathers. This really is my only friend, the Goddess of Ruin.

It's not possible. I raise my hands, seeking her wrists, to stop the hidden dagger that has to be coming. Nobody holds a grudge like Até. She's got to be using Heracles to lure me out of Olympos, to get me where I'm vulnerable. To get revenge on me for getting her cast down.

If Zeus is around, I need him right now.

"Hera! Darling!" She kisses my cheek, a dry gesture. No poison on her lips, unless it's a powder. Has she ever used powder poison before? "Seeing you is the best, but you've got to back off a minute. Let me work my magic here. I'm helping you."

"You're helping me?"

The distance between our faces increases, despite neither of us moving. The world feels wrong.

She releases my shoulders to twist around in her tattered white dress. The ends are all frayed and stained with yellow and swamp murk. It's the same dress she wore on Olympos. In all these eternal years, she hasn't changed from the last garment she had from home.

She waves her fingers at Heracles and his hydra, wrestling at each other with cleavers and burning refuse. As though this fight is something I'd want to see. Something we'd enjoy.

"Look, you annihilated his family. I know that was you; I was in Thebes planning to bring about his fall, but you upstaged me. That was genius vengeance. I thought you'd just make him kill himself and replace him with some hero your husband hates. This, though? This is next level."

I touch my cheek, both fearing and hoping for powder poison. My fingers find only my body oil waiting for me.

I stammer, "That's not it . . ."

She keeps going. "I know all the lesser gods think you're out to kill him with the labors. But I know better. I have a bet with Oceanus about this. You're totally not trying to kill Heracles, right?"

She asks that, and my instinct is to run in the opposite direction of the truth. To announce that I want him dead, in order to spook Zeus out of hiding. But any faith I have in Zeus being here is draining, and do I really want his son alive? Or dead? Is there a truth to run from, other than being confounded as to what I really want with him?

"No," I say. "I don't think I am trying to kill him."

"I knew it." She snaps her fingers at my fingers—our old gesture, urging the other to join in and snap together. It's been so long since I felt that joyous connection with someone that now I don't know what to do with it. "I fucking knew it. Nobody knows you better than me. Oceanus is full of shit. You're not trying to kill him off. You're driving him to kill Zeus."

Those words give me a pleasant tingle—inappropriate, beneath me, and pleasant, all at once. The feeling quickly fades into something unpleasant.

I say, "Hang on."

Até hangs onto nothing save my elbow, gesturing down at the receding murk of the marsh and the stone columns sunken beneath it. "That's why I've been pitching in from down here in the mortal world. I'm going to reveal this temple of Zeus that's submerged in the marsh, and he's going to connect that with the Temple of Zeus in Nemea, and with your brilliant inspiration of making him think the Nemean Lion is a child of Zeus."

"Wait, I didn't make him think that the Nemean Lion was from Zeus."

She blinks, then gets an even smugger smile. "Was that a coincidence? Because it's too good. He'll connect these dots and think the divine plan is pointing to Zeus as the one who annihilated his family. Then the war will be on, and Daddy will pay. A ruin like no other."

Listening to her plot makes me need to wash my hands, and all I have is a poisoned swamp. I grip at my elbows, feeling filthier than the swamp could make anyone. I need a full bath. An eon of baths.

I say, "My revenge? I don't need revenge."

"Every generation slays their parents. Zeus did it to Kronos. Kronos did it to that guy who came before him. You're going to show your dipshit husband that he's nothing but destiny's next domino."

Até never hates in a straight line. Her causes wind and curve like unruly rivers, until no one knows why they're drowning in the flood. This is all bigger than the incident of Heracles's birth. If she hates me and my husband, there are more twisted reasons than she's letting on. She doesn't ruin anyone for simple causes.

It's not just that I let Zeus banish her. I left her to rot down here, and toil with the lower gods and mortal affairs. Mortals could never know how interminable just one year as a god in their midst is. She doesn't just hate us for stranding her down here. I never came back for her. I haven't even thought about her this entire time.

I've been too preoccupied. And by what?

By the revenge that she's preoccupied with.

I think of Mount Olympos, and of the marble palace that allows only the bidden within. Not even an unbidden god can set foot there without perishing. Since her banishment, Até has been without a home. She couldn't return to me, and I never once thought to invite her back. I never once thought of her. Only of my own anger about her.

I take Até by both hands, my fingertips on her palms. I draw her to stand in the sky, on an errant beam of starlight. All that lustrous hair. That youth that defies time. Against the radiance of night, she looks too excited to realize how tired she is, like a log that doesn't realize what the flames it enables are doing to it.

"Até. I never visited you because I forgot you were down here. I betrayed you. You're right to be wrathful at us."

All the fatigue in her face refuses to direct at me. "I'm not mad at *you*."

"You always put up an act. You're out to get revenge for being banished."

"This isn't an act! We have a bond. We're families and ruin; nothing is more intrinsically linked than us. And you did nothing wrong. We were wronged. This is about what was done to us."

I feel a tremor run through me, so sharp it must have traveled through every generation of my family.

"To us?"

Até steps so close to me that she could go right through me. "Where is the fearsome queen who used to start wars just to end them? The queen who eradicated Heracles's children to break him? Why are you meek now? What did Zeus do to you while I was gone?"

I have to ask her. "How long have you been in the mortal world?"

"Your dipshit husband has stranded me here for twenty-eight years. Which was *his* fault."

Twenty-eight years without a word from me. Twenty-eight years and she's still loyal. And to what?

I say, "There are mortals that don't live that long. All that time, I left you here. You were in my entourage. You were doing my bidding when he brought the hammer down on you."

She shakes her head so sharply that the splay of her hair threatens to fell the stars from the sky. "We were standing up to him. Somebody had to."

I let the hair slash my cheek. I don't care if it bleeds. "You should be furious at me. You should be raining ruin on every temple that bears my name. You're not even raising your voice. Why don't you hate me?"

"I see what he did to you," she says, her hands moving as though to cup my cheeks, and then stopping. "This isn't you. He'll pay for making you doubt yourself."

Then she reassesses me, with a coolness that no one has dared cast on me in ages. No one save Zeus and Athena. It's like she's realized I am a shoddy statue, a visage left on the roadside, chiseled by an amateur.

"Don't you worry, Hera. I know what'll help."

Then she's gone. Gone from the stars in the sky, and gone from the marshes. So, too, are Heracles and the monster. I have no notion where any of them have gone. In their absence, I realize Até isn't the only one I used. Not the only one I used and forgot existed in my passion. Not the only one who's suffered without amends. Not the only one I've ignored so long.

I have to find Granny before Heracles does.

Our campsite is already packed when I arrive. Megara has unbeliev-able foresight; she should be an oracle. She's tying up the last of our provisions, getting them ready for when Iolaus brings the chariot around. We'll need to make more space so Logy can fit inside. The good thing is they've dropped a lot of weight today, and with their flexible body they ought to be able to fit anywhere.

I clap my hands together like I'm a kid again, and trot right up to Megara. I can't wait to tell her the good news. It all goes by so quickly. I run to the revelation that the hydra can think and knows all about other monsters, and she reacts so little that it feels like I should keep talking. Like I haven't said enough.

Through her veil, Megara gives me an appraising look. No, it's more than a look. Her whole posture is rigid, like she's tied herself up to throw on the chariot.

"Here's the best part," I say. "This hydra knows of a creature, a deer blessed by Artemis herself. The deer is so cagey that it can sense any pred-ator coming. Orion couldn't track it down. It can sense every possible predator, which means it can tell where the furies are. We can get this deer to point us to them. This is why we were sent after the hydra. We've almost got it, Megara."

The veil hides her face, but I can tell she's not looking at me. I crouch toward her, trying to look into where her eyes have to be.

She says, "You still believe in all this. You went out there and had me shoot burning arrows in your direction, and you still believe."

"Of course I do. I'm doing this for *us*."

"You're going to follow the advice of a hydra? For us?"

"Their name is Logy, and they're wise. They know a lot more than we do and they're willing to help. Aren't you the one who always felt sympathy for monsters?"

"Did I feel sympathy?" She touches her fingertips to the veil over her face, as though testing that it is still there. "I don't feel much at all anymore, Alcides."

Despite myself, I step closer. "We can work on that. Together. What do you need?"

"You're too quick to help. To run in and solve the problem. It used to be one of my favorite things about you." She steps away from me, toward the parcels of our belongings. Now I recognize all my equipment is grouped in one roll. "I need you to keep doing what is keeping you afloat. Find the deer, and whatever the deer points you toward, and whatever that points you toward, so long as it keeps you alive."

Atlas has it easy. It would be easier to hold the sky on my shoulders than keep my distance from her right now. But I'm not the only one afraid here. She wants the gap, too, and so she gets it.

I ask, "What are you going to do?"

"Iolaus is taking me to Corinth, where my father has an envoy. We'll return to Thebes and I'll start my own plot there. I have some ideas."

I wait, so curious for what she's thought up. She's always been cunning.

She says, "I don't want to tell you, because anyone could be listening."

Anyone? Any god?

She moves her veil aside, revealing how puffy her eyes are. How sallow her skin, and how gaunt her neck and cheeks. I see her waking before everyone every day in those features, and I have nothing but boiling guilt.

Still refusing to answer me, she casts her gaze upon the sky, almost as though she's concerned about who is listening to her words. As though the gods are untrustworthy.

If that were so, they'd kill her in an instant. A landslide or a thunderbolt would end her whole blasphemy. If she was right, wouldn't another fury drive me mad right now and make me . . . ?

I can't finish the thought. I rub at my eyelids, which are sore for no reason.

She's really going to leave. We'll never see the boys again, and now we'll wake up without seeing each other. How can I help her if I'm not there?

Auntie Hera, please . . .

"No."

Megara's word startles me so hard I almost fall over.

I ask, "What?"

"I can tell when you're praying, Alcides."

I scratch at my beard. "I'm that obvious?"

She comes closer now, until I can smell her unwashed skin. I missed her smell, like pomegranates on the last day before they turn. That smell has always done things to me.

She asks, "You were praying for me, weren't you?"

"Well, yeah. I care about you. I should say it more."

"You always do this. You want the gods to look after others, but look what they made you do. You need to take care of yourself. Pray for yourself."

Pray for myself?

It takes an embarrassingly long time for me to realize my answer.

"I don't know how."

My wife kisses me. Our mouths don't fit together, and I tilt my head, trying to make it work. It's like one of us grew, or both of us shrank. I keep repeating what my lips used to do, and none of it works.

It's over before I can fix it.

Pulling her veil over her face again, she whispers, "Find a way. Then tell me about it when I see you again."

Hera 18

Olympos is warmer than sunshine, and cooler than savanna breezes. This place was built to adulate me. Its comfort hits me like a club, dizzying me. It doesn't feel right on my skin, like I should remain down in the mortal world working. Searching.

But to find Granny, I need the help of the heavens.

"Athena?"

I call for her, expecting her to immediately arrive. The only nearby divinities are vague senses of music and sport—Apollo must be around the next corner of the marble palace, eavesdropping, wanting to know more of my tale without having the decency to come out and ask. This is why nobody likes Apollo.

I part my lips to beckon her again, and without speaking the word, there she is. The gray-eyed goddess in her great helm.

"Your Grace?"

"You watched all of that. Don't lie."

"I saw enough. I assumed you would desire privacy for some of the exchange."

No, privacy is far from my desires. If anything, I want to shed other people's privacy.

I ask her, "Is it possible Zeus is doing all of this?"

"No."

One word. Seldom has one word been so unsatisfactory.

I ask, "Why?"

"Because I've seen you doing much of this yourself, including what you're doing to yourself, and what you've done to others."

She is lucky I need her. Balling up one fist at my side, I formulate my next question. It takes too long. Could Zeus be manipulating Até and

Heracles and all the rest of us? How much of this is a contest, and to what end?

But I need to focus. Where did Granny go? Who can find her?

A clatter of metal against marble distracts us both. Athena and I turn to the looming presence of another god. My son Ares, God of War, tramps across Olympos toward us, his brows a portrait of ire. Seeing him bear down on us, I remember that he inherited his father's wide and knotty shoulders. He is fully dressed, with a war belt of hides of ancient beasts covering his hips, and a cape of flowing blood on his shoulders, as though a wound perpetually weeps across his back, a representation of the fate of his devotees.

In his right hand he clutches a helm to his chest, with a brush plume so prickly it could be hedgehog quills.

He looks past me, eyes upon Athena, his gaze like a volley of arrows. "You have given my mother enough failed counsel. Be gone from her."

Athena is unmoving, yet I feel her in my orbit, waiting for me to dismiss her.

I do not. Rather I wave to dismiss him and his inherited shoulders. "Shouldn't you be with Aphrodite? Helping her be unfaithful?"

"Don't try to push me away when you need me, Mom. This one is poisoning you."

When is the last time my son spoke this ferociously in my defense? I cover my own lips, uncertain what will fall out of them.

Athena's tongue is not so bound. "I answer every question that my queen puts to me. I counsel her at her beckoning. I have done nothing but help."

"You let her be embarrassed by that Goddess of Ruin," he says, free hand jabbing down at the mortal world, at the marshes. "You let her quake and question herself. Mother, know that I'll go kill that Goddess of Ruin right now if you ask. I'll add her domain to yours, or to mine. War and Ruin often ride together. Otherwise, we can throw it to Apollo."

"No," I say. "You leave Até alone. She's suffered enough."

"The wrong sides are suffering this whole saga," he says, those arrows in his eyes still trained on Athena. They have never liked each other, but it's been an age since he challenged her to a fight like this.

Athena brushes the backs of her fingernails against her senatorial robe, like there is dust on it she would shake off. "What advice would you have given my queen that I have not? What insights would you share with the cause?"

"Don't try to confuse me. I didn't know how hurt she was until I heard Apollo gossiping. But now, I'm here."

Athena's voice is a sword sliding out of its leather. "I'm sure that is a relief to her."

"You think you're smart." He says it in the same tone that I always use when I cut her down. When did he get that from me?

Athena says, "You think you could have provided better counsel than myself?"

"You had Mom send Heracles after lions and hydras. I've got a monster in Crete that would kill him dead. I could summon it right now and the affair would be over."

"That thing would destroy half of Greece in their battle. There's no conscience sending Heracles to fight it."

Ares sucks air between his teeth as he looks at her. "You're too timid to be of service in these matters."

Athena lifts her chin, eyes assessing him. "Why are you here? Do you want to lose another war with me?"

"Is that supposed to be clever? You're so smart because you stole my domain?"

He comes closer to her, no weapon in his hands, save the helmet of porcupine quills, as though he'll swing it at her.

He swings his words instead.

"Mortals think you're the virtuous one, but I know you're just a coward. You're smarter than I am, and I've never pretended otherwise. Smart has never meant good. Through tactics and strategy, you became the god of generals, and high ground, and markers moving across maps. You stole what I didn't have to focus on. You stole from me while I was deep in the shit, being the god of men bleeding out from belly wounds. The god of amputated limbs. The god of ships catching fire when no soldier aboard knows how to swim. I'm the one who lives the reality of war. You're the lies, and so victors love you. You're a coward and you'll never have what it takes to replace me, because you don't want to get blood on your outfit."

A storm brews on Athena's tongue—now she's ready to argue with him.

I am not ready for that.

"Enough," I say, in the tone that is law. "If you two want to be of service? I don't want you clubbing each other. I don't want Até harmed. You need to find someone for me."

Athena slows. The storm on her tongue cycles down, until her question to me is a murmur of wind. "Whom do you seek?"

"I hurt Até, but I shattered Granny. My personal fury, who should have spent eternity in retirement. She hasn't returned to Olympos in all the time since I ordered her into Heracles's head, has she?"

Ares grips tighter on his helmet. He doesn't know the answer.

Athena does. "No, Your Grace. No fury has touched the marble rim since that day."

I say, "I never banished her. The curse of Olympos still would have let her in. She could have returned here at any time."

Ares asks, "She disobeys your summons?"

"This is not about obedience. I made her do things she knew better than to do. And now, Heracles is after her."

Athena says, "We can find her."

"*I* can find her," says Ares. "Furies don't sleep in peaceful places. Where would a fury hide other than a war zone? My son Diomedes in Thrace always has at least a couple campaigns going."

The insistence in his voice. Does he feel a war coming that he needs to be a part of?

I touch the tips of my fingers to the porcupine quills of his helm. It's the best way I have to appreciate that he really cares.

As though he understands what I can't put into words, he says, "The Goddess of Ruin doesn't care. The Goddess of Wisdom doesn't care. Whatever Dad is doing, wherever he's gone, know that I care. I'll find this fury for you. We'll do what has to be done. Your secrets will be kept."

"Do not kill her," I say. "Do not harm one scale on her head."

"What do you want done?"

I catch myself looking to Athena. Catch myself hoping she has the answer. Because until this instant, I realize, I haven't thought about it. I don't know.

Athena doesn't say anything. She simply gets to work.

It's hard to keep secrets on a chariot. So little space, even with Megara and Iolaus gone for Thebes. It's down to myself and Logy, who still reeks of charred serpent flesh. It's not so different from human flesh. They coil on one side behind the driving shield, out of view of all passersby. In my space on the stand, I keep shuffling my feet, trying not to think certain thoughts.

Regardless of how the hydra hides, we're still conspicuous. Passersby still gape at the chariot drawn by a great lion. Purrseus enjoys the exercise, and I insisted Megara take the horses.

Logy asks, "You miss her already, huh?"

I rub my wrist at my brow. "I'm told I'm an obvious man."

"I was close with somebody, too. Once."

It's something to do other than worry that they didn't make it to the Theban envoy. And it is an unusual thing to hear a monster say.

I ask, "You were close with your other heads?"

"So now you're a funny guy." Logy stretches their body so that more of their coils remain in the sun. Their blood can boil anything, but apparently they're chilly. "No, I was close with another person. She was truly something else. Inquisitive enough to wonder how monsters felt. What our internal lives were like. That's how we fell in together."

"She sounds interesting."

"She suspected there was a passage to the underworld somewhere underneath the Lake of Lerna. We debunked it together—as far as I've ever found, the one passage to the underworld lies beneath Mount Olympos. Still, it was a great adventure."

I wonder. "With how poisoned the lake got, you must have been looking for a while."

"Love makes a lot of things feel worth it. I don't even remember how we broke up; the migraine swallowed my whole being for years. I suspect she just became curious about some other hypothesis and moved on. She followed anyone around if they made her curious. She really was special."

I don't say that if she was special, she could have tried to save Logy from their many-headed migraine. If Megara suffered like that, could I have let her go on her own?

But why did I let her out of my sight? What kind of husband am I, allowing us to part when we're both still shattered?

Logy interrupts my dwelling, saying, "The Hind of Ceryneia is the right choice. I'm sure of it."

The Hind of Ceryneia. We've been on the road for days and only now, only with Logy inferring that I doubt it's the right choice, do I think to question it. I agreed to chase this creature without thinking. I was too eager to relapse into doing things rather than thinking.

Megara, I hope you're doing better than I am.

To be better and to be present, I ask, "What makes you certain she can help us hunt the furies?"

"She's so fleet that even Poseidon failed to capture her."

Rather than imagining that, I ask, "She can outrun the gods?"

"Because she always has a head start. The Hind of Ceryneia smells danger. She senses all things hazardous. It's a gift from Artemis, Goddess of Hunters. Because of these divine senses, nothing can creep up on her. Do you know how many monsters tried to eat that damned thing? She knew I was coming before I—that is, before they were hungry."

I ponder that. You see the trouble here, Auntie Hera.

"So she knows we're coming. This is a lot of trouble to find a creature that specializes in running away from peril."

I've never had a snake look down on me before, Auntie Hera. I swear they roll their eyes at me.

"Think bigger. She can sense any predator anywhere, and so it will know where your furies are. They are the most dangerous creatures in the world. If you want to hunt them, then you look which way the Hind of Ceryneia is running, and go the opposite direction. Her fear will be our compass."

I rest my weight against the rim of the chariot, watching Purrseus's haunches. He's been at it for hours, and never stops even to lick the muck from his fur. So many gnats have died struggling in the sticky mess on his invulnerable hide. It's got to feel terrible. How I want to wash his paws.

I say, "I don't know if I can use someone's fear like that, just for my gain. It's not the same as you two agreeing to work with me. This is a scared animal."

"She's not an animal. She's a monster, like your lion, and . . ."

Logy trails off. Were they going to suggest themself, or me?

A peal of ecstatic cries rises from nowhere, like my memories of glorious hunt. Purrseus halts at the noise, and the chariot lurches, and I have to grab the rim to steady it with my weight. I haven't heard so many voices crying like that since the siege of Thebes. It's like there's a one-sided war somewhere out in Ceryneia's woodlands.

I ask, "What is that?"

Logy says, "We may not be the only ones hunting today."

I start with the mad kings. Every region has its notorious monarch who has lost their mind, who the faithful and vigilant pray will be restored to reason. Any of them could be a harbor for a fury who won't leave.

But mad kings are always disappointments when you meet them. One after the next, I meet rulers who are just assholes. They are people with too much power and too little fear of consequences. They are wholly sane; they simply don't care about the people they can exploit. One king by the sea fabled for his cattle has let his entire stables turn into a mountain of shit because he's made it other people's problem.

He doesn't have furies. He has privilege and apathy. That ruler, I curse. Whenever his stables are cleaned, he'll be washed out to sea with the rest of the shit.

Disappointed, I search for new legends. Nemea is allegedly plagued by a great killer, who some say is the ghost of the great lion whom Heracles slew. But the lion isn't dead, and there isn't a great killer, either. It's easy to track down the one-armed man who has spent years pretending to build his house, and who has used that affable ruse to trick so many people into the jaws of the Lion of Nemea. With the lion gone, he's beginning to do the dirty work himself.

I break down his front door with an omen. One of the blunt omens. He's robbed too many families of fathers. He will turn his house into a home for broken families, where babies can grow up with better than they would otherwise have. He will go hungry before any wet nurse does.

It does the deed. He's soliciting needy mothers that very dawn.

But fixing people's problems does not fix a god's problems. How do you find a fury in a world of aggrieved people?

"Well? Ares?"

I feel him avoiding my eyes from two islands away. He's up to his elbows in a skirmish, examining those who lust for blood and glory in the hope that one is appropriately mad. I know when my son is making busywork.

"Are you any better, Athena?"

Because I can feel the smugness in her silence. She is on street corners, and in places of learning, sitting at the knees of teachers. Prophets of original ideas. Are any of them more inspired than they should be?

If they were, I'd know. And I don't waste my time listening to mortals talk about the meaning of life. They always make a mess of it.

There is no head that I can find that seems a proper home for Granny. Could she have found someone so insignificant that we wouldn't notice them?

Either that, or she's walking naked around Greece. Which is even less likely. Right this instant, I feel Até sowing discord among the Amazons in another of her ploys. If I'm listening for a god, I should be able to find them. No one can defy me.

"Granny? Please come home."

Beckoning her is like calling the raindrops back into the cloud. Not one drop reverses course. There is no answer. No tired old woman who will listen to me.

A decent distance ahead of their encampments, armed men gather to stop our entry. I don't know who rules Ceryneia, and I don't need more strife. I stop the chariot, scratching behind Purrseus's ears. There's no need to scare the locals with my monsters.

I tell Logy, "I'll go alone."

A plaintive breeze carries the scents of roasting fowl through the conifers, out from any of the six different campfires visible across the woodlands' canopies. The camps are distanced thanks to how steeply hilly this region is, breaking from the plains in a series of sharp inclines and declines. It goes on farther than I can see. Our chariot wouldn't make it much further into any of this. It's the perfect dwelling for an uncatchable deer; no one hunter could keep up pace with it without falling and breaking their neck.

I approach the nearest camp with empty hands. No club over my shoulder, and no sword on my belt.

Still, the two guards cross their spear tips together, signaling me to stop. They're both tall men, broad of hip and shoulder, wearing rough hide war belts and wolf pelts over their shoulders. The closest camp is a long trek. They don't want me anywhere near what's happening here.

"We're doing you a favor," says the man on the left. "Don't bother crossing any deeper. The greatest hunter in the world labors within, and you do not want to disturb him. He is in a shitty mood."

I crane my neck, judging the distance of the nearest smoke. "How many of those camps are in service of the one hunter?"

"All of them." The guard on the left again. His voice is sore, like he hasn't slept in days. "And he's not hiring additional hands. We're leaving as soon as he bags this stupid deer."

I think of all the journeying hunters who came through Thebes. Several had entourages, but none had the small army this one must employ. Have you put someone meaningful to my journey in my path, Auntie Hera?

"I don't mean any trouble, gentlemen. Who do you serve?"

It isn't Lefty who answers me this time. Righty raises his chin, staring directly forward with the intensity of an oracle. "We serve the greatest son of Zeus. We serve Lord Heracles himself."

"Heracles?" I haven't said my own name in so long that it feels like it almost belongs to someone else. Reflexively, I look down at myself, at my protruding belly and hairy chest. I don't recall hiring these men. This is going to be interesting.

Righty chastises me, "Say his name with the appropriate awe."

I hold my breath so that I don't guffaw at them and start a fight. Both of them look at me with deadly seriousness. I should order my devotees here to fetch me some of that bird they're roasting.

Lefty's tone is at least more conversational, if still pregnant with potential conflict. "Lord Heracles has been hunting this thing in the woods for nearly a year. We haven't so much as caught its tail fluff."

I ask, "You're hunting for the magical hind?"

"Yeah, that thing. Faster than your first lay. And the more time goes on hunting it, the more wrathful Lord Heracles gets. You do not want to invite his attention."

I scratch my beard to cover my mouth, not wanting a smile to be taken the wrong way.

Auntie Hera, I have an impostor. Someone has stolen my fame to go on an adventure, while I've been out adventuring as well. And he beat me to the monster I'm after. How surprised would he be if I showed up in one of his camps?

I'll be gentle in this approach, like my mother raised me to be. No need to give it away immediately and get into a brawl.

Lefty leans forward on his spear, upnodding at my chariot in the distance. "If you know what's good for you, you'll take that tamed lion and get out of here before dusk. He hates lions. He slew a giant one in Nemea and wears it like a cowl and cape."

My chest quakes, and tears threaten the corners of my eyes. Auntie Hera, something tells me that he might not have killed that lion. Please don't let me break and laugh at these armed men.

I should get moving. Go scout how to find a deer that a giant hunting party has failed to snare in a year. Still, I'm so curious about this impostor. What is he using my name to accomplish?

"He fought the Lion of Nemea? And pursues the Hind of Ceryneia?" I hang my head in ersatz awe, to hide my actual expression. "I'll be on my way. But what moves him to fight such monsters? What has Lord Heracles hunting this hind?"

Righty snaps, "Forgiveness."

My smile shrinks as I repeat, "Forgiveness?"

Lefty says, "You'll be smart not to ask about it. Nothing pisses him off worse."

Righty wipes something from his eye, his voice heavy like he might sob. "He needs to earn the forgiveness of the gods. He murdered his wife and children. Now he devotes his life to clearing his conscience of the sin, through these labors."

His wife and children?

Forgiveness?

The air turns solid on my tongue, and my lungs go chill as ice. I blink, trying to clear the world away from my vision. It will not go away. It's a fight not to let my legs buckle.

The guards look at me like a problem that needs solving.

"I'm sorry," I say, and stagger off, leaving them to serve their hero.

I head into another patch of woodlands, avoiding the chariot. I can't bring myself to look at Purrseus or Logy right now. Logy understands everything about the world, and it would hurt too much to have someone understand what I feel before I do. Groping along the trees, my hands are covered in sap and thorns. I leave prickers sticking out of me.

Without looking where my feet are going, I kick over a tall conifer. It swooshes down to the forest floor, letting out a sigh as though it's exhausted from standing so long. I mean to pick it up, and wind up falling to sit on its upturned roots.

Why did that hurt so badly?

Why is a liar who pretends to be me also defined by sorrow for lost children?

What am I even feeling?

Auntie Hera, I . . .

I keep trying to ask you the right question and failing. Neither my lips nor my mind can express what just happened. What a man did without meeting me. I can't reach you.

When did I forget how to pray?

I keep trying to beseech you. To beg for guidance. What am I, without you?

Without Megara?

Without my boys?

The tears of laughter are still in my eyes, and finally they spill with my keening. I rake at my chest, crying wordlessly, soundlessly. I've forgotten how to weep. Perhaps that is too much of a prayer for me to make.

I don't know how to do this alone. I don't know how to be anything. Whoever that impostor is, he might as well take my name. He'll glorify you better than I can.

My poor sons. Someone like me can never avenge you.

What am I supposed to do?

Something wet runs down my left elbow. Did I cut myself on this fallen tree? Did I rend my skin in my crying?

No, because that wetness is cold. It's not blood.

It's a damp nose.

She's a young doe, so small she could fit under my armpit and her hooves would not reach my knees. Her fur is the orange of fallen pine needles, with an undercoating of white toward her fluffy tail. Her nose is white as well, except the nostrils, which are black as the caves great lions live in.

Along the top of her head are fleshy buds. There the fur is thinnest, revealing raw pink skin where she has rubbed for unknown time. Her antlers are two small protrusions of bone, hardly the rack of legend. Yet as she nuzzles at me, those antler buds illuminate with the gold of the gods' own glory. They are as brilliant as gold heated to liquid intensity.

It can't be.

And it is.

No deer has ever come this close to me, especially not when I'm this noisy. In the vast hunting grounds, the Hind of Ceryneia should be running. There's no one more dangerous than me out here. I killed my own boys with the hands she's leaning into. She knows every predator in this world. If this really is that creature, she's known how dangerous every human is since the day before we were born.

I stare into her moist eyes, imploring her to make sense. How am I not a threat?

I want to warn her that she's made a mistake.

But it comes out, "I won't hurt you."

Her wet nose cools a spot where my knuckles are raw.

An audience with the prize no hunter can catch. I can't let it pass. Can she understand me? Will she fly away if I ask her for help hunting the furies? What does one even offer in trade to a sociable deer?

"You!"

It's the voice of a righteous soldier. Both Lefty and Righty are stamping through brush so far off that the company following them is barely visible. It's more than ten hunters, all fanning out across one of the steep hills, fighting for handholds.

Righty says, "Spotters said she's is on the move. It may have escaped in this direction. Did you see its antlers?"

She doesn't flee, not with me between her and the host. The coldness of her nose drags across my belly, like a sliver of melting winter.

I loop an arm under her flank to lift her, and she leans comfortably into me. Like she has never been less afraid. I become drunk on whatever her faith has given me.

Lefty says, "He asked if you saw our hind."

"I only bagged a stray fawn." I stand to my full height. Like I expected, her hooves don't reach my knees. Her golden buds are hidden against my breast. "Catching the Hind of Ceryneia will be up to Lord Heracles."

W here did we first meet?"
I talk to you without expectation of reply. I have to believe you're still alive, and that you can still hear me. I want few things more than to lay my head on your thighs and chat until all the kingdoms on the Aegean Sea fall. Please let me hear your voice, Granny. Just one reply.

"It was that frigid mountaintop, wasn't it? The one surrounded by bluffs of flowerless thornbushes, as though protecting anyone from having to experience its chill?"

It fills my vision before I am close to its feet. The formidable brow of white-dusted firs that climbs up, across the unforgiving range of mountains. The wild brush that snares badgers as though the plants are growing hands. Upward and upward it goes, not as imposing as the divine Mount Olympos, still tall enough that we saw Atlas himself holding up the sky in the distance from where we stood.

Why were we here, Granny? Why did you want to flee out into the sea and the islands that day?

I didn't send you on a mission to Mount Erymanthos. You weren't doing my bidding, I'm sure of that. We didn't know each other yet.

"That first dawn, we met on the summit. Do you remember?"

Because I don't. Fog rolls over where I should have clarity. Now I stroll across the bluffs, across the tiny villages that dot the surrounding spaces. I dwell there long enough to make sure all the children sleep in an extra hour, so their mothers can have some rest themselves. We need time.

That first time, I only came here because of a family problem. What was it that caught my attention from the marble rim? Did you have family here, Granny? Other furies whom you were in battle against?

That doesn't sound right. I would remember fighting furies. It had to be something else.

"What was it that brought me up here? Why were you here?"

I say it as though it's not a prayer for you to be here now. To be hiding behind the next rock, or for there to be a mortal I've missed on the mountainside whose mind you're camping inside.

The snow comes down thicker, despite the warmth everywhere but the slopes here. Just a few clouds pause in the sky to dump across the summit. There has to be something peculiar up there to summon such weather.

With naked feet, I touch down on the idea of the mountain. I shed no physical presence to disturb a single bird on these slopes. If you are in someone's mind out there, I want you to hear only my intentions.

"You were trembling that day like a newly blossomed flower in its first storm. Like your wings and arms would fall off in the tempest of your own mind. You were distraught the way your victims should have been. It must have been a long career. You'd been working for the Olympians since my father fell. But why was this the end of it all for you?"

I tilt an ear to the summit, begging the wind to whisper the truth to me. It's the best apology I can make, for never having asked these questions before. In all our time together, I never asked why you were so ruined by your life of ruin.

Something is off about this mountain. It's not you, so what is it? The snowflakes falling across my shoulders feel wrong. The air weighs too much upon the stones. There is a presence here that isn't mine.

No sooner am I suspicious, than my suspicions are confirmed. I notice the figures far below the summit, climbing from stone to stone and beating a path through the boundless brush. There is a deer, and a lion, and . . .

I bend over the mountaintop until I nearly topple at the sight of him. If you're not on this mountain, Granny, then why is fucking Heracles climbing it?

Heracles 20

Mount Erymanthos is so tall that it feels like a mortal on its summit could reach up and climb into the heavens. The higher we climb its face, the less I feel I belong on the earth. We follow the Hind halfway up, to the mountain's sprawling brush regions, where the air is thinner, and the cedars grow gnarled as though they are clutching at themselves. Denser than tree coverage are widespread thorny vines that scrape at any bare skin, so overgrown that passage is impossible without my great cleaver. The brush grows far above my head, so I can't see the nearest encampment of locals. Between the chill and the scraping brush, I've bundled up in every hide I own, and Purrseus keeps rubbing against my side for warmth.

There's so much inhospitable mountain left above us. Clouds drift above like hair on a scalp, idly dumping snow on the peaks above. The whole mountaintop looks covered in snow. Of course the furies would make such a miserable, frigid place their home.

Besides the peaks, the one visible thing over all this brush are the twin golden glows of the Hind of Ceryneia's antler buds. She beckons us onward.

And I will follow the Hind anywhere. That's become her name. Simply "The Hind." The one I trust.

Logy despises this place most of all. Their blood would burn a hole in the sun, but still they writhe against the chill. "When we agreed to work together, you were going to follow me. Not replace my guidance with a deer."

"She has the scent of the furies. It can't be much further."

"How do you know? You don't speak deer."

I reach for the next handhold in the rocks. "Then you talk to her."

I swear, it sounds like the serpent spits. "She won't talk to me."

"Why?"

"She has the foolish notion that I've considered eating her."

I don't doubt that Logy has eaten their fill of venison over the years. The Hind always keeps her distance from both Logy and Purrseus; Purrseus is at least more honest about his cravings. This same moment, he looks at the glowing lights on her scalp and licks his muzzle.

Logy continues, "And I still don't know if this is where the furies live, or where they last touched the world. She could be smelling their victims. And if she's so worried about being devoured, she wouldn't lead us to the lair of the most ferocious boar ever born."

I stop, catching my breath and listening for the grunts of wild game. I don't hear any boars. "Could this boar serve the furies? Drive away any unwanted guests and leave them with their privacy on the mountain?"

"Anything is possible. But the boar is under Artemis's watch. It's one of her most esteemed creatures. She always takes a liking to beasts that everyone else hates, so long as they survive."

"She's the Goddess of Hunters, not Goddess of the Hunted."

Logy flicks their tongue at me. "Isn't it true that a hunter likes nothing so much as a challenge? And this boar has challenged plenty. It's killed humans and centaurs and anyone else foolish enough to come after it."

"Are there specific legends of what it's done to people?"

"None from before I was stranded in Lerna. And it's not exactly a hydra or chimera, you know? It's just a big boar that eats people. Great creatures are usually human-eaters. The Lion of Nemea eats people. The Boar of Erymanthos eats people. The only animal of unusual size that doesn't eat people is Poseidon's son, the Bull of Crete, and that's because he's so strong he splits the earth open when he walks and sends all his victims down into the canyons before he can bite them. Be grateful you're not dealing with him up here."

I heft the great cleaver to my shoulder, preparing to carve the rest of our path. "You can't tell me anything about this boar? About why the furies would fancy it?"

"I said: it's a big boar. There's not a lot complicated about big animals."

I make a display of rubbing Purrseus behind an ear. "They're complicated enough for me."

In turn, Purrseus rubs against my side, shoving his neck under my armpit. I could almost laugh—I fit in better with these creatures than with people. In that brief silence before mirth can leave my throat, I hear a heavy breath. It's to my left, through the brambles, low to the ground.

I have just enough time to see Logy's coils go rigid, like they want to warn me. There isn't time.

The bushes tear apart with the sound of crashing waves, and I barely get my hands down in time to catch its head. The brown fur and black eyes come forward, along with yellowed tusks that swing up to gore me. I catch the tusks in both of my hands, forcing the creature to stop, great furrows opening in the moss below our feet. The boar shoves me back and groans out a fetid breath, trying to send me off the mountain.

I don't want to kill it. I just need it to lead me back to its masters.

I push down on the tusks, testing the thing's strength. I can only get through to the creature if I can hold it still until it calms, like when I met my lion.

Under my grip those tusks slip, skewing to one side like they're coming loose from the creature's body. The boar growls, and two hands reach up, punching at my wrists to wrestle them off the tusks.

Do boars have hands?

Bewildered, I try to look over this monster, to grasp what I'm seeing. The hide along its flanks sags, loose as though not attached by sinew or bone. It's not even that large by the standards of boars; it has more hide than insides. Then the snout tips up, and I see plainly: the face of a gray-bearded man, snarling at me from underneath the helmet he has made from a boar's head.

I can't think of what to say to this wild man, who continues to buck and grapple with me. Before words find me, Purrseus surges inward, gnashing his jaws at the man.

"No!" I say, throwing an elbow up beneath Purrseus's jaws to prevent him from killing this boar-dressed man. I release the tusks to get between them, and Purrseus climbs right over me, growling like the fury of an earthquake.

The boar-dressed man turns from Purrseus, hide cloak flapping around his shoulders, and flees through the brush.

Purrseus tries to go right after him, into the maze of thorns waiting ahead. I barely catch him around his rear haunches, squeezing as tightly as I can. Even if the boar-dressed man attacked me, I'm not going to recklessly kill anyone. Especially not in his own home.

Above me stands the Hind, all four hooves perched on a single tree branch, as though the divine beast is weightless. Her antler buds glow as gold as a greedy man's soul. She points her snout into the maze the boar-dressed man disappeared down.

I say, "But that wasn't a great boar."

"Yes," says Logy. "But our friend says that guy smells like furies."

Hera 21

There's more going on here than just my dipshit husband's child chasing a man wearing boar skins. The higher they go, the harder it snows, until I'm nearly blown off the face of the mountain. And I'm in divine presence, not a physical one. Snow should pass right through me unless I bid its touch. Some god just gave themselves away.

There is scarcely a cloud anywhere save for above Erymanthos. This isn't nature. This is an insult to my intelligence.

"Stop this instant," I say, in the tone that is law. "Show yourself."

Oh, she shows herself. I only didn't recognize Artemis because I wasn't looking for her. No god can hide their presence from me—except possibly my dipshit husband—no matter how much Artemis prides herself on being discreet and undetectable until she strikes. Once I suspect her, I try to see her, and immediately she is revealed.

She is not hiding behind the snowstorm. She *is* the snowstorm. The closer Heracles gets to the man in boar skins, the harder she blasts them with sleet and snowdrifts. She gets in Heracles's eyes so he'll lose track of the otherwise unmistakable hulk of a man.

"I wasn't hiding. If you wanted me, you just had to call," Artemis says, with the petulance of a pubescent. Some part of her has never matured beyond the young goddess who spends all day tailing impossible prey. "Is this about hunting King Zeus?"

"No. This is not about Zeus."

"Are you sure?" say the divine snow clouds. "Because all of recorded history feels like it's always about you and Zeus. And honestly, Athena and Ares aren't who I'd ask to hunt a missing god. Even Apollo thinks you should have come to me."

I rub the bridge of my nose. Nobody likes Apollo.

I measure my tone. "Athena and Ares are helping me with something else."

"He's an elusive quarry. I spent a year and a half looking for him around the Aegean and couldn't find a trace. I was hoping you'd have a lead."

All of Artemis's storm continues to bear down on the two men who run across the mountain range below. Heracles is as pink in the face as a newborn baby, except he's crying that he won't hurt this man. I can hear his voice wanting to pray, and being unable to muster it. I know who he'd pray to.

Artemis pauses to catch her breath after a particularly cruel gust that leaves icicles on Heracles's beard. "He adores you. What did he say when you talked to him?"

Now I have to catch my breath. "Talked to him?"

"To Heracles. What did he say when you told him it was you he was after?"

Some part of me seizes up, and I fold my arms at this impetuous cloud. "Why would I talk to him? A mortal couldn't understand what a god goes through."

"You were afraid you'd be misunderstood?" There is the faintest hint of slyness in her voice. Any more than that, and I'd show her what a real storm is like. "You send omens to mortals all the time. No god sends a clearer message than the queen."

She inhales deeply, and I grab hold of her, to cease the gale before it blows. The men below have fought fate enough for now.

I ask her, "Why are you messing with him?"

"I have no fight with Heracles," she says, and then waits too long to follow up. "The other one is a personal project of mine."

Her entire endeavor as a storm has slowed Heracles in chasing the man. I thought Heracles might kill him, but already my dipshit husband's son is building a fire for them both. He's making a cozy spot in the miserable wilderness, witless that a god may dump a maelstrom on them in a moment. How dare he be cute in a time like this?

"You don't recognize him?" Artemis says, like she's skeptical and I'm feigning confusion. "That was the darkest thing that ever happened on this mountain. But it was just a blink of the eye in your schedule? I am glad I'm not the queen."

"I remember coming here. It's how I met my personal fury."

"Yes. You stole her from me," she says, and I can hear her sucking on her teeth that don't exist. "There was a time when I fed a great boar until it was the largest that any mortal had seen. People mistook him charging for Poseidon rising out of the seas and shaking the earth. He was one of my favorite critters. He could eat half an armored legion if they trifled with him."

It doesn't take much to give away how that story ended. Watching the man swaddled in the enormous boar skin, wearing an enormous boar-skin helmet, I say, "What made you let your boar die?"

"I didn't mean to. But there was one hunter who was too damned clever. He used his wife and kid as bait, then pounced on the starving boar when it came to eat them." She growls like she might flatten the mountain in the next moment, just to wipe away the memory. "You were pissed at him, too, for doing that to his family. Didn't say a word against me when I demanded the fury go avenge my boar. She whined and kicked for me to not make her do it."

I don't remember any of this. Granny struck madness into a man who sacrificed his family for glory? And I was here, losing my mind at what the hunter did to his family? Too much has happened since. History is a fog I can't clear.

Sounding defensive, Artemis says, "You were there the whole time, you know? I thought you were going to intervene and fight me. I sweated blood at the thought of it."

"I wouldn't harm you."

Not today, I wouldn't. But depending on how much weighed on me at the time . . . ?

Artemis says, "Instead you waited until the work was over, and the family was avenged, and the man wasn't himself anymore. Until he was babbling and broken, and sure he was something else. He was so good at surviving, too. At playing the boar. The legend of the Boar of Eryman-thos has never waned, for all the time it's been about him. He's no longer my victim. Now he's another of my creatures. I look after him, some-times. Know that if Heracles harms him, I will step in."

I should put her in her place. Threaten her until she remembers it is me stepping in that everyone should worry about.

But my gaze surveys the mountaintop, begging for someone who isn't here to come out.

"Did I take care of Granny? That day?"

"You stepped right in," she says. "You put your cape around her shoulders and did the flying for you both. She was immediately smitten with you. It wasn't just soaking up the retirement being in your entourage provided, either. I could tell."

I look this waning snowstorm in the face. "What do you mean?"

"I always assumed she liked you because you kept families safe."

"Fuck."

Without meaning to, my expletive sends a shelf of snow falling over a cliffside. I could dissolve into my own weather pattern for the rest of the week, tearing out my hair and weeping lightning.

Artemis says, "I thought you wanted King Zeus, or the hero down there. You're looking for Granny?"

"Of course I am. I did worse to her than you did, because I should have known better."

"Well, let me answer your prayers. Because that fury has been a pain in my ass for several seasons now."

"Wait," I say. "You know where she is? Is it in that boar man's head?"

"She's not in any human being's mind. It's not a human's mind at all. If you promise to leave the boar-man alone, I'll show you her hiding place. But I warn you, she's not in a social mood."

Heracles 21

Logy warns me, "Whatever he is, he knows the mountain like no other. Don't take this place lightly."

Logy is a cold-blooded hydra and cannot make the ascent, and Purrseus will simply attack the man again if I bring him. I leave them all below in the brambles on the mountainside. The Hind follows me just long enough to keep pointing me after the man, as though I could doubt her. Following is the only purpose I can hold onto right now.

New snow falls as I climb, flakes sticking under my fingernails. The man's tracks are obvious, a trench in the snow bluffs. He's not stopping to fight again. He's spooked.

"I'm not here to hurt you. I seek the Boar of Erymanthos. And the furies. Do you know the furies?"

In this pathetic, slow chase through walls of snow, we find the apex. It's all flatness and false contours, hiding the real edges of the top of the mountain in high drifts of snow. The man is a dark blur in the whiteness, and I try to warn him. As my mouth opens, he stumbles, footing unsure, all the snow hiding where it is safe to run. He won't stop running.

"Slow down. Please. Who are you?"

I scan the apex for any other living creatures, expecting something to waylay us both and send us toppling off the mountain. He's moving so frantically that he's inviting the attack.

But what stops him is his own body. Eventually he stumbles again, and the hide cloak on his shoulders flaps like a flag in the winds up here. Falling snow immediately gathers on that cloak and his exposed back, and his head bows with strain. His snorting is rapid; he is desperate for more air.

Whereas my father's gifts would let me knock this entire mountain over if I craved it.

I lower one shoulder and force the snow away, until it furls up into a wall ten times our height. I force the whole embankment up against that north wind. It's the beginnings of a shelter.

The man stares up at me from under the boar's-head cowl with an animal fear. Gray hair is thick, sprouting from his chest, shoulders, and cheeks, those few bits of him I can see beneath his boar hide. His face is so lined with age that it should have come apart long ago. The fear keeps willing him to move, and all he can do is flinch. If there is a goddess of despair, then this man is her favorite son.

I've been desperate before. If I weren't desperate, I wouldn't have chased him up here until I couldn't feel my toes. Let's be desperate together.

I uproot two trees, shaking the snow off of them until they are relatively dry. Then I strike them together, trunk against trunk, with enough force that the claps send the snow flurrying off the man's cowl. In a few more strikes, the sudden friction sets both trees ablaze. I use them to build a fire for us both, under the embankment.

I crouch on the opposite side of the burning trees from him, gesturing for him to join.

He pulls the boar pelt closer to himself and shuffles closer to the fire, while still squatting at an angle. His posture threatens that he'll bolt whenever he likes. He may only be warming up enough to flee.

I'll make do with that.

"I'm sorry that I scared you. Your pain is my fault. You're welcome at my fire for as long as you want." I gesture to the gap between myself and the fire; I won't even get to close to it. "Many people call me Heracles."

He doesn't like it enough to call me it, or to call me anything. Dark eyes, as pitch as the sea itself, study me. His arms vanish inside the boar hide.

I ask, "What do people call you?"

"Boar."

That's his entire answer. So I try again.

"And what is your name?"

He says, "Boar."

I look up to the matching pair of dark eyes on the boar-skull cowl of his garb. "You are a boar?"

"I am Boar."

He looks at me dubiously, like I'm a foreigner who doesn't speak the local language. My mother taught me to be considerate to folks who don't have a common tongue with us. I try to pull myself toward that family ideal.

"All right." I put a hand to my chest. "I grew up with two names. Alcides, and Heracles. You can call me either. Do you have multiple names?"

"I am Boar."

"Are you injured?"

"Boar is tired. Need to warm up."

I snap a limb off one of the trees and toss it onto the center of the fire. It's the best gesture I have. I'll collect more firewood as necessary.

I regard the hide wrapped so snugly around his human form. He's a burly man, nearly as hairy and unkempt beneath the boar hide as above. I think of Logy bringing up the legendary Bull of Crete earlier. That divine bull impregnated a human woman and sired the Minotaur. He is a monster so powerful he bent reality around his lust. Could there be other such creatures? Could this man actually be part boar?

It's worth asking. "Was one of your parents a boar?"

"Both of Boar's parents were boar. Obviously."

Obviously. How silly of me.

"I'm the son of a human woman," I say, rubbing my hands over the fire, less to warm them, and more to show they need to be warmed. "And the son of an Olympian. You never know what children unusual couples will make. Do you have any children, Boar?"

Dark eyes cut at me in the firelight, like he suspects I'm suggesting something. "No. Boar has no children. Never had children."

"I see," I say, to calm him. My own heart starts hammering, and I don't know why.

The man doesn't calm down. He leans his head backward, so that more of the face under his boar helmet can stare at me. His face is streaked with grime and scabs.

He asks, "Do you have children?"

"Yes."

I say it before I think, and my heart is going harder. The reason I'm upset hits me like a club upside the head, and I have to hold onto myself as I shake. The cold is overwhelming, sudden, like I had shut it out until now. It coats my legs, like so many small hands grabbing onto me from out on the mountain.

"No," I correct myself. "I once did, and I keep trying to forget the loss. As though forgetting would help anything. I had three beautiful sons. Therimachus, Creontiades, and Deicoon. One of the Olympians became angry with me. I still don't know which one, or what I did. But the god sent the furies to drive me mad, and under their influence, I . . . hurt my boys."

I want to cover my eyes and shut the world out, but I don't allow myself to. I will not weaken. My boys deserve better.

With my eyes open, I see the other man's eyes growing darker in the firelight. They are deep brown, so deep they are mistakable for the black pitch of the sea. So too they are moist, as though sculpted from thawing ice. The only thing on this entire mountaintop melting is his attention.

I tell him, "I've been trying to find the fury that did this. That made me do this. I thought you might know something about the furies. But it led me to scare you and drive you out here. I'm sorry, Boar."

Snowflakes catch in my eyelashes. I rub at them until they melt. Wind shrieks its mournful song to fill the world after I run out of words to say. It's the only sound I expect to hear until I descend the mountain.

Then the man speaks. "I know about furies."

"You do?"

"Yes. A long time ago, they saved Boar."

I lick my lips, and the saliva instantly freezes on my skin. "They helped you? You met them?"

I've never thought about furies helping anyone. That's not in the poems. Logy never mentioned such a story.

The man says, "There was a wicked hunter from Aegea who wanted to become king. He was clever and cruel. He brought all his traps and his wife and his son to my mountain. He thought to kill me, and skin me, and wear me as a trophy. He would inspire fear in all who saw him, and return home a king."

I force a neutral expression to stay on my face, striving to look as though I'm just listening, and not judging what I'm hearing. I try not to look at either of his two faces too intently, the man or the boar cowl. I can't risk offending either of his selves.

He says, "After weeks of failures, the hunter used his son for bait. Starved Boar, then drew Boar out when Boar was hungry."

He stretches his arms out at the wrists as though something is trying to dislocate them. The physical memory of being captured in a snare.

Then he draws a thumb down, to the left side of his throat, as though preparing to slit it.

"His kingdom was in his grasp when the hunter had a delusion. An old woman with wings and flesh of leather descended on him, and made him think he was claiming his prize. He slit a throat, but not Boar's. It was something he should have treasured more than crowns."

He swallows hard, and he covers the dead eyes of his boar cowl for a moment. His entire cloak trembles. His mouth opens, then closes, then shudders open again like he's wrestling with the words.

"He was a terrible man. It is good he died that night."

I've wrestled with enough words. I put my hand halfway to his, offering to steady him. He doesn't need to share more with me.

I say, "So the gods made the hunter destroy his family and himself. And now Boar lives safe in the mountains, where no one hunts him any further."

He stares at my offered hand. His fingers tremble like he wants to take it. He doesn't.

But he does pull himself to sit closer to me. He may not believe he has hands to take mine, so he sits closer.

He murmurs, "Boar is safe. Boar never hurt anyone."

Please don't judge me too harshly, Hera. I know you are the protector of families, and we are two men who destroyed ours. You may despise him. Try not to despise me for weeping with him.

Too many snowflakes have fallen in Boar's pelt. The right eye of his cowl is completely clotted with snow. His shivering is not only from grief. A part of me comes to despise the cold for existing. The winds of the world could lay off a poor man for one hard night.

I rise, saying, "Let's get off this mountain. It's warmer below. I can carry you, if you want."

When he tries to rise, his legs buckle. He refuses my hands, instead climbing onto all fours, snorting in the direction of the nearest slope. "Boar would like to be warm."

"Are you sure you're good to walk?"

"Boar has walked plenty of times," he says, again, like I'm a fool. Maybe I am. Then he adds, "You have two names. Alcides and Heracles."

It makes my ears tingle, hearing someone call me both those names. I say, "Yes. They're both me."

"Which do you want me to call you?"

I don't need to leave the snow anymore. Not with the warmth that question gives me.

"You can call me Heracles."

"Hello, Heracles."

"Hello, Boar."

Artemis guides me through Arcadia's plains, down a dwindling and rocky stream, where the grass gets patchier and patchier, until it terminates into the swampy remains of an abandoned farm. Empty homes with caved-in roofs wait in a crowd of rotting barley. Egrets and herons shy around ponds, poking about for food beneath the darkest cloud to never thunder. It casts an impressive shadow over the swamp, making the waters seem black.

The cloud undulates, swirling up in the sky. Strands swirl off from its body and dive back in, and whenever they do, they are revealed to be lustrous as polished bronze, rather than dark at all. It is so dense a cloud that I think they must be insects. But these things are too large.

Artemis tells me, "Each one has the wingspan of an adult crane. Their beaks and talons are made from a shiny chitin the like of which I've never seen elsewhere. It can punch through a bronze shield when they're hungry enough. Those talons are attached to enough muscle that they can wrestle a wolf to the ground with one foot. They love the taste of wolves."

For want of something better to say, I give her, "Impressive fowl."

"Their feathers are definitely some kind of metal fiber, but thin enough to let them fly. How the whole creature is light enough to fly is one of those things Athena is never going to figure out. Because who is going to catch and dissect one of these?"

"You bred these birds?"

"Ares did. Then he got bored with them after they ate the generals he intended to have use them in war. After he abandoned them, I adopted them." She leans on one end of her bow, smiling beatifically at the beasts. There's a shine that could replace the moon in her eyes. "I love an unloved animal."

Such a cloud of creatures could block out the sun while diving at their victims. Ares had a good idea; they'd make amazing weapons of war. I say, "I don't imagine they need much protection."

"They don't," she says with a hiccup of a laugh. "I only inspire hunters to come here if I want them humbled."

I've had enough giant creatures for this age of humanity. I can't regard the cloud of murderous birds without thinking how many children they have stolen from loving homes.

I ask, "These birds serve Granny? They're protecting her lair? She never mentioned keeping pets."

"Not exactly," she says. "Any one of these birds is just intelligent enough to be a pain in the ass. Roughly as smart as a fox, but with the social instincts of birds. Which means they have enough of a mind for . . ." She trails off, waggling her fingers for me to come along and finish the idea.

It takes me a moment. I've been hunting for the human mind she's in, but Granny has been hiding somewhere else. I'd never check inside a monster.

Artemis says, "You'll never convince me they aren't related to harpies. It doesn't make sense otherwise."

I don't care about harpies, or clever foxes, or most of these birds. There are so many that it overwhelms me to look at them.

"Which one is she inside?"

Artemis still leans on her bow, lackadaisically pointing a finger into the flock. Her finger could be directing at any two dozen of them at any moment. It's not like the beasts sit still.

She says, "That one."

"Which?"

"You can sense her, can't you? It's the one with the fury in its head."

I can. I mean, I probably can. I'm the Queen of Olympos. I just didn't think to do it, yes? That's it. I'm overworked and didn't think to try to sense her divine presence in that flock. Now that I know where to look, it'll be easy. Just as soon as I try it.

"Well, thank you, Artemis," I say, brushing off my robes. "You are dismissed."

She stiffens on her bow, like she was looking forward to seeing me wrangle the birds and have my showdown with the fury. I give her the message by not bothering to look at her. I am not her entertainment.

"My pleasure," she says in syllables so measured she sounds like she's afraid to spill one. "And let me know if you figure out where King Zeus is hiding. All of Olympos is curious about it."

No, she doesn't get any more attention. I don't look her way until she is good and gone. I need to focus.

Then I am alone in a swamp overcast by giant bronze-rending birds. Granny is in my reach. It's time.

Except, in the northern plains, a great-grandmother has gone missing. Her entire extended family fan out along cliffs, clapping and beating drums, praying to catch her attention. She is wandering near a stream, feeling bewildered by life, only sure in this moment that the warm mud of the bank soothes a little of the ache in her sore feet.

With a few nudges to the fleetest of the children, I make sure the family will discover her before nightfall. They will sup together.

That's done. Just a little work for the Goddess of Family. When the great-grandmother is safe, my attention returns to the distant birds. No village dares settle anywhere near their territory. The swamp is so overgrown with tall trees that no one could find just one of their nests. No one, save an Olympian such as myself. It will be easy for me to reach into the midst of their cloud and capture the one who harbors Granny. And then I'll say to her . . .

It's not safe with the birds diving every which way, snatching up egrets for snacks. If the winds suggested they stray outside their normal feeding patterns, then an unfinished roof would be the end of all the children that lived under it. So I attentively urge every household in the region to make sure their roofs are patched and reinforced. No newborns need a shiny beak punching through and snatching them.

Parents simply do not think enough about the safety of their children. If they didn't have me, what would they do?

That's what I will tell Granny. That I am the Goddess of Family, perpetually overworked, overlabored, looking after so many thoughtless and thankless souls. I never have a moment to myself. So of course I was going to eventually break under the pressure of it all, *she* needs to understand what I've . . .

Who let this toddler out? She's as naked as when she slipped out of her mother, honey and crumbs all over her face, and she is trotting herself up to the family shrine. She could knock over any of the figurines of the gods and bring our anger down on her entire family. I snatch her up to my breast before she can do anything regrettable.

Do not worry, little one. I will keep you safe. When you're fed, and happy, and asleep, then I'll go talk to Granny. But you need me. You're a lucky thing.

Heracles 22

The first thing I do is intercept Purrseus. I get ahead of Boar, coming around a craggy outcropping and circling both arms around the lion's neck, scratching at his ears to placate him. He strains against my side, and I don't let him go to pounce on the man. After a while of passive time in his presence, the defensive lion will grasp that this isn't prey or an enemy. Boar is one of us.

This clarity came from somewhere. Thank you, Auntie Hera. I feel shreds of myself pulling together, like strands of who I should be, twining and braiding. They pull together like muscle and sinew in a wrist. The fist I make is the one you helped me make.

I think I can pray again. Am I doing it?

It must be a sign from you when the Hind trots up around Purrseus, and comes straight to Boar. Her legs are so long she's nearly taller than he is. Her crown of antler buds is dim. She's unafraid. She knows he's not a predator; he just smells like the one that touched him.

She rubs the auburn flat of her muzzle against the nose of his helmet, as though to kiss the dead boar's skull. Then her nose lowers and she snuffles, drinking in the air of the person under the hide. Boar stares at me, with both sets of his eyes, his arms struggling to remain at his sides.

I smile for him. "You're doing great."

He asks, "What is Boar doing?"

"You're making friends. Everybody?" I call to them, squeezing Purrseus's neck to make sure he's paying attention to me and not planning to make a meal out of anybody. "This here is Boar. He's met the fury who drove me to madness in Thebes. That's what the Hind smells on him."

Gradually, the Hind's antler buds flicker, like two lightning bugs live in her mind and are waking up. The glow grows, illuminating all the fur of the top of her head. She has the scent of something. She already knew what the fury smelled like to bring us here, so what is it she senses now?

She tilts her antler buds toward my father's sky and turns her head slowly, like the shadowy point of a sundial. The motion is so gradual that she could be still, and her decisiveness could be a trick of my mind. Then her eyes set on a direction, and her snatch of yellow and auburn tail prickles. Then she springs off.

Boar marches to my side, looking warily between me and the direction the Hind left. I expect Purrseus to snap at him, but it's Logy who interjects.

"You're coming with us? You don't want to stay on Mount Erymanthos?"

Boar looks at me as he answers, "Gods are hunting this man. Boar does not like hunters. Boar knows how they work and how to thwart them. Boar is coming with you, to make sure Heracles remains safe. Someone has to look after him."

It's such a sudden thing to say. All I can see is Megara's black hair, swaying as she climbs into the chariot, to ride away from me with Iolaus. Did I let her leave me? Or did I send her? The worry pinches in my chest, like the claws of a small paw.

Logy says, "You know, we kind of look after him."

Before, it was up to question. Now it is obvious that Boar is refusing to look at Logy. "You stayed below the mountain while he climbed alone."

"He was fine. He would've knocked your head off if you misbehaved."

Boar touches the rear of my shoulder. Nobody has touched my skin that way in years, curling into the muscle there, trusting how strong and unyielding I am. Not since Megara.

Boar says, "He is gentler than that."

"Sure," says Logy. "The son of Zeus inherited his father's famous light touch."

Boar looks around Purrseus's rear haunches, and then ahead of us, to the empty path beyond the Hind. "Heracles? Is this all your retinue? Where is your wife?"

He asks like there is an easy answer. My tongue disagrees. It takes me too long to come up with, "She had her own ideas of how to hunt for the truth. She went her own way."

Just as quickly, Boar asks, "What about your lovers?"

I don't remember the last lover I had. I shake my head at him. "I don't have any."

"Not one lover? Hmph." Boar pauses by a narrow patch in the path, letting me go around the bend ahead of him. "If Boar was human, he would take you as his lover. He would give you what you deserve."

I suddenly feel less comfortable with the old man dressed as a boar being directly behind me. Heat wells up in my scalp. Something about his breathing on my neck is abruptly complicated.

Logy makes it less complicated in a single sentence. "What is it that makes you want to fuck a man the gods are trying to ruin?"

From Purrseus's glowering, Logy isn't the only skeptic walking down the mountainside.

Boar answers, "Not many men will chase you into the snow just to build a fire to save you."

Is that true? It shouldn't be. More people should care. Thinking about it, I grope my beard, and find myself smiling at the compliment. It makes the chapped corners of my mouth crack. The sting doesn't stop me.

I tell him, "It was my pleasure, Boar. I'm sorry I frightened you."

"Boar is glad you did. The fright was the start of something better. And you would enjoy me greatly." Boar moves to look me in the face. "If I was human."

"I'm sure."

"Have you ever lain down with a boar?"

Because they are the wisest person I know, Logy intercedes. "So we're hunting this fury, to get justice and all that? Maybe you've heard? Tell us what you know about her."

A field hand drops his rake to bicker with another over who has done the most work on their lord's field, and the other responds by flipping her rake so its teeth point upward, as though she'll use it as a weapon. On the north side of the same field, people begin chattering about reducing their tribute to King Eurystheus this season, for how little protection he provides. Not one of them cares that simply broaching the idea is courting a war they can't win. Aren't they afraid enough of the monstrous birds over the next hill?

"Just go to her."

Oh, that's what it is. The unseen influence. While I was distracted caring for needy families, my son found me.

Ares stands to my right, resting a hand on a stalk of grain. None of the mortals see his flowing cape of blood, nor the porcupine quill helm held at his side. Many of the needles prick his own flesh. They don't know it's his presence that leaves them bellicose with each other.

Ares ignores those angered mortals, his eyes cast toward me and the cloud of birds.

I put my back to the birds, staring down my son. This is one of few times his avatar has appeared shorter than mine. He still has his father's shoulders, though.

I ask, "How did you find me?"

He closes his eyes, and still I can tell he's rolling them behind his lids. "It wasn't me. Athena found you."

Fucking Athena. I begin to snarl, sensing her. She's watching me, from somewhere.

Ares continues, "She hesitated over the wisest move. So I jumped ahead of her in line."

"Because you think you're wiser?"

His eyes open, revealing too much depth. "Because I think you need family."

"You were wrong."

"You found her, Mom." He gestures behind me, as though trying to get me to look at the sky. I decline. "She was family to you in ways we haven't been in a long time. I know she's an arrow sticking out of your chest, and we ransacked the world to find her. Now she's within your reach. It's time to pull the arrow out and tend the wound. Go to her."

He is lucky I don't command lightning, or there would be scorches all over his hairy shoulders. I almost spit out the question. "Why do you care?"

"I don't know why what happened with Dad this time shook you up, or why breaking Heracles bothered you so badly, but I get this part. I get what Granny means to you."

Oh, for one thunderbolt. Just one.

I say, "Don't pretend you care about that. You were busy fucking Aphrodite behind her husband's back while I was keeping heaven together."

Maybe I do have a thunderbolt. Ares shakes for a second, and reaches to his eyelashes. He pulls away nothing, examining it like it's the ashes of his own remains. "Mom, you only regretted this all after it happened. Is it so hard to believe that made me realize the things I should have regretted? That I should take more of a position in the family?"

This, from a god with a cape of perpetually weeping blood. How hard it is to juxtapose wanting to shut him up and wanting to hold him to my shoulder until he falls asleep, like I used to ages ago.

But he's not a child anymore.

Neither am I.

So I confess it to him. "I don't know what to say to her."

"Is it that you want to apologize for making her do her job?"

He asks so incredulously, like caring for Granny is beneath us. It's a caustic question.

And yet in the question being asked out loud, its answers become simpler than they were before. When I wouldn't ask the questions, I didn't know how few of them there were. Granny was always dutiful in my service. It was wrong of me to send her after Heracles in the first place, and it's my fault that things didn't go the way I intended, and it was wrong to send her on a task that would shatter her, and it was wrong for me to ignore that it would shatter her. All of that is true at once, where a sentence ago, I couldn't think any of it.

I can't go to her and wave my hand. I don't know how to tell her any of this. Or how to get her to listen.

So I say, "I've been choking on what to say to her."

"Trust me," says the most vulgar of my children. "You can say anything to her. It will mean the world."

He didn't learn to talk like that from Zeus. And I don't buy that it comes from Aphrodite.

I ask him, "Where is this coming from?"

"I've suffered hearing so many philosophers in war councils, and their endless blathering about the relationships of our domains. Not a single one of them has ever asked why War is the son of Family. Do you know how many families are destroyed by war?"

I've felt too many of them. How many times he and I have been at odds, and I've never thought about us like this. My hand wants to reach for his. I pull something intangible from my eyelashes instead.

He says, "But a veteran still loves his mother."

Damn it. Your children will always surprise you, even when you're the god of them.

I reach for his hand. I kiss my son, then I fly to the birds, to collect my family.

Heracles 23

What odor is this? It's like an army of men with rotting teeth all exhaled in the same direction at once, and then all died. My eyes water until I'm blind and I have to lean on Purrseus and Boar to get by. I was deep to my knees in Lerna and never felt so swallowed in stench.

At first I think it's Logy, for they ooze some truly offensive substances, especially when we have to re-cauterize their stumps. But this isn't a single beast. It's a vast stink that no single being alone could create.

I look at it through my bleary eyes. I ask, "Is that a mountain?"

It can't be, for its peaks are sunken too low. The humps on the horizons are a broad range of dank hills, several of them tall enough that buildings jut out of their surfaces. The smell is earthier as we come closer, until I taste it in my stomach.

I ask Logy, "Are those mounds of dead animals left untended in the elements?"

Logy says, "No. Those smell more appetizing."

"Some physical manifestation of the furies upon the earth? Could this be their lair?"

Boar stops in his tracks, shielding the dead eyes of his boar helm. He takes one more sniff.

"It's shit."

Pardon his language, Auntie Hera. But he's right. It's too simple an answer for my nose to have believed, but once he says it, I can't smell anything other than vast tracts of spoiling manure.

I should have recognized the city of Elis. Atop one tower is a marble statue of Hermes that was sent long ago as a gift from King Amphitryon of Thebes, in exchange for a herd. I helped pack that statue. I knew Elis had more cattle than all the rest of the world combined, and they were sometimes overwhelmed in caring for them. I didn't know it was such a dire area.

Purrseus refuses to accompany us any further. Where he might hunt on a few droppings, this many is too much. He's the one monster too civilized, and he heads off to the beaches. I pet his mane and promise to find him.

I keep wondering at the sheer disaster of this place. You'd have to be driven mad to let half a city be buried in such filth. Nearly all of it spills from the great stables, where the greatest herd in human history should be boarded.

"Would furies do this?"

Logy says, "I'm not sure."

"Could they?"

"That's what I'm not sure about. They're pre-Olympian gods, from before the Olympians warred with their parents. I'm pretty sure gods don't have to defecate."

"If they chose to, would it be this much?"

"If they did it in this plenty, I think we'd have more records of them doing it at all."

The Hind brushes against my left arm and then pitter-patters right up to the great stone walls of the stables, fearless of the stench. Stretching out her neck, she points her golden antler buds through the walls. The buds are glowing brightly. It's obvious where she thinks we're supposed to go.

Thankfully, the citizens aren't deranged and in worship over the manure. When I ask around, none of them objects to my excavating it. One of the princesses of the city, Epicaste, waylays me in the road. She's a handsome young woman with a broad chin and some telltale brown stains on her garments. She dresses like a laborer. When I offer to help clean the stables, she brightens and asks my price.

"My father, King Augeas, has made deals to let all cattle in the region board here. Millions of cows have come swaying their udders and bowels into our home. Father doesn't care that he's buried Elis in filth. What little profit he lets slip through his fingers to public works goes to prison for dissenters."

What a shameful king. I ask her, "Where is your father?"

Epicaste guffaws and spits at the stable walls. "Who cares? The real question is: what does Heracles require to start cleaning?"

I ask Logy, "Do you enjoy wine?"

They say, "My favorite part is throwing it back up. No, thank you."

I ask Boar. "Do you enjoy wine?"

He says, "Boars do not sully ourselves with intoxicants. We need to stay canny, so we can watch for gods and hunters."

Purrseus and the Hind don't seem like drinkers, either. So I smile to Princess Epicaste. "It will cost you one cup of wine. Mix it with water. I'll be thirsty."

Your solution would have been more clever. But Papa Zeus gave me two hands, and I work with them. I grab the largest boulder I can find and crack it into a great wedge. Dragging it behind me works up a little perspiration after an hour, making your breeze upon my brow so much sweeter. This is the same way I carved rivers back in Thebes. I make two trips back and forth, until I have a good trench.

Is there a God of Municipal Infrastructure? That feels like Athena's domain, or Apollo's. Apollo seems like a busy fellow.

I barely have time to consider that one of those gods may be our secret enemy, before the project is over. I sweep around north to dig a second trench toward the sounds of the nearest river up there. Soon the waters crash down into my canal, spraying me and rinsing all the grime from my person. I stand at the bottom of the canal for several moments, holding my breath in the bracing flow.

South of me gets a worse show of it. I climb out in time to find a hill and watch as the new canal crashes down through the stables. Several posts and boards from the walls come loose, too, but nothing King Augeas can't afford to replace. Most of the uncovered stables are wrought from heavy stones that refuse to budge. The water pools up high with only one way in and one way out: the two entrances of the stables. Out the second entrance goes the tide, carrying years of excrement down to the second river and out to sea.

It's quite something to watch as I savor my cup of wine. I close my eyes, and imagine offering this cup to Megara. Wherever she is, I hope you're looking over her, Auntie Hera. I wonder what plan she's hatching.

If what lies below the stables is our answer, I'll need to find her next. We're almost there.

The Hind is the first one to find me. She's on the shore of the new canal, stamping her hooves for attention again. I come to her side, and she points her head and her glowing antler buds into the water.

I ask, "What is it?"

Whatever she senses, it's under my handywork. The stables are as clean as they'll get, so I take my boulder and stop up the stable canal. Excrement is still floating in the dregs washing out from the stables as the Hind climbs down, turning her head this way and that. Her antler buds flicker as though struggling, as though she's looking for one holy turd in particular.

Toward one embankment wall is a floor made entirely of one flat stone. It's like it was constructed to slide away when some hidden lever is pulled. This is much older than the stables themselves; it's a ruin they must have housed the cattle on top of. After some searching, I think any ancient lever is long gone.

The Hind doesn't help in hunting for it. She keeps tapping her hooves on the floor.

Logy joins us eventually, scrunching up their face, insofar as a serpentine face can scrunch. "What could possibly be down here that's worth the smell?"

"That's the big question."

While the Fates didn't leave me a lever, my father gave me strength. Once the area is dried off, I punch right through the slate floor. The air beneath is stagnant and musky, frankly refreshing compared to what's above. The chamber below must have been airtight.

"Here," Logy says, slithering up to my side. "Lower me in."

I take them by their forked tails, tickling my arm as they wind around me. Down goes their one remaining head, tongue flicking around. I brace my knees, ready to spring up if a fury flies out of that chamber. My palms only start to sweat when I dread her getting inside my head again.

"Do you see anyone?"

"Hang on," Logy says. Then, muffled, they say, "Uh."

I ask, "Uh?"

"Uh. Uh."

It's like their mouth is stuffed. Did they find ages-old lunch down there? If they bit onto a god, we'd hear the protest.

I reel the hydra upward to me, creaking and clattering following them, echoing in the dark. Logy almost drops the object, and I grab it from them. It's not a fury. It's a device.

There are strips of hide from animals I don't recognize, latching around several braided ropes made from hair that shines without light source, as though they stole some blood of the sun itself. They're surprisingly heavy in my hands—I doubt any mortal living in this city could lift them.

The Hind bows her head over the device, antler buds glowing bright gold. This is what she wanted us to find. If only she'd explain herself.

Logy says, "I haven't seen these in a while."

I'm tempted to touch those odd chains again. "What are they?"

"Restraints made from titan flesh and hair, from long before the time humanity ruled these lands. From when I was young. Before the Olympians warred with their parents."

It's an amazing relic, and that odd hair makes more sense now. But the whole device doesn't make sense. I look at the Hind. "Why did you smell the furies on this thing? Did it belong to them in their fight against the titans?"

Logy answers for her. "These were tools of the titans, not used against them. They slew each other and made weapons out of their remains. These shackles are how the ruling titans first captured the furies and forced them to do their bidding. If she smelled our fury on this thing, there's only one reason. At some point, someone used this device to restrain her."

Until now I haven't really considered how to battle a fury. The one who made me into a weapon came from nowhere. I didn't see her come or go. I've just wanted to find her this whole time. What am I supposed to do when we come face to face?

From above the stables, I see Boar looking down at us. The expression under his cowl isn't so different from the Hind's. How can such different faces look the same?

Boar asks, "What did you find?"

Logy says, "This is a tool for capturing gods."

Why is the flock circling so aggressively? An hour ago they swooped in tight patterns, and now they spin as though caught in a whirlwind, snapping their beaks at each other and flinging bronze feathers in needless battle. When they pass before the sun, not a single beam of its radiance passes through their maelstrom. What whipped them into a storm of wings?

But I know. It's you. I'm trying to confuse myself to avoid just coming to you, Granny. Just as you're whipping them into a frenzy to avoid me.

You don't have to be afraid of me anymore. Never again.

I don't have to be the Goddess of the Families of Wildlife to break into their flock. I press on the heads of those birds in the lead, guiding their eyes toward the needs of their young, who are tiring from the frenzy. To remind them of the respite that is a nest. What is a nest if not a home?

As the flock slows, it becomes obvious which head you're living in. One bird who keeps squawking and biting at the others to spur them into more unrest. There's a crack running down her beak, and the bottom half of the tip is gone. She's an older creature, her feathers thinning such that she's bald around her neck and down the center of her back. It's a wonder she can still fly. You may be the only reason she can still take flight.

We Olympians don't send furies to keep people going. Perhaps we should.

"We should have asked you what you should do."

I say it to you, and your bird soars away from me, like you don't hear me. But that's your voice, creaking and pointed.

Your essence speaks from the bird's gullet. "I could have been born from an egg. I would miss the shell. I would miss being nestled and groomed. Fed chewed-up entrails from the beak of my mother."

You snap your beak at others, to less effect than before. They are tiring well ahead of dusk. They have young to shelter. I warm the branches and stolen hides that make their nests down in the dilapidated farm, so that avian joints find relief upon landing. The smallest nestle into the largest.

I follow you to your resting place. A god can take many forms. I don't have to be a hurricane or lion. Tonight, I will be the oil slicking the wings of a bird. I will be a balm, soothing aging joints. Do you feel the cooling effect on her skin, Granny?

You say, "I don't have to be a bird. Let me be a lop, spending all my time tunneling in a prairie. Let me be a snake. Let me slither on my belly until all heat drains from the world and I forget how to move."

"Granny. I want you to be yourself."

"Please don't make me," you say, your voice caught in a sudden rush. "Let me be a bull and I will never turn my horns on anyone."

Your bird's entire form shudders, until for an instant, its heart stops. I cup its ventricles and massage life into them. Her blood resumes its current.

I say, "You don't need to be anything other than yourself."

"I am never myself. My lot is to be others, and to make them suffer."

I want to tell you that you are more than that. But I can't draw you out of your anguish by arguing that it isn't there. I can't talk truth by telling favorable lies. We did what we did. Even now the ire rises in me, the desire to demand you face me and end this nonsense.

Instead of giving in, I face the urge for what it is. I will be better.

"I made you take Heracles's hands away from himself. I made you do those things. Whatever other Olympians or titans did to you before, I made a choice. I treated you like a tool."

Your words sharpen, like you'll stab yourself with them. "Please don't make me do it again."

"No. You'll come home to Olympos and no one will ever do that to you again. I will never—"

"Please don't make me!"

This time the words sound like they sink into your flesh. Are you hearing me at all? Your possessed bird lets out a racking cough, as if her lungs are coming loose and need to be expelled. As if she may expel you entirely.

I bring cooling hands down along her feverish scalp, hoping you can feel an iota of this touch. To know an instant of relief. You've spent this whole time blaming yourself for Heracles's pain.

I'm collecting what to say to you next when another presence looms. Somewhere in this roost of a thousand bronze-feathered birds is an owl. A gray-eyed owl.

Athena says, "You are engaged, but you need to know—"

"Not now," is the gentlest way I can put it, my tongue measured so that you don't hear my frustration. If Athena wants to help pacify you, let her speak directly. But my attention is on you. "I am with family."

You plead, "Please don't make me destroy another family."

The weeping in your voice is so strong that dew drips down every leaf in Stymphalia. If this isn't your doing, then it is mine. How I want to haul you out of this bird and hold you.

I say, "It was me. It was my rage. My fight with Zeus, and our ugliness that burned you all."

"Burning. That's why you brought him here. You want me to burn him like I did his boys? Please don't make me."

"It's just me, Granny. Nobody else is here."

Athena chooses to butt in again. "Your Grace?"

"Shut the fuck up, Athena!"

The anger flies out of me too quickly to rein in. She's lucky I don't reflexively go from oil to a wildcat, to some predator that dines on owls. Why bother me now? After all this time of quiet watching, she has to disturb me as I'm trying to get through to Granny? What wisdom is that?

Turning toward the owl is what makes me realize all the other great birds of Stymphalia have taken flight into the night sky, their wings beating in fear. We are trapped in gusts of their air. The whole flock has abandoned us.

What has spooked them?

At first, all I see is that man charging across the nests. That face. That unmistakable beard.

Heracles 24

This is equal parts prayer and battle plan.

"Night has lower visibility," I say, gesturing to a cloud rolling across the moon, "but it is when they roost. All of the birds in that flock are on the ground and reachable. Once they're spooked, they'll scatter and we'll lose our chance at finding the fury in their midst. Quietly, Boar and I will spread oil around the easterly side of the farm. On my signal, Boar will ignite the oil so that the birds will all scatter westward, where we'll be waiting.

"These creatures have metallic feathers they can shed like darts. We've found them lodged in skeletons around the farm. No doubt they can shred any man in seconds. That is why it's imperative you all stay back while I go in. Let me be the only one to take this risk tonight.

"My arrows are tipped in Logy's blood. No matter how armored their feathers are, they won't stand up to your poison. If it all descends into chaos, I'll loose my full quiver and strike down as many birds as I have to, until we find the right target. If we're lucky, we'll find the true target, and cause the fury to leave the bird and come into the open where we can catch her with the harness.

"But I'll need guidance. With the Hind pointing me at it, I can loose my arrows in the direction of the fury's host bird and we'll have the best chance of driving her out. I won't risk your health, hind. That is where Purrseus comes in. Your impenetrable hide will . . ."

I lose my concentration looking for Purrseus. Boar, Logy, and the Hind are all clustered around the camp with me. Purrseus always curls up by my side to leach my warmth. He especially wouldn't abandon me tonight.

"Where is Purrseus?"

Logy says, "He wasn't listening."

"What?"

"Have you never had a cat before?"

Before my mind can wrap around the question, the night is shattered. The blunt force that shatters it is Purrseus's guttural roar, hurtling far away from camp. It's so loud it shakes the boughs on the trees and flattens grass to the ground.

"Purrseus," I call in a foolish whisper. "No."

The silhouette of his haunches bolts across the barren field, tail whipping, paws trampling dead crops. He's going straight for the nests. What got into him?

Hundreds of shadowed wings beat at the air, sending a volley of figures up from the ground, heading into the sky. Their bronze feathers rain down on Purrseus, tearing divots into the earth. When they hit his mane and flank, though, the metal snaps against his god-blessed hide. They've never met a beast like him.

One bird gets a little height above the others, and Purrseus leaps up into the air, jaws clamping down on its breast. He drags the bird back down into the mess of their nests, slamming it into several more of its kind. He shakes it vigorously before throwing it at the next birds that try to fly.

They all try to fly, those terrifying wings fleeing against the stars.

And then Purrseus goes scampering across the nests after them.

He wasn't thinking of anything, other than the same thing every pet cat ever thought when it found the pigeon's cage open.

Boar says, "Just because he's a giant animal doesn't mean he isn't an animal."

My faint smile melts away into dread, and I go chasing after him. How are we supposed to capture the fury if he scatters every bird whose head it could be in? They take to the skies like each star is another home they will hide in.

My feet pound at the earth, and I wade right into the befouled mess of their nests, branches and dried reeds cracking. In my haste I forget my shield and bow, and carry only the harness. I'm ready to whip the titan shackles at anything that moves. Can I draw the birds back down to earth, with my flesh as bait?

A sound too like words crackles nearby, as if an old woman is arguing with Purrseus. It could be a strangled bird's shrill cry.

Tucked under the limp boughs of a desiccated olive tree, I spy one feathered silhouette. One of the creatures still lurks in this abandoned place. Its long dagger of a beak is cast to the right, as though it still doesn't know I'm here. Why wasn't it afraid of the rampaging lion? Is it sick? Is it guarding eggs?

The bird squawks something, again too much like words. Like, "Don't make me."

Two small bits of light move in my peripheral vision, like two stars forgot where they belonged. They glow gold enough for me to see the contour of the Hind's head. She followed me in here, into the peril.

She points her antler buds at the whispering bird.

I swear it speaks to us. It rasps, "That's why you brought him here."

The only bird not afraid of a giant lion is one host to a greater predator. I know it in my bones. My fingers curl around the chains. They clink together so softly, for a noise at the end of all of this.

The beak wavers, then turns its dagger point right at my heart. In the faint moonlight, and the fainter light of the Hind, I see the sheen of its eyes. It's doing more than looking at me.

It recognizes me.

No.

She recognizes me.

I lunge for her with the titan shackles, and a wing catches me in the face. Streaks of blood tear across my cheek and into my beard, and down my chest. Her feathers rend me like I'm a soap bubble. My whole front feels aflame, and still I reach for her, to bind her wings.

"Hera!"

Do I call your name, or does she?

In my shock, she slips upward, wings splaying. One beat of them and wind gusts across my body, sending her up into the air. I stretch out my hands, grasping for her tail, for a feather, for anything. I can't let her get away, but my arms aren't long enough. I leap with all the breath I have in me, blood streaming into my eyes. Anything. Auntie Hera, let me catch anything.

And like a prayer, my hand finds an ankle.

We've got her, Auntie Hera. We've got her.

I can fix this. Granny, can you hear me? Feel me holding onto you? Take my strength. Every drop of bitter resolve against a world run by a shitty pantheon. Don't give in to the shackles. I'll get you out of this.

What force could break titanic shackles? They reek like my father's unwashed crotch. I know these things, made from strips of godly hide. When we waged war to bring the titans down, floods barely made them stumble in their hundred-footed steps. They were unshaken by hurricanes. I can't solve this as a storm, or a beast. Even the Lion of Nemea couldn't bite through these things.

What creature can I send that will break these?

None, short of Heracles himself. And he's busy.

"You could do it."

I didn't notice Athena was still here. No other gods lollygagging around this disaster. It's her, Goddess of Wisdom, here to see everything fall apart. Here to taunt me.

"And how the fuck could I do that, Athena? What form do you want me to take?"

Her eyes are too murky, like rainless gray clouds. "Your own."

"What?"

"The Queen of Olympos has the power to break those shackles. King Poseidon did it once, to free the titans' furies into his service. You are a match for him. No god is greater than you."

My spirit opens up to lash at her, to scream obscenities. To abuse the goddess who's here to help me. Because it's easier than listening. It always has been.

I could make a divine appearance. Bring my full presence down in that dilapidated farm, splitting the earth and the bonds at once. Step between a fury and a father. I could rescue Granny right now. No, I have to.

The notion freezes me in place.

If I go, they'll know it was me. Heracles will know. And then I would have to . . .

Athena says, "You can either reveal yourself, or Heracles will torture her into revealing you. You came to spare her suffering, didn't you?"

"You're the smart goddess," I say. "Can those birds break the bonds?"

"No. Not even the entire flock put together."

"What creatures besides Olympians can break them? What in all of Stymphalia?"

I will reach my arm across the landscape and drag a hero here if I have to. We don't have time for this.

"No creature in Stymphalia. I'm afraid we're out of options."

I grab at her, insisting. There has to be a way. "What in all of Greece? You would know. You love knowing shit. What in the whole mortal world can break aging, decaying shackles made by fallen gods?"

Her gray gaze shifts, just for an instant. Southward. What is south of here?

"What is it?" I ask. "What do you know?"

"Ares had one creature in mind. But it's too dangerous. It's got Poseidon's blood in its veins. All of Crete fears its presence."

I grab onto the entire allegory of her shoulders. "What is in Crete?"

Heracles 25

W hy does looking into this shriveled bird's face make me remember my wife? Its skin is strained and withered, bleeding in so many prickles where feathers no longer grow. There is nothing human about its metallic beak or the slope of its forehead. It has a smooth swoop of a head that doesn't seem fit to contain a life. There is nothing like Megara about it.

So why, Auntie Hera, do I keep seeing her in this thing?

Its eyes. The frantic intelligence, the pain that leads it to averting, like this bird too wishes to mount a chariot and ride out of my life.

That's not the bird. That's the fury inside.

I ask, "Do you recognize me? Are you remembering what you did to me?"

Not remembering. Reliving. Relishing.

I grab onto the bonds, clenching fists around braids of titan hair so coarse they cut through the calluses of my palms, like the taut wires of a harp. "Do you remember how their mother felt? Did you bore inside her psyche, too? Sink your claws into the soft meat of her loss?"

"Was . . . was never." The voice comes from the bird, but not from its beak. Somewhere inside its body. It's rasping, like the words are exhausted and climbing out of a hole in the ground. "Never touched her. Her pain is hers. Don't make me hurt her again."

A tear blurs the red smears in my vision. Me? Send a fury to hurt Megara?

I say, "You made me hurt them. You made me destroy my boys."

Is the bird choking, or is that noise coming from the fury? I can't tell. I'm too angry to tell.

"You did it. Say you turned me into a weapon."

"I . . ."

The bird's head shudders on its neck. The whole rest of its body is forced completely still by the bonds, wings and feet trapped up into one ball of flesh and bronze feathers. It jerks twice more, like it wants to wrench itself off.

"I did. I used you."

The titan's bonds hold true. The fury cannot escape this body. Boys, if you can hear me: we have her.

Squeezing the harness until it feels like my fingers will slice off against their taut fibers, I say, "Little Deicoon was the youngest. He was beautiful from the moment he was born. Before he could walk, he played with lyres. He took to it like none in Thebes, and everyone swore he had the singing voice of his great-grandmother. Year upon year, it didn't fade. He is going—he was going to be a man that kings traveled across the world to hear sing to the gods."

Which god ordered him to die? Which one?

Another shudder, bringing a popping sound from the bird's neck, vertebrae in argument with each other. The voice inside the bird simpers. Is it crying? Is it mocking my beautiful boy?

I command her, "Bring me to the god who ordered this."

The command comes out as smoothly as a sword from a scabbard. I'm holding the bonds. It can't disobey me.

The voice of the fury says, "I . . . can't."

"Do it. Bring me to him. Now."

"Don't know where she is. She's gone."

She? It was a goddess?

"How can you not know where the Gods of Olympos are?" I bring up a fist as though to threaten to cave in the bird's head. As though to threaten. Even then, I know I don't mean it. I put the hand down immediately, feeling sickness welling up in my guts.

I don't want to kill the fury. Looking into the face of a monster that hides another monster, I know how wretched she feels. I want to believe I know why. The fury made me a weapon, and that goddess made her a weapon. We were both used.

There's a brief urge to hold the bird to my chest. To weep with the fury that was used as I was. To ask what she remembers of the anguish of the time when she was in my mind. To ask if the anguish in her eyes is mine, and to ask how I don't recognize it.

Before I can, there is a touch on my shoulder. That gentle lover's touch, that Megara might use if she were here.

Boar says, "You're bleeding. Come."

I hold onto the bonds. "No. I'm fine."

"You're blinded from your own blood. The bird almost took your scalp off. Come. Let Boar care for you."

I rub knuckles into the pits of my eyes, and realize my whole face is slick. Two gashes sting along my forehead, stretching into my hair. I didn't notice.

Boar shoves a wadded cloth into my hand, and guides me to hold it in place to stop the bleeding. That's when I see Logy and the Hind are here, watching me. Even Purrseus has given up chasing the other great birds. He's so close, mane flattened to his back, head down and neck stretching out, like he wants to nudge his snout against me.

They're afraid to approach me. This new family I don't deserve.

Forgive me, Auntie Hera. I know you wanted me to smash this creature and kill it. But I don't know how to hate her. When I wasn't paying attention, I forgot how.

For a moment, my hand goes slack, and caresses the side of the bird's scrawny neck. The fury felt my hands do so many awful things that day. But she never felt how I held my sons. How I loved them.

The fury whimpers. "Please don't make me. Let me be a bird. Let me a snake. Let me be anything but that. I can't be that anymore."

I speak into those grief-panicked eyes, wondering if mine don't look the same. What is it the fury is afraid to be? Herself?

I ask, "What do you think you are?"

Gentle as I make my words, the bird resumes struggling against the bonds. "Please. Please."

"I'll let you go," I tell her. "But first: what goddess sent you to kill my boys?"

She jerks her beak down, snapping helplessly against a strand of titan-skin leather. Still the words spill from her.

"Wasn't supposed to kill your boys. I did it wrong."

That's not possible. She destroyed my sons. Who could do that on accident?

"What were you trying to do?"

Another snap of that beak, against leather that will not give. The harness holds her down.

"You heard me," I said. "What were you trying to do to my family?"

"She sent me to kill you."

I shake my head, send droplets of my own blood flying. They spatter against the beast's bronze feathers and balding hide.

"Kill me? You came to kill me and my family? Who sent you for that?"

That voice inside the bird keens and her wings beat against the bonds, undulating uselessly. "No, no, no. Don't make me."

Behind me, Logy speaks up. "Al. Let's go slowly here."

"Tell me who sent you after my family," I say, both hands gripping at the braided hair ropes of the harness. I lift the entire creature off the ground, forcing her tilting eyes to look at me. "Who did this to us?"

The creature's beak goes so wide it's like she will vomit up its own guts, and she thrusts hers head at the sky. The voice within goes shrill, like she's calling someone's name. "I'm sorry, H—"

Together with Athena, I ride on a sliver of time. The one sliver in which Granny has a chance to escape all this.

I won't fail you, Granny. We're bringing you home.

Moonlight is jarring against my hair, raking against my scalp as though to tear the visage from me. That harsh light looms large over the pillared temples and grazing lands of Crete, where it falls upon this creature.

Its hide is so white it nearly drinks the moon out of the sky, no pinkness of blood seen through its skin. The hairs along its back and flanks are even brighter white, blinding, as if I'm gazing upon the sun itself. The only darkness about it is its hooves and those two horns, glistening, black as ravens' feathers, jutting from its brow.

"This thing?" I ask, already turning back northward, toward Stymphalia, where Granny needs me. "This bull will do it?"

It's unusually large, yes, but beasts of unusual size haven't stopped Heracles yet. Bulls don't even eat human flesh. To free Granny from their clutches, it needs to possess unrivaled violence. This great white figure stands alone in an olive grove, still and tranquil as the stars above. Yes, its back is nearly as tall as some of the tree branches, but it's not picking any fights or terrifying the locals.

Athena says, "This is the Bull of Crete, who sired the Minotaur. It is a child of King Poseidon himself. Demeter and Artemis themselves once favored it, but it was too wrathful and frightened them from its presence."

I shake my head at that mental image. "Artemis doesn't scare, and this thing isn't doing anything."

"That's because no one in Crete will trifle where he stands. Every farm he stands in is guaranteed peace, because to upset the Bull of Crete is to court death."

Up in Stymphalia, a kindly old woman is being tortured because I'm too slow. I coax Athena to speed this up. "I don't have time for these sideshows. Are you sure this will do it?"

Her tone is perplexing, like she is arguing to convince me not to do this. "This is the beast that Ares thought to send after Heracles. Once he rages, he is prone to—"

I've heard enough. I'm already reaching through the mortal world, bending sea and space to my will as I ask, "And this thing can break her loose?"

I hurl it across the mortal world, aiming its horns true.

Heracles 26

An insect is singing in the center of my head. I rub at my ears, and still the whine continues, deafening me. I can't hear a thing as I look around me, trying to understand where I am, and which way is up. All the earth around me is charred, and I'm at the bottom of some pit I never climbed into. What happened?

I call for Logy and Boar, and can't hear my own words. I dig my fingers into the earthen walls of the pit and heave myself upward, climbing toward the surface, toward the twilight sky. There must be answers up there. It has to be a trick of that fury. I let my guard down and she slipped her bonds somehow.

The first sound that returns to my ears is the rumbling in the ground. An earthquake shakes the farmland, but in a rhythm, like a heartbeat in the soil. Like the titans have returned to Greece and resumed their rampage. What is up there?

This hole is fresh, punched deep into the earth, with smashed bits of nest in all the dirt of its walls, as though Papa Zeus hurled a thunderbolt down on us. Was he here to avenge my family, Auntie Hera? Did he hear the treacherous goddess's name before the fury could speak it?

Still the ground rumbles all around me, as though the earth has become a storm and thunders on the cosmos beneath it. Whatever is causing this is up there, with the others. I have to get out of this hole.

The cloth that Boar gave me is still wadded in my hand. I wrap it around my bleeding forehead, tie it tight, and then get to climbing. Every foothold I find is an invitation to jump higher.

Just as I clear the pit, the Hind streaks overhead, leaping across the gap and fleeing from the farmland. She moves as fast as a bolt of thunder. Is she running from the fury?

The next sound is unmistakable: the bone-rattling threat of Purrseus's roar. He hasn't sounded like that since the day I hunted him in his cave. Now he stands tall on his hind legs, every hair of his mane bristling on end. He faces away from me, in front of the pit, as though defending my domain. No one sober would stand up to him. I want to touch his hind paw, to let him know I'm here and it will be all right.

Then great whiteness rises up over him, a bulk twice as tall as Purrseus. What could even get that large? With a shock of a snort, it charges forward at him. The lion springs up, swatting down with a paw that would behead any man alive.

The white monster drives into Purrseus's belly, shoving him aside, revealing it's some giant bull, made of blinding light and rage. I yell for Purrseus to run, my words scarcely out when those pitch-black horns drive into his belly. His skin won't break, but the force lifts him off his paws and into the air. The horns dig against his hide, jamming it inward, like if they can't puncture him, then they'll use his hide to smash the ribs underneath.

With a single whip of its head, the bull flings Purrseus across the birds' nests. He yowls as he hits the ground, bouncing twice before falling in a heap. He struggles to rise up, and the bull rears around to charge again.

I lunge over the lip of the pit and clasp both hands around one of its legs, just above its black hoof. I've never wrestled a bull from so low on the ground, with no leverage. I try to yank with all the strength Papa Zeus gave me, but instead the bull kicks, dragging me the rest of the way out of pit and slamming my side into the ground. Brilliant reds and oranges pop in my vision, and I try to focus through the bursts to see the bull's legs and grab for a better hold.

"Off of him. Now."

A sound like a rainstorm suddenly hitting a wall, and the bull stumbles for an instant. Above me falls the shadow of a man—Boar's hides flap in the breeze as he braces, both fists linked together. He lowers his shoulders, aiming the tusks of his cowl at the bull.

I scramble to stand, and Boar steps into my path again, not letting the bull at me. The bull bolts forward, lowering its head like it will gore us in the knees. Just as quickly, it explodes upward, and I grab Boar's hips to pull him away. I'm too slow. One black horn tears through the hide, and rips it all the way down to Boar's navel. With a wet sound, his cowl flops off, revealing his balding scalp, and then drops into the pit behind us.

With a mortified scream, Boar covers his face and totters backward, only brown eyes staring out, looking frantically for the head he lost. He dives into the pit, after his sense of self.

"You can't make me!"

Another voice, not Boar's. Who is that? It's all too much. Too much is happening for me to follow.

The bull heads for the pit, to chase Boar down and finish the job. That can't happen. With knees bent the way my great-uncle taught me, I come sprinting in, flinging myself with all my strength. Please, Auntie Hera, let Papa Zeus's strength become the speed I need.

The horns come in, leading the monster. They drop low to the earth, the monster crouching suddenly, and I bring my hands to grab for them. With a thrash of its head, those horns go right through my fingers and aim for my guts. I barely catch them in time, near their base at the monster's skull, so that the tips scrape along my flesh and then have to stop. It bucks, and I widen my feet, refusing to let it move me again. When I try to twist my arms, it refuses to budge. I read its tensing neck and legs, as it's about to try to throw me off.

"No more!"

It tries to hurl me leftward, and I throw both of us in the same direction, with all my strength. The bull isn't ready for us both to move the same way, and goes tumbling along the swampy farmland, legs kicking up tall sprays of pond water.

"Al! Al, over here!"

That one is Logy's voice. They slither along the ground to me, head low to the ground as though they're afraid the bull will return any moment and spot them.

"Are you hurt?"

"Everybody's hurt," Logy says. They have a bleeding wound on their tail that the bull must have made. Their blood sends up noxious smoke as it dribbles on grass. "Quick, use my blood."

"Your blood?"

"Nothing survives the blood of a hydra. Dip your arrows in my wound and cut that beast down before it gets back up."

I touch my throbbing head, where bleeding has started again under the cloth bandage. A wound the bull didn't make. I don't know if I can stop that thing. I can't focus on it. My mind drifts to the sky, where the birds have long since scattered. Something's wrong that I can't grasp.

Logy insists, "Just stab an arrow into me and nock it. I'll be fine, so long as we win. That's the Bull of Crete. We can't fuck around here."

As though in agreement, the earth trembles under my feet. The bull is back on its feet, kicking and running in a wide circle, heading back toward me. The earth threatens to fall apart before it reaches us.

Logy says, "Let's find your bow."

More than my bow is missing. My eyes grope around the destroyed nests, trying to find what I can't put my finger on. The birds are long gone, but there's a bloody mess of a corpse in one of the nests. Gore and innards streaked with metal feathers.

I reach into the slick gore, and pull out several long strands of hair. At one end dangles a strip of leather that is heavier than any other I've lifted. I gather more of those hair strands and strips. They are torn apart like a child's toy.

The bird and the shackles are gone. That's what's missing.

Where did the fury go?

Over the earthshaking hoofbeats comes a shrill voice, ascending the crater. She yells, "No more!"

W ait."

Athena says, "The Bull of Crete freed her from the bonds. By some definitions, it was a success."

"She went from the bird to the fucking bull? We gave her a fucking invincible vessel?"

The Bull of Crete erupts from the swampland, sending up furrows of dirt with his horns. Except it's not the Bull of Crete flying through the air, or bringing his full weight down to try to shatter Heracles. It's Granny, feeding on the rage of a god-forsaken monster. Two god-forsaken monsters, panicking and lashing out together.

Heracles weaves to one side of the Bull of Crete, shouldering him in one knee so it buckles. Just as nimbly, Heracles grabs those horns and jerks the bull's head to the right, manhandling it with Zeus's own strength, forcing it further away from the hydra and his other friends. He keeps putting himself between his monsters and this one. Fists coil like he wants to shatter the horns, or wrench them to break the bull's neck.

My hands tremble at my sides, wanting to reach out and grab them both. Force the fury and the father apart. Because this is about to get worse.

"Athena," I ask. "What happens if a fury stays inside the mind of a host that dies?"

"It is like being any other thought in the head of someone when they die."

"What does that mean?"

"It won't be good for her."

Fuck. I'm not the Queen of Olympos. I'm a horsefly, a black dot fastened down on the white muzzle of the thrashing bull. As he throws

Heracles across the land, I whisper to her psyche. I know Granny is in there.

"You don't have to fight."

"Don't make me."

"No one is making you. I am making you not! I, your queen, command you to abandon this bull and retire. Be at peace."

"Please don't make me be a fury anymore."

"Then don't be. Leave the fight behind. I made you a tool when I should have made you loved. Go be whatever you want to be. You don't have to do any of this."

She stamps his hind legs down so fiercely that the earth actually splits open, sending a chasm from the farm all the way out to the nearest river. Water rushes in like an army of hissing snakes below us.

And Granny says, "You can't make me be anything anymore!"

I try saying, "You're right."

"You can't make me be!"

"You're right, Granny. I'm sorry."

Then the Bull of Crete is off, leaping over the freshly split chasm to try goring Heracles again. She can't stop raging. Just hearing me talk set her off worse. There's no magic phrase I can utter to restore the old friend I had. All I have scalds her.

Because I'm her problem.

I almost say it, but stifle myself for fear of making her worse. I can't help her by apologizing.

Then I see what's in Heracles's right hand.

Heracles 27

I don't know where my bow and arrows even are. On the ground lie several lengths of that shining black rope, braided titan hair with a few remaining straps of tanned titan hide. The harness that bound the fury is torn asunder, but it's still the remains of ancient gods. I wind all the strips and ropes together into a single cord. It's the tool I have.

Whenever the bull charges for me, it always dips its head low to the ground, just before its front hooves hit in the gallop. When the hooves hit, it flings itself upward with all the strength of its neck and legs, thrusting those horns.

It made that move when it hit Purrseus, and when it nearly killed Boar. It's tried it twice on me already. I know it'll do it again.

From the moment the bull comes racing across the nests, hooves trampling them into dust, I know it's coming. I see before the bull's shoulders tense to lower its head.

I stretch a length of my cord in both hands. I don't know if they can force the fury to submit like they did before they were broken. But I do know that Boar and Purrseus can't survive this thing. I have to put a stop to this. Prevent the fury from taking another life. Let my sons be the last.

Blood trickles into my left eye, and I ignore it. I stare into the frantic eyes of a giant bull that doesn't know what it is going to do. Its shoulders ripple, and its head starts to lower in its charge. I'm ready.

Auntie Hera, please let this work.

Hera 28

I shouldn't have sent the bull today.

I shouldn't have sent the fury then.

Every mistake is laid too bare. I never needed to put a snake in this man's crib, or to send him to fight a great lion. His whole life has been a misanswered prayer.

It's time to answer it correctly. The way only a goddess can.

Heracles wrestles the bull to the ground again, winding those scraps of titans around its throat. He can't see the eyes, but I can. Granny knows she's caught, and she can't think of how to separate herself from the bull. In her panic, they're the same creature. Kicking her hind legs does nothing to throw off a wrestler as strong as this son of the King of Olympos.

One thing can stop him. The right omen.

I appear in a flash of ash and white, a dance of cuckoo feathers in the wind. It carries the scents of pomegranates and lotus petals, those scents that for his entire life he grew up recognizing in my temples. Nothing should capture his reverence so quickly.

Nothing so quickly as this horrid avatar. A tall matron with a white robe, and white banners flowing from her polos crown, all the way down to sandals etched from bone. I am the source of the wind on this abandoned farm. Even as I sculpt my face, it is too haggard, too spent to be divine. He'll see the weight of all that has happened upon my brow, and he'll know in an instant that I am who is responsible for all this.

Parting my arms, I raise empty hands to him.

I part empty lips, my confession ready to spill out and turn his vengeance where it belongs. It's time.

Heracles 28

My elbow finds the base of the bull's neck, and I know I've got it. All my weight and strength goes down on that spot, so that the bull's horns jut up and hit nothing, all that momentum wasted, none left to resist what I'm doing. I bring its snout down into the ground, the impact shaking every bone in my body, but I have to move. Here go titan hairs and hide, looping first around the bull's throat, and next around those horns to anchor it. When it bucks again, it strangles itself, and doesn't have the air to fight me as I keep holding it down.

Through gritted teeth, I pray to the bull and the fury alike.

"Please."

Its brilliant white hide is dingy now, caked in mud and earth, rocks sticking into its skin. The same muck covers most of my body, like we're brothers. Like we're the same creature, thrashing around together.

The thrashing weakens, the bull's legs kicking feebly for purchase. Hooves scrape along earth and find nothing to help. Not even a monster can fight without breath.

Holding those shackles taut across its neck strangles me. I can't breathe, only exhale.

I've had enough blood.

Haven't we all had enough blood?

Are we doing this to ourselves? If not, who is making us make these choices? Who?

I ask both bull and fury, "Who did this to us? Which god was it?"

I listen for the voice that lives within the bull. It's the same that lived in the bird before, that fury that is so angry at herself above all things. I'll let her go. I'll wash her feet and comfort her if she'll just tell me the truth. Tell me before I drop dead atop this creature.

Despite myself, my fingers loosen their grip. I can't bring myself to put this beast down when it's another victim. No more than I want to strangle the fury.

The voice struggles, like she is clearing a throat that doesn't exist. Like she's sucking in spiritual breath to feed the bull that cannot breathe through its own nose. But there's a composure to it, too. Like the truth is coming.

I blink grime from my eyes and look up, praying to you, Auntie Hera, for the clarity. Wind makes me wince, and a figure appears in my blurry vision. She's so tall and grand, a great woman whose diadem is the sun. Her robes light up and fill the world with sun like no dawn has ever had the daring to carry. Her features are lined, her eyes so heavy it is a wonder they are open, like this miraculous figure has no idea how tired she is.

Who is she that would come to this battlefield, where it's not safe? I need to warn her, to run before the bull wakes up again. I've forgotten how to speak. She takes the words from me.

Her own lips part, and I want nothing more than to hear her song.

Before, in the ecstasy of interrogating the fury, I didn't pay attention. I didn't see the threats around us, and the bull surprised me. This time, I am ready for calamities to steal a precious moment.

For there is something else in the world, high above her. High in the sky, a spark that comes diving down, like a god of predator birds. It blazes so bright, like it will burn the world. An arrow of bright red feathers, its haft deep brown, and its tip blackened animal horn. It flies true, down at us.

I leap over the bull, standing in front of it and this radiant woman, defending them. I stand tall and in the path of this falling arrow.

Hera 29

Who shot a fucking arrow at me?

It streaks like a shooting star, except its hue burns with brilliant light, so bright it belongs only in thunderstorms. It breaks the clouds and turns raindrops to vapor. The shock of its appearance is so great that I lose my physical avatar immediately, and fly back to Mount Olympos.

There's nowhere else that arrow could have come from. It's too high in the cosmos, and I know the directions of heaven. That had to have been loosed by a god. A god who is about to get their ass kicked.

I bellow into the halls, "Athena, did you aim that arrow at Granny?"

But Athena is at my side, her voice infuriatingly placid. "No, my queen. I wouldn't interfere like that."

"Then who the fuck did?"

She gestures with one long arm over the marble rim of Olympos. Beyond her pale fingernails, that brilliant arrow has struck the earth and sent off a shock wave that fells all nearby trees.

From that wave emerges a man-shaped avatar. He has broad shoulders coated in thick hair, wearing a white robe around his waist and a wreath of olive leaves around the crown of his head. I cover my mouth at the sight. It can't be.

Athena says, "Your son."

Heracles 29

He was an arrow, a moment ago. Now he is a man of unbelievable musculature, hairier even than myself, in a robe that hangs off of his hips like a lover. I swear that lightning flickers on the sheen of his fingernails. His thick, black beard trains on me, along with a gaze that measures me down to my smallest bits.

When he steps forward, the chasm the bull opened creaks and slams back together, the earth obeying this man-arrow's footsteps. I stand my ground, shoulders spread, hands ready to grapple with him if he comes closer. Purrseus and Boar are in no shape to join a fight. He won't touch them.

YOU WANTED THE TRUTH?

His voice comes not from his lips. It's from everywhere, from every direction. I hear him in my psyche, with that simpering timbre.

YOUR BIRTH WAS A MISTAKE. YOU ARE A MISTAKE. I SENT THE FURY TO WIPE YOU FROM THE MORTAL REALM LIKE THE STAIN YOU ARE. BUT THE FURY FAILED ME. SHE SHOULD HAVE TAKEN YOU, AND YOUR WIFE. RATHER THAN JUST YOUR BRATS.

What blood is left under my skin goes hot in my cheeks. It is him. Megara. Hera. It's the god we've been hunting all this time.

"Who are you?"

YOU ARE MY FATHER'S MISTAKE. AND I AM THE CORRECTION.

"No," I say, not settling for metaphors. "Give me the name of the god who will pay for my children."

Where his sandaled feet touch the earth, the grass stains red, and broken shafts and arrowheads litter the ground. It is his wake.

I AM THE GOD OF MEN BLEEDING OUT FROM GUT

WOUNDS. THE GOD OF AMPUTATED LIMBS. THE GOD OF
SHIPS CATCHING FIRE WHEN NO SOLDIER ABOARD KNOWS
HOW TO SWIM.

He gives me bluster instead of his name. Even now, having brought
down his bull and his fury, he insults the memory of my children. He is
the one god without honor. The coward who showed his face.

I say his name limply, flatly, in vain.

"Ares."

A TRUE SON OF ZEUS. NOT A HUMAN MISTAKE.

I could tackle him down to his litter of arrowheads and symbolism,
and he could rend my head from my shoulders. We could do violence that
would leave Stymphalia unlivable for a hundred generations.

If I could get my hands coiled into fists. But they won't. They remain
slack at my sides. Too tired with everything I've had to do this night
and day.

I ask him, "What did I ever do to you, other than honor your father
and mother? The great King Zeus and Queen Hera have been my greatest pride. I served Thebes in constant sacrifice to them. I waged war and
never said a cross word to you. My wife reveres you. They were her sons,
too. Good boys."

YOU AVOID VIOLENCE WHEN IT IS NECESSARY. EVEN
NOW YOU'RE TOO SINFUL TO FIGHT ME LIKE YOU SHOULD.
YOUR PRESENCE RUINED WARS. YOU PUT STRENGTH TO
ENDING THEM RATHER THAN RIGHTEOUSNESS AND
GLORY.

"I fought for Papa Zeus and Auntie Hera," I say, immediately regretting using such informal names. "I am Hera's Glory. I did everything in
their honor."

YOU FOUGHT FOR FAME. TO BECOME A GREATER GOD
OF WAR THAN MYSELF. MORE MORTALS ASPIRE TO YOUR
FAVOR THAN MINE. I KNOW YOUR SCHEMES.

"I never aspired to godhood at all. I never meant to . . ."

I catch myself. I won't apologize to the god responsible for all this. As
ravenous as I am to understand why he did it, I will not give him quarter.

"You. You annihilated everything in my life over nothing?"

IT IS TIME FOR YOU TO UNDERSTAND. TO ALL GODS,

YOU WERE ALWAYS NOTHING. IF YOU SO MUCH AS UPSET MY MOTHER FOR AN AFTERNOON, I COULD SLAUGHTER YOUR ENTIRE FAMILY LINE TO APPEASE HER.

A tiny paw sticking out of a bonfire. Claws seeming to grow as his fur and skin shriveled from the heat. It will never touch anyone again.

YOUR TIME RUINING WAR IS OVER. YOU HAVE ONE WEEK.

A week?

"What is this week for?"

COME TO THRACE, KINGDOM OF MY SON, DIOMEDES. A GENUINE SON OF A GOD. SEE THE LIFE YOU SHOULD HAVE LIVED, AND THEN I WILL WRENCH THE VENGEANCE FROM YOUR HANDS AND SLAY YOU WITH IT.

Then he is that brilliant arrow once more, flinging up into the sky. So quick he moves, he could knock Helios from the sunbeams, and that arrow arcs deliberately, for the north. For where the land of Thrace lies.

A week? I rake my hand across my hair and the sticky bandage on my head.

We have a week, Auntie Hera. We have one week until we get justice.

Part Three

The War

Hera 30

From across Olympos, Apollo shrieks, "My king! King Zeus is back!"

I shove Apollo aside and head to the marble rim to meet my son. Ares rises over the rim, still wearing that white robe and crown of olive branches. Even the aegis on his left arm is made of simple goat skin. Of the gods, only my dipshit husband wears such a useless shield, as a sign that no one can hurt him and he needs no guarding.

Ares's figure always cuts a similar avatar to his father, but now he's dressing up like Daddy. He looks me in the eyes, and I know he's not playing impostor. Not trying to be mistaken for his father.

That's what cuts the curses down in my throat before they can leap out and lash at him.

Instead, all I can say is, "What were you thinking?"

Ares pauses with one foot on the marble rim and one foot on the mountain below. He holds my gaze for an instant, and then his eyes flick away, like a nervous child.

"The fury you treat like family is safe. Heracles won't harm her further. Everyone's leaving her alone. Your worries are over."

That's not an answer. It's something else, something that makes me fear something about my son. Fear him? Or fear for him? I'm not sure.

So I glare at him. "Who told you to interfere?"

"I wasn't going to watch you hurt yourself for another moment. It's fine, Mom. I'm handling this now."

"That's not an answer, either!"

He climbs the rest of the way onto the marble rim, standing on it with both feet. Another step and he'll be back in Olympos, where I gave him life. I should cut him down with a scowl, but my lips can't form it. My avatar betrays me, and I'm smaller than I should be again, like all those times Zeus came home and looked down on me.

Ares says, "I don't know why you can't face him. But if you can't, you have your reasons. I'll settle family business."

I grab onto a handhold of outrage. I hang onto it. "You dress up like your father and you pretend you're me? You're not the killer. You didn't send Granny. You've never even watched one of Heracles's battles."

"I've seen enough."

"I was handling it," I say, stepping forward, unsure if I'll shove him down into the mortal world or pull him into my arms and hold him in the heavens. "I went down there. I was going to tell him the truth."

"No one in Olympos has seen more soldiers freeze when they needed to save themselves than I," he says, and steps off the rim, onto Olympos, as though he can walk through me. "It gets them killed. I didn't want to see what would happen to you when, after a few heartfelt words, you froze. I don't know what his power is over you. He doesn't deserve it. So I'll kill this mortal piece of shit, and then it'll be done."

Kill him? Kill Heracles?

"I didn't ask you to fight my war."

"War and family," he says. "A veteran loves his mother."

He kisses me, then enters the shifting marble walls of our great temple. Aphrodite is waiting there for him; I didn't notice her presence until now. She wears a radiant dress of a million woven gold fibers, so that it shines nearly as brightly as her hair. Has she spent this entire time looking at me? Her gaze digs into me now, even as Ares approaches her. But she will not look me in the eyes.

The two of them enter the halls, and Apollo passes after them, asking something about the olive wreath in Ares's hair. He chases along with their footfalls, probably loosening them up to ask a favor, or pitch a scheme.

I'd follow after them and pry into what he's scheming, but Granny needs me.

Heracles 30

It takes a long time to work the titan hair and hide from my hand, revealing a welt so deep across my right palm that I can't see how it doesn't bleed. All the flesh there is a dull charcoal color, and it throbs wildly. I slump on the ground beside the monstrous bull, who lies with its snout down in the mud. I pluck at the remains of the harness carefully to loosen them, then slowly peel them away, revealing a deep purple crescent under the white hair of its hide.

Bending in sight of the bull's right eye, I kiss the bruise that I made. The bull lets out a depressive snort, as a dog that wants nothing but sleep. I rest my head between its horns for a time. Words of apology would be meaningless to it. Perhaps just as meaningless to the fury.

Is the fury still inside this bull? A tight knot in my chest, right between my lungs, refuses to let me feel any angrier at her for what she did than I should be with myself for what I did to the bull. We were caught in a current too swift for us.

If it's still possessed, the bull is weary and tranquil. Its rage has abandoned it. And if the fury hasn't fled, I have what I needed from her. I know what god used her. I know where justice has to come from.

"That was him," comes a voice behind me, low to the ground. Logy found me. "That was really Ares."

"It was."

Logy noses against my calf, and I sit squat in the mud to welcome them into the warmth of my side. They stay on that side, with me between them and the bull, tongue flicking rapidly.

Purrseus pads up to me, ginger when he walks on his left feet. His hide shows no war wounds, but internally he's aching. His lips pull from his teeth at the sight of the bull, like he'd strike if I weren't between them all. I put my hand up, welcoming him closer, and also ready to hold him away if he tries to start round two. The thought of more violence feels like bile pumping through my veins.

"Please. Come and sit."

Then I notice Boar is behind Purrseus, hands on the sides of his boar's head cowl. The gash in his pelt is ignored, as is the scabbed-up cut on his actual skin. All his attention is on his cowl, which he's secured to his scalp with several lengths of bandage, tying his second head in place. When I look at him, he tilts the eyes of the boar's cowl away, as though it's nervous. Both sets of eyes look like they're desperate for him to run over and hold me.

"You too," I tell him, patting the mud beside me. There's room for everyone to sit. "Will you be all right, Boar?"

He says, "Boar was shaken. But he has resolve."

"I'm glad to hear that. I like your resolve."

He comes closer, not touching me yet. "Boar will fight, if you will fight. Now we know what god has been hunting you. How will you kill him?"

Logy says, "He's got a plan."

Do I? Logy has too much faith in me. In the moment, all I can think to do is stroke the bull's neck, in the fashion I wish someone would do for me right now. If only I could spend the rest of my life soothing a creature.

Boar says, "Boar assumed that is why Heracles keeps a hydra around. Your blood can kill many things."

Logy sucks their tongue in, no longer flicking it at anyone. They give Boar a long look. "The poisons I bleed have killed enough heroes and spawn of gods. I always wondered what they would do to an Olympian."

One hand drops from Boar's cowl, instead stroking at his chin. "Do we climb Mount Olympos? Storm the marble rim?"

"No one can enter Olympos save the Olympians. The place tears mortals apart if they approach."

Boar says, "Mortals, maybe. What about monsters? Has Olympos's curse been tested by an army of monsters?"

Logy tilts their solitary head upward. "It's an interesting hypothesis."

Their chatter makes that knot in my chest tighten, until it feels like it will suck me inside it and shrink me down to a seed. I want to sit out of this. But I have to speak or I won't be able to breathe.

"No." It's my first word in how long? It feels so childish to say. "Ares told us he'll be in his son's stronghold. He summoned us to Thrace."

Boar gives me a flat look, both sets of eyes equally unimpressed. "Yes. That's why you don't go there."

Logy rises up against my knee, now looking at the welt on my palm. Their attention makes me flex my aching fingers.

They say, "Boar's right. Ares is craftier than people give him credit for. Fools think he's a fool. A bully and nothing more. He uses that impression to kill kings."

I ask, "How do you know?"

"I've known very few people who survived knowing him." They hesitate. Then they say, "You know his rival goddess of war? She puts on this fake aloof and calm exterior whenever she gets nervous. And whenever she talked about him, she always had to put that façade on first. She defeated him in so many battles, and still, she was scared shitless of him."

Boar says, "He's going to bring a war to you, if you don't bring it to him. The hunt is on."

I try to decide what to do, and the first image I have is Megara with her bow and quiver in hand. Would she travel to Thrace and face Ares's son, or rush at the heavens themselves? She was always so cunning and careful. That's why she had to leave me. What would she choose to do?

All I can think of is her bare breast in the dark, on all those nights when we could not get baby Therimachus to latch. How he wailed like his voice would knock down the walls, begging for food, while refusing the mother's milk right in front of him. Neither of his brothers were like that. But Therimachus starved himself because he didn't understand what he needed was right in front of him.

How did we finally get him to latch?

Without realizing my lips are moving, I say, "I'm going to Thrace."

Logy says, "Come on, man. Ares has to have a plot laid out for you. And if his son is the tribal king there, then he's got to have that herd of mares so ravenous for flesh they eat every stallion in sight. It's a land so hard even the herbivores chew you up."

The knot tightens until I have to hunch my shoulders to remain standing. Purrseus looks into my face with wide eyes, offering his back to rest on, and I give him some of my weight. Only some of it. The rest I carry myself, huffing breath, and looking down at the exhausted bull at my feet. At the fight that didn't help anything.

"Ares challenged me to kill his son. To avenge my sons by killing his. He is the son of Hera, Goddess of Family, and he spits in her face using his child to wet his tongue for the act. He killed my family to spite me and her."

"So you're going to give Ares what he wants? That makes no sense, Al."

"No," I say it again. "We're not giving him what he wants. We're taking it from him."

Hera 31

I am the touch of the sun's fingers that is too hot to bear. There is ample sunshine that refreshes; I am what wilts and cannot be withstood, scorching the flies that buzz around your haunches. So many bugs want to gnaw on your host, Granny. Not a single one of them will land. They drop to the ground, never to bother your ears again with their whining.

You have to still be in there. The Bull of Crete alone wouldn't be so gentle with a stranger like Heracles, especially if he had any memory of fighting him. And I see how you keep going ahead of the group to loiter around the Hind of Ceryneia. You're waiting for her to alert you to predators. You've got to be in there.

I haven't heard your voice in some time. I can scarcely feel your presence in there, under the Bull of Crete's own. Poseidon gave him quite the aura. You wanted to be nothing but an animal. If you thought the same thoughts, and felt the same urges, could you hide, pretending you two were the same?

Ares created such a distraction that I wouldn't have noticed you escaping. If you're gone, and hiding from me, then I deserve that.

If you're in there, let me help you. Let me at least keep the flies from troubling you.

I should have come to you sooner. I should have known what to say, and how to get through to you.

I shouldn't have needed to. We should have danced barefoot on Olympos's roof rather than spit wrathful in Zeus's wake.

You're still family, and that means—

"My queen."

Athena's serene voice.

Not now. She has the worst timing of any god I've ever known.

Except she's also been onto many things lately that I've missed. I can't afford to dismiss her.

"Yes, Athena?"

It is the politest I can be.

She is tall as ever, eyes gray and unreadable, charioteer's helmet in the crook of one arm like she's ready to ride at a moment's notice. We aren't riding anywhere. Not when Granny is here, and needs me.

"I have always endeavored to answer any need you have. To come to you only to answer your questions."

It feels more irritating than that, but it could be true. So I say, "Yes?"

"This time, I need to bring a matter to you."

"Is it about what we can do for Granny?"

"It is about the God of War."

My temper slips, just a knuckle's worth. "Plenty of people call you by that title already."

If anything, her visage only grows more placid. I do not know how she does it. "If Ares means to slay Heracles to spare you trouble, why doesn't he fight him immediately? When Heracles is at his weakest?"

I wave her to leave me. "Because my son knows I don't want him dead. He wants me to squabble with him and bond with him and all that over saving the little shit."

Do I believe that? I didn't know it was on my mind before it flew out of my lips. Ares always wants a fight. He could be begging for attention as conflict.

Rather than take the dismissal, Athena goes on. "He created a time-table in which word of the battle will spread across the sea. He has the attention of Olympos. Soon he'll have the attention of all civilization."

I catch a fly and hold it up to her. I make sure Athena sees me crush it. "What are you getting at?"

"He is going to fight and kill the most famous hero ever sired, in defense of the Queen of Olympos, in the stead of the absent King of Olympos."

"You've always envied him."

"King Zeus hasn't returned in all these years."

I warn her, "I don't like your tone."

"It is worth exploring whether your son wants the throne, and if he's using you to get to it."

"If you're the actual smart goddess, you're going to shut up right now."

That placid face has the audacity to do as I tell it. Her lips seal like she was carved out of bone. The gray eyes keep watching me, like an owl.

I am not a mouse, Granny. I swat more flies, slaying seven in one blow. They aren't enough, and I catch my gaze shifting around the world, and around the marble halls of Olympos. I didn't mean to look for him. But where is my son right now?

People are following us now, Auntie Hera. I first spotted them climbing two hills behind us near the Aliakmon, and by the time we got to the river itself, there were more. Some I recognize as farmers from Stymphalia, coming to pay their appreciation for us driving the giant birds out of their lands. Others carry colors from Volos and Epiros. There are several thousand this morning, so many that I wonder if some Thebans are in there. It'd bring a little slice of relief to feel like home followed me here.

The more people you send to watch us, the more right I know I am about what we're doing. It's almost done. My boys can almost rest.

The masses slow down when the Bull of Crete joins us. Purrseus and Boar give him a wide berth, neither slowing in their gait, while both keep their heads turned to watch him. He treads up with head bowed low, horns randomly gouging the earth. The wheels of my chariot rattle with his hoofbeats. Logy tenses up on the chariot against my right leg, and I pat their tail with my welted hand. I don't think they're here to fight.

I'm not alone. I don't see the Hind until she's in the middle of our path. She trots right up to the Bull of Crete, looking so small before his mass that she could be something that fell off his left horn. The Bull raises his head slightly, his bruised neck tensing.

The Hind raises her head as high as it will go, sniffing at him like he's fresh grass to munch. The antler buds on her scalp are so dormant you could forget they are there. Where once the Bull was a monster that scared her away, she doesn't see him as a predator anymore. She touches the tip of her nose to his. His dark eyes shift, and he turns his head away, just a bit. What does that mean?

"Ugh," says Logy. "At least do that in private."

Whenever I smile, the wound the birds left on my forehead opens again. It trickles coolly around my eyebrow and down my cheek. Right now, it's worth it.

I say, "If she vouches for his character, then the Bull is welcome."

Like that, the Bull is welcome, and "the Bull" is his name. Unless it turns out he can speak, and he offers an alternative. He seems preoccupied sniffing the Hind.

Logy slithers their tail around in the base of the chariot, turning their gaze behind us, upon the many people and banners that follow us.

"Well, he'll be useful in the war, anyway."

Boar drops back enough to walk alongside my chariot, his cowl still held on by my bandages wrapped under his chin. He nods with Logy's words. "You know that's what all those followers want. To see a great battle."

I keep watching as the Hind and the Bull turn to walk side by side, so close to Purrseus that he lifts a paw in the promise of a swipe. That swipe never comes.

"They want a battle," I say. "But they'll get something better."

Boar balks. "You didn't hunt a god across the entire world in order to not fight him."

"In fact, I did."

In fact, I came all this way unsure of what I'd do. What does justice look like? I fought the birds and the Bull, and came away sickened. More violence won't restore anything to me besides glory in the eyes of strangers. I've known enough soldiers to know how little return revenge gets you. My boys deserve more than that.

Now the path of justice is obvious. There couldn't be a simpler god to face than Ares.

Logy watches me for too long, probably waiting for me to say something they can argue with. When I don't give them anything, they say, "You know what a god calls an enemy who won't fight back?"

"What?"

"A victim."

They're afraid for me. Their sarcasm and undermining are all expressions of affection. But I'm not afraid for myself, because I'm not doing this for my own sake. This is more important. Once we reach Thrace, the God of War will be defied.

Logy says, "So you are going to tour the world ending all wars to spite him?"

Boar adds, "Anoint yourself as the God of Peace?"

"No," I say, flatly. My right hand coils as though around the shaft of an old Theban spear, borrowed from one of your temples a lifetime ago, Auntie Hera. "When I was young, a tribe of Minyans tried to invade Thebes. I fought to defend my homeland. The Minyans were wrong to wage war on us; we were not wrong to wage war in defense of ourselves. War is an essential part of every life around the Aegean Sea."

Boar looks me over again, like he didn't really see me before. "Then what are you planning?"

"It's Ares I defy, not war itself. He wants a war with me." I cast aside that imaginary spear, imagining it rolling into the muddy waters of the river. "And I am going to break his war. He's set the stage for everyone to watch more needless violence. I am going to let everyone see something better. This is not going to be settled by fighting."

Boar says, "Ares isn't just sending you against his son. He's creating a distraction so he can hunt you."

His son. It makes me put a knuckle against the cut in my forehead, to hold my mind in place.

I ask them, "Can you imagine how Diomedes was raised? How loveless his existence is? If his father would treat him like a tool now? It speaks to how he must have been treated his entire life."

Logy interjects, "He's a warlord from a lineage of warlords."

"Of course he would be. If he's never had family that cared about him, he'd seek a handhold anywhere. There's got to be a pain inside him, a constantly tightening cavity. This has to have made it even worse, knowing his purpose in life is so unimportant to both gods and family alike."

Boar starts to reach for me. "He has an army behind him."

"An army is a poor replacement for a purpose." I stay away from Boar's touch this time, spreading out my arms wide and flexing my shoulders. If I clapped my hands, I could deafen all the thousands of people following us. "Papa Zeus gave me his strength for a reason. He didn't make me King of All He Surveys like Eurystheus, but he placed power in my hands. I have to use it to give the world something better."

Boar says, "If it were him, Zeus would kill Ares."

Logy says, "I agree with our boar theologian. In your place, Zeus would *absolutely* kill Ares."

I almost say that I am not a god, just a father.

I almost say that I am a father.

But I am not a father anymore. It makes me close my eyes and heave out a breath—too harsh a breath, for it sends water splashing all the way across the river.

"Ares killed my sons, and now challenges me to kill his son. He wants it done in front of the entire world. Don't you see? I can't give him that. Dying to Diomedes, or making him die at my hands, is the same injustice. More destruction of family. If anything, what Diomedes needs is better family."

We can show him that, can't we, Auntie Hera?

I wish I could talk to you about this, Granny. This is the sort of thing you, myself, and Até would have schemed over for eons, back when we were something we could call "we." This would have been the juiciest fruit on the tree to chat and bicker about.

And I know you aren't listening. That if you can hear me, you're deciding to ignore me. And I earned that.

But I'd rather be ignored by you than talk to anyone else.

So let me ask you, Granny: what is my damned fool son doing?

Is he foolish enough to race for a throne, sure to get toppled by other gods in the fight? And if someone did win the race, they'll be toppled by my dipshit husband as soon as he and his thunderbolt get home.

My imagination drifts to the wound on Zeus's side that night. That last time that I saw him.

But he can't be dead. He's too annoying to die. I'd sooner believe this was all a game he concocted to toy with us. And if he was dead, we'd hear the gloating from Hades and Persephone. That the God of Death had the King of Olympos down in the underworld, in the depths below Olympos's feet, shackled beside the old kings. Zeus isn't down there. Our parents are, the gods we were supposed to be better than.

If only we could talk this over, Granny. What would you and Até say? If you two knew all this, how you would laugh. Especially Até.

Reflexively I grope around Olympos for the sensation of Até, like the Goddess of Ruin might have snuck back here when nobody was paying attention, since the god who banished her has vanished.

For an instant I think I feel her presence—her peculiar warmth. She's deep inside the marble temple, down where the mountain becomes metaphor. What is Até doing? Is she what's ruining my son?

No, wait. That's not her. Deep under the temple, that's Aphrodite's essence. The two have a similar false beauty in their essence, a certain imitation, like a bird that has figured out how to mimic the song of the harp to attract people to feed it. I suppose love and ruin have that in common.

She's in the depths because she's chattering at her husband. My brilliant son, Hephaistos, God of Blacksmiths and Invention, likes to work outside the purview of the sun, where the light comes from his coals and furnace. If he worked any deeper under Mount Olympos, he'd be in the underworld itself. Cracked hammers line the wall outside his door, like trophies commemorating past jobs. The walls down here glow orange from his furnaces, and the stone itself beads with sweat.

"Don't you have anything harder?"

Aphrodite's voice comes from the doorway. I clamp a hand over my mouth, dreading what I've walked in on. The last thing my son needs is his mother watching him hammer his wife.

"The copper is for hardness," says Hephaistos, in a tone that doesn't sound passionate. "The tin is for flexibility. We don't want a harder bronze. It would break."

Relief washes over me. They aren't hammering. Not each other, anyway.

Aphrodite scoffs. "Well, can't you invent a new metal?"

"Haven't you heard? Bronze will always be the strongest metal."

"You don't believe that. Come on, we could help the humans discover something better in their mines. The world can't run on bronze forever."

"It doesn't run on it now. It runs on people who carry bronze, and what they do with it."

"Don't be cute."

"I don't have to be. You're cute enough for us both."

I hear her shove his side. "He needs this to be worthy of a legendary event. Poets need to sing forever of its bite. Whenever blacksmiths hammer a new sword, they need to be thinking of this one."

So she's asking him to forge a special sword? They really are going all out in having Ares's son kill Heracles.

Hephaistos says, "I'll see what I can do."

"And have you thought over his proposal?"

"I'm still making his weapon. Now you want me in his politics?"

Politics? That's enough for me. I clear my throat, which is already clear. I let them know I'm walking through the doorway before I'm there, and my gaze is blade enough to menace them. Aphrodite stands stiff as her favorite pastime beside an anvil, one hand on a split soapstone cast. It must be the mold Hephaistos is working on.

Hephaistos looks me in the chin, like he always does. My chin is firm, but I know he's just looking for the closest thing to eye contact without the effort. He faces me casually, like he was already pointed in this direction and knew I was coming, standing away from his anvil, both hands clasping the handles of his four-pronged cane. His bare upper body glistens like he poured himself out of bronze, thickly muscled, while both of his legs bend awkwardly at the knees, and are gnarled and thin. When he was young, he once caught me and my dipshit husband quarreling, and thinking Zeus would attack me, Hephaistos grabbed him. Zeus responded by hurling him from Olympos with such force that the boy's legs were destroyed. It took him ages to climb back up Olympos. As an Olympian, he could alter his avatar at will. He could regrow his legs. He could grow a hundred legs if he desired. But Hephaistos didn't care. He simply crawled back to his anvil and resumed inventing things. He's the only Olympian who I have never seen change his avatar, as though he's too busy creating things more beautiful than divine forms.

"I always leave the politics to my queen," he says, too knowing a smile nesting in a beard that is more soot than hair. "I merely smith the tools. How lucky I am, to have two goddesses in my workshop."

"Don't flatter me," I say to them both, to cut off any follow-up of false praise from Aphrodite. "Tell me about this proposal."

"Nope," Aphrodite says immediately, flipping her hair and heading for the exit. "I am not getting in the middle of this."

It is not the best starter Aphrodite could have opened with, yet she looks at me like I'm somehow the transgressor here. Now I'm sure what she and Ares are after.

I step into her path, looking down at her with a gaze that should remind her I own many javelins. "You're running favors for him. How do you think you're not in the middle of this? You think I don't know what you and Ares are plotting?"

Oh, she stops. She knows she can't walk through me. Her slender hands fidget at her sides. "I am plotting nothing other than keeping my loved ones alive."

"Oh, right," I say. "You still think you're the Goddess of Love."

That gets her to stand up straighter, and give a brief glimpse of her teeth. The corner of her mouth dimples when she doesn't want it to.

"Queen Hera." Not *my queen*. She says *Queen Hera*. She looks me dead in the face. "You are not the only one who loves your son."

I have more than one son, and she's cheating on the one in this room. I tell her, "You're no Goddess of Family."

"We're not in competition." She reaches into her hair to fix the daffodils she's decorated herself with. "You have your narrow view about what family is allowed to be. I attend to the rest. Love breaks through old boundaries."

"You attend to mistakes? To all the mistresses you've left stranded with child and no help? No, I wind up looking after mothers."

That dimple again, and now a glance down at the cast on the anvil, like she'll snatch the whole parcel up and dash my head in with it. But I know what she really wants to say. She wants to throw my family—my husband—in my face.

I catch myself craving for her to do it. For the fight that will make me forget my guilt. The fight I should have had with Heracles. Something so catastrophic that it ends all of this.

Instead she dares say, "Love doesn't make mistakes."

Hephaistos audibly licks his lips, and adjusts his four-pronged cane so that it clacks against the marble. The sounds interrupt my window to retort. With my attention, he says, "My queen. I honor my wife."

That Ares calls me "Mom" is cloying, but that Hephaistos only addresses me by my title has always been worse. As though we aren't family. As though, before he created so many things, I didn't create him.

It comes out in my tone, hotter than I intended. "You know what she does with Ares behind your back."

"You mean to ask if I am aware that the wife who I never sleep with has numerous children, many of whom resemble another Olympian?"

There's a sternness in his gaze, even if it's fixed only on my chin. A refusal to back down; a pride in saying they haven't been hammering each other on his anvil. For a moment, I wonder if I shouldn't have set him up with Artemis, so they could be virgins forever.

Aphrodite has the gall to say, "He understands me."

Hephaistos's tone tries to move the conversation on. "My queen, I am not interested in litigating the kind of family you wish I kept. I have the one I want to keep, and I will keep it. I also don't think that's why you're here."

It's hard to swallow the pride I feel in him standing up to me. But he's wrong. I am here because of the family he keeps.

I warn Aphrodite, "Whatever power grab you are putting Ares up to, the harm that comes to this family will be on your head. And I have a long memory."

Half a laugh pierces the air, before Aphrodite catches herself. "You think it's my idea?"

I don't know how to answer that. My whole being freezes up at the genuine venom she has for being called a part of this.

She says, "I don't want any part of this. But since I can't stop him, I'm just trying to get him to avoid the worst mistakes. I—he needs you to do the rest."

Her eyes, widening and then narrowing. Signaling for me to stop fighting her and think.

Just as quickly, she says, "I'll excuse myself. I have several more errands to run. Love is a demanding business. Queen Hera."

Then she's gone, leaving me with my boy. Hephaistos already has his back to me, examining the soapstone cast. Two daffodils lie on top of it. He moves them aside to work on it, shoulders rippling with strength. From behind, his legs are even scrawnier, like two strings loose from the great rope of his torso. He heaves himself up naturally to lean against the anvil, and takes a tong to wedge inside the soapstone cast.

I visit the anvil, and hold one end of the cast for him. It's been a long time since I've helped him work. It's been a long time since I've visited at all.

I say, "You know I'm going to make you tell me everything."

"You'll never get me to tell you. I'm too loyal to family."

"What is it?"

"A sword."

Damn him, but I'm laughing. "What kind of sword?"

"Ares wants me to back his heading the pantheon, and to ceremonially acknowledge him by handing over a sword that can kill a hero."

He wrestles with the stuck edge of the cast, like the weapon inside is refusing to be born. I look at it with fresh fear. So this will be the thing that kills Heracles.

I have to ask. "What kind of sword did you envision?"

"A normal one," he says, sweat sputtering off his lips in his laugh. "That's the point of heroism: that heroes are mortal and can die. More heroes have been killed by infection after a wound than have ever been beheaded. But, you know, Ares and Aphrodite and all of them are dramatic."

I wonder if I'm part of *all of them.*

One end of the tongs finally parts the seams, and he cracks the two halves of the mold open. Inside is a dusky piece of bronze, longer than a short sword. All the dark impurities and char have risen to the surface, and both edges are grossly frayed, bronze fibers sticking out like so many weeds growing from the idea of a blade. Closer, they look like whiskers. It reminds me of a child's prayer I heard long ago, asking for me to show him cats.

The sword is entirely unfinished, as ugly as a killer's intentions. Back when Zeus and I fought the titans, we would have done anything for such a weapon, such a weapon that today looks like shit.

I wave his hands away, and reach down with my own strength. It can't resist me. I pry the tang of the sword at the bottom from the mold, then pull the whole thing loose. I hold it up, gripping the tang like a handle. Bronze is still hot under my fingers. I refuse to be scorched.

I say, "I'll take this. You make Ares another one."

"I am of service to my entire family. Always."

Heracles 32

The followers are so numerous I can't lay eyes on them all. We come down this long slope, almost as drawn out a decline as a mountainside, and there are still clearly mobs of them that are out of view. None are bold enough to approach us, and frankly Boar would probably charge and gore them if any did. I can't tell whether Purrseus or Boar hates being followed more. They growl at our admirers in roughly equally measure. All those people camp a safe distance from us every night, as though they're afraid to witness too much.

We see the army on the cusp of the Aegean Sea, where the grasses are tall and blond, but unyielding. There waits a wide bank of archers, so many in number it's as though they fear an island will uproot from the sea and attack. We're far shy of the nearest stone buildings, almost as distant as those islands out in the water. They don't want us any closer.

So I leave my monsters and my followers, and I walk alone out into the weeds and tall grasses. I take in the brine through my nose, mixed with horse dung and blossoming dittany and oregano. I don't see flowers anywhere, but they must grow them somewhere. The field itself is salted, all dead dirt, flat land awaiting conflict. Thrace was waiting for me.

Out in my open spot, under the watch of every archer, I wait for the king.

Diomedes rides up to me on a mare with a rich brown coat and a white mane around her neck. Instead of hide reins or rope, he steers the mare with dingy bronze chains wrapped around her head. As she stamps to a stop, she chews on a strip of something like leather or flesh. Blood drips around her muzzle, but I don't see any injury on her. She keeps chewing at her snack while the man addresses me.

I look up at that bloody mare's mouth and say, "I bring good news."

Diomedes would be taller than me on foot. On horseback, I have to lean back to look him in his eyes. Curly black hair spills from under his bowl-shaped bronze helmet, and a war belt with bronze plates sits over his navel and genitals. The plates are etched with the likenesses of serpents. Otherwise he is nude, no defense against the rainfall of arrows that could drop on us at any moment.

"I'd like some good news," Diomedes says, jabbing a callused finger past me and at the hills of people who followed me here. "Because right now all you've brought me is an enemy host."

Any smile threatens to break open the wound on my forehead. I risk it. "Here's the first piece of good news: that is not an army. Not one of them serves me. Not one of them means ill-intent to Thrace."

The king twines a hand in the bronze chains of his mare. "That would be great news, if I believed it."

"Here is a second piece of good news: I am not here to kill you."

He looks me over, eyes lingering on the paunch of my belly. "You should know that brings me great comfort."

"I'm not trying to condescend."

"Let me be the judge of that."

He's witty. Now I couldn't stop smiling if I wanted to. Let this be the beginning of a good friendship.

I say, "Your father summoned me here for us to battle. I want you to know that I won't hurt you. My name is Heracles, son of Zeus. Technically, I'm your uncle."

A hoot escapes him, like the mirth of a bird. A smile threatens to split his head and send it falling off his shoulders. "Oh, so you're the meddlesome Heracles? Well, then we have a problem."

That we do. I'm eager to get into it.

I say, "Tell me how we can solve it."

He gestures with that callused finger, back behind him, as though I'm supposed to see something through the mass of his archers. "You see, I'm full up on Heracleses. Three of you have already soiled my borders claiming to be the son of Zeus who honors Hera with his muscles. They claimed to wear the skin of invincible lions, and to have stolen the sky off of Atlas's shoulders."

The impostor again. But now there are more of them? Why would anyone want to pretend to be me?

I say, "Those are cases of mistaken identity."

"And they were much mightier of figure than you are. I have them in a dungeon right now, and it's getting crowded in there. So I don't need any more Heracleses in Thrace. Why don't you take your not-an-army and go run home?"

All right, Auntie Hera. Let's settle some of these things.

I ask, "Did these three other so-called Heracleses claim to have fought the Hydra of Lerna?"

"Yes. Each of them killed it in equally heroic fashion. Generous of the same monster to die in three separate battles."

I put two fingers to my lips and whistle. The sound makes Diomedes's mare stiffen, and my friends rise. There is the Bull of Crete, standing tall as a house, with the Hind sheltering underneath him like his sole occupant. Purrseus and Boar are pacing, clearly desiring to charge in. Thankfully they have the respect to keep their distance. The whistle is merely a summons to show themselves.

In their midst rises Logy, coiling the butt of their tail and sticking their head high in the air. They flick their tongue at me and Diomedes, and all those archers.

I call, "Logy?"

They call back, "Yeah?"

"What's my name?"

"I call you Al. Most people call you Heracles. I suspect people closer to Thebes refer to you by—"

They could be less helpful. I interrupt them, "Did I fight you?"

"Yeah. I lost a lot of heads that day. Thanks for that."

"No, thank you," I say, and gesture that my fellow monsters can stand at ease. Purrseus and Boar are still pacing, though, and Diomedes is staring at them. I tell him, "If I split the earth with my strength right now, it would only terrify the people who follow me, and the archers you have pointing arrows at us. Can I ask you to trust me that I am myself?"

Diomedes breathes out something caustic, half a syllable that clearly wants to be a curse. Then he bites the tip of his tongue, right hand fingering his war belt. I see the handles of two knives hidden inside, against his flesh. So he isn't unarmed.

"You really are the Heracles that Father told me to kill?" He returns both hands to the chains of his mare. "That killing you will bring me an army that will let me conquer the entire Aegean Sea? He was supposed to send me a weapon. He must be busy."

I put my hands up as though to calm his horse. "We don't have to fight, though. That's why I'm here. Your life is worth more than one fleeting moment of glory."

He hesitates a moment, eyes shifting between his archers and where Purrseus and Boar are pacing. Then he leans down, fingers coiling for me to join him in close.

He whispers, "Let me be honest with you. I have a problem with you that only you can solve."

I step close to the bloody muzzle of his mare, ready to listen.

"Conquest is not my passion. I have babies I'd rather spend my days playing around with. Thrace has ample farms to feed my citizens. My father wants me to conquer the world, but I don't want the same things he does. Do you ever tire of violence?"

I suck the saliva off of my tongue. It's like hearing my own voice. "Yes. Nothing wearies me more."

"So, look, my father wants me to kill you and go on to take over the world. If he doesn't get what he wants, I might be in trouble. Will you listen to a little proposal?"

"Of course. How can I help?"

He mimes as though holding a knife, and poking first at his chest and then mine.

"Let's do battle, and you'll let me get my licks in and make it look good. But you, son of Zeus, wind up being the stronger. You just wait until I give you the sign to knock me down."

I nod, whispering softly, hoping no other gods but you are listening. "So you won't lose face in front of your father."

He takes that mimed knife and pretends tapping it against his bowl-shaped helmet. "You're the smartest Heracles I've ever met."

I mull this all over. Ares won't be easily dissuaded. I tell him, "I'd rather not fight at all. So I'll let you do your worst, and I won't throw a punch. When you're ready, feign exhaustion and I'll pin you. That can be it."

A crack of a smile flits across his lips. "You swear on Zeus's name that I can trust you?"

I put a fist over my heart, wishing it was the touch of one of my sons. "You'll go back to your children tonight. You know, technically, I'm related to them too."

"Make it look good." He says it so quickly that I'm not ready for him to rear his mare and turn her around. Certainly not ready for the sudden eruption of his tone, into something haughty and careless.

"You're the most pathetic Heracles yet, and the last of them. I'm glad to be done with you. For Ares!"

Logy calls something I can't distinguish, and I turn to them to silence threats. Purrseus and Boar have gone still, both staring straight ahead, through me, at my newest ally. They need to know it's all a bluff. I haven't whistled a second time.

Even the Hind is standing, shining the golden antler buds at us. I hope she can convince the Bull to stay in place long enough for all of this to work. They have to trust me, like Diomedes is going to.

Then I hear the beating of more hooves. It isn't just Diomedes's mare; I turn to see him riding straight away from me, for the bank of archers. The archers part, and many more bronze chains rattle as at least a dozen more brown horses come stamping out, snapping like they'd bite their handlers. The chains slip, and all of the mares bolt past Diomedes. Is he sending me a mount for the fight?

They're getting closer. Close enough that I see their mouths. Every one of them drips blood.

"How did you beat him?"

Athena is always easy to find. When she isn't otherwise employed, she stands at the marble rim, watching some corner of the mortal world. I always imagined she would want a vast library, full of scrolls upon which every word ever spoken is written, or full of the shades of historians recounting the minutia of human exploits. Granny, do you remember when Apollo went hunting for her space, assuming she must have one, because he wanted to expose her secrets? As far back as I can remember, she has never made a space for herself in the Temple of Olympos.

She is the only Olympian who has not willed these walls to yield her a domain. She doesn't keep her knowledge on Olympos. She keeps it down there, in the mortal world. And she is always studying it.

Athena turns from the marble rim, gray eyes upon me. "My queen?"

This time, I stand at her side. "When you were newly born, you fought Ares over and over. He couldn't abide you, and the feeling was mutual. In every contest, you won. The story is that you embodied strategy, while he was mere force. It's a nice story. Now tell me the truth. How did you keep beating my son?"

Athena smooths her fingers along the skirts of her robes, pressing palms to her thighs. "You won't like the answer."

"I asked for the answer. Let me dislike it on my own time."

"He thought he knew everything." What a pivot, her tone going from insecure to blunt. Maybe that's how she beat him, too. "He'd never had true competition before. When I had my soldiers attack with a pincer, he was unprepared. In the next skirmish, he was certain I would use the pincer again. Instead I lured him into engaging on uneven ground. In the third skirmish, he was certain terrain was the key, and so was unprepared for my feint of engaging in melee and instead showering him with arrows."

I was there for that one, and the fight after. I say, "And next he thought it was all about arrows. But that's not all you did."

"The theme of his defeats wasn't surprise. It was exploiting his emotional state while he was anticipating surprise. He went from too sure of himself, to deeply unsure and overcompensating. Which is how I beat him with a pincer for the second time. The victory was not about the pincer attack."

I see. I say, "It was about his emotions leading him. He's not so different from his mother."

Now I look over the marble rim, down at the coast of Thrace. At a little shit who's about to start another fight, and this one won't be against some animal he can woo with hugs and friendship.

Athena stands closer to me, her eyes landing not so far from where my own look. Although I suspect she's not looking at the little shit. Is she eyeing Logy?

She asks, "Are you going to stand in Ares's way?"

"If he had a just plan for the future of the Olympians, he would have made me a part of it. Instead he fooled me into thinking no such plan existed. That this was all love of his mother. He pulled your old trick on me."

"And what will you do?"

What will I do, Granny?

I know.

"I'm going to spare his life." Heaving a sigh so hot it scorches my tongue, I tell her, "If he thinks the throne of Olympos is open, then my brothers are going to come marching up here. Poseidon will come climbing out of his sea, and Hades will come climbing out of his underworld. You know they're both calculating risks right now. They will want the throne for themselves, and they make my dipshit husband look gentle. They will kick the shit out of Ares and wipe their feet on his hair."

Athena asks, "You're afraid for your son's life?"

I can't take my eyes off of Heracles. He's walking onto the battlefield alone, with empty hands, and little more armor than the bandage on his forehead. I hate how clammy my hands get watching that little shit make mistakes.

I raise Hephaistos's sword, letting the many bronze fibers fan over my view of Thrace, like metal rays of sun. I shine on Heracles, and his family of monsters, and the army of onlookers who have come to see his war. They have no idea what's coming.

"Athena. You're supposed to be the smart god."

"So I'm told."

"What was I planning, when I appeared to Heracles? Before Ares interrupted me?"

She touches a pinky to her chin. "You planned to tell him the truth."

That's almost it. I add, "And to suffer the consequences. I was ready to give him the ending he wanted."

Athena's whole bullshit breaks for an instant—her gray eyes swing to me, to my hands, to my neck, like she didn't suspect something until now. Her eyes go so wide that she might as well be an owl again.

I like that I can surprise the omniscient.

"If my son needs me to sacrifice so he'll learn? Then he'll learn."

The mares come stampeding at me across the battlefield, more of them than I can count, every visible mouth gnashing teeth, saliva frothing and red with gore. All I can see are poor beasts.

Do you see it?

No horse in the Aegean eats flesh. They chew grasses that this field was salted to never grow. These are animals who were starved of what their mothers must have grown up grazing upon, who were subjected to meals of torture. How many times did they go sick from it? And now it's what they crave. If their mouths are truly red with gore, then they've already eaten, yet as soon as they are loosed from chains they are crazed with the prospect of my flesh.

That's not natural. That's a lifetime of cruelty forced on them until it became all they knew.

Two lead the herd, thrusting their necks forward as though to snatch out my heart. I catch each of them by the neck, above their throats, under where their heads begin, giving them as little room to wriggle as possible. They jerk to rise up and kick at me, but I don't let go, keeping them grounded. There's hunger in their eyes that verges on madness. Their breath reeks of entrails and they're desperate for more.

Behind them, more mares neigh erratically and fly around the leaders, trying to get at me. I'll be surrounded in an instant.

It'd be so easy to hoist these two both up like living clubs and swing them at the others. But they deserve better. We all do.

The two leaders buck again, trying to spring onto their hind legs to escape me, and this time I shove them on their way. They go teetering into the flanks of their fellow mares, whinnying and kicking their rough hooves. Every mare in the herd thrashes about, trying to get around them in the melee.

Before they can bring their feet down and kick at me, I drop to the ground with both fists. Once the Bull of Crete surprised me with an attack like this; now it's my surprise. I put all my strength into the ground, impacting so hard that everything beneath my feet caves in. My flesh shakes as in sudden thunder, hair whipping away from my face as I punch the crater deeper. A wide gulf opens under the mares, all too caught up in their eagerness for my flesh to get away.

While I hop away before I can fall, the mares slide down the sheer slopes. Just like the crater that the Bull once made, it's perilously steep. The mares charge at the walls and only make it worse. They'll be stuck down there, until I can bring them proper food.

Only now do I feel the sting on my left arm. Two crescent chunks are missing on my forearm, bleeding from where flat teeth punctured skin. One of the leaders got a bite on me. I cover my wound with a hand, and shake my head over the pit of mares. Those poor things.

I'm about to call for Boar and Logy to pay attention to them, when I catch the great shapes out in the waters to the south. In the Aegean Sea, three ships of reddish wood sweep our way, sails the color of an old man's armpits, headed for our shore. The sails are stained from use, and each ship also has an accompaniment of oars thrusting. The sailors are rushing toward us.

Does Diomedes have a navy? How good does he plan to make this battle look?

Twangs ring out, not from the sea, but from the east side of the battlefield. My hands go clammy at the sound of so many bowstrings loosing at once. Before I look up, I know the death that's coming down on me. A swarm of bronze-tipped arrows, shining in the sunlight, arch through the sky.

I have no time to run or find a shield.

I only have a pit, full of flesh-hungry mares. Still holding my bite wound, I jump down into that pit of hungry mouths.

They will the marble walls to give them privacy, but you taught me how to find any drama on Olympos, Granny. You just look for Apollo.

One turn shy of the entrance to their parlor, I let my presence be known. I catch him by the back of his beautiful hair, and shove his beautiful ass against the wall, staring down into his beautiful eyes. Apollo really could steal the God of Love shit from Aphrodite if he wanted—and he probably does. From the way he looks up at me, he reeks of entitlement. Like I'm about to steal a present from him.

He's another bastard child of my dipshit husband. Why didn't I snap and ruin this little shit's life instead of Heracles's? Ugh, but then I'd probably have gone on some journey of discovering his virtues and feel guilty over that instead. Feeling guilty for Apollo? I'm grateful I spared myself that fate.

I ask him, "Do you know what I'm going to do to you?"

His face implores another god to come out and intervene. But it's just him and me here, along with my new sword. All those pointy fibers jut from both edges, catching the radiance that shines from his hair.

He says, "Are you going to let me go because you mistook me for someone else? You know, I've always revered you."

It's that tone, like he only reveres my station. Like he wishes he was the God of Mothers. I am sure Ares and Aphrodite have lulled him to their side with offers of new domains.

"I'm thinking of taking sport from you."

His eyes widen, like he's more afraid of losing a domain than getting killed. "What? I tend to sports all the time. Wrestlers adore me."

"And dance and music. And probably healing."

"Tell me what mortals you want healed, and it's done. Look, I practically invented medicine."

"I'm going to take every domain from you until you're nothing but the God of Rats."

He tries to shake his head, but my hold on his hair makes it feeble. "My queen . . ."

"No, not God of Rats. You'll be God of Rat Shit. I'll make Athena the Goddess of Rats, and you'll have to consult her every time you want to observe your domain through a vermin's anus."

His eyes give away where the meeting is taking place, because he keeps shooting looks in that direction, like he can summon help. From the people who promised him more rather than less. Apollo won't be taking any domains from others today.

"Unless," I say.

"Unless? Anything, my queen."

"Unless you're on your way to the mortal world, to help inspire some new treatments for mothers with troubled births. Or some new fashions of music. That's what you were doing, right?"

"Of course. Of course. Drums will never be the same!"

He turns around in a perfect circle twice before hastening out of Olympos. His audience with the future King of Olympos is canceled.

And since there's an opening, I follow the last leg of the labyrinth. Time to look in on my son. I come to the doorway with the tip of my sword scraping along the floor, a cloying shriek of bronze on marble. A song for the appearance of a queen.

It's a vast chamber for only Ares and Aphrodite to be standing in it. The ceiling is too high for the dimensions of the place, creating a sense of an artificial sky. Thin ripples of gray run through the otherwise white marble, creating contours like overcast clouds. The space is clearly designed so that a dozen gods could easily hold audience in here.

The throne stands on four slender legs that take on the likenesses of gods holding up the armrests, and nude likenesses pose over the shoulders of the backrests. It is inlaid with ebony, and gold and ivory, and panels of gaudy green and red that devastate anyone with a sense of taste. I only know it isn't my dipshit husband's throne because that thing doesn't exist when he's not here. The marble walls of Olympos will not recreate it without his will.

So my son has instead conjured an imitation throne, with imitation godly likenesses, to match his imitation chiton, and his imitation crown of olive branches.

I look to Aphrodite, his imitation of me. She stares at my sword like I'm carrying my own spinal column out to battle. If Ares wanted to replace me, he should have picked Athena.

Don't tell her I said that, Granny.

"Oh, fuck this," says Aphrodite, and flings herself away from the throne with all the grace of a woman who's found herself sitting on an icicle. "Hera. It is not what it looks like, and I have even less to do with it than you think."

To their credit, neither of them was actually sitting on the throne. In their time alone from the other Olympians, I assume they don't use it for sitting. The golden oil from Aphrodite's right cheek is a shimmering smear in Ares's beard.

"Mom, I didn't want you to see this yet."

I let myself in, my avatar tall enough that I take the steps two by two. Hephaistos's sword sways idly by my left hip, and I can tell they're both staring at its ugly, unsharpened edges.

I say, "We have our privacy. It's just family here. Why don't you tell me now? What am I seeing? It looks like a chair. Does the chair look familiar to you, Aphrodite?"

It looks like her mouth is trying to swallow her lips. Then Ares gets in between the two of us. He says, "I was waiting for when the time was right."

I tap the dull tip of the sword on the marble floor. "And that time was after you propositioned Hephaistos and Apollo, and who knows how many other Olympians? You told them about your plot before telling me. You let me think you were taking the fall with Heracles and Granny. Let me think you were acting out of love."

"Then let's have it out right now," Ares says, to Aphrodite, and to me, and to the empty chair, like my dipshit husband is an actual party to these politics. "Dad's been gone for too long. There's a vacancy in the order of things, and it's been tearing you apart. You're obsessed with a single mortal. No single mortal matters."

"They all matter," I say, without being sure I believe it. "And saying otherwise is one reason why I better never catch you sitting in a chair like this one."

I'm too good at speaking in anger. My son doesn't stand a chance. I was verbally sparring with his father for ages before he was born. There's too much from before he was born that he hasn't weighed.

He says, "You're overburdened. Simple things are weighing too heavily on you. You need help managing your reign. Let me help."

"Help is usually offered," I remind him, twirling the sword in my palm. "It's not usually forged in secret. Do you think it eased my mind all these years when Zeus made decisions behind my back, never asking for my opinion for our fate?"

"I am taking care of the Heracles situation, and soon Thrace will conquer all civilization. A new age for us all."

Now that sounds like his father. It makes me measure my next words, because even now, I don't want to feel for my son like I do for that god.

I say, "You want to establish your reign by pretending to have done the worst things I've ever done. To become the proud inheritor of my regrets? The last thing that will bring me rest is my children growing into worse gods than we were."

"Mom," he says, and holds both of his palms up as though to receive a gift. "Let's not regret anything more. You know that sword is mine."

"This thing?" I say, tightening my fingers around the tang, metal biting into me. Oh, if we'd had this sword back at the beginning. It's time to teach my son.

I tell him, "Before there was anyone to turn truth into song, Ouranos ruled the cosmos. He was cruel to his children, and crueler to the cosmos. So one of his children, Kronos, fashioned a sickle out of the first stone ever dredged up from the sea. And he cut his father's balls off, and watched him bleed out, and thereby filled the first lake."

Aphrodite blanches, and even Ares starts to turn away. "Mom."

I go on, because I lived this part. "Kronos then ruled the cosmos. He thought being less cruel than his father was a license for all his cruelties. Figuring his own children were the same kind of threat that he had once been, he ate us. I remember the feeling of his tongue sliding over my belly as he swallowed me. Only your father, Zeus, was clever enough to trick him. He used a stone, swaddling it like a newborn. Kronos ate it, and never saw Zeus coming. Zeus killed him and set us free. That's when our war with the titans began. To be better than our parents."

Ares says, "If you think I killed Dad, I didn't. I don't know where he went. I'm doing what needs to be—"

I enjoy interrupting him. I put one foot against this imitation of my husband's throne, feeling it creak beneath my power. "Fighting them made us better than them. It made us what we are. Each generation of gods and titans has been killed by our children. It's an insult that was waiting for me, and the first thing I felt when I was born. How is the Goddess of Family supposed to reconcile that every generation hates the one that gave it life?"

He chews air, as though trying to find the words in his mouth. There's no apology that fixes all of this. He's going to have to grow, and I'm going to help. By the end of this, you're going to be better than you're plotting to be.

I kick the throne over and it clatters dramatically, as the calls of so many bats fleeing from a tree stump. I swing the sword up, all those bronze fibers glinting from its two edges. Ares freezes, his eyes trapped in a dance between my face and my weapon. Which one of us is more emotional?

"That's why I'm going to kill you."

H a! You really are Heracles."

A hand sticks over the edge of the crater. There is Diomedes's beard, his eyes swallowed by the shadow of his bronze bowl helmet as he reaches for me. He's abandoned his archers to fish me out of the crater.

The first time I climbed out of an impact crater, I was bewildered and rattled. This time it's far easier, as I grab handholds and kick my bodyweight up the slope. Diomedes reels back as I ascend, clearly unprepared for how quickly I make it.

Still, I pause for him. I don't need his hand, but I do need his help.

"Keep the fight to just the two of us from here on," I tell him, clasping his hand. "I don't want to hurt your horses, or agitate any of my friends. Some of them are highly protective of me."

Diomedes guffaws at me, his breath sweet with wine. "You want it to just be between us? When you brought a navy? I'm not that gullible."

He jerks his head southward, and, still hanging off the edge of the crater, I look to the sea. The three sailed ships have already made landfall, and human shapes skitter over their bows like sailors will descend any moment. While their figures are shadowy, metal glints on their persons. They're armored and ready. Don't they serve Diomedes?

I'm going to ask him, and then see he already has his answer. He was reading my face. Is he afraid of what his father is making me do? How much has he been reading me this entire time?

I can help him. We both need it.

"So Heracles feels fear?"

His eyes narrow, creases spanning all around his brow. His other hand reaches to his war belt.

I tell him, "If those ships don't serve you, we need to find out what they're here for. Ares is up to more than we anticipated."

"So you don't know anything?"

I'm going to tell him what I know: that we can't trust the God of War. Diomedes has to know what his father is capable of. We are in this together—

He releases his grip and kicks me in the chest. He shoves his heel with all his weight, the clap of sole on sternum like a drumbeat that jolts all my thoughts. He's flinging me down to the mares, who stand on their hind legs, snapping their jaws for more hunks of my flesh.

He lets me go.

But I don't let him go. My fingers stay clasped around his palm, whether he wants me or not. He gapes, trying to shake his arm, too late. I'm too startled to release him, and we go toppling into the crater together. The mares whinny with excitement for their meal.

Hera 35

My avatar hasn't been this much taller than Ares in ages. I tower over him until I shouldn't fit under these ceilings, kicking his imitation throne aside. The charred blade darkens as I swing it through the space, making him totter backward. His eyes latch onto Aphrodite, who has already turned herself into a dove and flutters against the ceiling. She is out of here. It's up to the God of War to fight back against his mother.

"Mom!"

"Don't call me that. Zeus never called Kronos 'Papa.' I'm going to swallow you whole, my baby boy."

I make another wide swipe that makes him throw himself to the ground. Every time I move to slash, I hesitate with my bicep up in the air, so that it couldn't be more obvious where it's coming from. I want the little shit to dodge.

Come on, little godling pretending to be his daddy. You're not Zeus. Take this sword from me and do something you'll regret. A regret that will make you a better person for the rest of your life.

"Stop this!"

He yells, but he doesn't come for the sword in my hands. He lunges for his throne. Is being like his daddy that precious to him? Pathetic.

Both of his hands wrap around the back of the throne and he hefts it up. In the middle of my next swing, he bats the blade aside with the seat. The next moment, he's up on his feet, wielding the Throne of Olympos like a club.

All right, his father might be proud of that. I'm almost proud.

Crown of olive branches askew, falling over one earlobe and sending his black curls spilling over his eyes, he says, "You're making me—"

No, I'm not listening to anyone tell me what I make them do. I reach back and then stab forward, as obvious a move as I've made in my life. He has to swing the throne down, hitting the flat of the blade and nearly knocking it out of my grip. He starts to stand a little taller, like he's remembering his power. This is the right time.

"Athena would have disarmed me."

His face buckles, jaw shooting up, eyes locking on me. That hurt worse than being impaled, didn't it?

"When I'm done with you, she'll be the only God of War. Like it always should have been. You were always—"

The throne. I couldn't avoid his swing if I wanted to. The throne spins around like it's trapped in a tornado, and he dashes the wood against my head. I forgot I was wearing my diadem until it clatters against the marble floor, amid a shower of splintered wood and bent gold plates. He destroyed the whole thing over my head.

And I don't fall. I stand straight as order itself, locking my gaze onto his.

"Is that all the King of the Gods has in him?"

Wrapping both hands around the tang, I direct the tip of the sword at him. I rear back, letting him see this coming. His hands are empty, the remains of the throne crumbling in them. He only has one choice.

Shrieking, I drive toward him. He's going to have to catch the sword and wrench it from me. We both know what he'll do with it once he gets hold of it.

This is how I make you a better god, my baby boy. Reign, over my dead body.

Heracles 35

Demanding neighs fill the air, and hooves beat toward us before we even land. The whole weight of the earth hits me in the ribs, and all I can do is cradle Diomedes, trying to soften his fall. If he dies, his army will riot and we'll have a real war. He twists and curses against me, then curses louder at the sight of the mares. From every angle, his horses dart in, trying to bite at him. No one is loyal down here.

This is what Ares wants, isn't it?

So I shove the man aside, and catch the nearest mare by the scruff of her neck, from behind her head so she can't thrash and get another bite on me. My arm is still bleeding from the first time one of these got at me, and it's inspiration enough to force her around, so that her flank is a shield against any other approaching horses.

I tell him, "Call them off."

"Call them off?"

Two more mares leap up, kicking their forelegs out against the first's hide, trying to climb her. At least they don't eat each other. The blood of their breakfast has dried into a dark scarlet on their muzzles, cracking and flaking away like gory dust. They keep trying to work around this one mare, no matter which direction I hold her. They'll find a way around soon. All those wide horse eyes fixate upon us.

"Right."

I hear the *shlick* of metal against hide, and just barely see Diomedes's dagger. I want to warn him he can't fight them all, but he's not coming at the mare. I turn my side into him, feeling the slender agony of the blade scraping my shoulder. Any slower and he'd have stuck me between the ribs. Even now? Why is he doing this?

Diomedes twists his wrist, trying to slice his dagger deeper into my shoulder, like he'll carve off the arm that's holding the mares at bay.

"Stop!" I beg him, even as I push that shoulder into him, knocking him against the wall. The shield of a horse is failing, several mares squirming over her back and biting at us. One gets my hair in her teeth and jerks a clump of it away.

How do I hold them all? How do I keep the mares from devouring us and keep him from giving his father what he wants? Why am I not strong enough?

"Make it look good!"

His voice, like he thinks he's mocking me. His proud expression, as he's fumbling to pull the dagger back and stab me again. Like he's fooled me, like he hasn't submitted to be a tool in someone's game. The chill pity in my chest nearly makes me apologize to him, for letting him be himself.

Instead, I grab him around the waist and hurl him like a toy. He doesn't know what's happening until he's flying out of the crater, up to safety. I hope he doesn't land on his dagger.

A mare darts in while my arm is still up, and it snaps its teeth onto my wrist. I howl and yank back, but three more mares skitter over her, hooves flailing, strings of saliva dripping from their loose lips. Their fetid breath smothers me as I try to force them all back, but no matter which way I push, they spill to the side and keep coming.

Two great horns shove into the crater, black as pitch, brushing the mares aside like they're puppies. Above are the weary eyes of the Bull of Crete, who tilts his head and sticks one horn under my armpit. He lifts me like I'm nothing. I shake my head the entire time, begging him not to get involved. Begging the others not to join this fight. I can't have more blood. We'll only make Diomedes worse.

They're all here. The Bull and the Hind, Logy, Purrseus, and Boar. They make a semicircle, all of their backs to me, like they know how ashamed I should be. Like I don't deserve to see their faces.

That's not it. They're facing toward a host of bronze-tipped spears on long shafts. The warriors in front are stocky, half-naked, all ready to drive forward. Three have their spear tips pointed at Diomedes's neck, forcing him to remain sitting on the ground like a child. Have his soldiers turned on him?

As this host of warriors fills the battlefield, many of them block the archers as well, threatening to advance on them if they loose a single arrow. They've come streaming off of the ships. These are the sailors who swept in while I was dealing with the mares.

Though my shoulder is killing me, I catch the Bull by the back of his neck, and Purrseus by his mane, physically imploring them to stand down. I'd rather end my life down in that pit of mares than give Ares this.

Knowing it can't work, I look across all those bronze spear tips, searching for eyes. Searching for a human face who can listen.

I tell them, "I don't want to hurt you."

"You don't? How blessed we are."

A woman's tone, smoky, with the faint hint of warmth. Like the voice of the last hot coal in a fire.

Hearing her makes me realize that all of these warriors holding weapons on us are women. I've never seen a ship sailed exclusively by women soldiers before, much less three such ships. I never thought Ares would empower so many like this.

Two banks of spearwomen part, allowing the speaker through. Her hair is frizzy and wild, and her eyes are like beads of topaz. She is spectacularly fat, her chest and belly bound up in a girdle lined with bone. Around her hips is a war belt with familiar markings.

All of my family rear up. I can feel Purrseus getting ready to dive out of my grip.

The large woman says, "You're going to want to make those animals stand down."

I stare at her war belt. Yes, those bronze plates have the signs of serpents—signs of Ares.

It feels like there's nothing of me left. I don't want to fight, but I don't have much peace left in me either. The ghosts of words pass my lips.

"Why did Ares send you?"

"Ares? I'm not here for him."

Then I catch Diomedes looking at her, almost sheepish. Like he recognizes her, and rues the recognition. Who is she? That's what I mean to ask her. Except it comes out, "Then why are you here?"

"Your wife asked me to find you."

I t happened, didn't it?

He saw my desperate thrust before I came at him. The God of War saw it coming, and knew every way to avoid it. So he caught my arms, and with one mighty hand wrenched the weapon from me. He drove the sword through my heart. Isn't that what happened?

"No."

Granny? Why didn't he take the sword from me?

"No, no, no."

He got a hand on my wrists, yes, but too late to slow the plunge. The point bit him, all the bronze fibers along the edges snapping off as the length of the blade drove into his belly.

Even now his flesh parts like a waiting mouth, like he welcomes this meal of pain inside himself. My son's warm blood speckles my hands, and it melts my grip. I lose the sword and step away, shaking my head, refusing to see this. This can't be happening.

His hands grab onto air, like someone will keep him aloft. Blood draws perverse arcs along his side and down his hip, like his body is too great for anything to wholly paint. His feet cross each other, and he tumbles down to the marble, onto his ruined throne. He sits in it for the first and final time, the king of broken things.

I reach for him, and my arms are too short. My hands too small. "This isn't what I wanted."

His smirk is smaller than his wound. Ares puts a hand onto the tang; he's ready to draw it from the scabbard that he's made out of himself.

"I won."

"No. No, you can survive that."

"Go ahead," he says. "Swallow me whole. I promise I'm not a rock disguised as a baby."

He doesn't sound afraid. His tone is mocking me. Mocking my whole plan to sacrifice myself in a lesson to make him a better god.

I ask, "How did you win?"

His hand leaves the weapon, gesturing to the only exit in his temple. "Go to your marble rim. Go watch your favorite mortal. That one who might as well be your son."

I can't look at the exit. Can't even contemplate leaving this place. Leaving him.

"You are my son."

He says, "Eventually, he was going to find out it was you. We couldn't hide it forever. Especially not after Dad gets back, whenever he does."

It doesn't make sense. Granny, what is he imagining? That me mauling him in a fight is somehow going to bring his father home?

Ares goes on. "If I told you, you would've stopped me. Heracles does strange things to your reasoning. So I let you fixate on me. Come fight me while what has to happen . . . happens."

"What are you saying?"

"I made Heracles think it was his own idea. I demanded violence and war. Why? Because of course he'd refuse the demands of his enemy. He disobeyed me all the way into peace. With each day, his insistence on peace felt more like righteous defiance. Now he thinks not getting revenge is a virtue. Now all his strength is useless."

It's the hollowest laugh I've ever heard. How dare it echo in this place?

I ask, "You were toying with him and me?"

"It was inevitable that he'd learn it was you. All of us can only fool him for so long. And with his strength, he would've knocked over Mount Olympos to get at you. But now, when he figures it out, he'll still think harming the one who did this to him is wrong. He'll refuse to fight you, no matter what it does to him. His strength will be useless. And you'll be safe." Another croak of a laugh. "Let's see Athena top that."

I kneel before my son, less sure than ever which of us was stabbed. I can feel the blade in my heart, even though it's so obviously sheathed in his skin.

I ask, "Why did you do all of this?"

When did he become the one holding my gaze? I want to look away from the soft, dripping wax heat of his expression.

"Because a veteran loves his mother."

Down from the ceiling flutters a dove, Aphrodite, gray of belly and pearly white everywhere else. Her avatar is so tiny, and yet she nudges her way under his right hand, and she lifts him up. He groans, thighs quivering like jelly, and rises up until he and I are at eye level. Have we ever been the same height before?

He holds an arm over the embedded sword, keeping it still. It's only as he limps past me, as blood pat-pat-patters on the marble floor, that I recognize the wound I gave him. My son is bleeding from the same place his father was, on the last day he left me behind.

That wound. Did Ares let me strike him there because it would make me freeze up? Or has that wound followed me across time?

It plagues my thoughts as I follow them out of the chamber and flee to the marble rim. I have to see what my son has been hiding from me. I see the melee, the frothing-mouthed mares, and foreign ships landing in Thrace. So many archers and spear-wielders and creatures.

Amid them all is that unique, honeyed warmth. That sucking, false vacuum of joy. None of the mortals down there see her. What is Até doing down there?

In Thebes they tell stories that the Amazons all cut off one breast to better shoulder their quivers of arrows. This is not the last untrue thing I've believed. Most of the women aboard these ships still have both breasts, save a couple of women who were born as men and have little chest to speak of. Altogether, few carry bows. They prefer these long, light spears, and they use them well enough to create a standoff with a whole team of monsters, so I can't say they made the wrong choice.

Boar announces, "Boar is not entering any of those ships. Too many hunters. You can't trust they won't see us as prey."

Queen Hippolyta gives him a dull expression, flicking the fingernails of one hand against the roundness of her left cheek. She is the large woman who commanded us to cease fighting before. "Fortunately, this invitation is for one. You can leave your band on the shore for an hour."

I want to make peace with Boar and the others. Calm them down. Logy rears up before I can dicker about it.

"Go," says Logy. "Follow the queen and see your wife. Do some human things. Most of us would rather stay out here and wrangle these flesh-eating mares."

I hesitate over Logy. "You're sure?"

"Absolutely. Somebody's got to teach those horses who it's polite to chew on. But observe whatever you can on that ship. The Amazons are secluded, and most information about them is heavily biased. I'm going to need you to tell me *everything*."

Boar lets me go, too, though he speaks no further. Instead of saying goodbye, he touches my shoulder in a way that gives me a pang of guilt. I wonder if, aboard one of those ships, Megara is watching that touch.

Then Queen Hippolyta is the one touching my shoulder. She takes me below the decks of her ship, into a private cabin, and jams a poultice against the dagger wound, followed by some colorful language for having let myself get injured. She doesn't even know that I literally did. Did I want Diomedes to kill me and end everything? If she'd arrived just in time to witness that, I'd spend all my time in the underworld in shame.

With the worst of the bleeding stopped, Hippolyta produces a basin of water and a rough cloth. I reach for the basin; it smells saltless, and shimmers differently than the sea, as though the Amazons have traveled with supplies of fresh water just for washing. That doesn't seem possible. A lot of things don't seem possible right now.

Hippolyta pushes my hands away, refusing to let me wash myself. I feel like a child as she works at my feet with a coarse stone, the fat of her arms jiggling. Then she digs into the creases and calluses with her fingernails. There is always more dirt.

"I think you have four different cities caked between these two toes," she says, her tone too bemused to befit a ruler. King Amphitryon of Thebes never treated guests this well. It makes me yearn to reciprocate, and I know she won't let me. My eyes fall to the bronze plates of her war belt, and I instinctively fear if I look too long, she'll offer it to me. My body tenses. It doesn't feel right, taking so much from anyone.

She must see the reticence in my face. "Your wife wants you tended to."

I ask, "Does the Queen of the Amazons often attend to the cleanliness of strangers? And go retrieve errant husbands?"

"No more frequently than the sons of Zeus go on such winding adventures that finding them is a pain in the ass." She rubs her hands in the basin. "That makes both of us exceptions."

I want to smile, and my lips are too weak. I find myself wondering about exceptions.

"Megara wants me bathed?"

"She asks very little."

"She'd make a queen do this? Why doesn't she do it herself?"

For the first time, she averts her eyes. "That's for her to say. Dry yourself."

The mare bites on my arm. The gash on my forehead from the giant birds. The dagger wound on my shoulder, which now feels like a finger is trying to stroke it whenever I tense my neck. Hippolyta finds a wound on my calf that looks like an arrow passed through it, and neither of us can explain it.

Everything is tended. I go through with this as though I am dressing for a reception. Instead of fine robes and laurels for my brow, I am hiding wounds. Megara deserves that much.

The bandages are the only clothing that adorns me. I walk under the beating sun, squinting against the light for a glimpse of her. Hippolyta takes me across the deck, then across a plank to a second ship. That's where she waits.

Her black hair is now streaked with gray, and somehow the rest of her hair has darkened. So has the flesh around her eyes. Her lips keep twisting, unable to settle on an expression, perhaps wrestling with words.

She smells the same as ever, though. She smells like hard work.

She leans into me, and holds me briefly. So briefly that before I can touch her in return, she is away from me. I forget how to say hello to her.

Her eyes dance over my injures. Her voice is too measured. "Alcides."

I almost greet her as "Mommy," because all I can think is Little Deicoon can't.

I muster, "I missed you."

She is at my nephew's side. They hold each other unusually close, although it may be usual for them now after all their travel squeezing onto a chariot together. Iolaus has filled out, thicker shoulders and legs, hair shorn around his ears to reveal how boyish his face still is. His father must be proud. He could be a statue of Apollo, or one of Apollo's lovers.

It's Hippolyta who sits first, yawning and spreading her knees like nobody else needs to fit on the deck. "You were right, Megara. Your foolish husband was going to war with Ares."

That ignites something in Megara, her eyes widening like I might start swinging swords here and now. "It's not him, Alcides. Ares didn't make you . . . didn't do this to us."

I tell her, "I know it's hard to believe. But Ares came to me in person. He confessed."

Iolaus steps a little closer to my side. "Uncle, this is going to sound strange. But another Olympian made him deceive you. They've been hiding from us all along. We can prove it."

He takes one of Megara's hands in his own. They squeeze each other's fingers in a way that makes mine twitch with envy. I don't remember how to touch anyone like that. How badly I want to bring affection to Megara's hand.

I need to focus. I rub at my eyes, and try to listen. Try to be open to his words. But I know what I saw. I know Ares is out there.

Megara only sits as close to me as Iolaus will go. They rest together, and she produces a small parcel from a rough hide bag. With the parcel still wrapped, she strokes over it, like it needs to be coaxed into showing itself.

She says, "While you had the attention of Olympos, Iolaus and I traveled. We tried to pry out their secrets while they were distracted."

"You didn't risk your safety, did you?"

I only know how ridiculous that sounds when I feel the bandage on my forehead crumple up. They could berate me until sunset.

Megara's voice goes chilly. "We all did what we had to."

Iolaus has forced optimism in his voice. "In our travels, we found someone the gods had tried to kill and failed to. It was amazing."

"My great-aunt," says Hippolyta, reclining on her bench. Her voice has a joy I'd forgotten was possible. "We were separated a long time ago, in a battle with Minyan raiders. I spent half my life thinking she was dead, and then these two came into our lands with her between them."

Megara reaches out, and touches fingertips with Hippolyta. Megara says, "She is a very wizened woman. An oracle."

Hippolyta adds, "The only oracle ever born to the Amazons. We'll never lose her again."

Megara sinks her fingers into the lip of the parcel, and starts to pull the hide flap open. "The Amazons were so grateful that they've done us some favors. The oracle herself had some insight into what happened to our family."

Why does the back of my neck prickle? Like the sun itself is leaning down onto my scalp? I say, "I already consulted the Oracle at Delphi. Who could be more trustworthy?"

Iolaus says, "Don't you see that it was a gift from the gods that we found her alive at all?"

"And this oracle had met furies before," Megara continues, her voice hardening, like she feels the same heat as I do, and refuses it. "And she gave us a gift. A stone said to be the last eye from a dying titan, cut from her head before she perished. The rest of her is in Tartarus. But this eye persists here, in our world, and still sees. It sees the truth."

She finishes unwrapping the crystalline ball. It's so glossy it's hard to believe it isn't covered in tears, or that film that surrounds the human eye. Mists swirl under its arcane surface. Looking upon it, immediately I know this isn't something I'm supposed to see.

I ask, "If this eye is so important, wouldn't the labors the Oracle at Delphi sent me on have pointed me toward it?"

Megara and Iolaus look at each other like neither wants to say it. That's what convinces me I'm wrong. I've been wrong so many times. Too often not to trust them now.

"Alcides?" Megara tenses her fingers over the crystalline eye's surface. "I think you couldn't have found it. Not if you walked the world for the rest of your life looking for it and knew what it was. Because the gods were misleading you. We only found this because they were distracted by you."

I turn my head away from them, out to the sea, where nobody stands. Out in the direction of Mount Olympos. I never thought about deceitful omens.

Megara says, "I couldn't look into this thing's gaze. To see what's in its depths. I kept trying." She takes a hand from the eye and touches a gray streak in her hair. "But I couldn't."

Iolaus says, "I did it. I couldn't look into it for long, but I could tell it wasn't Ares. It was the same day as we heard you were going to war with him, and we begged Hippolyta to get us here in time. We had to show you. Because I think you'll know who this is."

Megara cups the eye and lifts it toward me like it's a palmful of water to refresh me. Why do I want to see Ares's quill-plumed helm? Why do I crave the simplicity of continuing to face him, instead of the truth they've toiled to bring to me?

I can't look away. Not with Megara and Iolaus's gazes hanging off of me. I rub my eyes, and peer down at the figure in the stone eye.

Hera 37

I take inspiration from the Amazons and surround Até with spears. And I mean every bit of her—every strand of her hair, every pore on her ass, every relaxed iota of her posture gets a sharp tip pointed right at it. This armory of threats is my new avatar. She isn't going anywhere.

The Amazons can't see her. She stands unseen on their ship, between two rays of sunshine. If she was visible, I bet she'd pose as one of them, to feel superior as she snooped. It's easier, going unknown among the mortals. I don't know what I want them to know yet—I just know she isn't going to reveal shit to anyone today. If she squeezes out a single omen, all the Amazons will find is a bloody smear on their planks.

And she has the gall to get giddy, squirming amid the nest of spears, even letting a few of them poke into her. Her smile is equally proud and understated, like a cat who thinks it's going to be petted.

"Hera, baby, how much do you love me?"

"You?" I say, restraining myself from impaling her a thousand times. "You talked my son into this mess? You dragged out Heracles's whole ordeal?"

Até heaves a put-upon sigh, and reflexively I pull several of the spears from around her face, letting her dip her head. She's giving me the eyes. This is going to be a squabble.

She says, "Let's be clear: Ares sought *me* out! I still can't get into Olympos. This started with him. He came to me because he wanted me to talk him into something. He knows what you know."

"Which is?"

"That I always have a plan."

I hate her tone, making it sound like I've been in on this, too. She deserves a couple of impalements just for that. "You talked Ares into all of this. Your plan was to make Heracles and Ares fight to the death?"

"No way. I know you're protective of your kids. It was never going to get that far. And look: it didn't. Can I?"

She shrugs a shoulder, asking for space that she knows she can have. The spears would have shredded her tanned and thin-skinned avatar if I didn't pull them back subtly, letting her shoulder bob unharmed. No, I don't want to hurt her. I still have so much to make up to her. So of course, I dispel the spears and let her free.

For the moment, anyway.

Now freed, she skips right over to me, gesturing at the party gawking at that orb, and then at all the Amazons and Thracians and monsters negotiating on the beach. "See? Heracles is here, the monsters are liberating those sweet mares, Diomedes is fucking off back to his stronghold, and Ares is, what? I assume somewhere in a marble bedroom inventing a new position with Aphrodite. Everybody's alive and happy."

So the mastermind didn't account for everything. I nearly slew my son today. And that was because of the plan she set in motion. I summon all my poise to remain measured with her.

"You turned my son against me."

"Come on. We leaned into the tradition of Olympians fucking each other over to fool you. You know he's always going to be loyal to you until they run out of wars."

A veteran loves his mother. It's so haunting I almost repeat it out loud.

Até cups my cheeks, peering into my eyes with too much sincerity to be healthy for any one deity. "We had to mess with you a little. You wouldn't let us get away with this until you saw how wrong you were."

I give her a tone to remind her those spears can return anytime. "Is that so? And what was I wrong about?"

"This is all Zeus's fault, and he messed with you until you believed otherwise. He's trying to break you. But this is how we rescue the Queen of Olympos. Follow me," she says, miming walking her fingers over toward Heracles's family. "So first I followed Megara and that stud nephew around for a while. They were struggling at various great temples, trying to bait the gods into striking them down, figuring only the one who cursed Heracles would come after them. It didn't work, but all that existential peril turned out to be a major turn-on for them both."

I squint at her, and at Megara. "A major what?"

Except Até is too excited, and her pitch keeps building, like a punchline is coming. "So what I did was pretended to be the lost Oracle of the Amazons. Classic crone-in-a-cloak shit we used to do to send so many pilgrims on adventures. The real oracle is long dead because apparently her foresight sucked and she didn't see raiders coming. I pretended to have survived this whole huge ordeal, and had them heroically reunite me with my Amazonian sisters, and Hippolyta cried into my hair, and everybody was so elated that they all completely bought the reward I gave them."

Megara cups the orb in her palms like it's an offering to the gods. Something parents would sacrifice for their children. For now the stone is foggy, like unloved quartz carved into a sphere. But its cloudy interior shifts, promising to reveal things that Até has set in motion.

I ask, "What is that thing, anyway?"

She brushes a knuckle across her lips as though to prove her smile can't be killed. "That's a lump of pig shit from Hippolyta's own farm. With a little of my influence, all the mortals see it as a conduit of truth. As reward for rescuing the legendary oracle, she bestowed to them a seeing stone that will reveal which god had destroyed their shitty little family."

I could swipe the stone into the sea. Of course, Heracles would take anything like that as a sign of a god covering up truth, and dive in after it. Options are limited here.

I click my teeth together. "And you're going to make it reveal that Zeus was the one who sent Granny?"

She holds her arms out to me, clearly expecting a hug. "See? This is why we make a great team."

I need to tell her to stop. I know better than to let this keep going. But Até is drunk on her narrative, and I need to know how dark she'll make all of this.

So I gesture for her to go on.

Unhugged, Até mimes her fingers walking over toward Heracles. She points at the bandage on his forehead. "When this little shit gets all pissed about his daddy being the killer? That's when I'm going to appear as an Amazon belowdecks, and tell all the others that he's molesting Hippolyta. He's the son of Zeus. They all know he's capable. He's going to have to kill every last one of them to get ashore alive. And better yet, as soon as Amazons start charging, every monster on the shore is going to charge in here. Anybody Heracles doesn't kill, they will. I don't know whether the Lion of Nemea or that boar weirdo loves him more, but they'll sink a fleet for him. It'll be a massacre."

I want to say that Heracles doesn't deserve that. But my tongue goes to the last remnant of his family. It's where his concern would lie. For some reason, that matters.

"You don't care that his wife would die in all that, too?"

Finally I get a sour expression out of her, a pout like she's disappointed in me. "Is this because you're Goddess of Mothers? Come on, you hate adulterers. Look at Megara basically sitting on that stud nephew's lap. Do you know how many times she's fucked him since she's been apart from Heracles?"

I could know the truth about Megara and Iolaus in an instant. I could read the attachment between them. Get Athena to pour out their whole truth to me. But Até isn't lying about this, is she? The prospect pricks me, like a cold spear tip in the base of my spine.

Eventually I say, "No. Because I haven't had my attention on her, either."

"That's not surprising. I figured if you were watching, you would've showed up sooner. Heracles has been a great distraction. But let's make up for lost time. Let's get some revenge on his wife first. Want to set her on fire, pubic hair first? That's a classic."

All those labors. All those monsters. Climbing mountains, getting dashed into craters. He said it was to get justice for his sons, but it was always about getting justice for a mother who had motherhood stolen from her. He's covered in wounds, and right now he's sadder for her than for himself.

There was a time when I would have wanted to drown her and everyone on this ship to get revenge.

If I told Até, she'd chide me for changing. Where did the old Hera go?

She went nowhere. She's right here. She's right here, but she's wiser.

I say, "Tell me something."

"Anything! But let's be quick, because they're going to ask the pig shit orb for a god soon and I need to set up Zeus."

"Ares agreed to you fooling Heracles into thinking it was Zeus?" I ask her, because I know the answer.

Her expression shows she knows that I know.

Até bites the tip of her thumb. "Technically, I may have told him that I was going to frame somebody else. Possibly Athena. But what's he going to do? Declare war on me? Even if he does, it's worth it to do this for you."

Ares didn't say Heracles would go for Athena. He was sure that Heracles would figure out it was me, sooner or later. So maybe he didn't trust Até's schemes, either. That hurts, too, like another spear tip against my flesh. Because I want to trust Até.

I let some of that exhausted pain waft into my voice. "Até?"

"Yes?"

"When Ares confronted Heracles, he was actually interrupting me. I was on my way to tell him the truth."

Her arms tense, like she wants to hug onto me this time. "Well, I'm glad we stopped you."

"Family is accountable, Até."

"What does that mean?"

I pull my voice together, like so many loose branches crushed in a strap. "Do not harm a single mortal on this ship. Do not let anyone from the shore harm them, either. This isn't their fault."

The tip of her tongue swipes her bottom lip, like she tastes mischief. "You want me to set up another Olympian? Please tell me you're sending Heracles after Athena. I never liked her."

"I've always loved you. It's why I kept you close. For ages you were my revenge. My Goddess of Ruin."

I see the goosebumps flying across her flesh. "Hera? What are we doing?"

"You want to see the Queen of Olympos in her full glory? Then don't hide me. Don't shield me from what I did. Be my Goddess of Ruin. Ruin me."

Alcides 37

I stumble away from them with the heels of both palms digging into my face, rubbing my eyes flat to blot it out. The diadem that was bright as the sun? Robes so long and radiant, and eyes carrying the weight of all mothers?

They may as well have poured boiling tar into my mind. This is a trick. I'm being mocked again, just as when Ares pretended to be the killer. I swing wildly, hip striking the edge of the ship and nearly plunging overboard.

It's not her. Not family itself. Why would the one who loves children the most take mine? Why would the one who protects babies kill them in a home?

You'd never do such a thing. You couldn't. My whole life has been for you. They're all wrong, and I can't breathe. I keep clawing at my throat, squeezing at it, trying to remember how it opens. How do you forget something like breathing?

When I spill off of the ship, the Amazons pour aboard. They are the wine returning to the bottle, swarming around their queen, and around my wife and nephew. Around that lying stone eye.

The only people anywhere near my part of the shore are the monsters. The Hind nuzzling at the Bull, with Purrseus padding around them and toward me, his head low, sniffing like I must smell heartbroken to him. Somewhere behind them is Logy, asking a hundred questions at once.

It's Boar who gets to me first, carrying a bone with a wide hunk of pink meat so large he rests it over his shoulder. His other hand reaches for me.

"Come. Eat."

I used to roast meat with my boys. They were old enough to withhold portions to sacrifice to you. They pretended they were inviting you to dinner.

Take it. Take all the dinners I was ever to have in the rest of my days. Make this not true.

Boar gestures to my mouth with the stripped end of the bone. "You haven't eaten in too long. You've extended yourself too far. Boar took this from the Thracians. They say it's the most flavorful cut, and it's full of blood and everything that will restore you. So come. Cook your meat."

I say, "No."

"Or you can eat it raw. Boar prefers raw meat."

Purrseus pads closer, and I see a paw sticking out of a fire. The smell of skin and fur roasting as my son reaches for me. Family in need of a god, too late.

I look to Logy, and I see that all the questions that were in their face have been replaced. They already know the answers. I'm so obvious. Was it always so obvious?

I tell them, "An oracle says it was Hera. But it's not true. It isn't true. It can't be Hera."

Am I yelling? I can't hear my voice.

At Hera's name, the Bull of Crete bolts forward, horns lowering until they gouge the ground between us. His glossy eyes shine darkly into me. His air is stark, nostrils tense, refusing to breathe. It's like just hearing this thought has stopped his heart.

I can't fathom what he wants to express. I'm bound there, in his fright.

Boar says, "Of course it's not her."

I say, "I said it's not."

Boar tilts his head down, so that the dead eyes of his cowl stare me in the face. He steps around the Bull's great horns, reaching for me. "Yes. The gods deceive all the time. It is how they hunt. But you saw through their deception."

My legs make some mistake, and I fall to my knees in the sand. Sand mixed with salt from the battlefield and the sea. So much salt that it bites into the creases of my knees.

"What do I do now?"

Boar touches me. That delicate touch, that feels like it should be saved for privacy, on the bondage over my shoulder. As though he would dig the wound out of me. Pull the wound away and leave me whole.

And Boar says, "We'll find the god who's truly responsible. We'll get you the truth you need. First, you eat."

Part Four

The Peace

Hera 38

All those treacherous gods sent an audience larger than any army in the Aegean Sea to witness Ares conquer Heracles, and to see Ares rise to the throne as King of Olympos. People traveled from all across civilization for this. They aren't getting that revelation today.

But I'm not going to waste an audience.

Até moves in a thousand forms. She snakes her way through every nook and encampment. She is an old soup cook with a bottomless pot, dishing out spicy goat broth and slander about what an asshole I've been. She is a weary crone who always knew Queen Hera despised heroes even when they were slumbering in their cribs. She is a king from an island no one has heard of, who was there in Thebes the day Heracles's family was struck down, and who has never forgotten seeing my statue's visage twist into a smile as the children burned.

Her gossiping isn't halfway done before the crowds take up her work for her. All mortals need is a story, and then they do the work. They ruin me.

In the guise of a gaunt and furious Amazon, Até is about to announce what the titan's eye showed her aboard Hippolyta's ship, when she shrieks in unexpected pain. From nowhere, Ares grabs her by the hair and drags her to the divine plane. He tears her from the physical world, shredding her guise and forcing her into our realm, leaving all the mortals who'd turned to look at her wondering what miracle they witnessed. None of them know they just witnessed a tantrum.

Up on Olympos, Ares shakes her like a rattle. Being here unbidden by the monarch means her avatar immediately starts falling apart, her pretty tanned skin flaking away like clay. Olympos will kill anything not allowed here, and she's banished.

Ares bellows at her, "That wasn't our deal!"

The blunt sword is still embedded in the flesh of his side, the blood dried and turned to serpents that rise and hiss with his breathing. He always liked snakes.

"Hey! Hey!" Até says, prying at his fingers. Her hands are feeble, especially with Olympos's curse attacking her. "I didn't want to screw you over!"

"You know what happens to people who turn on me?"

I'm so done with all their plotting. Am I going to wrestle her free of the God of War?

No.

Instead I dart to his side and grip the tang of the sword. His entire avatar goes rigid with the sting, and before he can resist, I yank the sword out. The red snakes gasp and hiss, more blood flowing from his side. He loses his grip and staggers, but doesn't fall to a knee.

Even by the standards of gods, this is not what happens when someone is hewn with a sword. I lift the blade up, still murky with char from the forge, a few fibers of bronze sticking to the edges. It wasn't sharpened. It shouldn't have needed to be. Hephaistos designed this to cut down any foe. That it didn't even stop Ares from raging after Até makes me wonder. Did Hephaistos deliberately forge a faulty weapon to screw over all our scheming against each other?

He's a clever tinkerer. Ares would see that as a betrayal, even if the betrayal meant he survived.

Ares barks at me, "Stop. This is our business."

Rather than do battle, I hold the sword up, one hand on the tang and the other on the tip. Before their eyes, I slam it down over my knee. It snaps like metal kindling.

I tell him, "You want to know what happens when a goddess betrays you? She gets promoted."

Até sounds as baffled as Ares. "What?"

"You're unbanished from Olympos. You're in my entourage. I need you around."

"No," says Ares, standing up straighter, causing his wound to open further. The blood becomes serpents before it can even leave his flesh, and they all hiss at me in that juvenile way of his. "She remains in the

mortal world until she fixes this shit. Your scheming is going to rile Heracles up and make him dangerous again. He needs to be put down."

"Good news, Heaven," I say without thinking. It bubbles up out of
me like fresh bile. I take on the swagger of my dipshit husband, spitting
irony at my son. "I invented this new thing called 'accountability.' If you
want to be King of Olympos someday, you'd better study it. For now, I'm
the fucking queen and I say which gods walk the marble halls. You are
lucky I don't kick you out."

"I'm protecting you. You've lost yourself and you need us."

"I do need you, but not to scheme behind my back." That sounds
more like Zeus than I want to, too. I need to wash my mouth out with lye
and seawater after this. "You're trying to correct the wrong mistakes. I
fucked up, and I know I fucked up. I'm unfucking it. Your manipulations
didn't help anything. You hurt a grieving father worse than he was hurt
before, and you made me feel even more alone."

"I . . ." Even the snakes at his side go still. Several slither back inside
him. They look nearly as ashamed as his falling brow. "That's not what
we were doing."

"I don't blame you for resorting to manipulation. What you didn't
learn from Athena, you picked up from your father and me. But I'm dealing with Heracles now. You and Até are going to help me."

Até says, "We are?"

With a tone not unlike a sword shattering over a knee, I tell them
both, "Not by plotting behind my back, though. You two will do what I
tell you, or you'll stay out of it. This isn't your story."

It sounds so righteous that I'm warm for a fraction of a moment.
Then the cold chases after it, the realization that it's not just my story either. I fight not to look across the world for wherever Heracles is lurking
and plotting my death. Accountability will come for me, too. I'm ready
for it.

It's Ares who breaks my concentration. I can tell it's hard for him to
meet my gaze. "What do you want me to do?"

Alcides 38

I sit in wet earth and I'm running away. My eyes dash as fast as they can carry my soul, along the shoulders of my friends, along the tops of the firs that turn to silhouettes in dusk, out beyond where my attention can hold. Anything to be distracted. Any thought that requires not thinking. I pray to a goddess who detests me to teach me how to not be, if even for a moment.

Boar pulls a hunk of meat off a bone and sucks it between his lips, slurping so loud that I can't look away. With his eyes on mine, he tightens his jaw. His jaw's gaze is more intense than his eyes. I watch it, waiting for him to chew and swallow. That bristly, graying beard remains still, the dimple on his cheek so deep it could be a scar.

Why isn't he chewing? How long has he held his mouth like that, refusing to taste his own dinner?

I start to fade again, to reach for thoughtlessness, when a cold nose brushes along the naked crease of my spine. Purrseus returns to our clearing, rubbing against my back instead of stretching before the fire. I'm in the way of his warmth. Cool wetness drips from his muzzle, some flesh that isn't his or mine. It is a white-speckled owl, which he carries by its feet. He lifts it to my mouth, like I'm supposed to try a bite.

That's when I realize how many times Purrseus has visited and left the camp. On my left stinks a heap of offerings. A goat with its throat gashed open. A lynx in the same state, and a calf that has been torn in half. Purrseus has been trying to feed me for hours.

All the calf's legs have been stripped and roasted, and I didn't smell them until now. The bone in Boar's hand is one of those hanks of meat. The still-unchewed morsel in his mouth is one bite of a feast.

I gesture for Purrseus to have a bite off of the three calf's legs still roasting above the fire. He's tall enough to reach any of them without being singed.

He looks at me, owl still dangling from his mouth. I know if he doesn't get what he wants, he'll go hunting again. For the same reason that Boar hasn't chewed a mouthful of meat in an hour.

I stroke Purrseus's mane and kiss at one of his ears. They're all here. The Hind lies on her belly, and Logy curves their length around a quarter-circle of the fireside as though sunning themself. I want to stop thinking, to dissolve like the last light of the setting sun, and they won't let me.

There is no flavor in the food. Chewing it is like chewing my own tongue, hard to recognize that it is in my mouth at all. I tilt my head back and swallow all the same, and in that moment, Boar swallows for the first time.

Logy says, "Welcome back, my friend."

"I don't know where I was."

"We want you to know. We've all agreed. If it comes to it, we'll storm Olympos with you."

I pull my hands to my sides. "All of you?"

"Even the Hind says so, in her prickly way. Hard for Helios to outrun us with her on the battlefield."

The Hind's antler buds are dim. The fire makes her nose and eyes shiny black. She's unthreatened as she watches me. I realize this is the first time I've seen her apart from the Bull of Crete since the day they met.

"Where did the Bull go?"

The Hind turns her head, directing me from our camp. Out in the darkness, beyond the end of the firelight, thumps that great white shape. He could be a mountain, except he's on the move. He paces over pulverized earth, back and forth, toward us, and then away. Each time he turns away, his horns point at a distant mountain, as though part of him wants to rage off and flee to Olympos. But each time, his dark eyes return to us, to me, as though another part of him can't bear to leave us. So odd a sight, to see so enormous a creature torn in twain.

I want to ask what is on his mind. What troubles him so greatly. He's never spoken. I'd still listen. I should go to him. I should rise.

I try to curl my fingers, and I can't. They go weak on my knees. After the birds, and the Bull, and those horses raised to believe they hungered for flesh? The idea of a fist makes me retch dinner.

"I don't want you to fight."

Logy insists, "Even if it was the Queen of Olympos who came for your children. Even if she's who we have to face. You mean that much, Al. To all of us."

"I . . ."

"It wasn't her." It's Boar, his voice like a door slamming shut. "Heracles would know if Hera was hunting him. No one knows her like he does."

When Boar utters your name, the Bull exhales so sharply the air before his nose freezes. Icicles clink to the ground.

Auntie. It can't be you. It couldn't be. My mind starts to sink again at the idea, wanting to drown my thoughts before I hear them.

Because if you are behind this, then I really am at fault for everything, aren't I? Nobody made me a weapon. If I made a family to honor you, and I did it so terribly that you made me destroy it, it's because you thought I never deserved them. I offended family itself. I wasn't just the weapon; I was the cause for which it was unsheathed.

Auntie Hera, I'm sorry if I made you . . .

Purrseus bumps his head against my thigh, and I think I must not be eating enough. Boar touches the bandage behind my shoulder, a touch I don't deserve. Boar doesn't care what I think I deserve.

The Bull resumes his pacing, back and forth, every muscle along his pale back rigid. I can feel his legs wanting to break into a sprint, in one direction or another. He makes the world tremble.

Amid all that thumping, Logy slithers into the light, around the campfire and closer to me and Purrseus's assorted victims. They swallow the dropped owl whole; apparently they like birds. I didn't know. I've never heard a serpent belch before. It's more of a squeak.

"I'm willing to believe it wasn't Hera," says Logy, like a door creaking open. Do they sound like they believe what they're saying? "So we're going to take the answer from her."

I don't know what to say. Boar speaks more sharply than I wish. "Say more."

"Hera and Zeus got married at the very top of the world, in a place only gods can travel to. To celebrate their union, the nymphs and other

Olympians gifted them a tree upon which grew apples with flesh of solid gold. The juice inside the apple retained all possible knowledge. Anyone who chewed their flesh could know anything they pondered. Hera and Zeus each ate an apple to know for certain they truly loved one another. I've always assumed that true love is why they make each other so miserable."

I need a magic apple just to comprehend how a magic apple would work. Eating a thing to learn an answer? It's shameful, but it feels more like Logy is making something up to stave off facing something.

I ask, "You never brought this up before. Are you sure they're real?"

Logy flicks their tongue at the fire once, and then twice. "When you started your labors, I didn't know what you were capable of. I never would have recommended the apples, because even Poseidon's favored heroes drown trying to sail that far off the map. But you need your answer. The apples contain all answers, and they can't be tampered with the way oracles can."

Boar works his jaw, like he's imagining chewing gold. "That must be an observant fruit."

Logy keeps going. "What do you say, Al? Up for another labor?"

He hates doing it, so it's the right choice. My son, the God of War, visits the great Geryon, the three-headed giant so ferocious that he seizes cattle from all, and none dare seek reprisal. The flocks on his island are myriad, poached from any king that any of his three heads set their eyes upon. Geryon's every interaction with the mortal world is war.

And Ares has to tell the giant to calm his ass down and play nice.

I sit on the edge of the marble rim with Até, smirking as my broad-shouldered son imparts the giant to receive his next guest in peace, and to grant unto him whatever animals he requests. Geryon is not permitted to show this guest unkindness out of a single one of his mouths. Every club and spear in his palace must remain resting on the floor.

"If the guest asks why you show such hospitality," Ares says, with an audible loathing for every word he utters, "tell him you are a fellow enemy of Hera."

Penance? That's too grand a word. This is the beginning of Ares being a better God of War. To show that he knows how to make peace meaningful. He was born a grown warrior. Today, he actually grows up. I find myself laughing at how he disparages me, because he hates it far more than I do.

Até says, "You finally got him in line. And all it took was stabbing him?"

I don't mean to sound fond when I say, "He's like his father."

"Maybe if you didn't marry your brother . . ."

I stiffen. "Hey. Don't you judge me. There were twelve people alive back then."

"It's more than that, though, isn't it? King Zeus gets to you like nobody else."

Her words should sound more cutting. Her tone is idle, even distant.

This sort of drama should have her rapt. She better not be plotting something again.

I nudge her with my tone. "Até? Why are you thinking about my family?"

I glance at her shining essence, and find her directed across the land, to where Heracles rides. She's not looking at him in particular, though. It's like she's sorting through his family of monsters, trying to take stock. Down below, the Bull of Crete's horns turn up, almost like he's looking at us.

"I guess family's been on my mind since we reunited." As though nervous, Até's eyes tick from the monster and over to me. "Hey, did you ever track down Granny?"

Alcides 39

One thousand head of red-haired cattle thump along ahead of us, tamed from a life under a three-headed giant who could have hoisted any of them in a hand and bitten their head off if they misbehaved. Tame or not, Purrseus races along their west side, refusing to let them scatter along the streams of plains of the northlands. Boar runs along their east side, keeping up easily, a whip in one hand if they stray. A crack of a whip or a roar from a lion is all it takes to keep the cattle from straying.

I can't imagine any predators daring to pick them off. But Purrseus would love to meet them for dinner.

Logy thought it would be the Bull of Crete who would lead the herd of cattle, but he lags behind, dragging his hooves in the dirt. The Hind drops back to stay with him. I worry he's falling sick, but whenever I look, his dark eyes are right behind my chariot. It's as though he doesn't want to lose sight of me.

We drive the cattle from behind, riding in my chariot. Three of the cattle are eager to be yoked, and to drive it for me. Logy hangs along the rim of the shield, happily sunning themself. A few nodules press out between their scales—we'll have to shave and recauterize again soon. We don't want them to grow more heads and be waylaid by their migraines.

Together, Logy and I share the gorgeous view, cattle with fur the orange of sunset, their haunches swaying and bouncing as they rush ahead. It's like chasing the sun over the edge of the world. Like at any moment we can dive off this mortal plane and find the truth.

Logy turns their triangular head from the cattle to me for a moment. "I didn't expect the giant to be so enthusiastic."

"I guess he was. I've met very few giants to contrast him against."

I look away, to the faint sight of the great Atlas's hands holding up the sky, far to the south. From here, I can't even make out his head. We've got many weeks of riding before we get there. Time I don't have to do anything. It should be relaxing, but . . .

Logy interrupts my thoughts. "It sounded like Geryon would have joined your battle if you asked. I wonder what Atlas would think."

"I'm not interested in putting more lives at risk."

I'm not interested in talking about future conflicts at all, and I tell them through my tone. Thinking about it makes my hands feel too heavy.

A blast of cold air from behind me as the Bull snorts. The chariot fills up with his sour breath. I know this is wearing on everyone, but I need to find out what is eating at the Bull.

"Well," Logy says, clearly angling to keep me talking. "This should keep us out of trouble. There are a lot of states around this region that don't like random visitors. We bribe them with a few cattle, and they'll let us through without a raised fist. We'll probably have plenty to return to Geryon when we get back."

They're trying. Promising me a lack of conflict, because they know. They want to talk about it. It's me who doesn't.

I ask, "You're sure Atlas will help?"

"Either we sail across the seas to the top of the world, which nobody has ever done, or we ask the biggest living thing alive to wade across them for us. Those are the only two options for getting to those apples. I'm telling you, if you want to get one and be alive to eat it? We need Atlas."

I look again upon those upturned hands, holding aloft the heavens. Tendons have strained in their labor since before I was born. Since before Thebes was founded. A punishment for the failure of the titans that outstrips history.

There's an obvious question.

Logy says, "There is the question of payment, though. He's been trapped there all this time. Some particularly robust cattle aren't going to cut it. But I trust we'll come up with something."

They've been thinking the same thing I have. For once, I'm ahead of them.

My right hand still has the deep welt from where the cord dug into it. I turn that hand upward, daring the sky to drop into it.

"He wants relief."

Logy flicks their tongue at my hand, then recoils. "Hang on. What?"

"We're asking Atlas to venture to the top of the world anyway." I hold up my hand until it covers one of Atlas's distant ones. "Someone has to hold the sky aloft in his place. I'm going to offer him time to rest."

"Shit, no. Al, do not trust a titan to come and take the sky back from you. I don't even know if a mortal can hold it up, let alone that once Atlas doesn't have to hold it anymore, there's nothing to force him into ever touching it again. You'd be stuck."

In all our time retrieving the cattle and driving them south, this is the only answer I can think of. I'd hoped Logy would have another answer. But I'd also hoped they wouldn't.

"What else do you offer a suffering man, except relief?"

A deep grunt rolls from behind us, like the Bull is startled. But what else am I to offer Atlas?

"You know if Boar hears this plan, he's going to kick your ass." Logy lays their head flat on the shield, eyes turning to the Bull behind us. Their tongue still flicks at me. "Al? Is this about Atlas, or about our Olympian?"

I don't know what to say to that. The knot between my lungs pulls tighter.

"Is this about adding more time before you have to fight them? Because we're exposing the gods just to point a finger and accuse them. This is what you want, isn't it?"

"I need to do this. For my boys."

I say it, and know it's true, and don't know what I feel about it, beyond tired in a way sleep doesn't cure.

Logy asks, "Even if it's Hera?"

The world rattles so sharply that I think it's just me, in my head or losing my composure and thrashing around. Then the chariot dips, and I have to kick off a foot to steady us from overturning. Ahead of us, a hundred head of cattle jump into the air from the fright of the sudden earthquake.

The cattle are groaning in panic before they hit the ground, and Boar and Purrseus have to rush to keep them together. It's not an earthquake, just the first note of one rather than a chorus of tremors.

Behind us, the Bull of Crete has split the earth wide open with one of his hooves. He's stopped in the path, several lengths back. The Hind stands beside him, sniffing curiously up at his muzzle. He ignores her, remaining still on his spot, his dark eyes cast up.

I pull the reins and slow the chariot to a stop. I'm not leaving him behind.

"What do you see?"

He's not looking up at Atlas's hands. He's pointed in the wrong direction, his horns tilting north, maybe northwest. Mulling the geography makes the knot in my chest wind even tighter. All of Aegean civilization lies back there, but I know what mountain got his attention.

I step off the chariot, reaching for him, to tell him he's safe. This is my fight.

My foot is barely on the ground before the earth shakes again, and the Bull leaps into the sky. He erupts like a volcano, sending dirt spraying in all directions, and becomes a brilliant shock of white shooting through the heavens. I've never even thought of putting my strength into leaping like that.

"Where's he going?"

Logy has no answer, and the Hind isn't speaking. Already the Bull is gone, leaving a wide gulf in the earth where he'd been. A gulf, and the Hind.

She stands there, all four legs stiff, antler buds flickering, like she can't decide whether this is a threat. Like her mind is a candle in the wind.

I join her by the gulf. We can spare a moment. I don't touch her; I just let her know she is not alone. I stay with her until she is ready to move.

Hera 40

"You're making him what he isn't!"

Sound seldom carries from the mortal world across the marble rim, unless an Olympian deliberately wants to hear it. The mightiest floods are muted here, or else we would all be deafened by the constant maelstrom of creation below. So when I hear a voice shrieking up at us, I know there's trouble.

Claws the color of sewage scrape along the marble rim, and then the fingers they belong to reach further up and grab hold. Gray wings like those of a giant bat flutter, forcing their owner up. Granny is home.

"Leave him alone."

Até rushes in first, jumping, both arms outstretched to embrace her. There is no fear in her posture. The Goddess of Ruin has missed her old friend.

But Granny weaves around her, her glowing yellow eyes fastened on me and myself alone. She sticks two clawed fingers out, like the horns of a bull, threatening to gore me.

"Let him be what he is."

I'm beaming. I can't help myself. Laying eyes on her, no matter how angry she is, means too much. I'd let her gore me for the favor of a touch.

"Granny. Welcome home."

Cracks open along her knuckles, and at the corners of her mouth, like the flesh is wearing away a thousand times faster than it would in the mortal world. She's not an Olympian, and her permission must have lapsed. None unbidden can survive.

Still she comes along the marble floors, the claws on her feet clicking. Black bile leaks from lesions that open on the flesh of her feet and ankles, marking her footsteps.

No more. I jerk one fist to the right. "You are welcome in Olympos."

That is all the queen needs to do. Olympos will not harm Granny any further. She could heal the superficial damage to her avatar, if she was paying attention to it.

Instead she stamps up before me, and I make sure our heights are the same. I look her plain in the face, in that mouth streaked with black bile. She still smells like the manure and sweat of the Bull she inhabited.

"Leave him alone!"

"I'm not harming him, Granny. I want to make him whole. He needs to finish this with me. He needs to face me or it'll never be over."

Her shriek surrounds my head, like she speaks from a mouth that is the world. "You're not evil!"

My eyes twitch, but I try not to break her gaze. "I . . . I was. I used you like a tool to destroy his family."

Até comes around her left side, like she might grab one of Granny's wings and pry her away. I gesture for her to stay back. This isn't Até's fight. It's not even mine. It belongs to Granny alone.

"You're tearing him apart! Stop making him what he isn't!"

"I'm trying to make him be himself. All I've done is try to free him from his illusions about me, and let him confront me if he wants. No matter what it costs me."

Spittle flies from her cracked teeth and spatters my chin. I let it stay, and let her yell at me. "Let him be what he wants!"

"You've been with him. Don't you see that I'm guiding him to what he wants? To the truth?"

"No," she says, stamping a foot so hard one of the talons on her feet snaps off and skitters off across the marble. "You're bragging around the world about destroying him. I know you're spreading those lies about yourself. Lies about you as a wicked queen."

"They're not lies. Not really."

"Stop being what you aren't."

I want to explain, and my words all seize up in my throat. They strangle me. The excuse that I'm playing the villain for Heracles's good. That I'm righting a wrong. That I deserve to have the world hate me for what I've done. Self-deprecation soothes guilt, but only temporarily.

Granny can see through it. As I wrestle with my words, she gets even closer, eyes so furiously wide.

"I know what you really are. You're better than this."

"I'm not—" I can't finish. Just her eyes on me chokes me up, and I'm shaking down to my ankles. That scorn from this wonderful woman whom I wronged, scorn in the shape of defending me. I don't deserve this.

"Stop making us what we aren't!"

I can't stand it. I fall to my knees, landing on her broken talon. The heels of my hands press into my eyes, and tears spill down the veins of my wrists. How long have I been crying and not knowing it? I open my mouth to argue, and all I can do is sob. I'm suffocating on stupid feelings that should be beneath me. I force myself to pull it together, and just fall apart worse, clutching at my heart. Fuck. Fuck my weakness.

"Stop!"

I don't know how. I'm blinded, I can barely hear anything over my own insipid wailing. I can't make myself be strong anymore. I fucking killed that man's children, and the weapon I used is telling me to be good to myself. It's me who should be banished from Olympos. What am I doing?

"There."

Granny's voice again, except not at all again. One word, one syllable, calm as a dead ember in a doused fire. I don't know what to do with it.

I don't do anything. Is that what she wanted?

Her long talons tickle along my shoulders, and then through my hair. I'm ready for whatever she's going to do, no matter how she attacks me, no matter how it hurts.

And I'm wrong. I'm not ready for her to hold my head to the rough skin of her chest, and to cradle me. Her chin rests atop my head, and she hums such an infectious tune that I know how everyone she's ever possessed must feel. You can't resist. I can't. For this moment, I stop.

"Don't be what you aren't."

My chin trembles so much it takes a while to get the words out. "Thank you, Granny."

I missed her so badly, and now she's studying my eyes. One murky claw comes up, and it brushes the lower lid of my right eye, like she's gathering morning dew from a lotus.

"Granny?" I can't stop myself from asking. "What are you now? That you choose to be?"

"Tired. Very tired. It is not easy being a bull."

Thankfully Até sniffles, off in her eavesdropping corner, and that gives me permission to do the same. I gesture to the marble rim behind Granny. The endless bench where, once upon a time, we were inseparable.

"I am tired, too," I tell her. "Can we be tired together? Until he gets here?"

Glowing eyes narrow, the only two sources of light in my world, threatening to go out. Studying me. Knowing that wasn't a royal command. It was a request.

We sit together a long time, and Até joins us, and we talk about nothing, forever. This is all I could ever ask to be.

Alcides 40

Of all the impossible things I have done, finding Atlas is the easiest. I simply look where I have always seen him in the sky, and then I walk in that direction. It's a long path, by road and field and sea. Every day of it, I can tell Logy and Boar are waiting for me to say something I'm not ready to say.

This has to be it. This is how I clear your name, Auntie Hera. How I find the end.

For such an enormous being, Atlas lives atop a still more enormous mountain. You would think one so tall could reach the sky from lower down. His mountain is too steep, from all the pieces that have broken off in the ages of adjusting his footing. I have to leave my friends behind and climb alone, feeling Purrseus pacing below, wishing he could help me.

"He was one of the most cunning generals in the war against the Olympians," says Logy. "Be wary. Don't let him fool you into something you'll regret."

Three days and two nights it takes, with the sun growing closer each dawn. Bitter rocks rake at my palms, until little skin is left on them. As I wrap strips of hide around my fingers, I catch myself wishing the climb could last longer. There's a dread in seeing that titan grow closer in my vision. That on the second morning I can see his blue thighs and knees. And it's not for fear of his wrath, but what he'll enable me to do. To have to choose.

I start to pray to you, and physically jerk away from it, nearly falling back down the mountain. As though praying to you is an accidental touch of a boiling pot.

You're innocent. Why am I afraid to ask you for help?

Then I stand before him, directly below his mighty chin. The sky has never seemed so far away as when I stand beneath Atlas, taking in the height of him, the measure of what lies between me and the heavens. And still it is too close. The skies surpass all the treasures of all the kings Papa Zeus has ever blessed, home of every star someone has ever wondered about, like uncounted jewels that fell in the wrong direction, up to a better home than mortals know. Sunless night, twinkling eternal. This close, I can see the beginnings of dawn, and of every day and night the Fates ever sewed into the fabric of our times.

Atlas has the figure of a man, made too great for any set of eyes to see the whole of him. His neck is bent so that the ceiling of creation presses down across his shoulders, his upper back, and his hair. Hands rest with familiarity on the eternity up there. Limbs thick with muscle, his body hairless and flesh gone blue, as though taking on the hues that drip down to him from the world above. Only his beard and nails differ, being the black of the deepest bruises. Only his beard and nails, and his eyes.

Those great bruise-colored eyes find me before I finish my ascent.

"Great Atlas," I greet him, "I am a son of Zeus, once known as Heracles. I come to beg your hospitality."

"I know you."

His voice sounds so weary of speaking, even though I can't imagine he's had much conversation up here. I want to ask if I've bothered him, but another question falls out of my mouth first.

"How do you know me?"

"My eyes see as wide as the sky." He says it, still sounding exhausted with having to utter any words at all. "I have seen many of your adventures. Although even if I tried to ignore you, your melee with Poseidon's great white bull shook the earth even here. That is why night came earlier that day."

I never thought about how earthquakes would threaten Atlas's work.

"I'm sorry for the trouble I caused. Thank you for keeping the sky up in those circumstances."

His bruise-colored eyes squeeze shut. "Gratitude does not belong on this mountain."

It would be insulting to ask if he is sick. I can't know the toll it has taken on him to do this great task for so long. Reflexively, I almost offer to take the sky from him for a moment, so he can at least rub his eyes and stretch.

He says, "I know you've come to me for a favor."

"How did you guess?"

"If you were here to kill me, you would have tripped me by now."

Well, he's called me out. I can't avoid it. "Great Atlas, who holds the sky aloft so all life may continue underneath it, I do need a favor. I seek to know something not meant to be known by mortal minds, knowable only through biting into the golden apples from Hera's garden. I believe you know where it is."

"I do. I fought there once, in the midst of other mistakes." He opens one eye, just a crack, glimpsing toward the north. "I can see it now. No ship yet built can sail that far."

"My wisest counsel tells me that those waters are thick with dragons and older creatures. That no hero ever blessed by Poseidon himself has survived the journey, so bitter is it."

He closes that sliver of his eye. "I haven't seen one do it. I can say that much."

"I'll do whatever you ask," I tell him, and a cold part of me hopes he'll ask for years of labor. "If you will simply retrieve me one apple."

Atlas breathes. His ribs creak like the beams of a ship, and his chest expands like he might blow the whole countryside up to the north of the world. Behind his lids, his eyes move. Whatever memories he watches, his brow creases until cities could be built in them.

Eventually he speaks. "I had assumed you were you doing all of this for some great love. Some family. Was I right?"

That knot in my chest could snap, and leave my limbs loose for the rest of my life. It could break me. It takes me too long to recover my breath.

I say, "It is for family that I couldn't protect. I need to get them justice."

Out pours Atlas's breath, his belly going shallow, a hissing sound like the sea draining out through the bottom of the world. I recognize that pain, because he's recognizing mine, isn't he?

I don't inhale again until he does.

I tell him, "I will hold the sky for you, until you return. If Papa Zeus is angered by it, I will let him take it out on me."

Heat wells in my cheeks saying that. There are no shackles on his ankles. There is not a single chain on Atlas's mountain. To some measure that I don't understand, he has to be here of his own will.

"It is heavier than it looks," he says, "but still harder to let go of."

That's all he says before lowering the sky onto me. I spread my shoulders, standing at the center of the mountain, and think that all night will fall over the world and crush the birds in the valleys below.

Not a single star falls from the heavens. The world beyond Atlas's mountain is as tranquil and conflicting as it ever was, witless that anything has shifted. Moonlight continues to paint errant ripples across the sea, illuminating tides and night fishers.

It is up here where things change. Ribbons of celestial lights tickle the hairs on my neck, and inexplicable winds chill my spine. I push my palms up into the sky, finding no hardness, nothing to grab onto, and yet nothing falls. My legs start to buckle, despite it feeling to my arms as though this could weigh nothing. It is a beautiful weight that defies brawn's understanding.

Atlas is gone, out into the north. I can't lift my head to follow his path, nor even to look upon the stars that rest above my scalp. It's just me and the beautiful weight now.

When all this started, Auntie Hera, did you . . .

No.

I fidget my big toe against a pebble, something that has likely spent the last hundred years under Atlas's heel. Something I can pay attention to. Some part of the pebble is rough but every part I can see is round.

I cannot reach for it, or look closer. The sky demands everything. I move a hint of my right shoulder, and instantly it presses down, ready to crush all the world. I strain my back to stay straight, to keep my arms wide. The chill of the world above eats at the flesh of my back.

I wonder which stars are digging into me, the ones I cannot see. Were these constellations overhead the night my sons burned?

I try not to think about it, and immediately instead wonder if they were overhead the night Megara left me. Or were they overhead the night after I met her again, in Thrace, and found her more comforted by my nephew than by my touch?

How many times have I been wanting? How little do they think of me?

How many times have these stars watched me pray to you, Auntie Hera?

I can't help myself. I'm sorry. I want to do anything other than dwell on what the stars have seen, but there is nowhere left to walk, or sail, or climb. No monster to wrestle. No one to seek or help or consult.

The stars don't make any noise. They make no distractions.

This is Ares's fault, somehow, isn't it? He had to really be behind everything, and at the last instant he fooled the orb into showing you?

It's Apollo. It's Artemis. It's anybody else I offended in some way that made them come after my family.

How little do you think of me? When you hear me trying to believe it's someone other than you?

What am I supposed to do, really? Storm Olympos with a full army, slay all your worshippers, and then break you in my father's marble halls? In what way is that the answer to my sons never growing older? Generations of Theban heroes murdered villains in revenge and it never helped a single victim.

Then what? I say this was you and I do nothing? Am I to shackle you and stand behind you for the rest of time, until you remember that you are the protector of families? Pull on bonds of titan flesh and hair whenever you move to harm a family?

Or am I to somehow remind you that you are the one who looks after mourning parents, and who should care for the hurt? Who should follow all my labors with sympathy, and wish only to put sun on my path and wind in my sails? To remind you of all the virtues you should have?

"Give it back."

Atlas's words drag me out of my thought, and I bang my head against the sky hard enough that I may have knocked tomorrow's sun loose. The titan is nearly up on the summit, crouching over me, eyes the size of fortresses staring into me. A hand reaches, empty, no golden fruit in his grasp. He wants the sky back.

"What you wanted is at your feet. Now give me back my sky."

He pushes his way up onto the top of the mountain, hands greedily fondling along ribbons of waning evening light. The sun is nowhere to be seen, but its glow is starting to emerge somewhere in the east. Atlas cannot bend his neck fast enough to get under the ceiling and shoulder it all.

With his help to keep it all aloft, I'm able to glance down and see the golden apple between my feet. It is lustrous in the gloom, with a golden stem, and four little dimples at its base. The titan carried it here un-bruised.

Rather than reach for the apple, I touch one spot on his enormous heel. "Do you want me to hold it a while longer? You've done this so long."

"You know better."

He lifts it until I cannot reach a single shred of night, adjusting his arms to spread out the burden. Everywhere he trudges, the mountain below has shallow craters. I notice that where my own feet rested, there too are worn deep footprints.

"I'm not ready to face what I'll do when I'm done with the sky. Go. Get out of my domain before you are the same."

I pick up the apple, cool as a metal goblet. The rind is hard, and too light. As though there is nothing inside. Knowledge might well be as baffling to brawn as the sky.

"Eat it," Atlas says. "Learn what you want. And then act on that knowledge, before you can't."

I turn that tiny object in my hands. The golden apple truly feels like it doesn't belong in our world. Like it can't have my answer under its rind.

But the answer isn't in the apple, is it?

Because I already know the truth, Auntie Hera.

I ask him, "Are there questions you're afraid to answer?"

His silence tells me there are. It's too quiet up here to avoid the sound of guilt.

Lacking anything better to use, I rub the apple on my hair. Then I set it inside one of my tiny footprints, beside all his titanic ones.

"Someday, I'll return to you. And we'll get your answers, like you got me mine. I'll help you eat this apple, if that's what it takes."

His bruise-colored eyes are closed. He doesn't watch me when I kiss his ankle, or when I leave. But I see those eyes watching me, when I re-turn down to the bottom of the mountain and leave. I know Atlas is watching me.

Hera 41

You know it's me.

You knew it before you held that apple. You've known it since before I hurled the Bull of Crete at you. I think you've known it since the first prayer you made where you didn't mention my name.

I won't pretend I'm worse than I am.

But I won't pretend I'm innocent, either.

You know it's me, and you still don't want to go through with this. You won't return to your wife until you're done with me. You know your whole life is waiting for you. Every family you might create.

All the potential futures you have are waiting for you to climb my mountain. At the base of Mount Olympos, standing in the tall grasses, surrounded by gnats and sunshine, you can see the climb. It's no taller than Atlas. It's no taller than the sky you held aloft.

Come on.

But you can't. Your friends ask you, and counsel you, and promise to be there in the climb.

You reach a hand to the rocks, knowing your fingers can sink right into them. There's nothing you can't climb. You could hurl yourself upward and be here in moments.

And you flinch, because there are things neither of us can bear to do. You flinch, and you turn away. One foot lifts, ready to step away from Olympos, to hesitate and think this over, as though you haven't been thinking this over your whole life.

There's something you might have heard: the only entrance to Hades's underworld lies below Olympos. Nobody can find it because it only appears when an Olympian beckons it.

As you take that first step away from my domain, I beckon. You drop straight down into the abyss, into the domain of the dead. The hole is open for the blink of an eye, full of ash and the growling of a three-headed dog that does not like unwanted company. You'll hate me for this, but you need to.

When you climb out of there, you won't stop climbing. I'll see you soon.

Alcides 41

I fall so abruptly that I think I've lost consciousness. This has to be a dream, for solid ground to turn into bewildering fog. I can't see a thing beneath me, not through whatever swirls down here, so I look up, for the monsters, for the ground that betrayed me. There's no hole above me. This can't be real.

I land on a granite altar, surrounded by twelve pillars that hold nothing aloft. I grope my way to the pillars, squinting into the cave. What I breathe in isn't fog. It's something heavier, sootier, like everywhere is a vaporous ash. It refuses my eyes any purchase. I lean against one of the pillars, trying to fathom what could be out there.

"Where am I?"

My question travels so far that it never bounces back to me. It's swallowed in the ash fog. I reach into that substance, waving my hands, and the gray stuff swirls, only for more to replace it. I can't clear it away. All my eyes can find is more swirling, and vague shades out in the substance. Figures of black that pass through the gray.

"Hello?"

If they hear me, none pause. A cavern of infinite space, blinded by ash, where unknown figures move, all lying beneath Olympos. It can't be.

I think to call for him. For my uncle, King Hades, the lord of all who are never seen again. I inhale to speak, and that's when the noise comes.

Several growls roll so thickly through the ash fog, pealing over me until my ears ache. Those are not sounds of Purrseus. There are multiple animals, and the growls are more guttural, like wolves bred to be large enough to chase Helios's chariot across the sky. The growls carry on, until I can tell there are three of them.

I know what's stalking me. The creature that knows I don't belong down here.

I twist left and then right, trying to see the source. Just the shape of the creature. It must be enormous, and at that volume, it has to be close. It should be a looming black shape in this gray world. I cock my ear down, hoping its scampering feet will give it away and I can catch it in a pounce.

I hear thickly padded feet moving, but they shrink away from me. Off to the left, I think. Yes, definitely the left.

Slowly I slide my bare feet along the rough cave floor, lukewarm as dead embers, and bend my knees to lower my center, making myself a smaller target, hoping to get under the beast if it pounces. With three enormous jaws, I need to make sure I'm below where they go. While I'm mostly blind here, I don't believe Hades's guardian is. And most dogs hunt by scent. Surely it can smell the only living thing in the underworld.

"Cerberus? Can you help me?"

The three growls again, still close, but weaker. Is it listening to my plea?

"I don't mean to keep you from your watch for long. But I need to find the way out."

Is that actually a growl? Now it's more of a staccato keening, a whine that creases my brow. The sounds hitch, rising in pitch without intensity, until it doesn't sound like a beast at all.

"Stop it!"

That voice, huffing words out between a wheezing, whining laugh. It makes me widen my eyes, forcing myself to stare into the ash fog. Yes, I do see a huddled shape, but far too small to be the guardian of the underworld. It quakes, and kicks its legs. Its oddly human legs.

"No fair! I was supposed to ambush *you*."

The giggling young man reaches out, and stops me where I stand. He reaches for help he doesn't know is there. And he reaches with a hand shaped like the paw not of a dog, but of a cat. A boy's arm with a lion's paw.

I open my mouth to ask if it's him, and my lips crack from how dry they've gone.

Immediately two more figures, smaller and clearly not hounds, but human children, launch into the ash and tackle him. They tickle at the backs of his knees. That's where Therimachus was always most ticklish. Even after he hit puberty, it was his weak spot.

They can't be here. All three of them?

Of course they're here.

I sent them here.

I should be horrified, and split open, and overjoyed to hear their laughter one more time. But my ribs fill up with hot pride because those voices are together. They've been down here this entire time, in this unknowable space, and they found each other. They've banded together, even here.

"Boys?"

In all the ways I've tried to say how I love them, my voice captures what my words can't. How can't I sound this way all the time? Surely anyone who heard the love in these words would be warmed for the rest of their lives.

Those three shapes in the ash fog slow, hands no longer wrestling, but resting on each other. The littlest hands, Little Deicoon's, grab onto his brothers. All three of their faces are looking at me. Do they see the same shadow that I see of them?

"He's not real." The dry encouragement in Creontiades's voice, as he steps before his younger and older brothers, getting between them and me. "It's an illusion, guys. He can't be here."

What are they seeing? It makes Creontiades and Therimachus stand up, tall but not as tall as they should have grown. Behind them, Little Deicoon whimpers until I have to hold him. I have to comfort my poor little boy.

"Boys, it was a fury," I say, too hasty, words not soft enough. I've lost the voice they deserve to hear. "The gods drove me mad. It wasn't me. You don't have to be afraid."

A hiccup, and a clutched breath, like Little Deicoon is holding onto a whine. Like all the times he tried to be brave for me in Thebes, a lifetime ago.

Creontiades points to me with a long finger, and I realize he has a sword. A straight blade with two edges, a stark triangle pointed directly at me. I can see it more than I can see any of them.

It's Therimachus that asks, "Is it you? Did Mom kill you, for what you did?"

The pain under that curiosity. They don't believe about the fury. Some dark shape approached them and shattered their playtime, and abruptly reminded them of the father that hated them.

It makes me grope along my chest and belly, in search of a fatal wound that Megara never struck. For an instant I believe she did kill me. She should have. Why didn't she?

"No. We've been searching the world for justice. For you. I've dedicated my life to you. I came here for . . . for . . ."

It's not a lie, is it? Say it to them.

"For you."

No, it's the wrong tone. They need to believe me. They need to know.

"I've never stopped loving you. Please know. I've never stopped being sorry."

There's a wretched undercurrent in everything I say. I tip my chin up, exposing my throat to that sword that the shade of my son threatens me with. Everything I say to them asks if I can stay dead with them.

The answer is Little Deicoon piercing the ash fog, wailing in a way I didn't know that I missed. How Megara and I used to cuddle that little boy in these tantrums. He'd thrash for hours until he knew he was safe, with us. But he wasn't safe, was he?

The shapes of Creontiades and Therimachus shift, tipping toward their youngest brother. Each wraps an arm around him, and the hardest thing I do in my life is stay where I am and let them comfort him. Can they see on my face how proud I am that they do this for each other? Or do they see my throat seizing up, hating my own flesh for staying away and not joining them? Not sweeping them into my arms until oblivion makes us one?

"It's not him," Therimachus says this time, and swipes his free arm at me, and I see his feline claws fully extended from paws. I forgot how long they were. "Get away!"

That uncertainty, of whether he'd fear worse if I was a ghostly illusion or his real murderer.

I can't argue them into knowing. For me that night has been years of toiling and searching and doubt. For them, it was a betrayal and fire and over. There's no demanding they hear me out, and no evidence I can drag down into the underworld to prove they're wrong. There is nought but one thing I can give them.

I can leave.

I flee the sound of my crying child, not that it will ever stop echoing in my head. Because it was my face they saw chase them down, and my hands that did it to them. I rush blind away from them, into ash, daring any other shades to leap out and strike me down, because it was my hands. I've known all along that I'm as guilty as anyone, for what you made me do. So I let my boys see me shrink from them, and feel safe the guilty man is gone, secure in the knowledge that they are right. It's not true, but the lie is the only comfort I can bring them down here, until the day I die.

Auntie Hera.

It was my hands.

And it was your will.

You made my sons' eternal memory of me a horror. And I couldn't stop you.

The further I run, the less I am the man who descended here. Does some fury take my feet from me? For as I break into the world above, into the mists and the silky night air, something is gone. As though this whole time I had not returned the sky to Atlas, and now, only now does the beautiful weight slip from my shoulders. I can't stop running, don't pause to give a reassuring word to a single member of the family that waits for me, for I am not a good man. I am not a grieving father. I am the man who walked across the world with the hands that killed his sons, and kept every finger.

I don't notice when the hole opens above me, or when I pass the foot of Mount Olympos. I only climb, dragging my carcass away from the shades of my boys. Higher, and higher, where the air is thinner, with eagles crying, insects buzzing, wind breaking limbs from trees, and Purrseus and Boar chasing me, and Logy begging to know where I've been, and still I hear it. I have to go higher, to outrun the sounds.

But damn it, I can still hear Deicoon crying.

He hurls himself up the slopes by his arms, grabbing handfuls of rock no mortal has ever reached, and throwing himself higher. His eyes were not made to even perceive the marble glory of the Olympian Temples and still he comes straight at us. I wait on the marble rim for him.

I draw my finger across Até and Athena who wait at my side, and warn them, "Do not get in his way. Let him come."

From the twitch in Athena's left eye, I know someone has rushed around behind me. Down dives Ares, off the marble rim and down the cliffs, in the avatar of a red arrow that would sunder the ocean in half.

Heracles keeps climbing, moving so fast he might as well be running up the sheer mountainside. But he isn't running alone. When Ares comes to split his skull, up leaps the Lion of Nemea with hide unyielding. The lion drapes himself across Heracles's shoulders, and Ares's arrow tip skids off that invulnerable hide.

My loyal son goes toppling down the mountain, cursing and shifting his avatar into something more godly and suitable. But just as quickly, the Bull of Crete is on him, headbutting him in the groin and forcing him further down the slopes.

"What?"

I turn to make sure. Granny is still behind me, arms folded, as though she is ready to pounce at me if I join my son in battle. That means the Bull of Crete isn't operating under possession. Did it grow loyal to Heracles's kindness, too?

All Ares's pomp and thunder drew their attention so wilier gods could move. I wasn't expecting Artemis to come to my aid, yet I hear the creak of her bow, a frozen mountainside cracking at earliest spring's touch. She draws her own arrow, where Ares's failed.

Into her line of sight tromps a wretched man covered in the remains of a more wretched boar, both flesh and hide equally bristly. Wearing the boar's head as a cowl, he turns its dead eyes up on Artemis. He offers himself.

She'll loose no arrow today. I can tell by the wintry feeling on my neck, as though she is turning into weather. For the first time since we built it, snow falls on Olympos.

As Heracles's fingers dig into the stone just a few body lengths below the marble rim, Athena shakes her head. I warned her, and for the first time that fool disobeys me. Her right hand moves to her hip for a sword she has not yet conjured, and her hand is in argument with her coiling lips, like she cannot decide whether to unleash blade or argument.

The hydra speaks. "My dear owl. If we interfere, we'll never learn what will happen."

Athena's hands and lips seize up, and she stares over the rim at one face as though it were a thousand. The Hydra of Lerna gazes up at her, so proud with the flick of their tongue, as though they have been preparing the fateful swing of those words for years.

After that, it is as though each is a gorgon. Each becomes a statue, the serpentine beast unable to climb another bit higher, and the Goddess of Wisdom unable to budge any closer to the mortal realm. They are the keys that lock each other into place.

Two so obsessed with knowledge, and neither knows what to do next.

It's too appealing to fixate on what they're doing to each other, and to avoid the hairy knuckles that reach up. The pinkened raw fingers, nails torn off from the climb, that fasten down on the marble rim. It cracks like fresh thunder and plumes of dust fly from under his palm, as the rim itself gives way to his strength. Somehow his hand finds the only chipped spot on the entire marble rim, where his father long ago dropped a thunderbolt.

Heracles's thumb slides inside the chip, and he hauls himself up, chest heaving, cheeks hollowing from breath. His eyes have forgotten their lids, so overflowing with pink and blood that I can't make out their color. He has my husband's beard, that thickness flecked with stones that fell into it in his ascent.

He has my husband's beard, but on his shoulders and his forehead, he has his own scars.

Over the rim he comes, through the cloud of marble dust, feet thudding against the floor before me, and then his shoulders rear back, and he stares into my face, a determination that wasn't ready for the face he'd see. I couldn't wear a different avatar today.

Alcides 42

Helios could drop the sun atop me and my flesh would be no warmer, so boiling is every organ inside my breast. I cannot slow down, cannot keep up with the things hurtling around me, because you are up there. You who need to feel what I feel, what my sons felt upon seeing me. You need to know what makes fear seem a mere shadow. You are family itself, and you must know what my sons experience at the thought of what you made me. Isn't this what I'm supposed to do?

I claw my way over the crude chunks of marble defending Olympos's summit, ready for you to swing at my head. To feel you finally resort to striking me down like you should have at the beginning. Yes, I'm ready for a radiance that will burn out my eyes, and I will wrestle you blinded. I am ready for you to be a whirlwind of poisoned tips and talons. For a greatness that commands a palace of the ages, who made my father dread argument, who brought down titans and forced the world into civilization.

But what is this?

A cheap sculpture? A lump of limestone like I could have hauled out of a quarry in Thebes, with a proud chin, and eyes too soft for the venom I anticipated. Its lips are an uneven chiseled line, heavier on the left side, as though she holds a secret that one needs to pray out of her.

I look behind it, expecting you to be hiding somewhere else, because I recognize this figure, and you would never wear it. I recognize my work, because I sculpted it, again and again. This is the visage that I produced and placed so many times along the roads to Thebes, for wayward families to pray to for safety.

I look up into the chiseled hollows of your eyes. It's really you. The goddess who made me into a weapon greets me at heaven's border, wearing the shape I once gave you.

I took this avatar to show him that he was always right about me, and that he's helped me be something I forgot I was. It was to show humility, and yet there he is, unwittingly screwing his posture downward, making himself shorter so that he has to look up to meet my eyes. Even in this guise, even blaming me for his children, he puts himself below me.

But he didn't climb here to supplicate before me. He knows we have to battle. And I'll give him whatever he needs.

Before Até can intervene like she's totally plotting to, I summon the marble walls to serve their queen. The foundations tremble all the way down to Hephaistos's workshop, raising twelve barriers around us, wall upon wall of obedient marble. We stand in a circular arena with a twelve-layered ceiling, such that no one will stop us before this is done.

All the shaking of Olympos doesn't dissuade Heracles's gaze. His eyes are swollen, blood vessels bursting until I cannot make out the color of his irises anymore. His fists tremble before him, as he fights himself to keep them from motion. This poor man thinks he's overwhelmed with wrath, and doesn't know how strong his gentleness is.

I know the prayer before it leaves his lips. It's the most common prayer from anyone who is losing their faith.

"Tell me I'm wrong."

"No."

A simple refusal. An invitation for his fists to fly up and make history out of my face. A lesser man would charge me no matter what it did to him. Come on, Heracles. You deserve to be lesser for one moment in all your suffering life.

His breathing turns into rancid huffs, eyes flittering around my limestone face like even now he's trying to understand me. Blood drips from his eyes like tears, down the sides of his nose and into his beard.

That doesn't look right. How did he hurt his eyes so badly climbing up here?

"I dedicated their lives to you. We praised you every morning and at every meal." He drags a thumb across his teeth, as though physically recalling all the bites of food he held off in order to sacrifice to me. "Say they were innocent. Say they did nothing wrong. Tell me it was me."

His thumb comes away from his teeth torn open, down to the bone. He didn't bite himself. In fact his hands are nearly worn away, gory far beyond how they would have been torn in his climb. What is happening to him?

"Your sons did nothing wrong."

"You protect children!" He points a finger at me, and the fingernail comes loose. It falls away with a string of blood and clicks against the marble floor, painting the white with a dark blotch.

It's Olympos. The Palace of Olympos is killing him. He's the favored son of Zeus, strong enough to hold up the sky. How is this place rejecting him? I ordered everyone to let him enter. He wouldn't have been able to see this palace if not for my welcome. And it's still rejecting him?

I bring a fist up and jerk it to one side, commanding Olympos to obey me.

"You are welcome in Olympos."

He continues to watch my limestone features, ignoring the blessing. Blood weeps down the sides of his face and makes a ruin of his beard. It drips from his chin, onto his chest and down his thighs.

"Why did you take my boys? What did I do wrong?"

The loathing in his voice, like he wills me to set him on a pyre and end his story. Oh, no, you poor little dipshit. Olympos is obeying me. Its atmosphere destroys anyone unwelcome who enters, and you are welcome here. This isn't Olympos's fault.

It's *you*. *You're* refusing my welcome.

I say, "Accept the welcome. Olympos is killing you because you don't want to be here."

"I do!" you say, like the lie pains you passing through your throat. "Why didn't my family deserve to grow? Why not take me from it and leave Megara with happy, healthy boys? What was the point of giving Therimachus the hands and feet of a lion if he couldn't grow up to roar?"

I stamp one foot down, and the report is like my husband's own thunder. "Listen! Your throat is going to collapse around your words."

"Why didn't you take me?"

If I swing a weapon at you, we might battle in a way that gets you out of Olympos. I could drive you out, or you'll kill me and then leave of your own accord. I've been ready for you to kill me for a long time, haven't I? If that's what it takes?

One misplaced blow, though. With Olympos ripping into you, all it will take is one from a goddess to break your body. To steal what you deserve.

I can't do that to you.

You beat at your own breast, which immediately goes purple from the impact. "What did I do?"

So I tell you.

"You were born."

Those bloodshot eyes move like you've finally woken. Like I've shaken you out of an ill dream. "What?"

You deserve to live. You want the truth, and you deserve what you want.

"I am the Goddess of Family, and my dipshit husband fucked every hole in Greece. He overflowed the lands with children he never paid mind to, all as an insult to me. You were . . ." No, that's not quite right. "I mistook you for a living insult. One of too many insults."

Don't look at me like that. Don't wipe the blood from your eyes and pity me. The way your mouth opens, you're trying to understand my side of a story where I murdered your sons. Don't you dare turn this around.

I try to interrupt your empathy, "You praised me. You sacrificed to me. I tried to kill you, and you thanked me by surviving on your own. Do you understand? I despised you enough to put snakes in your crib, and you were dumb enough to thank me. I hated you more every day."

I am not tearing up at the memory of you praying that night, for your snake friends. Praying for the health of your first son in troubled labor. For all the love I could have accepted at any moment, if I'd simply been different. If I'd been who I am now.

If I told you that, you might keep believing in me. And you can't do that. You have to survive despite me, one more time.

"My father hurt you?" That can't be your answer. Yet here you come, treading over the fingernail that fell off your hand, the corners of your frown splitting open with concern for me. "What did he do to you? Where is he?"

"This isn't about him!" Again my foot brings the sound of thunder throughout our arena, as though anything about the Palace of Olympos is divorced from Zeus. But this isn't about him. "Me! Look at me. I did this to you. To your sons."

That does it. I mention your sons and the empathy crumbles, your face returning to concern and mystery. Ignore what the absent Zeus did, that he drove me to do what I did. This is about what I did. He doesn't overshadow me anymore, not even in accountability. His part is his. This is mine.

In the faintest whisper, like you think there could still be a decent answer, you ask, "Why did you take my boys?"

"It was supposed to be you."

Right into your blood-weeping eyes.

"I was sick of hearing your prayers, hearing this little shit for whom everything came easily act as though it was my doing. That's all there was."

There was more, wasn't there? But we don't have time. The flesh in your knees and the pits of your elbows thins like it may bleed at any time, and then fall off dead. I won't let you lose all your limbs for me. If we're going to fight, it has to be soon.

"I tormented one of my dearest friends," I tell him, wondering where in Olympos Granny is lurking. "I ripped this poor old fury from her comfort and sent her to destroy you. It broke her. I broke her, all in order to make you kill yourself. Because I didn't care about anything but my pain. My pain was special."

It's in your ruddy face. Harsh as I'm trying to be, you can tell in my voice that I care now. That I'm the Goddess of Regrets now. But I won't let you reduce me to some petty redemption.

"But I survived." You put a palm over your face, wiping the sweat and gore away. You hold dripping fingers up to me, dying, to show me that you still live. "I survived, Auntie Hera."

My entire limestone statue of a body quakes, like Olympos is tearing me apart now. How can you still call me that?

"You don't mean any of this," you say. "Whatever happened to you, I can hear it in your voice. You're heartbroken, too. You're not some evil queen. You never were. If you sent the fury to kill me, then how am I alive and my sons are not?"

You don't want this truth, but you're getting it.

"Because I didn't care."

You flinch. Yes, you do. You try to hide it, but you can't, not from your auntie.

"I am Goddess of Family. I protect children. Do you know why no goddess swept in to protect them? Therimachus? Creontiades? Not even the littlest one, Deicoon?"

You don't dare say anything. Your face begs me not to tell you what neither of us can avoid.

"Because I didn't care. The whole end of your world was something I did to shut you up because I was angry at someone else. That's how little you ever mattered to me."

That's how little you should care what I think. Can you even see me anymore, with all the juices pouring out of your head? They stream from your scalp now, too, filling your ears. You don't have time left.

You stare at me, blind from the pain Olympos puts you through, what your hatred of being here puts you through. Your determination is greater than any strength. You're mastering your anger, and today you end it.

Whatever you choose to do, you deserve it. I won't stop it.

Go on. Do it, my son.

Your right knee shakes like it is giving way from its socket, and I brace myself for your lunge. The tremble builds until your torso is vibrating, bright pink as cooked meat. You look up at me one last time.

Why are you turning away from me? What are you doing?

"Wait," I command you.

Your feet drag along the floor, pulling you toward one of the marble walls of the arena. You walk straight into it, leaving bloody smears on holy white stone. I reach for you, to drag you back to me, to have the climactic battle you deserve. That you don't want.

Olympos obeys me before I know it's what I want. The walls of the arena unfold into a triangular tunnel, precisely the right height for you to enter without stooping. The floor is rough hewn to catch your feet and keep you slipping in what you bleed.

I reach again, trying to catch your hair, to look you in the face. If I can't die for you, let me apologize. Let me tell you how you changed me. How you won our feud before you set foot here.

Your chin drops as you trudge down the hall. You got your truth, and you got your opportunity for revenge. All it makes you do is walk to the marble rim, the rock dust still hanging in the air from where you shattered it upon your entrance. The white flecks stick to your slickened flesh as you waver over the edge of the mortal world below you.

"Al?"

It's that hydra from Lerna, the one that used to fuck Athena. A single serpentine head stretches up, their body squirming from beyond the rim, trying to make eye contact with you.

"Alcides? Did you get her?"

You look over the edge, past the hydra.

Then you drop.

Part Five
The Fall

The fall is comforting. Wind whistling through my hair, cold raking its nails over my shoulders and across my neck, robbing me of all weight. For as long as I fall, nothing about me has to be real. I have no effect on anyone, no worth, and that's right because I am unworthy of family. The spirit of family itself detests me. Everything I ever wanted was a mistake.

The stop is sudden, blistering my flesh, ground shattering and sending shock waves from my body. My father's strength refuses to give up on me, refusing to let me shatter like I should, instead splitting the ground deeper and deeper. Soil fills my mouth and nostrils, and I punch through the ground as though in search of what lies beneath creation. Will I land in the underworld again? Amidst the sons who dread laying eyes on me?

Not today. The sun-warmed air tickles my scalp, and I stagger up from the hole. The foot of the mountain is a red blur, and I rub the gore and grime from my eyes, unsure whether I would rather stand or drop.

You hated me this whole time? You hated when I was little and made small figurines of you to give out to the neighbors? When I dedicated lions to you?

"Give him space."

Someone is talking. Has been talking, and only now do I hear them. Whose voice is that?

"I said space to breathe. He's a mammal. They like breathing."

Logy. How did you get down from the mountain so quickly? Did you fling yourself after me?

There you are, squirming along the broken earth toward me, a second tendril wriggling along your flank. Is that a second tail? I swear there's a new mouth. A new head trying to hatch from your back, and you don't notice. None of us caught it because we were distracted. Distracted by me. You need to get away from me.

"What did she do to you?"

That deep, hoarse voice. Boar is near, on my left. I turn to push him away, and there's Purrseus, crawling low to the ground, ears low and back, pushing his head against my belly. His rough tongue licking at my belly, trying to clean my blood. I didn't know how much I was bleeding until I felt how little of it his tongue collected.

Don't they know I don't deserve them? That I don't deserve family?

Logy stretches forward, looping their long body under Purrseus's maw, and around Boar's left arm, tugging the monsters away. "He'll be fine. Let him collect himself."

Trying to make it sound like this isn't a problem. That I haven't dragged them all on a quest to prove my own unworthiness. I don't honor Hera. I don't honor family. The pain I put you all through, for nothing. You deserve better than to be my family. I need to get away from you.

Boar shoves through Logy's grip, still reaching for me. "Is she dead? Is Hera's hunt over?"

My head splits at the thoughts pouring out, and I grab at my skull, squeezing. What did I do to all of you? Boar, you belong on a mountain, untroubled, protected. I ruin everything. You're not safe near me.

"Stop," I tell him. "You need to get away from me."

Those callused fingers push through the blood on my back, and find the scar on my shoulder. The dagger Diomedes drove into that spot didn't hurt nearly as much as your sweetness. The generosity of your stroke. Beckoning me into your arms.

"Stop."

"Come. Eat. We need to look after each other."

He holds onto me. I'm naked, so where did he catch purchase on me? Yet I can't get away, can't push away without breaking him in half. My ears still ring with Hera's words, and the pitch grows shriller the tighter he holds me. Those fingers caressing my shoulder as though in search of a place that no longer exists. It doesn't.

"No!"

Run. Run, you damned feet.

They won't, and as I'm trapped standing still, he dares wrap both arms around me, pushing his head in closer, the tusks of his cowl brushing the top of my head, both sets of his eyes trying to look into mine. I can't bear him thinking I deserve attention. He needs to get away from me. I put a hand between us, bumping one of the tusks, urging him to get to some safer place, somewhere that Hera won't attack.

"It's all right, Heracles."

The word falls from his mouth, and my hand jerks, and connects with his cowl. Numb fingers are under the cowl before I know it, slipping under the boar skull entirely, tearing the knots binding it apart, so that it slips from the hair of his scalp.

"Don't—"

We both say it at the same time, and I jerk from him, like he's made of fire, to get my curse away from him.

That's my last mistake. The jerk of my arm rips every knot tying his cowl in place, and the visage of the boar leaps from his brow. It tears free, leaving his bald scalp exposed, only stringy hairs flying up, as though reaching for his real face. The boar's-head cowl is out of our reach immediately, whisking into the air like an arrow. I didn't mean to throw it. I grab for it and see it vanish into a distant forest.

I can't look at Boar, not with the sounds erupting from him. The liquid anguish of his voice drowns me, and my feet finally wake, stumbling out of his grip. In my blood-bleared vision he darts, running on all fours to retrieve himself, still howling, too pained to be misunderstood.

"I am Boar! I am Boar!"

That keening will haunt me the rest of my life.

I do the best thing I can, and get away from him. From all of them. I flee from my second family, as fast as my limbs will take me.

Hera 44

I taste the frizz on my tongue. That stink of static that's so heavy in the air, a lack of moisture that makes everything dry. It stings my nostrils and threatens to tear them apart. For years I searched the Aegean kingdoms for a whiff of this smell again.

I'm so busy mulling that subtle clue that I almost miss the thunderclap. From a clear sky its golden arc zags down and smashes into the marble rim on the other side of Olympos. Your feet touch down in an unmistakable explosion, sending smoke and radiance everywhere.

The full-bodied reek of petrichor and testicle sweat spreads across the entire mountain.

You're home.

You piece of shit, you're home. You waited until I finished ruining Heracles's life before you set foot here, so you could lord it over me? You think you're going to shame me any worse than I have myself? You designed all of this. If you knew I was fucking up so badly, you should have protected your son. You put us up to the tragedy while you sat around, invisible and jacking off with your pleasure at yourself?

You think you can bring vengeance down on my palace? The fuck you do.

"Granny," I call, unsure where she is, yet sure she is nearby. "Get out of sight and stay there. He doesn't lay eyes on you. He doesn't get to blame you for any of this. This is for me to handle, and me alone."

Talons grate along the marble floor to my left, the dragging footfalls of a hesitant fury. I don't move, letting her run away without having to attend to me. But those clacking talons come closer, until I feel her heat behind me.

I tell her, "You should run."

Granny's wizened voice comes out, "Let me be what I am."

She gets to make her choices. Not that I deserve to have her backing me up right now. The thought of Zeus coming after Granny makes me command Olympos to shut itself. Every doorway must become a wall, and every window must shut its eyes. We need time to think this over, and make sure that thunderbolt isn't an illusion from yet another meddling fuck.

I close my right hand into a fist, but the hallway before me opens wider, the ceiling receding higher. Around me, every exit to the courtyard forms more tunnels and walkways, all angling around the palace so that they would take me to one destination. Everywhere heads toward him.

"Close, damn you."

I flex my fingers in that fist, but Olympos ignores me. It makes itself a physical summons for everyone to attend. The only will it obeys today is its king's.

Through those marble passages comes your familiar voice, a thousand marble throats carrying your unintelligible sentences. You bellow in that self-assured tone, a voice celebrating yourself. Carrying the implicit menace that your mood might shift, that undercurrent that in your songs is the desire for the next verse, about lashing out at whoever interrupts you.

Down one hallway flap the dark wings of an owl, coming straight to me. Athena beats her way up, and perches above the exit. Gray eyes turn down on me. She's his servant, but she's coming here? Is she summoning me, too?

"It really is him?"

I meant to ask that in a more dignified way, but today has sucked the eloquence from my tongue. Fuck this fucking day.

"It is him, indeed."

"Not a deception? Not an illusion?"

"At this moment, Apollo is sucking up to him. Lord Zeus is responding with bemusement to all flattery, clearly waiting to crush his hopes when he asks him the favor."

I dig my heels into the floor. "Fuck. It is him."

"That's why Apollo is sucking up to him. Apollo wouldn't waste his time trying to get favors out of an illusion. He's asking about dominions. He wants to be the God of Accountability."

You're here because I'm weak. Because these travails made me doubt myself. Whatever else you've been up to, you know now is the best time to get your way. I need to arm myself.

Alcides

Heavy breathing across a long tongue, and paws pattering along jagged slopes of cracked earth. Purrseus is pursuing, and probably more of them. They don't understand. I dragged them all from their lives for a mistake that I can't even think about anymore. Fast as I'm fleeing, what makes my heart rattle against my ribs is the thought of all those years of prayers falling on hostile ears, that family itself despised my having a family, that I deserved nothing I had. That I'm a lie. It's hard not to split the earth again with how hard my feet come down, and then I'm knee-deep in marshes, then splashing nose first into work and thrashing my way across to shores unknown. It doesn't matter where I land, just keep moving, keep putting distance between me and them, keep doing, keep doing anything rather than think. Drown myself not in water, but in action, in distraction, in the fervor of busy hands parting the water and thrusting me out to sea. Stroke with my right hand, my left, my right, my left, doing nothing but doing, until I forget that I'm

Hera 45

I pull my avatar together, restoring golden flesh, my royal polos, and robes that would repel the tips of spears. Mine are the hands that refuse tragedies, hardened from a hundred thousand assisted births. I become so large that I will not fit in any of the hallways your will carves. I will shatter them when I walk through and meet you.

Except the inside of my avatar keeps opening cavities. Every shape I pull together is hollow, no matter where I squeeze. This fucking illusion of resolve. I can't let doubt beat me.

Thinking of insecurities brings Até to mind.

"Athena, where is Até? Typically I'd expect she'd be at my side by now."

That owl remains perched above the entrance to the nearest hallway. "She was the first to notice his return, spying the distant light that became his thunderbolt. She lurks on the periphery of Lord Zeus's audience, ready to run distractions if he comes for you."

Até, you wily asshole. I would castrate every just king for the rest of time for you.

Running my hands to smooth the skirt over my thighs, I look up at that wise owl. "You serve him. You were always his favorite. Why are you here, rather than there?"

"I serve knowledge."

"He's been to some unknowable place for years. Knowledge doesn't care about that?"

She cocks her head in that frustrating manner of owls, like she might twist her own head off. Her beak clicks once. "Of all the knowledge I desire, my queen, I most want to see what you do to him."

Don't make me like you.

Fuck, it's too late.

"Fine," I say. "Then where is my ivory javelin?"

"Here, dear." Granny's voice, simultaneously soft and rough, like the longest-worn garment passed down in a family. She extends a taloned hand into my peripheral vision, extending that polished javelin for me to take. She holds it so far forward that I won't have to turn and look at her.

No, that won't do. I turn fully, and in taking the javelin I take her hand, and I clutch her thin body to mine, and I kiss where her cheek becomes her eye. She holds me, too, for a moment.

I give the javelin a good shake to prove its sturdiness, then turn to one of Olympos's many halls.

"Good. Now let's go greet the king."

Alcides

can't find it anywhere at the foot of Olympos, no matter how long I look. Legend said another entrance to the underworld exists somewhere in the Lake of Lerna, and I'll go there next, scour it, calling their names, begging to make amends, if only one of my boys will show me the way to

think I hear Purrseus following me again. If I have to, I'll resort to

"will not" keeps becoming "can not"

the foreman hollers that everyone is out of the cave, but still I hold the ceiling aloft for the comforting sensation of being smothered by its weight. If there is even one more person down there, they need

I lean forward on my oar, on one of many benches aboard a long ship of many rowers. A woman tends my oar bench with me, the only woman I see anywhere aboard; her drawing fingers are callused, and a bow is stashed below her seat. I mean to ask her how I joined the crew here when a great back breaks the waters of the sea

a lock of gorgon's hair that can be contained in an earthenware jar, yet that can repel the whole army that stands beyond the

decrees wise Apollo himself will sell me into the service of

Together we are swallowed in the shadow of the towering wall, something too grand to fathom mortals building. A veiled woman pulls me deeper into the shadow, a fist in my beard, imploring me, "How much of the city will you take to free my brother?"

                                                        awake wondering. Could the ash
fog ever rise from the land of the dead? Swallow us without our noticing?
I think

    I think it already has. We simply keep walking through it.

All the hallways lead to the same amphitheater, the marble stands dropping down flight after flight. The stands are chiseled so that the visages of Olympians emerge every two body lengths, inviting us to sit on ourselves. The drop from each stand to the next is so sharp that the amphitheater's stage is hidden from view in the hallway. We have to come closer to see the god who summons us. As I tread down my hallway, I'm still wary of your tricks, as though down on the stage there awaits a stone swaddled in robes pretending to be the King of Olympos.

Nevertheless, the Olympians turn out. Artemis crouches on the highest stand, quiver laid down beside her, both hands laced together over one knee. On the next stand below her wait Ares and Hephaistos, each of them holding one of Aphrodite's hands. The heavy atmospheric presence of other Olympians lurks in the wings of the place, of those still tentative and fearful enough to not show their faces. Even Zeus's brother Poseidon is somewhere on the palace grounds, polluting the air with briny sea spray.

"I don't pretend to know where you've been, great king."

Apollo's voice, simultaneously deep and nagging, like anyone is fooled that he didn't reshape his avatar to sound more authoritative than he deserves.

"But wherever you've been must have overloaded you with burdens. So many new dominions to consider. I could help you by shouldering the more demanding ones."

His voice echoes up from the stage of the amphitheater, like he's already trying to approach the center. Athena did warn me to expect his trifling.

Athena remains in the avatar of the owl, seated on my left shoulder. She's earned a free ride. Does she give me a squeeze as we exit the hallway?

Até appears as soon as I set foot in the court, stepping into my path with her golden curls and white dress. She gives half a nod upward, like she needs permission to move any further, wordlessly inquiring whether I want her to go in front of me. The Goddess of Ruin is asking to be my gilded shield.

I tell her, "Not today."

"You sure?"

"You've done enough."

I guide her to one side with the haft of my ivory javelin. She should scurry away. Instead, she falls into step with Granny behind me. I really hope the two of them have the good sense to flee my side before this gets gruesome.

"Great king." Apollo is still prattling on. "Was there anything hotter than fire where you've been? I've always thought we should replace fire with something. I could be god of that."

"How about God of Reading the Room? Go get some practice."

Your voice makes my calves itch. Only you do that to me.

Apollo asks, "Great king?"

"Everyone here wants to know the treasures I've brought home to Olympos. But you won't pry them out of me until the lady of honor is here."

More of my flesh itches, writhes, and tries to secede from my body. I don't have *a reaction* to hearing your voice again any more than a tempest has *a raindrop*. I forgot how I used to put my palms over your chest and shove to make you fight to get closer. I long for how your forearms would dig into my waist when you lifted me. I want to loop your hair around your neck and strangle you with it. How many lies will you spill in your homecoming? And that entices me? How I missed having you commit the same wrong over and over, so that I could easily stalk you and punish you, safe within the predictable boundaries of how you'd folly. So that neither of us ever had to grow.

I miss being smaller. Ignorance is easier.

I swell as I approach, making my avatar larger, ignoring that the hollow cavities inside me grow faster than my flesh. Insecurity is no excuse to shy from the right thing.

You stand at the base of the amphitheater, your head scarcely clearing the second stand, and yet you are somehow the tallest god in the place. It's how you look at everyone. A quick glance and smirk up at Ares, Aphrodite, and Hephaistos, that makes them shorter than you by estimation alone. By self-assuredness. It's on your plump lips, and in that beard no cleaver could hack a path through, and in shoulders only your lucky children inherited, that you let go slack because they don't need to heft anything.

You bolt up at me, shoving Apollo to one side.

"There she is!"

Abruptly you aren't on the stage anymore, disappearing without a trace. I raise my head to gaze around for you, and then you're in my vision—all of my vision. Wine-sweetened breath assaults my chin, and your grin tries to fill my mind. Before I can shove you away, your right hand snakes down my back. Your fingers molest my ass in a way that reminds me all an ass is for is pushing out shit.

What the fuck is going on here? There is no way you aren't irate about what I did to Heracles. This is duplicity. This is more of your bizarre power game.

"This was all for you," you say, getting too much hot breath up my nostrils. "Staying away was the hardest part. How's my princess?"

In a more private voice than you deserve, I whisper, "What are you doing?"

"What I've been dreaming of for years. Come on, I know you missed me. I bet I haven't left your thoughts for one single day."

You know you haven't. I search your face, your thick beard, your grin that waits as if entitled to its kiss. So proud of yourself, like you think I know what you're proud of. Judgment lurks under these looks. It's an omen.

Yes, you know what I did.

To Heracles, I might have sacrificed myself. But you? You aren't killing anything today.

I say, "You want this to happen in front of everybody?"

"Hera, baby. We deserve an audience."

"We both made mistakes." You better know that I'm not alone in this. I let my tone warn you. "But I've done my best to help your son heal."

That formidable brow creases. "Which son?"

That's a trap. I can hear it.

"I know you've been watching. Don't treat me like less than I am."

You put your hand over your breast like a bashful maiden. "Look, if this is about the mortals? I have lots of sons. It's true that I wander. But I only wander because there is a home. Those lesser things I do? They prove what we have. They accentuate the greatness that happens between us."

Those lesser things.

Let's get this over with. I hand you an obvious opening.

"Like making new kings of the mortals?"

"Huh?" Your cheeks rumple upward, then you shake your head stiffly. "I haven't made a single new king in . . . I don't even know how long. This is about us."

I don't know how to tell you to just fucking stab me already. We both know what this is about. I am sick of waiting for your long game to finish. Let's fight it out.

Your eyelids narrow, as though you are finally studying my face.

Then your voice booms.

"Olympos! Listen!"

All the gods are watching us. Ares, Aphrodite, and Hephaistos are several stands above us, and Artemis is a predator above all. Até and winged Granny are on the stairwell, where I should still be standing. Athena is her humanoid self again, plumed helmet in hand, on the lowest stand, like she's ready to dive down onto us.

You and I rest on the marble stage floor, with our feet above chiseled likenesses of our faces. My heels cover my eyes.

But I've still got my ivory javelin, and I know where your balls are. I know you were a trickster before you were a king.

"Listen!" You keep booming. "Bronze will not always be the strongest metal."

From the tops of the amphitheater, Até yells, "What does that even mean? Where were you?"

I really would rather die than let you touch a thread on her dress. You squint up at her like you're struggling to recognize her, and I step in the path of your sight, because you're not banishing her again.

"Enough games," I say, in a much less private tone. "She's right. Where have you been?"

"I said," you say, as though you've already explained yourself and we're the unreasonable ones, "I've been astride the greatest conquest yet in the history of our pantheon. Bronze will not always be the strongest metal. Kronos felled Ouranos. I felled Kronos, and we Olympians felled the titans. Before the Aegean civilizations, there were strongmen whom the Aegean heroes brought low. Today, their civilizations are the bronze of the mortal world. But everyone falls to someone else eventually."

From up in the stands, Ares stands. "Who's threatening our station? What war is looming?"

"The same thing threatens us and the mortals," you say. "Time."

I can feel Até about to yell at you again, and I don't think she'll survive a second outburst. So I say, "What about time?"

Because if you found a way outside time itself, that would explain why nobody could find you. You finding a way to cuckhold time itself sends winter through my bowels.

You wave a hand toward the marble rim as though nothing beyond it matters. "These kingdoms may destroy themselves. They may fall to invaders. If they get too irksome, we may even wipe them out. What I've found is the seat that will replace these kingdoms."

None beg the answer to his unspoken question. I hear all those divine lips pursing, wanting to speak, and none brave enough to. Only Athena clucks her tongue, like she's figured something out.

You say, "Out in the west, beyond Macedonia, between the ragged farms and warlords, are fertile lands and wise people. They don't know how clever they will become. Today they barely have kings. But when we send them the right heirs, theirs will be a seat that rules everywhere a sail can take you. Not merely the Aegean Sea. Not merely the Black Sea. Everywhere."

Boundless dominion makes no sense. I get dizzy trying to imagine the logistics of expanding our pantheon's reach that far.

I ask, "You think one people will rule all the seas? One king?"

"Hera, baby, you were the inspiration. You scorned my trying to crown what's-his-name King of All He Surveys. Because that's not enough ambition for a future that has to last through time. The king of what supplants these civilizations will not be the King of All He Surveys."

You frame Olympos in a tiny square made of your thumbs and

forefingers, before your left eye. You look at me through that gap. Gradually you spread your hands, until your arms yawn wide.

"He will be the King of All His Subjects Survey. Anything they know will be his empire. And we will be his gods."

Ares clears his throat, and releases Aphrodite's hand. He puts a hand across his bare chest, still bearing the gouge marks from the Bull of Crete's horns. He wears the wounds. Even where I stabbed him, there is still gaping flesh.

My son asks, "What gods live there now?"

"Now?" You bob your head, so satisfied with yourself. "None are alive now."

That day when you left me. When my heart finally broke and I sent Granny after your favored son, and you were bleeding from a mysterious wound. No mortal could have struck that, and no Olympian had. How did I not realize, as I chased you, trying to heal you?

You weren't attacked by some monster. That was a war wound. It was a foreign god who'd struck you in your campaign to steal their domain.

I glare at the space on your belly that is long healed. "Do you know how afraid I was for you?"

"You waged war?" Ares says, voice hotter than mine. "Without me? Without Mom?"

You say, "I had to do this in secret. A full-scale invasion made no tactical sense. I kept it so quiet that not one person heard about it. No one was ready for destiny."

Ares jabs a finger in Athena's direction, "You took her, didn't you? You've always favored her. You and your subterfuge."

Athena stiffens so quickly that her fleshy joints creak like stone about to give way. Her cheeks go high, and she's fighting the color moving to them. Those eyes can't pretend to be emotionless, not right now. The Goddess of Wisdom is actually embarrassed.

No. She wasn't in on this. If I ever had a doubt, her flustering at being left out of her daddy's plans proves her innocence.

All eyes in the amphitheater are on her, waiting for her to explain it all. All eyes, except yours.

You say, "I was winning wars before you two were urges in my loins."

Athena says, "I was born asexually."

She just couldn't help correcting him. I want to get her something expensive.

You say, "You're the smart goddess. You know what I mean."

You better be lying to me, you piece of shit. I ask, "You plan for us to leave Greece? Leave all our worshippers who pray to Olympos?"

"Olympos is wherever we will it to be. We deserve the most powerful adherents. Our favored cities may change. Our names may change. But this next empire will earn our favor and spread our glory further than ever before. The world will name the heavenly bodies for us, just to beg for our attention."

I think about a potbellied man walking away from a chasm, and leaving so many confused animals in his wake. I may have fucked up with him, but that doesn't mean I give up on every expectant mother on these shores. Every child whose birth I oversaw does not now fall on a bonfire.

I ask, "What about the mortals under your feet right now?"

"The whole world needs us."

"You'll just abandon them?"

You better hear how I'm accusing you of abandoning all of us, on your new conquest for glory. You better.

You gesture for me to come closer. "What matters is we will always be revered."

"You," I say. "You want to be grand."

That hand keeps approaching, as you patter barefoot across your visage-laden marble floor, toward me. "I did this all for you. You and I will reign over every age, from wherever power is seated. For as long as I stand, there will be a Father of All, and there will always be a Holy Mother."

I let my avatar remain visible, but not tangible. I'm goddess-colored mist. An illusion that lets your hand pass right through her. You keep walking, and before you can turn around, I open a tunnel in the stands before you. It's a triangular gape, the same kind that ushered your son out of this place.

I ask, "That's all you did? You ruined mortal and immortal lives yet again, and as a make-good, your idea was to run off and steal domains? You're no better than Apollo."

Apollo says, "Hey!"

You say, "Hey!"

"You want my attention? Be a better god at home."

You whirl around, swinging your arms to catch me. Your arms shimmer as you try to match the evanescent nature of my avatar, and no doubt you would, if I stuck around long enough. If I got angry and chased you. If I kept giving you power, you would take it. And neither of us would grow.

It's not easy to walk down this hallway, as the Goddess of Family, and the Goddess of Wives.

You call, "Where are you going?"

It's not easy, having spent so many years dreading that you'd never come back. That you were hurt. That you were lost in a way worse than death.

"Do you know what I've been through setting up our future? Get back here."

That you'd never hurt me again, when I was too accustomed to receiving that hurt. Of everything I could have cared about, I missed fighting you.

It brings a little crinkle to one corner of my mouth, hearing your fists bang on the walls as they seal the tunnel shut behind me. You want me to take you with me. You don't want to be the one left behind.

I'm glad you came back, so that I can leave you.

Ignore   .

sink down.   breathe

     . can't breathe.

    breathe.

  catch   .   refusing   .

      , snap   .

drop   .

    just rowing.   pull. Looking   .

close   .   squeeze

     . breathe.

Brushing   , remembering

     . shrink away   .   shying

 , running   .   breaks   .   can't

breathe   .

    dive   .   smothered, hiding   .

shutting out   . can't.

    hear   . get between   ,

lift   . carrying . can .   forcing   .

tremble.   ignore and surrender.

I recognize   . don't. But yes, I do.

       wretch   .

breathe. have to keep breathing.

peering through the branches, and I can't see

.   can't   .   won't   .

Yes I can   . I can't help myself.   withdraw?

No. It's too late to withdraw. I push further through the trees, toward the sound of all those people. The smell brings bile across my tongue. I can't stop thinking about it. Why is it so familiar?

I step from Olympos's heights and my first footfall lands in a stiflingly sweltering shack with goat skins covering the windows, and the thin thatched walls palpitating with the moaning of a mother in need. Neither she nor her midwife have the wherewithal to pray, but their despair is prayer enough. The gray-haired midwife rests on scabby knees, with her hands deep in the mother's birth canal. The baby doesn't know better and is facing the wrong way, and the umbilical cord has snagged around her neck. The midwife squeezes her eyes closed, trying to focus knotty, aged hands into obeying enough to free the child.

She doesn't feel me taking her hands, guiding her middle and forefingers to the one hint of slack under the baby's chin. She does the work. The success is hers, and the mother's. Just a few more heaves. Come on now.

Then the baby comes pink and raw and dripping into the midwife's grasp. She's done this many times, obvious from how casually she clears the detritus from the baby's mouth and gets her breathing properly. The baby is a burning coal of heat and wonder, beautiful in every wrinkle and gob of fluid, little hands wiggling with no idea of what they're for.

The midwife brings her into her mother's waiting arms, arms exhausted and weak, and so eager to hold onto this new life forever.

My heart. I could never leave these people.

The midwife's expression narrows, almost chills at the sight of newborn flesh squeezing against mother's breast. That expression is what reminds me of who this midwife is—who you are. I haven't seen you in years, and you didn't even know I was on the ship with you back then. How little thought I gave to how much damage I did. You're why I'm here now. I hoped he'd come running back to you.

From over the newborn's tiny head, the mother mutters, "You didn't say your name."

The midwife turns away, wiping her hands on her skirt, not that it cleans them. It's an excuse. "I didn't?"

"Please. What is it?"

After a long moment, the midwife answers, "Megara."

Some cavity inside me seizes up, hearing your name.

Megara says, "You should rest."

The new mother is a natural, cradling the baby's head in the perfect crook of her flabby elbow, protecting the newborn's neck. Her milky brown eyes are enraptured with this creature she just met. She can't look away. But she doesn't relent.

"That man said you wanted something from me. That we needed to speak urgently. Tell me what I can do for you. I know people all through the port."

Megara looks through veiny half-lidded eyes, toward the goat skins that shade the window, that hide the view of the wide world outside. That she wants this woman to focus on the child in her arms is obvious, but also she can't let this opportunity go. I touch her shoulder, to make she sure asks.

"I'm not trying to rush you. It's simply that Iolaus said that you had information about some sailors who have been through here."

"I've met half the people who set foot on every dock. Who are you looking for?"

"He doesn't look like he should be a sailor. He has thin arms, and chubby legs, and yet he would have been stronger than anyone aboard any vessel that came through here. He might answer to the name Alcides, or Heracles, or to nothing at all. From the people I've found, he's not responsive. He's lost his way. It's my fault."

No, it isn't. I want to grab you by the shoulders and shake you until you stop blaming yourself. Too many of us are blaming ourselves already.

You say, "He went too far, and it broke him. I should have told him he'd done enough a long time ago. Now I just want him to come home. Is there any chance he's here?"

Eagerness slams into reality. The mother's downcast look, like she's ashamed to fall short in front of her baby. As though the answer she's about to give can only disappoint. Outdated hearsay to hunt down a myth.

"There was a man here, perhaps three months ago, before he—"

It doesn't matter. I didn't come here by accident. I'm not about to make mistakes anymore. Heracles is still lost out there. But I'll find him, Megara. One way or another, he'll come home.

That smell pulls me out of myself.

Smoke carries something I can't forget, that summons me from across the wilds. I try to simply walk toward it, to trek thoughtlessly, but the smell keeps stirring my heart. There is nothing in the world like burning hair. It clings to the roof of my mouth. I can't lick it away, or spit it out. It overpowers the other odors of burning flesh and the defecation from the dead.

I push between the last pair of thin cypresses, where the forest finally surrenders to open land. Crowds mill together, clusters of people sprawling across the grass, all toward the source of the smoke. A funeral pyre, where young men treated with rich oils toss logs on to keep it going.

Who died that attracted this many mourners where there is no nearby village? For all I see besides this pyre and the mourners is the pregnant bend of a river, rushing louder in murmur than any of the clusters of people. Was it a king? What king would die this far away from the seat of his power?

A ridiculous part of me pushes through clusters of mourners, like I might arrive in time to pull the body free and rescue them from a death long done. It's the stink. It makes me wipe moisture from my eyelashes. Makes me dread that a small paw will reach out to me from the flames.

Instead a man reaches to me, wearing a lion's pelt around his broad shoulders. His face is too beautiful to be perceived in a single look, and his flesh is oddly lacking calluses and scars for one so muscular. His eyes are pinkened from more than smoke.

"Did you travel alone to pay respects?"

No. Or, I didn't know that I was coming somewhere where respects would have to be paid. How do I answer him?

I have forgotten how to talk to people. The best I can give them is, "I could not stop myself from coming."

It's true enough. Hopefully it won't offend.

He licks the inside of his lips. "All those with compassion for my father are welcome here today. Come. Have my wine and sheep's cheese."

He gestures to where sustenance must wait. My eyes won't leave the flames, seeking the amorphous figure within.

"Who was your father?"

"He was the greatest hero of all Thebes."

"Thebes?"

Come on. Say you were born there. Say that it's your home. That you may have accidentally found the funeral of an old comrade. How did I forget how to talk?

"Fire was the right way for him to end," the son says. "He was angry his whole life. Killed his music teacher when he was a little boy with his own lyre."

I never heard of anyone in Thebes doing that. Music is beloved there. Or it was, when I had a home.

"But it's all Hera's fault."

My arms tremble, legs begging me to get moving, to get acting again so that I don't have to think.

Still I ask, "What happened with her?"

"She was jealous of how much Zeus loved my father, so she struck him mad. He killed my older brothers and his first wife in his rage, and then crossed the world making amends."

No. No, that can't be who I'm looking for in the pyre.

I fear the words of my question will shatter. They're too thin.

"He did great labors to clear his conscience? He pursued Artemis's favorite hind?"

The man rests weight on his left foot and rubs under his hairless chin, like he's trying to soothe a bruise that isn't there. "Yeah. All the stories you've heard are true. Lopped the heads off the hydra. Slaughtered most of the centaurs at Mount Erymanthos and stole their prized boar. Wrestled King Diomedes into the dirt and killed him for his treachery. He never forgave anyone when they crossed him. He was too angry. Even the King of All He Surveys was terrified of him."

I keep looking at his chin, for the bruise that isn't there. I wonder who hit him, that would haunt him today.

"Did it bring your father peace before the end?"

His fingers turn into a fist under his chin, and his voice hardens so much that his words may fall to the ground from their weight. "One centaur from Erymanthos survived. Just one. And somehow he tracked my father down and tricked his bride. He got her to smear the hydra's blood inside his clothes, so that when he put them on, his flesh burned. My father died fighting his own flesh for betraying him."

His splayed arm remains outstretched, like he might somehow grab onto the river and sink his fingernails into its arteries. I try to touch this young man's palm. This son of a familiar man. But I hesitate, afraid any contact will break the spell that keeps his story alive. I can't touch him. I can't tell him that long ago his father and I nearly met in the same wilderness. That we were so close to meeting. That on many stray nights I've wondered what our faces would look like if we witnessed each other.

Failing to comfort the son I never had, the urge to escape rises. To slink away, to run, to return to thoughtless action.

But the smell of burning hair pulls me into the roots of this. To faces I'll never see again, and to faces I never saw at all. To anger I never witnessed.

I decline the son's wine and sit on my knees before the funeral pyre, regarding the ashes of a man who borrowed my name for reasons I'll never learn. I find myself praying that I could meet him. I wish I'd known this version of myself who knew how to be angry.

A ll right, kid. Get your shit together."

Not that you hear my chiding. All the mortals at this funeral hear is the shushing of my currents, for I've taken the avatar of the Evinos flowing through this region. I blessed the river before any village on its banks was built, back when the locals' gods were quaint and kept throwing parties as an excuse to hang out with me, so I'm entitled to embody it all I want. Any side-eye the mourners throw my way is more valid than they think.

It took me long enough to track you down. Whatever fugue state you've been moping through made you almost as impossible to hunt as my husband. Being a pain in the ass must run in the family.

"Lord Zeus demands you return to Olympos immediately."

It's fucking midday out here. The guise of an owl is so obvious it should draw the attention of all the mourners, but they're busy with their little pyre. As though that body hasn't been roasted down to ashes. It's not getting up. Come look at this clearly diseased owl and maybe you'll notice she's talking.

"Shut up, Athena."

"I am merely relaying my king's message," she says, adjusting her feet on a low tree branch. "He was insistent I deliver it."

Further into the forest there sniffs an enormous predator. One that doesn't belong in such woodlands, or this climate at all. I'll laugh if he catches an owl for lunch.

But Athena is making great bait, and that's what I need.

I say, "I bet Zeus is as pissed as a punctured bladder."

Athena says, "He is waiting for you to come storming back to him."

"Because that's what I always do."

"Because that's what you always do. And you aren't doing it this time. It upsets him."

A little splash over my shore. The river equivalent of a smirk. "And it interests you?"

"It does."

"You're the smart goddess. If he wants my attention, he'll have to earn it."

"One could assume you are here to harass Heracles until Lord Zeus comes after you. To pick a fight on your own terms."

"Well, one is wrong. I'm harassing Heracles for totally other reasons."

You get down on your knees before the pyre, careless of just how close to my banks the pyre is. All you care about is communing with the smoldering ash of an impostor. Six times in the last century this river has flooded far over its banks. Once, it actually reached where the corpse of that imitator is now smoldering ash. What's happened once can happen again.

Dry twigs snap on the forest floor. Our guest is trying to sneak closer, but he's far too large to go unnoticed by the both of us. He's got his feline eyes on a tasty owl. It won't be long before he pounces.

The owl keeps her gray gaze on the ribbons of smoke rising from the pyre. Did she know where to find me, or was she already looking in on this funeral? I've had my suspicions before. Now, I have some certainty.

I say, "I wonder who was behind that impostor. He showed up at the right time to basically flush the Hind out for the real Heracles. And he died at the right time to lull the real Heracles out of his stupor."

"It wasn't you, my queen?"

My current almost slows to a stop. Athena is admitting to not knowing things? I'd rub it in, if I didn't know better. "I can see why you'd say it was me. It was an awfully *smart* plan."

Your words slow. "This is why I never tire of the mortal world. There are always new things to be confused by."

"Really? You don't have any idea which goddess was behind it?"

"I don't know what you mean. It's just as likely that some scurrilous human stole his name in a quest for glory."

"So now you're the Goddess of Plausible Deniability?"

You shuffle your taloned feet on that branch. It doesn't have any answers for you. "Once it was clear that you wanted better things for Heracles, some Olympians may have tried to ease his journey. Discreetly."

It's easier to roll a boulder uphill forever than get a confession out of this wily bird. That's wisdom for you. So I hit her from the side.

"I'm done with discretion. There's going to be a flood," I tell Athena, and grin in the undercurrent when her entire avatar stiffens up. "The worst flood this region has seen since Poseidon cursed it."

"You won't kill all those mourners just to cajole him."

Like I said, she *is* the smart goddess.

I make like a river, and babble. "The Evinos will swallow that funeral pyre and destroy the remains of the vaunted Heracles. It will come from the north, so none will see it coming before it deluges them. Fortunately, as you may have noticed, all the children and elders are far from the shores, enjoying the food. Only a couple of people will be swept in. Like that one alleged son of the dead Heracles. Mentor?"

"That is his name. He seems interesting."

She says it so quickly, eyes on the man in the lion skin. She utterly ignores the creature at the base of her tree, too interested by her people in her mortal world. There are more than people. Purrseus rests on his hind legs, raising one forepaw for a strike that would reduce any normal owl into a guano-encrusted stain.

A shame that at just that moment, the river breaks into a freak flood that engulfs the woodlands. He doesn't have time to roar before he's swept away in my current.

The eruption across the banks shakes me to life. Before I can turn, the waters spill over my body, thrusting me toward a pair of boulders. But I brace my heels, letting the sudden flood crash around me, spreading my arms to further divert the waters while people flee closer to the forest for cover. I refuse to yield when these people need me.

It's the river. Hera's river has surged from its path, sucking the entire pyre into its current, dragging smoldering logs away so that smoke and mist rise as twins. The flood keeps up the cacophony of a proper storm, and hands stretch out from the foaming spray, people begging for help.

I dive in, letting the fierce current swipe me to the riverbed. I kick off with enough strength to send me faster than the waters can match, and snatch each soul. Only one man went under—that handsome one who'd offered me wine if I grieved for myself. The son of another self.

I gather the son I never sired from the waters and slam my feet into the soft riverbed again, refusing to be moved another hair's width. Carrying this son against my chest like a baby, it takes me three heavy steps to deliver us to the air. He hacks and wails, and I pat at his sodden back. It's almost funny—he's the only man alive who was given life by two Heracleses.

As he recovers, I wonder. Can I rescue any of his father's ashes? Even a palmful would help him grieve in the years ahead, after this seeming attack from Hera's river.

I squint along the churning surface, seeking sign of the logs. Just a log from the pyre could become an object of comfort, couldn't it? But they're gone. Long carried down the flood, probably smashed to bits.

Just as I'm about to turn, a paw springs from the water. It flails as though the river has birthed a monster, and next rises the great muzzle. A giant lion with mane pitifully flattened to his flesh—there's no mistaking who this is. He tries to paddle against the spray and the current sucks him under, head and paws alike.

What is he doing? Invulnerable skin doesn't mean he can't drown. And he doesn't surface in the next moment.

"Purrseus!"

I'm diving in before I know I've left my feet.

A thena and I are quite dry. I twist my hair in both hands, squeezing out the last droplets of my river avatar. All the mortals are so afraid of the flood that came from nowhere that they hardly mind two women on the opposite bank. They're cursing how horrible a certain god is for ruining the great Heracles's funeral.

Athena asks, "You were helping him?"

I give my head a little proud wiggle. "Yes."

"By drowning his pet lion?"

"By *trying* to drown his pet lion. Yes. Haven't you heard all the legends about me? I'm a horrible villain. That lion had been following Heracles from a distance for who-knows-how-long, making him an easy target. Clearly I possessed the river, which everyone knows is my domain, and used it to harm that defenseless apex predator in order to harm Heracles."

I see her trying not to smile. Go ahead, try to keep a straight face as you piece this together.

Athena says, "How did you know he wouldn't drown in the current?"

"Maybe I didn't. Maybe I meant to kill him and failed. Heracles better be careful to protect it from my next attack. He'd better stick by its side. Anything else would be unsafe."

You don't want to lie on your back, but your limbs are too weak to fight me today. I push one hand to your tender underbelly, feeling as gingerly as I can against your hide. There it is. Your swollen stomach. Two fingers brushing it makes your entire body convulse.

I beg you, "Come on. Breathe with me."

And I push, soft and unyielding. I cup your belly upward, into your ribs until . . .

You barf all over my chest. It's a stream of fetid river water. The first of many blasts, as everything you swallowed in your failed drowning comes up. I work your belly until I hear your inhale, a wet sound from your nostrils, and your flesh pushes against me. Good lungs. I love your lungs. They kept any lions from perishing in this river today.

I nestle by your side to share warmth, and look to the orange sky. Your breath strokes my knee. It won't be light much longer, which means it's going to get colder.

A couple of dead trees volunteer to help. I strike them together so quickly that the friction turns their dry pulp into char and flames. Kindling is plentiful, and soon we've got a fire taller than either of us.

In the firelight your vomit becomes more evident on the mossy earth. What isn't straight water are clumps of fur. In our travels together I saw enough hairballs. But there should be more substance here. You expelled everything in your stomach. Where are the bones? The half-digested flesh and livers and hearts?

You're not just weak from drowning in that flood.

I sit with you against my side, one of your bony limbs digging into my right kidney. I make sure you're always angled at the fire, to dry off and get warmer. A stray rumble rises from your chest.

You're half-dead. You can't be pleased right now. Be honest.

"You haven't been eating," I accuse you. "What is a lion who doesn't eat?"

Not that you can answer. You don't need to.

"You've been following me for a long time. But you see how being around me put you in jeopardy? Am I worth that?"

You expel a heavy breath, sending feline snot down the back of my calf. Thanks for that.

You lay your long chin on my lap, right in the snot you just dribbled and the vomit I never wiped away. There's another of your exhales, this one of eye-watering breath. I missed how atrocious you smelled.

"I'll look after you until morning. Just until morning."

I don't mean to pet you. My hand moves to your scalp thoughtlessly. But knowing what I'm doing, I still can't stop stroking, from your ears down to your damp mane. You won't budge from me, either. Not even when I start weeping onto your fur. I hold onto you, until the sky lights up again.

Hera 50

This part is easy. Multiple cults that worship me in this region need to get outside their villages and mingle, to freshen up their minds and their dating prospects. New families will be born from this day if only their patron goddess Hera will give them a worthy endeavor to unite them. They cross paths answering a summons to do a deed that will prove their worthiness of my grace.

Not that any of them prayed for a dragon. But that's what they get.

Three cults of hormonal mistake-makers have to drive the seven-headed beast out of the valleys, and into the dark forest where it belongs. They don't have to kill it, because really, they don't stand a chance. Just goad it in the right direction, and then go home together and examine their marital options. From the looks I catch some of them giving each other, that's already on their minds.

"My queen?"

My owl-flavored lion bait has returned. This time Athena is invisible to the mortals, like myself, but in her humanoid guise. She pulls her plumed helm from disheveled hair, like she's been in a melee recently.

"What are you doing with those mortals? They don't usually go this far south."

"Testing their faith and having them fend off a dragon."

Athena leans closer over the landscape. "That's not a dragon."

"You are the smart goddess." I point up at the sky. "How's the homestead?"

She tries to fix some of her sweaty hair. That her avatar is in disarray is a great sign. "There are some distractions in Olympos today."

"I assume my dipshit husband has reformed and is taking a vow of not-fucking-up."

"Not yet. He's engaged in spirited argument with your sons."

My sons? I lean a little closer. "Which ones?"

"Ares and Hephaistos."

No way.

"Those two are united on something?"

She gazes more intensely along the path of the cultists, as though pleading to forget her morning. "Ares feels Lord Zeus has disrespected you. He's spent considerable time up in Lord Zeus's face demanding that he make amends."

"That much tracks, but Hephaistos? It's hard to imagine him arguing."

Athena puts a fist to her mouth and pretends to cough into it. She's not hiding her expression from anybody. "He hasn't argued, so much as he's smithed Lord Zeus a new throne."

"That's him defending me?"

"It's a peculiar throne. Once you sit in it, it's nearly impossible to stand up from it again. Which means Lord Zeus has not been able to escape Ares's arguments."

I put a splayed hand under my smirk. It deserves a display.

"I raised a pretty good God of War."

"He would like it if you would return. Many of us would."

Uh-huh. I know one goddess who's in that many-of-us. But I have work to do in Greece, and Athena has more potential to live up to.

I say, "I'll come back when I want to. Until then, I need your service."

Finally she looks at me. "My queen?"

"You've been studying me for a while."

"You make history. I could not turn away from you if I wanted."

"Well, next, you're going to turn into me."

Her avatar shrinks by a head, and she curls a hand in her robes. "You don't suspect I'm going to commit a coup?"

I wave her fear away. "A coup, with my consent."

"My queen?"

"Quit acting surprised. You're the Goddess of Wisdom. Olympos could use more ruling from the place of wisdom for once. I want you to take my robes, and my ambrosial oils, and fashion an avatar like mine. When the times arise that I am not around and my dipshit husband or

Apollo or Ares is going to make a terrible mistake? You're not going to stand there and watch."

She shakes her head so thoughtlessly that the helmet in her arms shakes, too. "I couldn't impersonate you. You're a unique being in the cosmos."

"You already fooled the world into thinking another Heracles was running around having adventures. Want to be me? Get pissed at bad people and you'll be halfway there. Até already knows the plan, and she'll be your shadow anytime you're playing the role. If you stray toward a mistake, she'll step in. Nobody knows my marriage like the Goddess of Ruin."

She looks inside her empty helmet, as though someone will crawl out and offer to take this job off her hands. "Why not have Até play your role instead?"

"I love her, but she screws around too much. I want ruin guided by wisdom, not the other way around."

Athena steps toward me, wise eyes imploring me to reconsider. "Lord Zeus would see through it. He'll figure out that it's me."

I remember him running off to the west, bleeding, refusing my help. "Lord Zeus doesn't pay enough attention to me to know."

"He loves you, you know?"

"Loving someone has never been enough. Don't pretend you don't know that."

Being the smart goddess, she doesn't argue that point. She presses her lips together and gazes over the cultists fleeing from the sight of the screaming "dragon" down there in Greece.

"May I think the proposal over?"

"Take your time. We make mistakes when we're hasty, don't we?"

"While I do, may I ask you one more thing?"

Oh, I hope this isn't about Zeus's sexual appetites. The plan is that between Athena's chastity and Até's wiliness, he'll never make it to bed with my divine understudy.

Dreading what it will be, I say, "Yes?"

She points downward. "You know that's not a dragon those people are harassing. So what are you doing this for?"

Alcides 50

awn's touch doesn't stir you. Your breathing is still shallow. When I pet you in the sun's full light, it's apparent the flesh under your coat of fur is too pale. No bronze spear or blade is strong enough to pierce your hide. Something is eating away at it, from the inside. I've held you near the fire all night, and given you all the heat in my body. This should be clearing up.

"Ahhhhhhh!"

For a moment, I think I hear my soul.

"Ahhhhhhhhhhhhhhhhhh!"

Okay, that's not me. What else is in this wilderness?

Wooded lands play tricks with sound, but those cries both sounded like they came from the north. It's worth knowing, just to keep you safe. But if I'm going to investigate, I'm not leaving you behind.

I slide two arms under your belly, then pull you onto my shoulders. You're definitely lighter than you used to be. It's not the first time I've worn you. This time I have to be careful in walking, mindful not to let you spill off my back. Doing so, I notice my own legs are skinnier, too. When did my thighs stop rubbing together?

"Ahhhhhhh!"

Yes, that's a good point. There are more pressing questions. Especially because I recognize those crying voices now. They wail together, like a phlegmy chorus. It's easy to mistake them for a singular pained tone. Especially since they all belong to the same body.

Behind a bank of pines, in a needle-strewn depression that decades of rain carved into the earth, the hydra's necks writhe against each other. So many lily-white scales and underflesh going pinkened and raw, with dark blood seeping from random bite wounds. Several heads joust with each other, each biting at the neck of another.

The sight makes my guts clench. Are they eating each other?

They fasten onto each other's necks and yank, that smoking poisonous blood pouring out of their mouths and digging new holes in the earth. None swallow. Their eyes wince and clench whenever sunlight falls on them. Two heads break away to cry at the sun.

"Ahhhhhhh!"

You grunt on my shoulders, turning your head away and flattening your ears. I don't blame you. It's not the most pleasant sound. But this clearly isn't from famine.

"Come here. Biting off your heads will only make twice as many grow."

Not that I can afford to touch them, with all the poisoned blood they're spilling. I'm afraid this is a job for fire at the end of a very long stick.

I smother the heads one by one, using the burning end of a log, pulverizing them and then cauterizing the stumps on their main body. I know I'm doing the right thing when their screams turn almost erotic.

"Ohhhhhhh yes. Right there. Like an itch you can't reach."

Down to one head, Logy is clearly canny enough to talk. That means I can ask.

"How did you get here? Of all places?"

The serpentine head startles, and they flick their tongue at me. The tongue keeps flicking, over and over, like they don't believe their eyes. "Al?"

My guts clench up again.

"It's me," I say, like it's an apology.

"How about that? My prayers were answered."

Both you and I tilt our heads down at the monster. "You prayed to see me again?"

"Well, no." Logy slithers out of the depression in the earth, coming closer to me. Char streaks their scales. "But the last thing I remember before the migraines hit was that I was developing an equation to predict the movements of the sun. I always thought equations were a sort of prayer. Now here you are, shading me from sunshine that was killing my senses, so you've proved me right. Math is divine."

They sound exactly the same. I have to ask, "Is this the head I went on adventures with?"

"No. You killed that one, along with two of its siblings. But I don't take it personally."

I missed how confounding they were. I say, "I'm sorry, nonetheless. Feels rude to decapitate the wrong heads."

"From my perspective, the right head survived. You're my hero."

Their tone dips, praise giving way to concern. They're looking me over, sensing how I've lost so much body weight in my travels. It's not me they have to be concerned with.

I set you down between myself and Logy, and smooth a hand along the fur of your side. I push your fur apart to reveal how your hide underneath is going yellow.

"I rescued him from drowning, but that's not the only sickness he's suffering from. You know everything."

"Not everything. Just most things."

"Can you help him?"

They flick their tongue at me again. "You left us. The only family most of us ever had fell apart without you. You were what kept us together. Loneliness is a disease in itself, you know?"

I can't argue with them, not when I need their help to cure you.

"I'm sorry."

"No, I'm sorry that you were in so much pain. The man on fire owes no apologies to those who can't extinguish him." Logy noses at your side, like they might take a taste of you to diagnose the disease. "What name do you go by now, anyway?"

I think, and can't recall. Most of what I've done is as lost as shades in the ash fog.

"Nobody has called me by any name in a long time."

"All right then, Al. Want to save this invincible lion with me?"

There is a perfectly good valley on the opposite side of the forest, through which these starving monsters can stroll once they have their strength again. It's far from any other human interference, so they won't have to trifle with hunters or my cultists. I make bright red berries grow near a sheltered pond, so they'll find plenty of fresh water. It's amateur god stuff, but I'm still pleased with myself, up until I glimpse the metal in the air.

They're high up, flinging across the clouds. That's not my dipshit husband. That's a flock of wings beating with the shine of bronze. What the fuck are—

"Dear."

Your voice behind me makes me shoot bolt upright and almost go visible again. Yours is one of few voices that could do that to me.

You stand with your wings wrapped around your shoulders, limp as a dress, bundled up for your journey. Are you cold? I left you in warm Olympos, blessedly free from the turmoil of the mortal world. Your jagged teeth nibble at your upper up like this is going to be hard on you. Like you know I'll send you away.

I say, "Thank you for coming, Granny, but I'll handle this. I won't put you to work again. You're free to be whatever you want to be. I promise."

You brush the backs of two talons along my cheek, your eyes shimmering. "Thank you. But I am doing what I want."

I do not want to argue with you. Send me anyone else, and I'll bicker them into a hole in the ground. But not you. I hope you're not here to stop me.

I measure my words. "What can I do for you?"

"I'm leaving Olympos."

That hits me right in the chest, as though I've been gored by words.

Of course you should go wherever you want. But I tucked you away in a safe place for reasons, and now I realize one of those reasons was my own. Selfishly I'd been anticipating that when I came back to Olympos, vindicated and restored, you would be there waiting for me. Yours is the face I wanted to see in the heavens.

It's too little, to distill all those sentiments into a childish question. Still I ask. "Why?"

You push into my space, shoulder brushing my chest, and extend a wing. You unfold it to gesture across to Heracles feeding palmfuls of blood to a sickly lion. Are you out to defend Heracles from me again?

You say, "I never understood you Olympians. Admired you, but didn't understand. Not until today."

"Are we really that complicated? Much of the time, it doesn't feel like it."

"It was simpler in the old eras. The titans were self-assured. They didn't need mortals to live out history underneath them. They didn't even want you to be born, not really."

I scoff at the memory of my father's teeth. "They showed it. I'll never forget being swallowed whole."

You go on, "It's part of why my sisters and I switched sides to serve you. You confounded all of creation, which is why you wound up ruling it. More powerful and more clever than the titans, but you weren't enough for yourselves. You were always watching the mortals."

I realize my hands are moving on their own, miming cupping warm fluid to feed the needy. I smooth them out against the hips of my robes. "They need to be guided, from time to time."

"You let them make their own choices more than they know."

"I try."

You point with the very tip of that wing, jabbing accusations in Heracles's direction. "They barely exist, and then their lifetime is over. In a few generations, none of their descendants will know any of their names. That was the first thing that made me feel I needed to look after you. You were too hard on yourself."

How am I supposed to respond to that?

"It wasn't until I possessed the Bull of Crete that I understood. I stayed in his mind for so long, not ruining him. Helping him be himself.

The longer I watched over him, the more I felt like myself. The more I understood myself, through this other creature. That's what the Olympians figured out. That the self comes to us through others."

There's more truth in that than is comfortable. Before I can argue the philosophy, though, you're crossing the valley, headed to the mountains underneath winged shadows. You know those birds better than I do. You bare your broken teeth up at them.

I follow after you, asking, "The Bull needed your help? Doing what? All bulls like is eating, shitting, rutting, and fighting."

"He wanted peace more than he knew. And eventually, he wanted something else more than he wanted peace. An attraction he couldn't otherwise face."

I put a hand over my eyes. "Please tell me the Bull doesn't want to fuck Heracles."

"I'll see you again, dear. The Bull needs me."

I wanted you to banter with me. Instead you said goodbye. I'm happy for you in a way that aches.

But I'm also curious.

I ask, "What is the problem with the Bull?"

You give me this look of gentle piercing, as though you're relieved some horrid thing isn't my fault. Your wings unfurl, like you're about to dash into the sky. You've got to take me with you. Show me what's wrong.

"Granny? What's wrong with the Bull?"

I follow Purrseus from his left side, stretching both arms under his belly, not making contact, but ready to catch him. My eyes pin to his shoulders, following their twitching and fluid sway, for the sign that his next step will fail. His head hangs low, like he's using all his strength to keep his body aloft.

"Look at that. You're doing great."

I hug the air under his belly as he takes his first padding steps out of the shade of the forest. The heat tickles my scalp through my hair, and shows how deep the color of his fur is. You'd never know the flesh beneath was sallow.

He keeps going, head twisting to the right, sniffing. How much I want him to have scented prey. That'd mean his appetite is truly back. I wish I had someone to pray to, for him. But right now, imagining reaching my hopes to the skies tightens a knot in my chest.

Logy slithers alongside me. "Much stronger. I wish I had wide hips like that. Give him another week or two and he'll be terrorizing some countryside like nothing was ever wrong."

Purrseus steps a little quicker, and I have to withdraw an arm to let him go. When I do, Purrseus jerks his head toward me. Dark eyes ask something.

I rub his fuzzy butt, right above his tail. I say, "He wasn't just suffering from starvation."

Logy flicks their tongue at my belly, which has filled out a bit, too. "No, it wasn't just starvation, or drowning. Do you know what it would do to some of us if you died?"

There's a possessiveness in their voice that almost warms me. And suddenly, I can't look the hydra in the face.

"You? You'd be shaken?"

"Al, we're just ourselves around each other. I haven't felt so comfortable around anybody since Athena."

"Really?"

"Mind you, my average social experience is being stabbed with tridents."

"I *did* cut off some of your heads."

"Have I thanked you for that lately?"

They're teasing me, and I can't keep up. I close my eyes against the warmth they offer, still dreading that I don't deserve—

The ground jumps under my feet, like it's trying to throw me into the trees. I spread my arms to brace my fall and whip my head to Purrseus, thinking he must have butted into me. But he's hunkered close to the earth, paws splayed, fur standing on end. Behind us, trees topple from the shock wave that ran through.

It's over as quick as it came. I reach and touch the back of Logy's head, gathering them to me in case that happens again.

They ask, "What's that shadow?"

A funny thing to call an earthquake. I mean to ask, until I see the triangular shadow sweeping across the grass. Purrseus rears back to look into the sky with an expectant violence in his face.

Up above is a huge bird, its plumage glinting of bronze. It flies northward, off to the mountain range. There are far more of them out there. The creatures that the fury once hid amongst. I knew we'd spooked them from the farm where she'd hidden, and they had to go somewhere. Those distant shapes keep diving, hunting prey that has no hope.

The world jumps again, and this time I'm ready. It's a definite quake, one that forces me and Purrseus to hold onto each other. I dig my feet into the earth, trying to steady my family.

We've all been through enough bizarre circumstances to know this isn't a coincidence. I hold my arms out to both Purrseus and Logy, upnodding toward the birds and their mountains.

"May I?"

I'm not done asking before Purrseus climbs aboard my shoulders. Logy makes a self-satisfied sound, like they're winning an argument by allowing themselves to be carried. It's the only way for us to all get there before those quakes get any worse.

I leap with all my strength, clearing the valley, trampling perfectly nice berry bushes. Purrseus nuzzles his wet nose into the crook of my neck as I send us up the slopes. I see the deep impact marks there, where something else fled. They're hoof-shaped, and yes, I know what I'm getting into before I see him.

On a shattered stretch of mountainside lurk the twin black antlers, swinging my way before my feet touch the ground. Then the Bull's snowy hide turns away, ignoring me in favor of those circling birds. His hide isn't all snow white anymore. There are streaks of red from deep wounds. It makes no sense why the Bull hasn't crushed all those birds at this point.

Three dive at him, straight down. He bucks and punts one with his rear hooves, sending the bird splattering against the stones until there's little left of it. The other two come right in, driving their beaks into his back and beating at him with their wings. More shadows stir as another group breaks off from the flock to dive.

Purrseus roars, a proud sound that shakes my bones and makes several birds flee back into the air. But he's too weak to chase them. As soon as he's finished his roar, his chin rests on my bicep.

Those spooked birds circle, swooping just outside the Bull's bucking range. One snaps its beak, trying to distract him so others can bite his sides again.

I pet Purrseus's mane and say, "Let me chase them for you."

The next bird that dives for the Bull's haunches gets a surprise. I fling forward, punching the bird square in the tail feathers—punching it with an invulnerable lion for a gauntlet. Purrseus happily snaps his jaws, showing his appetite by crushing bronze feathers and bones alike. I swing Purrseus, and he releases the mauled bird so it can strike the others.

The Bull's black horns turn at me again, eyes checking. I stand by his side, with Purrseus and Logy clinging to me. I'll cover what he can't see. We can work together, if he'll trust me.

Logy calls, "We're friends! Friends! Remember when I ate bugs out of your fur?"

A grunt. That's all we get, for those horns turn to the sky. The Bull should just leap into the sky with his impossible strength and gore them. It makes no sense that he's staying so close to the ground.

It makes no sense until I see the glowing gold light under him. Down below him is the Hind's auburn form and glowing antler buds, blazing at the sign of predators around. She kneels below him, like she's hurt.

That's why the Bull is staying put. He's sheltering his family.

Well, that family isn't alone anymore. Not so long as I'm standing. So I spread my shoulders and offer Purrseus's growling maw to the bronze flocks above. Let them come.

Hera 52

Granny, I swear I didn't plan for this. I didn't even remember those fucking birds were still out there. The last time I checked, they were feasting on the drifting island of cow shit that Heracles flushed into the sea from the stables of Elis. I can't keep track of every single weird animal stalking the known world.

With the Bull and the Hind accounted for, there's only one mythical creature I still planned on messing with. And since they're all going to blame this on me anyway, I lean into it.

That poor bastard fell asleep on one side of the Aegean Sea, and wakes on this side of it all, on the side of a mountain. If its chill doesn't rouse him, all that noxious squawking does. He's near the apex of the mountain with a great view of that lion tearing a bronze bird apart, of the man carrying that lion. You could run down and join them for the great battle.

I said you could join them.

Why are you freezing up? I hate you mortals. You have almost no lifespan. Quit procrastinating!

Fuck, you're not going anywhere, are you? All right, new plan: some extraordinarily thoughtful goddess has left a horn near his campsite. Go ahead. Give it a blow and bring all the attention of the birds your way. Sacrifice yourself for misplaced virtue.

At least you're doing something now. That's loud enough that every bird who's spooked by Heracles's company suddenly takes notice of this free meal. The flock swirls upward, flinging bronze feathers like darts at the horn-blower. You'd better run!

Not that you could outrun those birds. Nobody would believe a man could beat the Birds of Stymphalia on foot. You are officially breakfast.

Fortunately nobody's watching, and nobody's seeing me help you cheat. Just run toward that walled city you see in the distance. I might even help you make it to the gates.

Alcides 52

I put a hand over my eyes to shield them from the sun, trying to see the trumpeter up the slopes. Yet the birds are a whirlwind of metal, all darting upward, and he's gone. The man should've joined our fight. Now he's made it all his own.

I stand up from the Bull's side, saying, "I have to go."

Logy says, "No. *We* have to go."

The Bull of Crete already kneels for this, scraping the tips of his horns along the ground, offering his injured side for us to climb. The Hind breathes heavily for her tiny frame and puts trembling legs up against him, an animal ready to mount an animal. Her sides are swollen, and the flesh around her eyes and nose are pinker than I remember.

"What's wrong?" I ask her, stroking her back, half wanting to help her ascend and half wanting to forbid her to join a fight. "There's no time when you couldn't have outrun those birds. How did they catch up to you?"

Logy says, "Things have changed for a lot of us. Why, she could be . . ."

They flick their tongue idly from their mouth, and their words dry up.

They flick their tongue again.

"Hang on."

I ask, "What is it?"

Logy slithers up the Bull's side, tongue tasting the air in the Hind's direction. She climbs up to the fat-ripples at the back of the Bull's neck. She won't look at the hydra.

Logy says, "I'll be sloughed. Who's the father? Please tell me it isn't Zeus."

A father?

Her heavy breathing. The strain in her limbs. Abruptly, my eyes ache, and I reach for her again, although any embrace I gave her would crush her. "You're pregnant?"

Logy says, "She's almost due. That'd slow anybody down. When I laid my first clutch of eggs, I wasn't good for anything for a year."

I walk around the Bull, trying to look either him or the Hind in the face. "I don't know who that was that drew the ire of the birds, but I have to go help him. You can stay here. In your condition, you shouldn't risk anything."

The Hind responds by pushing up on her forelegs and pressing her head eastward. Her antler buds glow ominous gold, in the exact direction the birds flew. There's no easier way to find them. No faster way to pursue a winged legion than with her direction and the Bull of Crete's power. I just hope we catch up to that man before it's too late.

Hera 53

This isn't about the fight. Some ornery birds were never going to challenge a veteran with Zeus's own strength, riding a bull with Poseidon's own strength, teaming up with an invincible lion, an omniscient deer, and an immortal hydra that bleeds liquid fire.

Some families reunite around a sporting event. Some require good food and song.

My idiot babies simply need to reunite more dramatically than that.

I'd originally planned for the final reunion to happen in Thebes anyway. Nothing more dramatic than forcing Heracles to defend this new family of monsters in his old home. I promised Megara that I'd bring him back to her. But you don't bring a hero home with milk and honey. This is a battle they'll always remember. Something to remind the whole world of this family man's convictions. And more importantly, to remind his dumb ass of the same.

I wish everyone could feel the tension in Thebes as that shining flock beats closer on their horizon. It's not an illusion. It's not even an omen. It's more than a hundred hungry birds that can't wait to meet all of you. Archers race to the tops of the walls, and I can't wait to watch the first arrowhead bounce off of those feathers. The tension is delicious.

My quarry, that horn-blower who tried to sacrifice himself and draw the birds away from Heracles, arrives at gates that won't open. They won't let a soul inside. The Thebans are so panicked by the oncoming flock that they've forgotten that these birds don't need to walk in. Other farmers are stranded outside the gates, too, and my horn-blower looks at their wizened faces, and then steps up in front of them. He's got an old tusk in one hand, like a dagger. Maybe he'll take one of those birds out before the end.

Or Heracles could come slamming down like a meteor riding the least conventional weapon: one of his friends.

The Bull of Crete comes plowing down through the cloud of the glittering birds, crushing several of them into paste. Heracles grabs one of the fallen birds and immediately lobs it back into the sky, smashing through several more. The day is saved. The lion roars, the archers aim for the exposed necks of the birds, and everyone looks exceptionally attractive.

Attractive to everyone else. I'm a little tired of epic battles, myself. I'm only here waiting for Heracles to recognize the man he chased all the way to Thebes. This is going to be the good part.

I t's you, isn't it? The morning light turns the gray hair on your chest into silver as you try to slink around the people at the gates. You keep turning your head, watching me instead of the fight. That's your face, or one of them. Why are you more afraid of me than the birds?

"Boar?"

I nearly don't recognize you, because I've barely ever seen you undressed like this. The stringy hair from the sides of your otherwise bald head is drenched with sweat. One of the tusks from your old cowl is in your left hand, but the rest of the thing is gone. There's a furtive quality in your face, that insecurity that you'll be seen. I feel echoes of it in myself. That's why I come after you. The birds are already fleeing, uninterested in getting any more intimate with Purrseus and the Bull.

So I put my back to them, and pursue you. I need to make sure you're all right.

"How did you make it that far on foot? I was sure the birds would catch you."

You hold a hand in front of your face, like you've got a gorgon's curse on you. "Don't."

I'm good at not doing things. I drop my eyes to your bare feet, caked in so many layers of filth. You haven't washed your feet since I ran away from you. Since I ripped off your cowl in my heartbreak. I'm sure that's why I'm not allowed to lay eyes on you.

Then you say, "She cursed Boar. Don't look."

Despite what you just said, I almost look up. Almost. Cursed?

I ask, "Who cursed you?"

"Hera must be behind all this."

I remember that cowl flying into the distance. I must have obliterated it with my swat, so that you tracked down the last remaining tusk. I was too hurt to be accountable for stealing what you are.

I can do better now.

"Boar, I'm the one who lost control of myself. I'm not making excuses. I'm sorry."

"No," you say, words clipped and snub. You snort like you want to charge something. "Hera saw Boar forcing comfort on you when you weren't ready for it. She already despises Boar for siding with you against Olympos. Then she did this. This!"

You wave your hands at yourself. From what I can see of your hide-wrapped hips and bare belly, you look the same as before. I don't think I missed you having hair of snakes or eyes of flame.

I ask, "What happened to you?"

The only hissing sound is your voice. "Hera used her power to transform Boar into a human."

Oh, Auntie Hera. The things you let yourself be blamed for.

Still keeping my gaze low, I ask, "Are you sure you were transformed?"

You snort at me again, and thump a fist on your chest. In all the time I've known you, using your hands has never seemed to change your opinion that you were an animal. Yet here the gesture is clearly to demonstrate your humanity.

"What else do you call this? These feet with toes? This head full of conflicted nonsense? Boar never felt like this before. Boar has been defiled."

I raise my eyes, up your chest and to the scraggly beard on your chin. More gray hairs on a monster's hide. I won't look at your eyes if you don't want me to. But I have to tell you.

"When we traveled together, we knew each other well, didn't we?"

"Yes. So you should easily recognize Boar has been transformed."

"So I can tell you what I see."

Your hands grope at your own cheeks. "What is it? What does Boar look like now? Is it getting worse?"

I look further up, into those dark eyes. Only one set of eyes. You never needed the other one.

"You blew that horn to get everyone to chase you, to protect me. You recognized your family. Even now, you're unmistakable." I offer a tentative smile, praying it catches on. "You look like Boar to me."

Your eyes get even darker when you weep. Tears do that to some of us. You shove them away with the knuckles of a fist, and they keep coming. It must be difficult for boars to handle emotions.

Your eyes are hungry on me, hungry with the need to believe. "You are sure? You have not gone blind?"

"If I'm blind, I'm having amazing hallucinations. But you should stay by my side, until we're sure."

You rub at your chin, assessing something in me. "Hmm. You look like you could be hallucinating."

"How's that?"

You pick at your teeth using that tusk again, your eyes roaming down my belly and thighs. "Boar has a second concern."

Now I can't stop smiling. Your tone is tentative, like you're walking on a slender rope toward me, and any syllable may make you fall. It's so good to look you in the eyes, even if there is only one pair of them. They're as dark as they ever were under your cowl. Like freshly unearthed gems.

I say, "You can tell me anything, Boar."

"Are you dying?" No more tightrope tone. You go right into protective umbrage. "You look malnourished. You should be eating more. Boar will feed you if you have forgotten how to chew."

I can't help kissing you. It's hard and brief, there and then over. You touch your fingers to your bottom lip like it's the first part of humanity you've ever enjoyed.

The kiss ends that quickly because as soon as you put the idea in my head, I know you're right. I'm famished so that my limbs burn icily. For the first time in a long time, I could eat.

And I know good places for food in Thebes. Places that will suit all of us, because I can't eat alone. My family eats with me.

Hera 54

I am not going to watch those two clumsily flirt themselves into oblivion, no matter how cute it is. It makes parts of me clammy that I want un-clammed. And in the melee with the birds, I keep noticing the rough breathing of the Hind. Her golden antler buds flash too brightly, attracting the very birds they should be warning her to flee. From the way she's walking, it's almost like . . .

No. It can't be.

No mate could chase her down. All she does is avoid predators, and when it comes to bucks, they're little better. She's the favorite beast of a virgin goddess. There's no other creature alive as fast as her.

Impossible as it is, the fluids spill down the fur of her rear legs. I can feel the searing pain coursing her spine—it's happening, and it's happening wrong.

Now, I'm the Goddess of Family, and that usually means human family. But Heracles is half human, and these idiots are his family. You know what this means?

This means the left half of the gate to Thebes, which hasn't been properly maintained ever since Heracles departed this place for his labors, is about to fail. Look at that. The hinges have cracks that were probably always there, and . . .

Good thing it didn't fall on anybody. That was needlessly loud.

Now get your fluffy tail inside the city walls, you gold-headed deer thing. I know a woman in this city who's helped deliver plenty of lives into the world, both human and animal. And if she can't do the job, well, I know an expert.

Alcides 54

old! Slow your butt down!"

The Bull does not care how I beg him to stop. He knocks the other half of the gates off of the city, sending Thebans fleeing for their lives. I wave at the archers on the high walls, and they are wise enough not to loose arrows upon him. The Bull has had a long enough day. If they get in the way of him finding the Hind, there won't be a Thebes left for them to defend.

Boar races alongside us, grabbing at the Bull's tail to help. It gets him dragged right off his feet, and I scoop him up, holding him close, with Purrseus butting into my other side.

"Don't worry," Logy says, body wrapped around one of the Bull's horns. "We'll find your bride. We won't leave her be*hind*."

It's an actual laugh. It bubbles up, like pleasant bile. I swear I'm throwing up on a familiar road, and the noise passes my teeth. I squeeze Purrseus and Boar under each of my arms. I could follow that big guy for the rest of my life, and never sit down again. Let's keep walking, no matter where our feet take us.

Boar says, "Heracles?"

"No, let's keep going. Let's find the Hind."

It's more than that corner of the road. The worn paths in the middle of the road, like the hump on the neck of a man who spent his whole life over in accounting numbers and planning city life. The washed-out grooves on the side of the road are deeper, but I recognize them.

Logy flicks their tongue down at me. "Al? What's going on?"

"Nothing. Let's find her and see the . . . the baby."

How long have I been standing still? They're all looking at me, Purrseus and Logy, Bull and Boar, waiting for me to resume our march. Action usually makes me lose track of my mind. This is a rare time when I was thinking so intensely that I forgot to do anything. Silly, losing myself here, of all places. Here.

Hyacinths and anemones overwhelm the eyes in three separate gardens, flattening out the courtyard where the altar once stood, and the fire pit. Someone redid the stones leading up to the landing, but those are the same walls I laid, baked clay brick by brick, merely painted a yellowy white that reminds me of the morning sun through my eyelashes. There are the same windows, leading to the same rooms where the same boys can't live.

I've been standing in front of my own house for time unknown, looking directly at you. Your face is broader, your hair totally overtaken by gray. When I imagine you, I still think of your hair as pure black as the day we met during those arm-wrestling matches. Gray suits you better.

The wrinkles in the corners of your eyes deepen. Have you been standing here this entire time? Looking me in the eyes, waiting for me to wake out of my stupor and recognize my wife?

Iolaus steps out of the house, his smile too genuine. His face has filled out further, and time has made his biceps sag. He looks comfortable. He doesn't even notice the monsters around me. My nephew walks up beside you, just happy I've come home.

"I knew it."

Your voice has dried so much with time, and it's still unmistakable. Then I'm walking toward you, and you're running to the fence, and we meet at the border of our home. My toes stand the closest to our marriage that any part of me has in years. You take me by the cheeks, holding me like I'm just a head. Just a set of tired eyes for you to commune with. You kiss my beard, and my arms remember how to hold you. You fit in weary arms.

You ask, "You brought that enchanted deer?"

"The Hind?" Of course it's the Hind. "She's here?"

"She's having the worst labor I've ever seen an animal bear. Fortunately, the gods sent some wild midwife who's tending to her. They brought you back to me, too. To us."

"I . . ."

I'm fumbling for words when the Bull of Crete butts right past me. He waddles along the road to get to the stable. Some simple part of me loves that he wants to see his child, but feels he needs to be introduced first.

"That's the Bull of Crete. We are, well, we're distant cousins. He'll behave."

"I remember him. I remember all of them."

Right. You saw all of these monsters in Thrace. It's so hard to reconcile that you exist in the same world as they do. That the same sky under which we made meaning for each other also saw the meaning I made with them. Blood goes to my cheeks, just thinking about you all knowing what you've meant to me.

I wouldn't be here without you.

No. I might have come through Thebes. But I wouldn't have been myself. I would have been a ghost, walking through the world, simply doing, refusing thought and feeling.

You say, "They're welcome here. Do they have . . . names?"

Who do I introduce first? Whose name belongs on my lips?

How do I thank everyone here?

"A pleasure, madame," says Logy, slithering up to the fence. "People call me a lot of things. I promise I'll only repeat the polite ones."

I hold the gate of our fence open, and Iolaus steps back so the guests can enter. You shy to Iolaus's side, eyes curious upon all these visitors.

Into my yard goes Logy, straight for the brightest sunbeam that breaks through the trees.

Into my yard comes Boar, trying to fix his stringy hair. Iolaus has to teach him how to shake hands.

Into my yard pads Purrseus, dipping his head and deliberately rubbing against your side. You pet him, and laugh at the unique rumble he makes.

I keep holding the gate, waiting for them without thinking. It catches up to me so quickly, that I'm looking down, at the heights they were back then. Expecting three boys who will never set foot in this home again.

Part of me will always be waiting for them, until I am a shade who walks in their midst in the world below. I didn't leave this place to forget them. And their memory will never leave me. I take a moment to still my breathing, watching everyone who walked into the yard, and everyone who can't.

Hera 55

This should be easier. Deer have birthed in the wild since before gods first discovered them scampering around and eating all the pretty flora. I should have had to point Megara in your direction and she should have cooed about the wonders of nature as you pushed out a couple of new calves. What is so wrong here?

In the guise of a woman with cyst-covered knees and hands, I barge my way in. I get down on the ground and brush cool water across your muzzle. I've witnessed plenty of silent deer births, yet your every inhalation is a rickety wheeze, and you whine like I'm whipping you with thorns. The sounds are larger than your whole body. I have to shoo Megara away just so I won't be distracted or have to explain what I'm about to do. We need to know what's inside you and why it hasn't poked its head out yet.

Yeah, you're dilated enough that you could push out your own spinal column. This should be over by now. If I reach in, I can . . .

What the fuck is that?

Its body is like clay bricks that are still baking, blazing hot and way too hard to be flesh. That's not bone, either; it ripples. Two plates catch my fingers and nearly crush them before I yank them out.

That is not a calf. What is this thing?

Your answer is a long wheeze, and your head vibrates like your neck bones will shatter from the stretch. Your forelegs bend and shove your hooves into your sides like you're trying to expel the calf from the outside.

This time I reach in with both arms, palms brushing over jagged edges. They feel like volcanic stones, or hundreds of broken antlers and horns. My arms keep sinking in, too, past the elbows, and the calf keeps going. I stare at you from the outside while trying to find a handhold, and I'm right. The reason you're having so much trouble is this calf is bigger than you are. It's warping the dimensions of your belly.

I feel around for any limbs, something to gain purchase on. Deer come out feet first all the time. The keening yelp you give brings tears to my eyes. No. I'm not going to let this tear you apart. I am watching over you, damn it.

You bring your head halfway down to the straw-strewn ground, so tense, like you'll bolt at every moment. I couldn't urge you to push harder than you are. Come on, this thing has to have a . . .

A hoof! I grab onto it, squeeze, and it kicks into my palm. That's fine. I'm an evil goddess. Fight me!

I squeeze again, and the fawn kicks again—and kicks outward. The narrow, sinewy leg glistens with amniotic juices, and I grope along it, to find its twin. The next hoof kicks me before I can even find it, and I'm cackling *go*. Keep the violence coming, kiddo. I take hold of both hoofed feet and tug in rhythm with your pushes. Deep breath and tug. One more heave and . . .

The calf flops on top of me, so heavy that my avatar is crushed to the ground beneath it. Its skin is terribly bright, like burning flames that keep rolling. But that's not fire. I try to push it off of myself, gently, to get a look at it.

Already you're up on your feet, ribs quaking a bit, but breathing more smoothly, like you didn't almost split in half. You step over my face, pushing your nose into your fawn and licking away at that glowing skin to clean it. And that's not just skin. Every bit of your calf's hide is covered in those golden bits of bone. They're antler buds, just like what adorn your scalp. This creature didn't wait to be born to develop them, on every piece of flesh, on every leg and joint. It was born with brilliant armor.

Its eyes open and its head twitches, as it realizes it has a head. It's always amazing that animals are ready to go within moments of birthing, whereas human children often aren't ready to live when they're full adults. The calf rolls onto all fours, facing you.

Yes, it's a calf, but not a deer calf. I've never seen such a cow-shaped thing in my life.

Don't worry about infidelity, though. I'm pretty sure this calf is yours. Nearly its entire hide is covered in glowing antler buds. I've never seen a thing like it.

The father looms at the far side of the stables. A snow-white visage with horns too large to fit inside the stable without destroying the place. The Bull of Crete's first exhalation fills the stables and blows my hair and robe from my face.

There are my questions. All answered. It's time for the wicked Hera to retreat into the shadows again.

You nuzzle at your calf, pushing her toward her gigantic father. At least she wasn't born his size. I'll have to look in on her, from time to time, to make sure she has a happier life than his other children. The Minotaur deserved better. Your child will receive better.

I rise to walk out the other side of the stables, and freeze. There, in my only free path out of here, stands Heracles.

I hoped you'd still be here. You're wise to step away from the baby, because the Bull is breathing aggressively and clearly hankers to be alone with his child. The Hind's antler buds are dormant, dull in color, a good sign that she appreciated your help. But I don't want to take any risks with you. I step in to collect you, an arm between you and the monsters, to ward off any needless protectiveness, and to give them privacy.

I can't help pausing at the sight of their baby. I don't know what I expected from these two parents. But this?

"A golden calf? Is that a good omen?"

I wipe at the smile on my face. We're out of the shade of the stables before I realize what I've said. The last thing our family needs is more omens.

But you look more unsettled by what I said than I am. Your slender body, legs and arms so thin you could have been built out of broomsticks. The skin on your face is so thin, and it furrows and purses up at me. Are you more afraid of me than of the Bull of Crete?

Especially here, I don't blame you. I exhale slowly, drooping my shoulders, trying to look smaller.

"Can I offer you wine? After all you've done, I'm sure Megara will let you stay the night."

You pull your robe over your head, making yourself smaller in kind. The two of us are competing at who can be less obtrusive. I like you already.

"My work here is at its end," you say, in a wan tone that I can't quite place. "I'm only passing through."

"I don't think I'll be staying long, either. We could travel together. Make sure you get to your destination safely."

You won't look me in the eyes. Clearly I'm pushing too much on you.

After the birds descended on Thebes, I'm sure we're all wired tighter than we wanted. I withdraw a couple steps to give you space, but I'm serious about that wine.

Your eyes come up for a moment, like you're worried for me. "You're not staying here? I thought this was your home. Shouldn't you be with your family?"

So you do know me, and that's why you're nervous. I get it. I make myself nervous, too.

Words come out of me unbidden, in an attempt to help you relax. "I should be in there, yes. Right now my nephew is getting an earful from a chatty one-headed hydra. But seeing them all together, all right in front of me? I got overwhelmed. I needed to be away from them, just for a moment."

Your tone actually nags me. "You're not going to go wandering again?"

That a stranger could be that concerned for my health makes me smile. Maybe you should come join our motley family, too. I wonder what your home looks like. But I decide not to ask, and not to turn away from thinking about my own home.

"I don't know what you heard about my wanderings. The worst of them, though, were wandering through nothingness, where I just did anything to avoid facing how much family could hurt me, and how much I could fail family. This isn't that." To illustrate, I lean against the faded paint on the side of a house wall that used to be mine. There are scratch marks on the bricks near the base, like a lion cub had a tantrum here. "This is me catching my breath, before I rejoin them."

Your eyes move up for the first time, probing past me, like you're seeking something in the sky. "Reunions destroy my nerves, too."

My smile is back. I touch it to make sure it's real. "Thank you for being my excuse to take a moment."

"The older I get, the more moments it seems I have. I should give more of them away."

"Giving away your moments. I like that. Are you sure you don't want that wine?"

Your eyes drop. Maybe you have trouble with wine. I should be more thoughtful of that.

You ask, "You're really pulling yourself together. After everything she did to you?"

Oh, so it wasn't the wine. The concern in your voice makes me search your face again. That stub of a chin, those blotchy lips. I don't think we've met, unless it was during my fugues.

I don't have that much to say. I tell you what I'd tell her. "The truth is that I hurt for Hera."

"You do?"

"She's trapped believing she has to be wicked and vile." I gesture to the stables, where the golden calf is giving her first flute-pitched grunts. "When you look around, and see all the happy children born? All the families she's surely helped make it to another day? That she put you here, right when the Hind needed you? The most tragic thing about her is that she thinks she needs to be defined by her worst. She's a curse on herself, and she can't know it."

Your left hand trembles, a few fingers sliding out like you'll argue with me. I know hearing that kind of blasphemy is hard on many people. But you haven't seen the side of my aunt that I have.

Your hand comes up to your mouth, covering a choked sound. I come closer, wanting to pat your back or get you water. You're not young to have been through everything you have today.

"I'm sorry. I said too much."

Hugging your robe to your shoulders, you croak out, "Will you pray to her again?"

"I don't know. I keep wanting to."

"What would you pray to her for?"

This is not the right line of questioning for the moment. You look like you have the chills, and it's blazing hot out here. We need to get you to sit down, and you definitely need something to drink. I hold out my hands for you to take them, to steady yourself.

I assure you, "It's going to be fine."

"What do you wish she'd do?"

"I don't know."

I do, though. I can't look down at the scratch marks on that wall and pretend that I don't.

You insist. "What?"

"For her to let herself be better. To climb over whatever barriers godhood has given her, and be the goddess I believed she was."

"If she does that, she'll learn it by watching you." For the briefest instant, she touches my chest with her fingernails. Every hair on my body goes stiff. She pushes herself clear of me by that little prickling touch. "Do you know what she'd want for you?"

In your distress, I'll let you have whatever answer you like. For my part, I say, "I can't imagine."

"For you to go be with your family."

As though in agreement, a table inside scrapes across the floor, as monsters make room for their brewing party. Megara probably has some opinions about this that I need to hear, and soon.

I ask you, "You're sure you won't stay?"

"This place isn't for me. If it's meant to be, we'll see each other again."

We start walking together, step for step together in the blinding lack of shade. There isn't any arguing a busy traveler into doing what she doesn't want. You'll do what you want.

"Well, madame, thank you, for what you did today."

Quick as lightning, you say, "And thank you, for what you'll keep doing."

We walk around the house together and part. I go home. She goes somewhere else. In my doorway, I overhear someone telling an embarrassing story about when I took lyre lessons as a child. My family is waiting. I hesitate, and watch you go, and feel a familiar tingle in my thoughts. I catch myself praying, to her, for you.

ACKNOWLEDGMENTS

Found family is at the heart of this book, just as it is at the heart of my life. I am blessed by the people who have stuck by me, no matter how weird I got. Whether we're goofing around in video games or driving to the emergency room in the middle of the night, the value of having people you can trust is immutable. Among my found family, I number Nat Sylva, Nicholas Sabin, Kelly Allen, Cass Williams, Michelle Fleming, Key Dyson, Max Cantor, Beverly Fox, Vanessa McKittrick, Jane Briars, Leigh Wallace, Alex Haist, Devin Singer, Marissa Lingen, Meg Frank, and Will Frank. I adore you folks. I'll keep sending you puns until they shut off the internet.

Along the way to getting *Wearing the Lion* into the hands of readers, it was helped along by folks at DAW including Ben Schrank, Katie Hoffman, Leah Spann, Aranya Jain, Joshua Starr, Laura Fitzgerald, Madeline Goldberg, and at Arcadia Books by Anne Perry, Alex Haywood, Ella Patel, and Beth Wright. All throughout writing this book, I was kept steady by my brilliant agent, Hannah Bowman (hey, I wrote you some more serpents!). The U.S. cover art was created by Adam Auerbach, while the U.K. cover art was created by Tyler Miles Lockett. And because many readers picked this book up because they picked up *Someone You Can Build a Nest In* previously, thanks go to James Fenner for its stunning U.S. cover art, and to Stephen Player for its enchanting U.K. cover. Thank you all for helping bring my monsters to the world.

For this book in particular, I have to thank the influences of Jim Starlin, George Pérez, Ron Lim, and an ancient poet named Homer. You see, Starlin wrote the original *Infinity Gauntlet* for Marvel Comics, penciled and illustrated by Pérez and Lim. It was this gorgeous crossover about the Hulk and Wolverine and Captain America joining forces in an epic war. It so captured my childhood imagination that I cut the illustrations of the infinity gems out of my copy and glued them onto one of my mom's gloves.

Then a few years later I read Homer's *Iliad* for the first time. Reading about Ajax and Diomedes and Odysseus joining forces against Troy, I sat bolt upright in bed. To my young brain, this was just like *Infinity Gauntlet*. Something clicked. That day, a vast amount of classical literature opened up for me. My library card was never the same again.

Many of the ancient Greek writers have inspired me for years. This obviously includes Homer, but also Sophocles, Euripides, Aristophanes, and Aeschylus. Little inspirations from them nest all around this book.

One ought not to delve into the world of ancient Greek myth retellings without considering the many great contemporary Greek SciFi and Fantasy writers. I am privileged to write during the same period as them. Some of my favorites include Natalia Theodoridou, Ioanna Papadopoulou, Eleanna Castroianni, Avra Margariti, and Eugenia Triantafyllou. If you don't know their work, you're one web search away from discovering something great.

I also want to thank Eugenia Triantafyllou in particular, who performed a critical reading of this book for me. She was one of the first people I turned to when I seriously started laying the groundwork for my Hera and Heracles. Thank you for all your help, Eugenia. It is a privilege to be your peer.

Wearing the Lion wouldn't exist without great translators of classics, such as Emily Wilson, Robert Fagles, and Seamus Heaney (Heaney's *The Cure at Troy* remains a treat). Translators keep an essential part of humanity in the humanities. They honestly should get more hugs than they do. I'm trying to do my part when I see them.